ingh lives just outside Boston, USA, with her
..d, children, and a very rumbunctious Yorkie.
several years in the corporate world she finally
..ved the advice of family and friends to 'give the
..ng a go, already'. She's oh-so-happy she did. When
..t her keyboard she likes to spend time on the tennis
..or the golf course. Or immersed in a good read.

..d-winning author **Jennifer Faye** pens fun
..mporary romances. Internationally published,
..ooks translated into more than a dozen
..ages, she is a two-time winner of the *RT Book*
.*ws* Reviewers' Choice Award and winner of the
..omance Reviewers' Choice Award. Now living
..ream, she resides with her very patient husband
..Vriter Kitty. When she's not plotting out her next
..nce, you can find her with a mug of tea and a book.
..n more at jenniferfaye.com.

N
L
I !\
C

Also by Nina Singh

Spanish Tycoon's Convenient Bride
Her Inconvenient Christmas Reunion
From Tropical Fling to Forever
From Wedding Fling to Baby Surprise

Also by Jennifer Faye

Fairytale Christmas with the Millionaire

Wedding Bells at Lake Como miniseries

Bound by a Ring and a Secret
Falling for Her Convenient Groom

Discover more at millsandboon.co.uk.

AROUND THE WORLD WITH THE MILLIONAIRE

NINA SINGH

GREEK HEIR TO CLAIM HER HEART

JENNIFER FAYE

MILLS & BOON

First Published in Great Britain 2022
by Mills & Boon, an imprint of HarperCollins*Publishers* Ltd,
1 London Bridge Street, London, SE1 9GF

www.harpercollins.co.uk

HarperCollins*Publishers*
1st Floor, Watermarque Building,
Ringsend Road, Dublin 4, Ireland

Around the World with the Millionaire © 2022 Nilay Nina Singh

Greek Heir to Claim Her Heart © 2022 Jennifer F. Stroka

ISBN: 978-0-263-30210-3

01/22

AROUND THE WORLD WITH THE MILLIONAIRE

NINA SINGH

MILLS & BOON

To all those who don't fit the regular molds,
who live their lives full of spirit.

And to all the polar opposite types who love them.

CHAPTER ONE

A PIECE WAS MISSING. A very valuable piece.

Zeke Manning pulled out the inventory list that had originally been prepared for him when the estate was first appraised years ago. Then he compared it once again to the items on the antique mahogany desk in front of him. Yep, something was very, very wrong.

Biting off a curse, he brushed a wayward strand of hair off his forehead. He was here as a personal favor. As the owner of his firm, he never really did fieldwork as an estate attorney anymore. This was supposed to be a quick and easy task coupled with a friendly visit to one of his grandmother's oldest and dearest friends. But now it appeared he had a problem on his hands.

Hopefully, it was merely a simple misunderstanding. Maybe Esther knew exactly where the antique necklace was. She might even have it on her person and had merely neglected to tell him. Esther wasn't remembering much of anything these days.

Well, there was only one way to find out. With a sigh of resignation, Zeke made his way out of the study and toward the parlor, where Esther Truneau, patriarch of the once prominent and highly regarded Truneau family of New Orleans, was taking her afternoon tea.

He arrived to find one of the housemaids pouring tea for

her out of a delicate ceramic teapot into a porcelain cup. The aroma of fresh-brewed Earl Grey hovered in the air.

"Hello, Esther," he said after clearing his throat to get her attention. He'd found out the hard way upon his arrival that she was rather easily startled.

She looked up from her cup upon hearing his voice. Zeke paused and waited for the confusion in her eyes to clear. When it finally did, a warm smile spread over her lips.

"Zeke, dear. I'd forgotten you were here."

Zeke made sure to hide his concern. He'd suspected as much. He'd have to follow up with a medical professional to make sure she was getting the proper care and attention for what he suspected had begun a while ago. Returning her smile, he pulled out a newly upholstered chair across from where she was sitting on a love seat.

Without asking, the young lady waiting on her retrieved a cup from the bottom of the serving cart and poured for him. She set the tea on the coffee table by his side, then gave him a quick smile before leaving the room.

"Esther," he began, his focus fully on the matron who had been one of his beloved grandmother's dearest friends for decades. "I was hoping we might have a little chat."

"Of course, dear. It's so nice of you to visit. Are you in New Orleans on a business trip, then?"

This wasn't good. She'd clearly forgotten the reason he was here. Suddenly, his trip to New Orleans had gone from performing a quick favor for his grandmother's dearest friend to a wellness check that would require further follow-up. As far as he knew, Esther had no relatives in the States.

He leaned forward to make sure he had her full attention. "Esther, you asked me here, remember? After speaking with my grandmother."

She blinked up at him in confusion. Which was answer enough, of course. Finally, she seemed to gather some clarity.

"Oh, yes. Norma mentioned you were coming. That was today, then, was it?"

Zeke summoned his patience and responded as gently as he could. "It's today. That's right. You asked if I would come over and inventory the house and other properties to get an updated valuation of the estate."

Esther blinked again. "I did?"

Zeke nodded. "Yes. After speaking with Norma."

"I know Norma!" She clapped her hands together then patted his knee. "You're her grandson, aren't you? She looked after you and your sister."

Zeke couldn't believe this was turning into an unwanted trip down memory lane. He simply nodded.

"She was so intimidated, you know," Esther continued. "I remember her telling me how anxious she was about having to raise two preteens at her advanced age. We spoke on the phone about it almost daily."

"She did quite well with us," Zeke answered, not voicing the added thought that Grandmother had done much better than her daughter, who had abandoned Zeke and his sibling after destroying the family.

"Norma said you could help me get my affairs in order with the house."

"That's why I'm here, Esther," Zeke said, as gently as he could manage.

"How kind of you. Carry on, then."

Zeke cleared his throat. "Esther, we need to have a chat first."

"A chat about what exactly, dear?"

"Your estate. Or to be more specific, some of the pieces that belong to the estate."

"Pieces?"

How was he to put this without making her overly upset? Zeke couldn't guess how it might have happened, but Esther had managed to lose an extremely valuable item. Or it had somehow been taken. Not the kind of news he relished delivering to a nice little old lady. "Yes, I'm afraid I've run into something of a snag. An item is missing, Esther. A very valuable item."

Some clarity seemed to appear in the blue depths of her eyes. "Valuable, you say?"

"Very valuable."

She lifted an eyebrow. "What kind of piece?"

"Jewelry. A necklace from sixteenth-century France. Your records say it had been passed through several generations of the Truneau family. I'm afraid there's no sign of it in your possessions. While the paperwork says it should be right here in your house safe."

Her eyes finally lost all signs of cloudiness and grew wide with shock. For the first time since Zeke had walked through Truneau Manor's doors this morning, Esther appeared completely lucid.

"Oh, dear. That's quite bad, isn't it?"

Zeke took her hand gently and patted it reassuringly.

"I'm sure it was a simple misunderstanding. Probably merely a mistake," he insisted in an attempt to quell her fears. He hadn't meant to alarm her.

"I just need your help to determine exactly what might have happened to it."

She blinked at him once more. "Of course."

"Can you think of the last time you might have seen it?" As clichéd as the question seemed, Zeke figured it wasn't a bad way to start an investigation.

Esther shrugged, her forehead scrunched in concentration. "All the valuable jewelry is always under constant lock and key. Only taken out to be polished, which I only allow my most trusted staff to do. People I've employed for decades."

First off, he would need to look into all her staff members. He really didn't want to get the authorities involved until he was a bit clearer as to what was going on here, exactly. And there were other avenues to explore still.

"I see. Is there a chance you might have lent it out?" he asked her. "Temporarily? To a gallery or museum perhaps?"

Esther immediately shook her head. "Oh, no. I don't lend out valuables."

Zeke racked his mind for another avenue to pursue when her next words stopped him. And they sent alarm bells ringing in his head.

Without any irony whatsoever, Esther added, "I have been known to give things away occasionally, however."

Fifteen minutes later, Zeke had a name and was looking at a photo online of a dark-haired, brown-eyed woman with shoulder-length curly hair. She wore dramatically dark eyeliner and appeared to be in her mid-to-late twenties.

All in all, she looked like she might very well fit the type. A type he knew all too well. If Zeke's suspicions were correct, he was looking at a photo of the kind of person who would take and take until there was no more left to give.

"I'm almost positive he'll propose this weekend. What do you think, Vivi?"

Vivienne Ducarne flipped six cards in a semicircle on the velvet table cover between her and the client who came in every Thursday for a reading. Sally's question this morning was the same as it had been all too often in the past.

"Well, let's look at what the cards say, shall we?"

Sally McNeill had become a regular customer over the last several months, ever since meeting Lance. Or was it Luke? Vivi knew she should pay better attention, but the man's name hardly seemed to matter. Sally usually referred to him as her stud muffin.

Sally had made her way into Lucien's Magic Shop and Gift Store the morning after their first blind date to see where things might lead between them. So far, the two of them had been enjoying a whirlwind romance according to Sally's rather TMI descriptions. The woman was more than ready for the relationship to move on to the next level. Vivi didn't have the heart to tell her that she just didn't see that happening in any of her readings so far.

Of course, she wasn't about to tell Sally that. Not directly, anyway. It would crush the other woman's excitement. Why dash her hopes?

Vivi pointed to a card in the center. "The Empress. That card could mean a few different things."

The other woman released a long sigh. "Ooh, like what?"

"Well, in your case, I think it means a strengthening of bonds. Growth in your relationships in general."

Sally clapped her hands in front of her chest. "That's great. I knew it!"

Before Sally could get too worked up, Vivi pointed to the card right of center. "The Seven of Pentacles. That's something of a cautionary card."

Sally's eyebrows drew together. "Cautionary?"

"It usually refers to patience and perseverance. A message not to try and rush things, but approach matters with more of a long-term mindset."

Sally seemed to deflate in her chair, her smile faltering. "Huh. Long-term?"

Vivi merely nodded.

"So what do you think, then, Vivi?" Sally repeated. She asked that question a lot, in fact.

Vivi tapped her chin. "I think you're in store for some good tidings coming your way. A lot to look forward to."

Just like that, the smile reappeared.

"The cards seem to be advising you to try and be a bit patient. For now," Vivi reassured her.

Ten minutes later, after some more questions from Sally and a bit of random chitchat, her customer left. Sally seemed content with what fate had chosen to show her today through the tarot cards. A lot of folks looked down upon oracle cards, such as tarot or runes, even in a city as spiritual as New Orleans. But Vivi saw it as a craft, an art almost. Not only did Vivi interpret what the cards displayed in a manner that felt relevant to her clients, but she also knew she was just as talented at providing conversation or simple reassurance. Sometimes, her clients just needed someone to talk to.

Esther Truneau came to mind. Vivi had been giving the nice old lady personal readings for the last several months. Sometimes she wondered if Vivi was the only source of meaningful human contact the older woman had in her life. Her staff seemed to mostly ignore her when Vivi was there.

Vivi packed up the cards and started tidying the shop. It was a pretty slow day, with not too many shoppers strolling in, and Sally had been her only prebooked appointment.

The chimes above the door sounded as someone entered.

Vivi looked up with a smile to greet the customer—finally, some action. Slow days bored her to tears.

Her breath caught in her throat before she could offer a greeting. The man walking in was strikingly handsome. Which was saying a lot for someone who worked in a magic-and-gift shop in the heart of one of the world's most famous cities. This area drew visitors from all over the world.

Tall with jet-black hair and chestnut eyes, he had a strong jawline and ruggedly sharp cheekbones. He wasn't overly muscular, but was fit and toned.

He obviously wasn't any kind of typical tourist. That much was abundantly clear. Dressed in a black collared shirt, which appeared to be silk, with pressed gray pants that had a perfect crease line, he seemed to fit the picture of an accomplished, successful businessman.

So what was someone like him doing in a quaint tourist trap of a shop in the middle of the morning? Had he gotten lost on his way to a high-powered acquisition meeting?

Vivi shook off the beginning of a giggle and cleared her throat. "May I help you find something, sir?"

His eyes narrowed on her and she suddenly had the strange urge to duck behind the nearest counter. A shiver of iciness ran along her spine. His gaze was clearly not a friendly one. And he certainly didn't appear to like what he was looking at.

She wasn't imagining it. She didn't even need her so-called "seer" skills to be able to tell as much.

Working hard not to bristle at his hostility, she forced a smile on her lips. "Was there something in particular you were looking for?"

"Oh, I'd say so," he answered with a cryptic clip in his tone.

What was that supposed to mean? "I beg your pardon?"

"Are you Vivienne Ducarne?" he asked without any hint of cordiality.

Vivi's heart pounded in her chest. He had to be a cop, maybe a detective. But why would an officer of the law be dressed as impeccably as he was?

Ha! Like that was the most pressing question she had at the moment. A better one would be what would a cop want with her?

Her days of hiding from the law were well in her past. She'd left that part of her life behind years ago, when she'd finally cleaned up her act and wised up enough to dump the charming yet toxic ex-boyfriend who'd led her down so many objectionable paths. There was absolutely no reason she could think of as to why a law-enforcement officer might be seeking her out at this moment in time.

But she realized her mistaken assumption the more she studied him. Now that she took a good look at him, she knew one thing for certain. He was no cop. Every inch of him screamed that he was a professional man with privilege and clout. Just the pants he was wearing would probably cover a beat cop's monthly salary.

So if his visit wasn't about her past, what was it about?

He was staring back at her just as intently. That's right—he'd asked her a question. Her name. He was still waiting for an answer.

"My friends call me Vivi. So you can call me Vivienne. Not that it's any of your business." She had a question or two of her own. "And who might you be?"

"The name is Zeke Manning. Esquire."

An attorney. She should have known. She'd had to interact with more than enough criminal lawyers in her lifetime. But something told her criminal law wasn't this man's specialty.

"What can I do for you, exactly, Mr. Manning? I gather you're not here for a tarot reading?"

"A what?" He gave his head a shake. "Never mind. You gather correctly. That's not why I'm here."

She tilted her head in his direction, the perfect picture of unaffected patience. But inside, she was a trembling mess. This stranger really had her rattled. The last time someone had looked at her so accusingly, so disdainfully, she'd been a scared teen at the full mercy of the court.

It also didn't help matters that the man looked like something out of a cologne ad in a high-end magazine.

"Then please enlighten me."

"For one, you can start by handing over that which doesn't belong to you."

Vivi summoned all her will and strength to try and get her rapid heartbeat under control. Who was this man? And who did he think he was talking to?

Well, if he thought he could intimidate her, he had another think coming. Vivi had survived and prevailed against far scarier people in her lifetime. Not to downplay his sheer presence, but she knew how to handle bullies.

And this man was clearly trying to bully her.

"I have no idea what you may be referring to, Mr. Manning." That was the absolute truth. The days of being accused of any kind of crime were well in her rearview mirror. Or so she'd thought. "But I think I'd like you to leave."

He quirked an eyebrow. "I can come back with the proper authorities."

What the…? *Authorities?* What was his game? She'd done nothing wrong! Not in the recent past, anyway. And she'd absolutely paid her dues for all that had come before.

Anger and frustration raged inside of her. Along with what she had to admit was a mild curiosity. What in heaven's name was he referring to, exactly? She really shouldn't care. The sooner she got him out of the store, the better she could breathe. He was starting to make her feel really unsettled.

"Like I said, I have no idea what you're talking about. Come back if you feel you must. With whoever you wish to bring." She managed to fill her voice with false bravado somehow, though the prospect of seeing this man again was making her shudder. She wanted to kick herself for feeling even the slightest bit intimidated. She'd handled far worse in her lifetime, including tense questioning in dimly lit rooms by trained officers. There was no reason for this man to make her feel quite so shaken up. It was hard not to feel those old insecurities and fears bubble up to the surface when confronted, but she forced them away.

"But right now, I'd like you gone."

She would not be hassled here, of all places. Lucien's Magic Shop was one of her safe spots. A second home. A haven. It had been so for years. She would not allow this man to desecrate the sacredness of this store.

Too late, a little voice whispered in her mind's ear. The voice was right, of course. She could hardly deny that she was rattled.

Lucien chose that moment to step out from the inventory room, a grave look of concern marking his face. "Vivi? Is everything all right? Is this man bothering you?"

She must have raised her voice when she'd asked this Zeke to leave. Vivi sent a reassuring smile in Lucien's direction. The last thing she wanted was for things to escalate and have her boss involved in some type of altercation.

Something told her Zeke Manning wouldn't shirk away from a fight, physical or otherwise. Lucien wasn't exactly in his prime, or the violent type.

"He was just leaving," she said with clear force, shifting her gaze back to Zeke.

He appeared ready to argue, staring at Lucien intently. Then he gave his head a brisk shake.

Zeke Manning's next words did nothing to alleviate her disquiet, however. "Fine. I'll go for now. But trust me, this isn't over."

He might have overdone it.

Zeke poured an inch of bourbon into a glass from his hotel room's well-stocked bar rack and contemplated the day's events. Perhaps he'd been a bit overzealous in confronting the young lady. He probably should have called a colleague more familiar with this sort of thing. It's not as if he practiced criminal law. His specialty was in estate and trust planning, a completely different field.

Ms. Ducarne's face kept reappearing in his mind's eye. Her expression was as clear as if she stood in front of him at this very moment. If he didn't know any better, he might say she'd looked scared.

Or maybe she was just a good actress and he was being influenced by a pretty face. A *very* pretty face. It had shocked him when he'd first walked into the shop just how attractive she was. The photos he'd found online had not done her justice. She had striking features—dark, almond-shaped eyes and curves in all the right places.

It had thrown him off, he had to admit.

Damn it.

He had no reason to feel guilty. Even if he had been a bit over-the-top. A highly valuable antique was missing. Just because Vivienne Ducarne was attractive didn't mean something ugly hadn't gone down involving her and Esther. Zeke owed it to his grandmother—and to Esther—to uncover the mystery.

He just might have if the shop owner hadn't shown up at that moment. Zeke had never been afraid of a fight and had gotten into more than a few skirmishes in his lifetime. The man had certainly looked ready to defend his employee in any way necessary, despite having several years on him. Not that Zeke could blame him, given what the man must have been thinking if he'd overheard them. At that point, Zeke had figured the best thing to do was leave. He could have told the shop owner the truth about why he was there, but something made him hesitate. He hadn't been quite ready to jeopardize Vivienne's livelihood right then and there. Esther had given Vivienne the necklace, after all.

This isn't over.

He'd actually uttered those very words as a parting

warning before he left. How utterly dramatic. Like a scene out of a bad movie.

Still, he refused to feel remorseful. He'd learned the hard way, more than once, that when it came to a certain type of person—the type that had no qualms about taking advantage of others—it was always better to be safe rather than sorry.

Zeke had seen it firsthand, starting when he was only a child, how letting one's guard down could not only destroy the life of those most gullible, but also everyone else within range.

To be trusting was to play the fool.

Zeke had no doubt in his mind that Ms. Ducarne was exactly the type who should make others wary. Sure, he could have handled things better today. But the facts were the facts. Vivienne Ducarne had somehow finagled her way into being gifted a near priceless piece of jewelry.

Well, there was one way to find out exactly what kind of person she was. It was high time he called in a professional.

Zeke pulled his phone out of his pocket and pulled up his contact list. He only called Bill Wolfson under the most pressing of circumstances. And the current scenario certainly seemed to qualify.

The other man answered on the first ring. "Wasn't expecting a call from you, Ezekiel. What's on the horizon, then?"

Bill was one of the few people who insisted on using Zeke's proper name. He'd long ago accepted it as just another of the man's many quirks. Along with the catch phrase he often used: *What's on the horizon, then?*

"I could use your help to get to the bottom of something."

"Hmm. Kind of figured that or you wouldn't be calling. Any specifics?"

Right. Bill was the type where if you didn't get right to the point, he would be sure to call you on it.

"I have a name I'd like you to investigate. Along with her place of employment."

Zeke heard the other man's resigned sigh over the tiny speaker. "And I don't suppose you're willing to share anything more than that? Like why I'm looking into this person?"

"Not just yet. I'll text you the info you need for now."

Bill didn't have any more questions. They'd worked together for a long time now. Knew each other fairly well.

Zeke clicked off the call and dropped his phone on the hotel-room bureau. There, he felt better already. Bill would be able to uncover some answers for him. Hopefully it wouldn't even take that long. Zeke had enough going on between his responsibilities at the firm and his latest investments. Not to mention the French-winery acquisition that needed his focus before his trip to Provence. He didn't need a headache like Vivienne Ducarne right now.

Speaking of pressing responsibilities… Zeke picked up his cell phone again to check his latest emails and review updates on his pending projects. A message from his grandmother stood out among the others. She'd used several smiley-face emojis as her subject line. He clicked on the body of the message.

Hope you're enjoying New Orleans. Thanks again for handling Esther's affairs personally. She's a true friend who has always been there whenever I needed her throughout the decades.

Zeke bit out a curse and sighed.

He supposed he could do some investigating on his own in the meantime while Bill did his own thing.

Looked like he'd have to pay another visit to Lucien's on Bourbon Street. The sooner, the better.

The magic store was closed when Zeke made his way back there three hours later. A strange feeling of disappointment swelled in his chest—a feeling he didn't want to examine too closely. He was merely disappointed about having wasted his time coming here on a futile errand. He should have called first.

Zeke resisted the urge to swear out loud as his agitation grew. It had nothing to do with missing an opportunity to see *her* again. That would be downright silly. He'd only laid eyes on the woman for the span of a few short minutes. And their encounter could be described as contentious at best. Still, an image of Vivienne's almond-shaped eyes and sparkling smile appeared in his mind's eye, though her smile had faded when he'd confronted her.

No. This impulsive trip had nothing to do with her. He was here for one reason only. For Esther. To make sure she wasn't being taken advantage of.

Surprising, really. The shop seemed to be the only thing shut down as far as the eye could see. Around him the street bustled with both noisy tourists and what appeared to be locals. Jazzy music blared from every direction. A makeshift percussion band performed on the corner, using everything from large plastic buckets to aluminum cans. Neon lights lit up the night in every direction.

Bourbon Street seemed to have an energy Zeke would be hard-pressed to compare to anywhere else he'd been in his extensive travels. Sure, he'd visited New Orleans several times in the past. But he was usually at one business meeting after another before retiring to his hotel room in a quieter part of the French Quarter, only to do it all again the next day before he had to return to Manhattan.

Well, his fact-finding would have to wait another day, at least. Would she even be here if he came back tomorrow? He had no way of knowing if she worked every day. What sort of hours did tarot-card readers keep, anyway? To think, there were people out there who actually paid to have someone interpret what a bunch of cards meant as it pertained to their future. Just another grifter, as far as Zeke was concerned. It was a big clue into this Vivienne Ducarne's character that she made her living off gullible people.

How did Vivienne even happen to meet Esther and grow close enough to the old woman that she was being given valuable jewelry as a gift?

Zeke shook his head in consternation. Perhaps the better question was, why was he so curious about her in the first place? He couldn't deny that something about her had called to him. Even during their brief, rather volatile conversation, everything from her manner to her attire had piqued an interest that he felt rather confused about. His grandmother's affection toward Esther aside, if he was smart, he would wish the elder lady the best, wrap up the appraisal of the estate as best he could and simply wait for Bill's answers about the beguiling Ms. Ducarne while more qualified professionals dealt with the mystery of the missing necklace.

Whoa. Where had that come from? He was thinking of her as beguiling now?

That did it. He had to get out of this city. Maybe it was the bewitching atmosphere. New Orleans was known to have a certain mystical energy. That's what the locals always said, anyway. He'd never given it much credence or thought, for that matter, that the city's main attractions involved hexes and paranormal influences.

Or maybe it was simply the strong Louisiana bourbon he'd indulged in back in his hotel room. Zeke didn't know.

But he couldn't even recall a previous time he'd ever described a woman as "beguiling." It simply wouldn't do.

He was going to drop this matter. Let the expert investigator deal with it. But as he was turning away from the store window, a colorful flyer caught his eye. A classic-looking tourist steamship floating on the majestic Mississippi River. The poster was an advertisement for a party cruise that featured dinner, an open bar and a live band.

But the image that really drew his attention was a black-and-white thumbnail-size photo at the bottom corner of the paper.

Ms. Vivienne Ducarne was apparently a part of the river-cruise entertainment being offered this evening.

CHAPTER TWO

VIVI'S EARS STILL burned with anger as she made her way down the concrete steps and across the boardwalk to the River Rider steamboat's usual docking spot. She had to find a way to calm down. As part of the evening's entertainment, it wouldn't do to appear furious and frazzled as she sang onstage. Sure, she wasn't even the main act. That would be the jazz band with whom she added vocals on a handful of songs. Still, she would stick out like a sore thumb onstage if she appeared angry or perturbed. The whole atmosphere on the boat was supposed to be one of fun and joviality.

Still, calming down was going to take some work. The more she thought about…that man, whoever he was, the more her ire grew. Who did he think he'd been speaking to?

On top of apparently trying to accuse her of some kind of wrongdoing, there had also been an undercurrent of disdain. People like him always did that—approached her with a dismissive attitude, as if people like Vivi were hardly worth their time. For most of her childhood and teen years, she'd been nothing but a loose bolt in the system. A variable that needed to be addressed and then set aside. No one had been there to look out for her or stand up on her behalf. She'd had to do it all herself, not that anyone bothered to do much listening when she tried to stick up for herself.

The sting of tears burned her eyes before she could fully

steel herself against the onslaught of bitter emotion. Hadn't she sworn all afternoon that she was going to do her best to forget about Zeke Manning? She had a job to do, and she couldn't jeopardize this gig. People had paid good money for an evening of entertainment and fun.

Looked like it was a good crowd, too. She could see the line of people waiting to board snake around the dividers leading up to the entrance plank. Not bad for a Thursday evening. Vivi wasn't quite in demand enough to win one of the coveted weekend slots, or even be billed as the head-liner on the evenings she was here. But this continued to be a great opportunity for her. With her past, she didn't dare pursue any kind of career that might put her on a national stage. But the opportunity to sing on a busy tourist attrac-tion was the next best thing. Despite the late hours and the occasional overzealous male patron who'd overindulged in the bourbon punch the bartender specialized in, she en-joyed being up there on the small corner stage.

Not surprised you don't have any kind of real job.

The unwanted voice of her last foster father invaded her thoughts before she could stop it. Much to Vivi's dismay, she still ran into the man around town now and again. Their unwelcome conversations always ended with some kind of insult about how Vivi lived her life. As if it was any of the man's business. She'd turned eighteen and aged out of the system years ago.

Real job or not, Vivi was proud that she worked hard at what she did. So what if it was a collection of gigs here and there? Tarot readings and retail sales at the magic shop. Waitressing for the lunch crowd at the Crawdad Café and performing two nights a week on a steamship earned her enough money to pay her rent and buy her groceries. The waitressing even got her a free lunch every afternoon.

It wasn't much. But it was a far cry from the days when

she couldn't guess when her next meal would be, or where it would come from. Someone like Zeke Manning had probably never gone hungry a day in his life.

Now, why had her brain drifted back to that insufferable man yet again? The sooner she eradicated him from her mind, the sooner she could get on with her evening. He'd made it clear that they'd be meeting again at some point. That prospect sent an icy shiver traveling up her spine. But she certainly didn't need to dwell on his existence in the meantime. She'd deal with him when she had to.

Or maybe he would figure out she had nothing to hide and be on his way. She may never even see him again. For some inexplicable reason, that notion didn't bring the level of satisfaction it would have warranted. Frustrating as it was, she was a warm-blooded woman. And Zeke Manning was certainly easy on the eyes.

Don't. You. Dare.

How many times in one lifetime could she err on the side of sheer stupidity when it came to men? She'd barely laid eyes on this Zeke, had no business thinking about how handsome he was. Especially not after the way he'd treated her.

By the time she reached the boat and made her way on board, she was still chastising herself. How could she even think about the attractiveness of a man who had just that morning shown up at her place of employment to berate her without so much as an explanation as to why. Handsome though he was.

Stop it.

Anyway, something told her she hadn't seen the last of him by any means. Zeke Manning didn't seem the type to let things go.

The friendly faces of the crew greeted her as she made her way to the staff cabin below deck. The engine slowly

roared to life as billows of steam drifted in the air. The excited sounds of passengers as they slowly boarded became
louder and louder as the crowd grew. Excitement hummed
through her veins as Vivi mentally prepared herself for the
performance later this evening. Being onstage made her
feel vibrant and alive. Any nervous energy quickly turned
to excitement when she let her voice simply take over and
she became Vivi the vocal artist.

Some might say she was nothing more than a lounge
singer belting out tunes for some extra cash and a few mea-
sly tips. But Vivi knew it was much more than that.

Up onstage she became someone else—the music took
over her soul, the melody allowed her to temporarily stop
thinking about her past and the daily struggle it was to
make ends meet, along with all the negativity that had followed her around since childhood.

She forgot about the voices of those people who wanted
to belittle her. Vivi doubted herself about many things. But
she was certain she could carry a tune. And that she had a
voice. Maybe it wasn't one that would make her famous or
any real amount of money. She didn't want any of that, anyway. She just loved who she became when she was onstage.

Today, she hoped being up there and performing would
allow her to forget about the clear derision she'd seen in
Zeke Manning's eyes earlier that day.

He almost missed it. Zeke took a moment to catch his breath
as he watched the boarding plank be lifted much too close
after he'd just cleared it. He'd never been an impulsive sort.
Yet he'd surprised himself by calling a car to make it to the
square, then fought the throngs of tourists along the river
walk that led to the dock.

But it had been close. In fact, the agent in the ticket booth
had been reluctant to sell him a ticket, explaining he'd cut it

much too close, that the crew was making the final preparations before setting sail.

It had taken quite a bit of convincing and no small amount of charm to persuade her. Now that he was aboard and the boat was en route, Zeke had to wonder what had gotten into him. How had he ended up on a tourist steamship cruise when he had so much to do? Still, there were worse ways he could be spending the evening than a tour of the Mississippi. Not to mention, it was a dinner cruise and he had to eat, didn't he?

He took a moment to study his fellow passengers. All the coveted spots along the railing had been taken. The smaller tables sat two or three. Most of them were inhabited by lovestruck couples holding hands, or sharing a snack and a drink. One couple appeared to be in the throes of a passionate kiss.

Get a room.

The larger tables were occupied by noisy families with laughing, screaming kids and indulgent parents.

Yep. He was the only person on board who appeared to be here by himself. He hadn't really thought this through. Not that he had any kind of qualm about spending time alone—he just didn't like to stick out. And in a crowd such as the one on the steamship, he stuck out like a sore thumb. A small trickle of discomfort drifted over his skin. He'd spent most of his childhood making sure to attract as little attention as he could, constantly trying to be seen or heard as little as possible.

The least conspicuous thing would be to hang out at the freestanding bar in the center area of the upper deck. He could chat with the bartender. Small talk always came easy for a man who was used to dealing with all manner of clientele. He'd worked hard over the years to perfect the art.

After making his way to the serving area, he pulled out

one of the barstools and sat. The bartender approached immediately. He was a tall, wide-shouldered man with a thick ponytail made up of elaborate braids, and his wrists were covered with gold jewelry.

"I know what you want, my man," he told Zeke with a smile, pointing a finger at him. "Our specialty, the bourbon punch."

"You're the expert. I'll take it."

"You're gonna love it, man."

Zeke watched as he walked to the other side of the bar and pulled out a plastic pour container and a gold glass bottle of liquor. He mixed the two expertly then poured the mixture into a tall, frosty glass.

This was good. The bartender was chatty and friendly with a perpetual smile, and it made him feel less like the lonely tourist.

He could always take out his phone, but he didn't want to waste this beautiful evening staring at a small screen. The scene around him was too majestic. The sky was a beautiful, deep shade of pearly blue as the sun got ready to set. Thin, cotton-white clouds formed various patterns above.

"You in NOLA on business?" the bartender asked, sliding his drink across the wooden surface. The glass stopped expertly in front of him, not a drop spilling over the side.

Zeke nodded. "I am. Thought I'd do something fun while I'm here."

"Good for you," he said. "It's good to explore this city. Too many business people come here and don't bother to check out all the wonderful things New Orleans has to offer. I'm Tomas, if you need anything else," he added with another friendly grin.

Zeke took a sip of his drink. Tomas was right. It was good. A bit fruitier and sweeter than his usual fare, but the tangy flavor hit the spot.

"I'm actually on board looking for someone," he told Tomas. "There's something we need to discuss and we didn't exactly get off on the right foot." Why he'd admitted such a thing to a virtual stranger, friendly or not, he had no idea.

"Oh, yeah? That happens sometimes in life," Tomas offered wisely.

"Wanna talk about it?" Tomas asked. "You can tell me."

Before Zeke could answer, a recently familiar voice sounded behind him. A voice he'd heard echoing in his head more than once over the last few hours.

"Hey, Tomas. Nice night, huh? Could I get a glass of lemon water?"

He wouldn't have thought it possible, but the bartender's smile grew even wider, and a softening Zeke would describe as tenderness washed over the other man's features. Yet another one loyal to Vivienne Ducarne, it seemed. First the shop owner, now the bartender. Her ability to elicit such loyalty reminded him of someone he'd rather forget.

"Coming right up, Vivi."

Taking another large gulp of his drink for some liquid fortitude, Zeke turned slowly to face her, bracing himself for her sure-to-be-volatile reaction. He wouldn't be surprised if the woman chose to fling her lemon water in his face rather than drink it.

It would probably be less than what he deserved.

She glanced past him at first, tilting her head in a friendly nod. She appeared to do a double take a mere second later. Then her focus found his face again. Her eyes grew wide and her mouth fell open.

"You!"

"What are you doing here?" Vivi felt her pulse shoot clear to the sky and the heat of anger travel clear down to her toes. "Are you trailing me?"

Zeke held his hands up in the air, palms facing her. "It's not like that."

Oh, she couldn't wait to hear his explanation, then. Considering he was here now at yet another place of her employment. "Then how is it exactly?"

"I went about things the wrong way earlier today."

She'd say so. "Get off this boat. I want you gone."

His head tilted to the side, one ear nearly touching his shoulder. "Where to, exactly? If you happen to have forgotten, we're on a boat in the middle of one of the USA's longest and deepest rivers."

"A boat you have no business being on. Now leave."

"I would have to jump into the water."

"That suits me just fine." She knew she wasn't making any sense. But shock and trepidation were making it hard to think straight. She hadn't expected to see him here. He'd caught her off guard. She felt frazzled and unprepared. Along with something else she didn't exactly want to name. Heaven help her, she did want to know what his deal was. Why was he after her? She knew without any doubt whatsoever that she wasn't in any kind of danger from this man. Not physically, anyway. With the life she'd led, she could spot such peril miles away. No, he wasn't that kind of a threat.

But that didn't mean he wasn't dangerous.

"Look, I went to the magic shop on Bourbon and it was closed. A flyer on the window advertised that you'd be here."

She gave her head a shake in a futile attempt to clear it. "I'm sorry. How does any of that sound like you're not trailing me?"

Tomas appeared on the other side of the bar with her lemon water. He set it in front of her, but his eyes were trained squarely on Zeke's face. "Is there a problem here,

Vivi?" the bartender asked, his voice laced with clear concern.

Great. She didn't want any of her friends involved in whatever this mess was. No one who worked on the boat, the magic shop, or the café knew anything about her past. Except for Bessa, her roommate, who also happened to be her best friend. No one else had a clue.

She wanted to keep it that way.

She took a deep breath to try and calm down. The last thing she needed was any kind of scene here, similar to the one earlier, at the magic store. "Nothing I can't handle, Tomas. Thank you."

Tomas didn't so much as shift his glaring gaze from Zeke. "Are you sure?"

"Yes," she assured him, grateful that he was looking out for her. It was a strange feeling. She was still getting used to the concept of having friends who actually cared about her well-being. "Thanks."

She couldn't help but laugh out loud when Tomas, with complete and utter seriousness, pointed two fingers toward his own eyes and then one at Zeke's chest. The universal sign that said, "I've got my eyes on you." He lingered a few seconds after the gesture, then finally turned away to attend to other thirsty customers.

"Thanks a lot," Zeke said with a wistful tone, watching the other man retreat. "We were just starting to become friends."

"I find that hard to believe."

He turned back to her and took a drink of his cocktail. "What? That I can make friends?"

Calm and charming. While she was shaking inside. What kind of effect did this man have on her and why? Sure, he was handsome in a striking and disarming way. Tall and dark. Piercing expressive eyes. She'd been right in her earlier assessment. He wouldn't be described as muscular, per se. But he was certainly in shape. He probably belonged to the best gyms and could afford the most exclusive trainers. But there was nothing soft about him. The edge was there. It was in his voice, in his mannerisms. He wasn't the type one wanted to tangle with.

She should probably do her best not to goad him.

Just figure out what he wants and move on with your life.

But she couldn't seem to help herself.

"Let's just say I've yet to see your friendly side," she answered, taking a sip of her water.

He ducked his head. "You have me there. It's why I'm here. I came to find you to say I was out of line. I should have handled our first meeting much better than I did."

"That is a very weak apology, Mr. Manning."

He merely quirked an eyebrow at her. This wasn't a man used to being repudiated in any way, she wagered.

"If you're here to tell me you're sorry," she continued, "then just say it."

The slightest hint of a smile tugged at the corners of his lips. He lifted his drink to her in a salute. "I'm sorry."

Before she could feel any kind of satisfaction, he added, "For the way I went about things."

Implied was the suggestion that he wasn't sorry for his reasoning.

Vivi rolled her eyes at him. She should have known better. After downing half her glass of water, she turned to tell him their interaction was over for now.

She really shouldn't be sparring with him—she should be resting her voice instead. The band was due to start in ten short minutes. She was on twenty minutes after that.

Whatever his issue was, she was going to have to deal with it later.

"I hope you enjoy your evening, Mr. Manning. I have a

show to do." With that, she turned and walked away to the steps that led to the lower deck to start to get ready.

Maybe she was putting off the inevitable, but there wasn't any other choice right now. Whatever Zeke Manning wanted with her it was going to have to wait.

She was really something, all right. Zeke had no doubt about it as he watched Vivi's back as she left the bar area. He couldn't help but notice the other appreciative male gazes that followed her exit. She wasn't quite sashaying, but her movements somehow screamed out her allure and sex appeal. Long, shapely legs leading to a rounded, luscious bottom. Her waist was cinched by a thin gold chain that served as a threadlike belt around her silky black dress.

He squeezed his eyes shut. He really had no business looking at her dress or her curves.

Tomas was still glaring at him from the other side of the bar. Zeke held up his hands in mock surrender. He hadn't really done anything wrong. For all he knew, Vivi had indeed taken advantage of Esther when she was most vulnerable. Zeke just hadn't handled his suspicions well. But, truth be told, even their brief interactions had sewn a seed of doubt about her guilt. Not to mention, she certainly had a loyal friend in the bartender. Women who took advantage of little old ladies didn't usually inspire that kind of loyalty, did they?

He let out a disgusted grunt. What kind of question was that? He, of all people, knew how some individuals were charismatic and duplicitous enough to attract lost souls. Souls like his mother.

Still, Vivi didn't strike him as anyone who resembled his "uncle." Quote, unquote. Even calling the man by that title sent a surge of bile rising up in Zeke's throat. The ever-present memories dancing on the edge of his mind threatened to trot to the center before he squashed them back down. He dragged himself back to the present.

Tomas was clearly done serving him any more cocktails. He hadn't so much as acknowledged Zeke's existence since Vivienne had walked off, other than to send a withering glare in his direction. Shame. He could have used another glass of the punch. Just as well, he needed his wits about him when they finally had the conversation about Esther and the missing necklace. He hoped she had a good explanation. In fact, he wanted that to be true more than he would have imagined when he first boarded the boat. Which made absolutely no sense. That one scenario would be the fastest way to be done with the whole mess and get back to all the pressing matters waiting for him at the firm. He still had that trip to France coming up in a few short days. All the documents needed for the winery acquisition still needed to be drawn up and finalized. He really had no business drifting on a steamship on the Mississippi.

With a sigh, he pulled out his wallet and left a generous tip for the man who apparently didn't think him worthy of another minute of his time. He could hear the band starting up one deck below. The programs on the back of the plastic-coated menus indicated Vivienne wouldn't be onstage until after they played for a little while as dinner was served.

Well, he'd paid for said dinner. So he might as well eat.

A wall of aroma greeted him when he opened the double-wide door that led to the main ballroom. Buffet tables were set up in a half rectangle on the opposite side. Steam wafted from shiny silver trays. The band was between numbers, but struck up the first chord to the next song as Zeke shut the door behind him. A bouncy jazz number started to play with a trumpet blaring to accompany the rapid notes of the banjo. A drummer accentuated the rhythmic beat, and a piano player rounded out the foursome. Just like by the bar, Zeke didn't know anyone. And there'd be no bartender with a friendly smile to help keep him company. Not that that had lasted long.

At least the food looked good. In fact, between the scents of seafood, rice and gumbo, and the colorful array of salads and fruit, Zeke's mouth started to water.

Striding over to the buffet area, he grabbed a plate and stepped forward to the start of the line. He couldn't remember the last time he'd eaten buffet-style. This trip was turning into one big slew of surprises.

The touchy-feely couple he'd seen earlier was right in front of him. The man had one hand gripping a plate as he waited his turn, and the other wrapped around his lady's waist. She stood leaning tight against his side. Every few seconds, they faced each other for a quick yet ardent kiss on the lips.

What would that be like? Zeke had to wonder, making sure not to stare. To be that enamored of someone. Not the way his mother had been with Rex—that wasn't healthy or natural. That had been the type of relationship that ruined lives. No, there'd been nothing affectionate about that relationship. Just his mother's rampant gullibility and blatant disregard for all those who had the misfortune of depending on her.

Zeke made himself turn away from the couple and concentrated on filling his plate. Before he knew it, he was back up for seconds. The food was good—really good. The band was entertaining, and he couldn't deny that he was enjoying himself. He was debating going back for yet another helping when the lights in the room dimmed slightly. The band played out of the latest song and its members shifted to make more room in the center.

A moment later, Zeke found himself grateful that he hadn't gone up for more food. He didn't think he could swallow anything down. Vivienne stepped onto the stage and though she was wearing the same dress, her entire look had somehow morphed into something even sexier. She'd taken off the flat checkered Chucks and donned stilettos. Her hair was piled on top of her head. Scarlet red lipstick covered her mouth. That had to be the sexiest shade of red he'd ever seen.

Zeke shifted in his seat to somehow quell the unwelcome surge of desire storming thorough his core. This wouldn't do. It had to be the novelty of the atmosphere. The fact that he was on a boat surrounded by arduous couples. Once he left New Orleans, and the business with the necklace was resolved, he would forget any kind of attraction he was feeling at the moment for Ms. Ducarne. He was convinced. But then she began to sing.

CHAPTER THREE

SHE'D NEVER HAD this much trouble concentrating on her performance. How many notes had she missed already? And the song she was performing was one she knew in her heart. It was her warm-up song, for heaven's sake. There was no excuse for messing up the way she was.

She knew exactly whom to blame.

Vivi tried to keep her gaze roaming around the entire audience and not on one individual in particular. The man who just happened to be sitting at one of the tables closest to the stage. He hadn't seemed to have taken his eyes off her. Which was disconcerting to say the least. Not that it should have been. She was onstage, after all. It was just that the way he was looking at her was making her think all sorts of wayward thoughts. Thoughts like how the dark hue of his eyes seemed even more dramatic in the dimly lit ballroom. And of the way she'd noticed his scent when she'd been sitting next to him at the bar. Like spearmint mixed with some kind of woodsy, rich scent she'd be hard-pressed to name. How his dark hair fell haphazardly across his forehead and had her fingertips itching with the desire to gently swipe the strands off his face.

She'd just sung off-key again. The audience seemed too distracted to notice, or maybe they didn't care, given all the food and drink distracting them. But both the drummer and piano player were giving her quizzical looks from under the brims of their straw hats.

Vivi somehow managed to finish the set without slipping up too badly. But her lackluster performance had her feeling out of sorts to say the least.

Enough was enough. After taking a bow to the applauding audience, she made a beeline to where Zeke Manning was still sitting at the same table.

"Why are you still here?"

He didn't so much as blink in reaction. "What? You were hoping Tomas might have thrown me overboard perhaps?"

"The thought is not without appeal."

"Sorry. No such luck." He pushed out a chair with his leg, motioned for her to sit down. "Why don't you join me?"

"You know what? I think I will." It was high time they had a little chat about what it was, exactly, that had Zeke Manning's knickers all twisted. Whatever it was, Vivi just knew she wasn't going to like it. Nothing like ripping the bandage right off. Ignoring the chair he'd kicked out for her, she pulled out the one farthest from him and sat. Though only a matter of inches, the petty gesture gave a small manner of satisfaction.

"Why exactly are you here, Mr. Manning?" she began without any preamble. "What is it that you want with me?"

She thought she saw a flicker of something pass behind his eyes. Probably just a trick of the light. Right now, all she wanted was some answers.

"I'm an estate attorney who specializes in appraisals."

"And?"

"And I'm here in New Orleans as a favor to my grandmother."

It was her turn to blink in confusion. Zeke wouldn't have struck her as the type who did favors for their grandmothers. "Come again?"

He nodded. "She's a friend of Esther Truneau."

"The sweet lady I do weekly readings for?"

"That's the one. You do the readings at her mansion, I was told."

Alarm bells started to ring in Vivi's head. "That's right. She used to come to the shop at first, but at her age, I offered to go to her instead. She's not terribly mobile, if you hadn't noticed."

Zeke casually rubbed his jaw, drawing her attention to the dark stubble of his five-o'clock shadow. The facial hair added another layer of edginess to his already jagged aura. "Hmm" was all he said in response.

Vivi really didn't like the way he said it. "What exactly does that mean?"

Zeke gave a small shrug. "I'm just curious. Do many fortune-tellers make house calls?"

Vivi crossed her arms in front of her chest. "First of all, I'm not a fortune-teller. I read tarot cards."

He waved that off with dismissal. "Six of one…"

She didn't bother to explain how wrong he was. Zeke made it sound as if she sat in a darkened tent at the traveling carnival with a crystal ball between her and a lovestruck teenager. Not that there was anything wrong with that. But Vivi had spent years studying the tarot. She took care to interpret and explain what she thought the cards meant in such a way as to make a real impact on her clients and how they lived their lives.

He motioned to the stage. "And obviously that's not all you do to earn a living."

The way he said the last three words sounded downright condescending. Of course he looked down at her. Everything about this man screamed prestigious attorney for the rich and powerful. He was clearly no ambulance chaser like the ones advertising on daytime television every afternoon who promised to "win you your due without even having to go to court!"

"I'm sure you've heard of the new gig economy in the US these days. Now, what's all this got to do with you being here in the city and following me to said gigs twice in one day?"

He leaned over the table, his elbows on the wrinkled paper mat. "Esther mentioned she's sometimes gifted you various items."

The alarm bells suddenly increased in both frequency and volume. "That's true. She told me she's ready to downsize and wants to get rid of some odds and ends."

He grunted out a laugh, but darned if she was in on the joke. "I believe she recently gave you a necklace."

Vivi nodded. "That's right. She said the red stones would go well with my dark hair."

Zeke quirked an eyebrow at her. "Those stones happen to be red rubies. On a platinum chain."

Vivi's mouth went dry. "Wait. Real rubies? On a real platinum chain?"

"That's right. The piece happens to be an antique crafted in the eighteenth century in France."

Vivi swallowed past the heavy lump that had formed in her throat. "Are you telling me that wasn't costume jewelry? I—I thought it was a trinket, just a small token of Esther's appreciation."

Zeke leaned closer to her over the table. Vivi resisted the urge to draw back or to drop her gaze. She knew she had to meet this man eye-to-eye. Still, it was hard not to show any kind of reaction at his next words.

"It just so happens that the small trinket Esther gave you is highly valuable, and would probably fetch high six figures at auction."

She was good. Zeke had to give her that much. She'd barely reacted when he'd told her the estimated value of the item she'd so casually referred to as a "trinket." Still, he hadn't missed the near imperceptible flinch when he'd mentioned the actual sum.

Either Vivienne Ducarne was an actress of Oscar-worthy caliber or he really had shocked her with the revelation.

Now she sat across from him with her mouth agape, seemingly at a loss for words.

"Is this someone's idea of a sick joke?" she demanded finally after several silent seconds.

He shook his head in answer. "No joke. You have in your possession an extremely valuable piece, which should fetch close to a million dollars at any international auction."

She squeezed her eyes shut tight, took a deep breath. "But why would Esther give me something so valuable?"

Did she really have to ask? It was clear Vivienne was a bright, intelligent young woman. Clearly, she had to see what was happening to Esther right in front of her eyes.

Vivienne had to have noticed that Esther wasn't always speaking sensibly or remembering things. Just today, Zeke had noticed all the times she hadn't been quite lucid. "Because she's gradually losing her faculties. It might be the onset of dementia of some sort." He couldn't try and guess, since he was no medically trained professional. But even a layman could see what was obvious.

"Poor Esther," Vivienne said simply. Suddenly, her eyes grew wide. "Wait. You don't think I somehow tricked her to give me something that priceless. I didn't even know! How could I?" She clasped a hand to her mouth in horror. "Oh, my God! You threatened in the shop to come back with the authorities. You were ready to accuse me of theft, weren't you?"

She leaned closer to him over the table. "Valuable or not, I was given that necklace!"

Zeke ducked his head—she had him there. The threat

had been a bit much coming from him before he'd so much as gathered any facts. "Yeah, look. About that."

Her palm remained on her mouth—he had her full attention. "I admit I may have been a bit…overzealous back there earlier today."

"Oh, you think?" she asked, her voice dripping with sarcasm. "You didn't even bother to explain or ask me my side of the story."

Zeke cleared his throat—she was right. He should have done more asking and less threatening. "I admit it. I didn't handle that very well."

She tilted her head, studying him. "You're not very good at apologizing, are you?"

An apology wasn't quite what he'd intended when he boarded the steamship, but he didn't bother to correct the assumption she'd jumped to. Again, he had to wonder if she was a gifted actress or really did consider herself to be the slighted party. Maybe it was both.

"I'm guessing you haven't had much practice apologizing to people," she added.

He had to laugh at that. She had no idea. He'd been made to apologize so often as a child. For even the smallest of slights. "I'm sorry for the way I behaved when we first met. Maybe we can do that part over."

Her eyes narrowed on him. "How do you propose we do that? You were ready to throw me to the wolves because you thought I was low enough to take advantage of a vulnerable old lady. You didn't even ask if I was innocent."

Not many guilty folks would actually admit it. Zeke kept that thought to himself. He wasn't quite ready to accept her total innocence. But he could give her the benefit of the doubt. He'd humor her until he learned more, at least. For now.

"How about we try to start over?" He stuck his hand out. "Hello. I'm Ezekiel Manning. Everyone calls me Zeke."

She looked at his outstretched hand with clear wariness, but made no move to take it for several moments. Finally, she took the end of his fingertips in a quick shake before pulling away. "I'm Vivienne Ducarne. As you know. Everyone calls me Vivi. And I did not knowingly take a priceless necklace."

"Nice to meet you, Vivi. Please just tell me it's in a safe place."

She nodded. "Yes. It's at my apartment. I gave it to my roommate because she admired it so much when I brought it home."

A surge of panic shot through Zeke's core. "You did what?"

"Don't worry. She wouldn't be wearing it tonight. She's waitressing the night shift at the Crawdad Café. No need for even costume jewelry there. We get covered from head to toe in powdered sugar and coffee syrup before our shifts ends."

"We? Our? You have yet another job, then?"

"This is a very expensive city, Mr. Manning. It takes a lot simply to make ends meet." Her voice was full of emotion and grievance as she said the words. He'd wounded her pride.

Great. Yet another slight he would have to find a way and time to apologize for. If he ever got the chance, he might have to explain to Ms. Ducarne just how little he came from. Though he went through extreme pains to make sure to hide it.

Vivienne changed the subject. "I'm sure it's on her dresser bureau, where she keeps her baubles."

Zeke had to suppress a shudder at the thought of such a priceless antique sitting among a slew of discount-store knickknacks. All that mattered was he'd discovered the location of the necklace. At least the mystery was over.

Vivi continued, "As soon as we dock, I'll head straight back to my place. I'll leave Bessa a text to tell her why I had to take it back. She's not going to believe this!"

Zeke could hardly blame her.

"We can get it back to Esther tonight," Vivi continued. "I have no desire to have anything that valuable in my possession a moment longer."

They took a cab from the Toulouse Street wharf to Vivi's neighborhood. Zeke studied the buildings they passed as the taxi came to a stop in front of her residence. Nestled between a restaurant and a candle shop, her house looked like something out of a children's storybook. A porch with hanging spider plants, pink-and-white shutters and two matching rocking chairs. The siding was a bright powder blue. The street held an eclectic mix of businesses and residential houses.

"Wait for me here," Vivi ordered as they exited the car and reached the sidewalk. "I'll be right down with it."

It was past eleven o'clock, yet the street bustled with activity. Different types of music poured out of every open window. A For Sale sign hung off a pole in front of the house across the street. A smaller sign in the window read Haunted in bright red letters. Interesting disclosure. Quite the selling point.

A group of teenagers walked by him, laughing and talking loudly. One of them sported a thick yellow boa wrapped around his neck. Zeke did a double take upon closer inspection. It was moving. The boa wasn't a decorative accessory, after all. Rather, it was a very large python. Vivi must have noticed his reaction to the reptile as she pulled her house key out of her purse.

"That's Nessie," she called back to him. "You can pet him if you'd like. I'm sure Tim will let you."

Zeke hoped his shiver wasn't terribly obvious. "No, thanks. I'll pass."

Vivi laughed, unlocking her door and pushing it open. It occurred to him that this was the first time he'd heard her laugh. Hearty yet soft. It sounded almost melodic...

He gave himself a mental smack. What in the world was wrong with him? Waxing poetic about the way a woman laughed?

The sooner this night was over with and the sooner he got the necklace back to its rightful owner, the sooner he could get back to normal.

He was unable to recognize this version of himself. Overindulging at a buffet, boarding steamships on a whim, noticing the sway of a woman's gait when she walked. The sound she made when she laughed.

Practically swooning while watching her sing onstage. He was acting like some hormonal teenager.

When was the last time he'd dated? It had been too long apparently. Maybe that was the problem. He'd been so busy with the firm and his growing clientele, not to mention his investment portfolio. He needed to get out more, as his ex, Marnie, had so loudly pointed out after he'd turned her down for yet another red-carpet event. Right before she'd stormed out of his apartment, cursing at him over her shoulder. He'd thought about calling her to apologize, but figured it was best they go their separate ways. An up-and-coming actress needed more time and effort than Zeke was ready to give.

A light came on upstairs on the second floor. Zeke glanced at his watch. Hopefully, this wouldn't take long. It was already too late to wake Esther, but he could at least get the necklace back to the Truneau estate sometime tonight. He'd sleep well knowing it was back where it belonged.

And what of Vivi?

The question nagged at him because it wasn't one he had any business asking. Twenty-four hours ago, he hadn't even known the woman existed. He had the firm's investigator looking into her and if the vetting proved unsatisfactory in any way, if anything unscrupulous turned up in her past, Zeke would make sure Esther knew and was protected. Other than that, after tonight, there was no reason to think about Vivienne Ducarne, let alone ever see her again.

A coil of displeasure tightened in his gut. What might have transpired between them under different circumstances? he wondered. They belonged in such different worlds. It was a wonder their paths had crossed at all. If he had happened to run into her during one of his business trips to Louisiana, would he even have noticed her?

Something told him the opposite was definitely not likely. A free spirit like Vivi would probably not look twice at a businessman like himself. The guys she dated were probably all as eclectic as she was.

They really had nothing in common. And their first encounter had been less than cordial. Still, imagining running into her at a different time and in a different place brought all sorts of intriguing pictures to his imagination.

The taxi driver rolled down his window, interrupting Zeke's musings.

"How much longer, man? I got calls coming in from dispatch."

Zeke glanced at his watch. How long had it been? More than the couple of minutes it should have taken for her to retrieve the necklace, then head back down. Even accounting for a potential run to her restroom, or a quick stop in the kitchen, Vivi should have come back by now.

"I'm sure she'll be down in no time," he answered the cabbie, somehow managing to keep the uncertainty out of his voice.

But several more minutes passed. A curl of unease ran down his spine. She definitely should have been down by now. Possibilities he didn't want to explore tried invading his mind. Had he been duped? Was he standing here like an idiot on the sidewalk because she had no intention of coming back down? Maybe she'd even cut and run using a back door.

That made no sense. She clearly lived here—she'd entered with a key. Why would she bring him to her home only to try and ditch him when he could come back to find her at any time?

There was one way to find out.

He was about to run up the steps to ring her doorbell when she finally reappeared. Even in the dim glow of the porch tea lights, he could tell by her pallor that something was terribly wrong. She was pale as a sheet. The unease he'd been feeling turned into full-blown trepidation as she spoke.

"It's not here."

CHAPTER FOUR

ZEKE DIDN'T EVEN know why he was surprised. Why had he expected things to go without a hitch in the first place? Nothing that had happened since he'd first laid eyes on Vivienne Ducarne should have ever given him the impression that things would run smoothly where she was concerned.

"Are you sure?" he asked her, though he was certain of the answer.

She nodded briskly, her head bobbing up and down. "Positive. I looked everywhere. Pretty much tore the apartment upside down. Esther's necklace is nowhere to be found. It's gone."

In a colossal case of bad timing, the cabbie bleeped his car horn twice. What was wrong with the man? The meter was running, after all. Zeke held his hands up, asking him to wait.

"What about your roommate? Maybe she is indeed wearing it. Have you tried calling her?"

Vivi glared at him in response to his question. "Of course. What do you take me for?"

Zeke threw his hands up in frustration. "And? What did she say? Does she have it?"

"Don't you think I would have told you if I had an answer to that?" she demanded. "She didn't answer her phone.

I didn't really expect her to. We're not allowed to carry our phones on the dining floor when we're serving. And I know she would have taken her only break by now."

Zeke pinched the bridge of his nose. "You could have led with that information when I asked about your roommate."

The cabbie interrupted yet again. Rolling down his window, he leaned his head out to yell at them. "Listen, man. Y'all ain't paying me enough to just sit here idle."

Zeke walked over to the open window and handed the man several bills as a tip to add to the meter reading. But without waiting any longer, as soon as he took the cash, the cabbie rolled the car forward and drove off. None too slowly.

Zeke swore under his breath. "Great. Now we have to find another ride." He rounded on Vivi, a little more abruptly than he'd meant to. "How could this have happened?"

She didn't so much as flinch. Rather, her chin jutted upward. "Our driver got tired of waiting for us and he left."

Zeke sucked in a deep breath, aiming for some semblance of calm. If she was trying to aggravate him, it was working. "You know very well our loss of transportation is not what I'm referring to. How could the necklace not be where you were certain it would be?"

Clearly, giving Vivienne Ducarne the benefit of the doubt had been a mistake. Zeke wanted to kick himself for playing the fool. Was she playing some kind of game with him, trying to dupe him somehow? But if that was the case, why would she have brought him to her house in the first place?

Curiosity mingled with irritation and churned in his core. Maybe she was lying about where she thought the necklace would be. But he'd play along for now. In for a penny and all that.

"Don't snap at me," she growled. "That's not exactly helping matters. We just need to talk to Bessa. Ask where she's put it." She pulled her bangs off her forehead. "I wish I'd never laid eyes on the confounded thing."

"How can we ask this Bessa anything if she's not answering her phone?" Zeke asked.

She puffed out a breath before answering. "Let's just go to the café. Talk to her directly. Her shift doesn't end for another two hours."

Zeke pulled his phone out of his pocket, swearing once more, this time at the disloyal and impatient cab driver. "I'll call for another car."

She touched him on the wrist before he could dial. A strange current seemed to travel over his skin where her hand made contact. And wasn't this a fine time to be noticing such a thing.

"Don't bother. It's just as easy to walk. It's just through the main square."

She dropped her hand and turned on her heel. "Be forewarned, though."

Warned? What fresh peril awaited them now? "About what?" he asked, following in her path.

"The French Quarter is a chaotic party zoo this time of night."

Despite the more pressing matters they were dealing with at the moment, her statement struck Zeke as rather odd. "Why do you feel the need to warn me about that?"

She shrugged. "Something tells me you're not exactly the outdoor, citywide-partying type."

She had no idea how loaded her comment was. Zeke didn't bother to try and elaborate. Vivi was right. He didn't like crowds. He didn't like chaos. Another reason why Marnie had broken up with him. He'd worked hard all his life for order and structure and discipline. Because he'd been exposed to too much of the opposite in his younger years. If they'd met under different circumstances, he might very well have told Vivi about all the ways his childhood could have been a disturbing movie. But tonight wasn't the night. And it made no sense to rehash any of his past, anyway. That's exactly where he'd put it all—squarely in his past.

She wasn't kidding about the rowdiness. As they approached the cross street, the level of noise grew gradually louder and the handful of people out and about slowly grew to parade-size crowd numbers.

Vivi must have sensed his thoughts. "You should see it at Mardi Gras. This is nothing."

"How do you know I've never been to New Orleans for Mardi Gras?"

A small smile danced at the corners of her mouth. "Again. You don't seem the type."

"You're making quite a few assumptions about me, Ms. Ducarne. Might I remind you that we just met?" Little did she know, he'd grown up with quite the partiers.

"Well, that's rich," she replied as they passed a juggler entertaining a small crowd. The tall thin man in a tracksuit tossed several sharp objects in the air and caught them effortlessly to the sounds of oohs and aahs from those watching him.

"What's that?"

"Considering how you made a major assumption about me before you'd even met me."

Zeke sighed slowly. "Yes, we've already established I was being a—"

She supplied a noun that didn't bear repeating. "And it was more than that," she countered. "You accused me of being a thief."

So she still held a grudge about that first meeting. Zeke didn't bother to voice his thoughts aloud—for someone who still hadn't produced the necklace, Vivi certainly played the part of the injured party very well.

They didn't bother to speak the rest of the way. It would have been near impossible to hear over the noise that surrounded them as they walked through the massive crowds.

Finally, Vivi turned a corner, passing a group of tap dancers using flattened soda cans as makeshift tap shoes. Half a crowded block later, they approached a glass-walled diner-style café with open-air seating. Every table was full, the hum of conversations accompanying a single pianist on the stage in the corner. The man's fingers moved furiously over the keys as he played a fast-paced jazz number that sounded vaguely familiar to Zeke's ears. He finally recognized the tune as an instrumental version of a popular hip-hop song. Two couples were dancing a complicated number between the tables.

One thing about New Orleans—the music and dancing never seemed to stop. Vivi spotted a group leaving their chairs and immediately nabbed the table. The woman sure could move fast when she needed to.

"This isn't her section, but we can try and steal her away," she explained as Zeke pulled out his own chair to sit. The sweet scent of sugar and fried dough wafted in the air. His taste buds reacted in response. He didn't possess much of a sweet tooth, but the smell of freshly fried beignets was hard to ignore.

"You want something to eat or drink?" she asked, somewhat surprising him. "The beignets are as good as they smell." She really was rather intuitive. Maybe it had something to do with her fortune-telling. He'd have to remind himself not to refer to that particular job that way if it came up again. She hadn't liked that description.

He shook his head in answer. "Maybe later. Let's just find your roommate and be on with it."

"There she is," Vivi suddenly exclaimed and jumped up. "Bessa! Over here!"

The other woman smiled immediately as soon as she spotted where Vivi was standing. She was over by their side in less than half a dozen strides.

"Hey, sugar!" Bessa yelled over the noise, then clutched Vivi in a tight embrace as if they hadn't seen each other in weeks. "Whatcha doin' here?" Bessa asked when she finally let Vivi go. Her gaze darted in Zeke's direction. "And who is this fine-looking gentleman you've brought with you?"

Zeke stood to introduce himself. "Zeke Manning. I'm here from Manhattan on business." He held out his hand, but Bessa surprised him when she ignored it. Instead, she stepped closer, grabbing him in the same bear hug she'd just released Vivi from and squeezing him tight. "Uh, nice to meet you," Zeke said over the woman's shoulder right before she let him go. "As for why we're here…" He motioned over to Vivi to take over and explain.

"Bessa, I know it's super busy here," Vivi began. "But can you spare a moment? It's important."

Bessa glanced around to the other side of the café, then over to the bar area. "The barista is shorthanded and way behind. So I've got a minute or two until she puts out my table's orders. What's going on?" Immediate concern flushed over her features as she studied Vivi's agitated state. "Everything all right? You look like you've been caught doing something you shouldn't have been doing." She gave Zeke a loaded look, adding a mischievous smile.

Zeke grunted out an unamused laugh. She had no idea how accurate her description was.

"If you only knew," Vivi answered.

Bessa pulled out a chair and all three of them sat. "Tell me."

Vivi quickly explained the situation, luckily leaving out the part where Zeke had confronted her in the magic shop before it all began. There was clearly a lot of affection between the two women and he didn't feel like landing on the roommate's bad side so soon upon meeting. He recalled Tomas's earlier visual warning at the steamship bar.

Vivi certainly seemed to be emotionally close to the people in her life. Now Bessa's eyes grew wide as she listened to her explain the events of the past twelve hours. When she was done, the other woman was completely still, her mouth agape.

"It's true," Vivi emphasized. "The necklace is worth a ton of money. We have to get it back to Ms. Truneau."

Bessa seemed at a loss for words. "Oh, my," she finally said, somewhat hesitantly.

"I had no idea it was so valuable," Vivi repeated for what had to be the tenth time.

"Now, why would that ol' lady just hand you something like that? Like it was nothing more than a carnival bead chain or something?" Bessa asked.

Zeke decided to step in. "She's not quite herself lately," he said vaguely. "What matters is we return her property."

Vivi nodded with solemn agreement. "As much as I hate to reclaim a gift I gave you, it can't be helped. I'll make it up to you, Bessa."

"Girl." Bessa slammed her palms on her hips, seemingly offended. "That's not it. You know I wouldn't ever hold you to something like that."

"Then what is it? Can you tell me where the necklace is?"

Bessa's eyebrows drew together and she clasped her hands in front of her powdered-sugar-covered apron.

For the second time in under an hour, a feeling of low dread washed through Zeke's chest. He didn't have any idea what Bessa was about to tell them. But he was certain she wasn't about to say the exact location of Esther's antique necklace.

It appeared their journey wasn't quite over yet.

Vivi really just wanted this all to be over. But everything about Bessa's expression and demeanor told her she was about to deliver some really bad news. Bessa confirmed that suspicion as soon as she spoke again.

"Listen, sugar. I don't know how to tell you this..."

Vivi resisted the urge to stick her fingers in her ears like a petulant toddler who didn't want to hear a reprimand. She could just guess what was coming. "I no longer have the necklace," Bessa informed them.

Bingo.

In the chair next to her, Zeke wearily rubbed his forehead. He didn't seem particularly surprised at the latest turn of events.

"What do you mean you don't have it?" Vivi asked past the lump in her throat.

Bessa leaned closer to her over the table. "Well, you know how Roxie's getting married, right?"

Vivi nodded absentmindedly, though she was decidedly confused. What did any of this have to do with Roxie's impending nuptials to the mechanic she'd met two months ago, when he'd towed her car after it had broken down on Canal Street?

"Who is Roxie?" Zeke asked. As if that really made any kind of difference in the overall scheme of things.

"She's one of the other servers here," Bessa answered. "Really sweet girl. Plans on eloping with her beau, whom she met a few weeks back. I hope the marriage lasts—I do. She deserves some happiness."

Vivi cleared her throat to interrupt the tangent. Zeke was looking at both of them with utter bewilderment on his face. "Perhaps you could tell us what Roxie has to do with this," Vivi said.

Bessa visibly cringed as she answered. "Well, it's like you said. Just like you, I had no idea how valuable this piece of jewelry was. And Roxie's about to get married. Even though the happy couple plans to elope, it's still only proper to give them a wedding gift, right?"

Vivi's blood turned to ice in her veins. *Oh, no.* This couldn't be happening.

"Let me guess," Zeke began, pinching the bridge of his nose. "You gave said piece of jewelry to the bride-to-be."

Bessa nodded slowly. "I'm afraid so."

Zeke swore elaborately next to her. A rather descriptive curse that involved sharp objects and places that saw no sunlight. Honestly, the man spoke like a sailor on leave. She'd grown up in New Orleans and had heard more than her fair share of colorful language. But coming from someone as sophisticated and polished as he appeared to be, it was just a tad jarring.

Not that she could blame him in this particular instance.

Bessa grabbed her hand over the table in reassurance. "But don't worry. They haven't left yet. I'll just sneak my phone and go call her to explain what's happened. Tell her she needs to give the necklace back." She gave Vivi's hand a squeeze. "You two just wait here and relax."

Easier said than done, Vivi thought as she watched her friend walk away. "Do you want a beignet while we wait?" Vivi asked, more for something to say than any kind of attempt at hospitality. "My treat. It's on the house. Employee perk."

"Sure. Why not?"

Vivi raised her arm and the section's server appeared at their table within moments. The woman was a relatively new hire, and Vivi didn't know her well, but she seemed nice enough. "What can I get y'all?" she asked in a thick Creole accent.

Vivi ordered beignets and coffee for both of them. Though rather late to be drinking coffee, Vivi had a hunch they were going to be up for a while longer and needed the boost. It was relatively early by NOLA standards, but she felt like this day had lasted a fortnight already.

Bessa still hadn't returned by the time their food arrived. In between giving her looks of consternation, Zeke kept glancing at his watch. To his credit, he hadn't made any cutting remarks yet about their lack of success in retrieving Esther's necklace.

Neither of them touched the beignets, though he downed about half the strong chicory roast within moments of it being placed in front of him. Vivi guessed he probably wasn't really tasting it. He probably wanted this night to be done with as much as she did.

Simply to give herself something to do, Vivi reached for a beignet and took a small bite. She nearly moaned in delight despite herself. Jess was at the fryer tonight. The man somehow made magic with dough and hot oil.

Zeke lifted both eyebrows at her reaction. "That good, huh?"

She swallowed, savoring the sweet concoction melting on her tongue. "You have to try one to believe how good they are."

Giving a small shrug, Zeke reached for one of the pastries. His eyes grew wide when he took a bite.

"Wow."

Vivi couldn't help the bubble of laughter that escaped

her lips. The expression on his face reminded her of a toddler who'd just had his first taste of ice cream. Or a some-one from New York who'd just bit into his first authentic Louisiana beignet.

Through her chuckle, she took another bite of her own treat. Zeke had his finished in two quick bites. "Please, have the other two," she insisted. "I have these daily."

"Don't mind if I do," he replied, but stopped in the act of reaching for another. His eyes narrowed on her face.

Oh, Lord. Vivi knew what he had to be staring at. She no doubt had powdered sugar all over her face. She'd been eating these things her whole life, worked in a café that employed a man who specialized in making them to perfection and she still hadn't learned to consume them without making a complete mess.

In horrified embarrassment, she reached for the napkin dispenser and pulled out more than a few, then hurriedly began trying to clean herself up.

"You missed a bit," Zeke told her, and before she could react, his hand reached out and rubbed a spot right above her lip. The touch of his warm fingers so near her mouth sent a strange sensation through her center. Despite the heavy scent of sugar and hot oil, she could still smell the woodsy mint hint of his aftershave. He'd undone the top two buttons of his shirt sometime over the evening, revealing a tan vee of skin. Was it her imagination, or had his hand lingered near her mouth a scant second longer than it had to?

Time seemed to stand still and neither of them moved. Finally, Zeke dropped his arm.

What had just happened? Sure, Zeke happened to be a very attractive man. But she couldn't be attracted to him. He lived in Manhattan. He was a high-powered attorney who clearly did very well for himself. While she had three undependable jobs.

Her roommate chose that moment to reappear at the table. Vivi dropped the bunched-up napkins on the table and stood.

"Bessa, what did Roxie say? Can we get the necklace from her tonight?"

Bessa rubbed a palm down her face. "I'm sorry, sugar. I'm afraid I have more bad news."

CHAPTER FIVE

Zeke figured he must have misheard what Bessa had just said. "If you want that necklace, you're gonna have to go to Niagara Falls."

He could only repeat the last two words, dumbfounded. "Niagara Falls?"

Bessa nodded. "Yeah. But don't worry. It's the US side. You don't have to cross the border or anything."

Right, as if that had been Zeke's main concern at this latest, strange new turn of events.

Maybe Bessa was making complete sense and the problem was him. He wasn't processing correctly. His head still felt like it was spinning, after all. What had possessed him to reach out and touch Vivi the way he had just prior to Bess returning? He could have just as easily pointed out to her where to wipe the sugar off her mouth. But before he knew he'd intended to do it, his fingers were on her skin.

Heaven help him, he hadn't wanted to stop. He'd wanted to linger on her face, then trail his fingers along her soft, feminine jawline. He wanted to taste that small speck of sugar right off her lips.

Zeke gave himself a mental shake. He had to stop the treacherous line of thought. None of it made any sense. For one, he'd only just met the woman. Oh, and there was also the small matter of a major antique having gone missing that he was somehow responsible for finding.

Speaking of said missing antique, Bessa was now saying something about a chapel. Right, the wedding of Roxie and her mechanic beau. It was hard to keep track of all the details. Especially considering how fast they were coming at him.

Vivi looked just as perplexed as he was. "But I thought they weren't due to leave until early tomorrow. And why are they in Niagara Falls? Don't people usually elope in Las Vegas?"

Bessa clapped her hands once in front of her chest. "See! That's what I thought. But it turns out there's plenty of twenty-four-hour chapels in Niagara Falls, New York. It is the honeymoon capital of the world, after all, you know."

"Huh," Vivi replied. "I didn't actually know that."

Zeke might have heard that fact once or twice. Simply because he made his life in Manhattan now. Though Niagara Falls was farther north. A hop and a skip from the Canadian border. Apparently, couples in a rush to get married found something romantic about gushing, loud waterfalls. The city served as an alternative to those who found Vegas too bawdy.

"Sure," Bessa said, breaking in to Zeke's thoughts. "Couples go there, get married, then start their honeymoon right away. Turns out that's what Roxie and Rocky decided to do. And they didn't want to wait until tomorrow."

Zeke knew he shouldn't even go there, but he couldn't seem to help himself. "Did you say Roxie is marrying someone named Rocky?"

Both women looked at him like they didn't understand the question. "Never mind." Yep, he should have known better.

"Anyway," Bessa continued, "Roxie's mom told me all

that. It took me so long because I couldn't get a hold of Roxie herself. I had to track down her momma. She said the happy couple doesn't want to be disturbed during this special time, so they're probably not checking their phones. They haven't even sent the poor woman any photos of their vow taking. Can you believe that?"

"I find all of this pretty hard to believe," Zeke muttered under his breath.

"What was that?" Bessa asked.

"Nothing. Forget it."

She turned back to face Vivi. "I'm sorry about all this, hon. I'd have never given it to her if I'd known."

Vivi reached over and rubbed her roommate's upper arm. "It's not your fault, Bessa. I'm the one who should be apologizing."

Zeke found himself wanting to apologize as well. Though for the life of him he couldn't say why or what for. But it was hard not to feel as if part of this was somehow his fault, too.

Bessa squeezed Vivi's hand on her arm. "Well, I better get back to work. My tables are getting antsy and at least one café au lait is probably too cold by now."

Vivi nodded as the other woman walked away.

She turned to him finally, rubbing a hand down her face. "Now what do we do?"

If this was some kind of con or hoax, then Vivi would have to be the most talented hustler this side of the equator. There was no way anyone could have planned something so convoluted with so many people in such a short amount of time. As ridiculous as it was, there didn't seem to be anything nefarious going on. Esther's necklace had really somehow traveled all the way from New Orleans, Louisiana, to Niagara Falls, New York. He almost had to laugh.

Zeke weighed the possible options. He could hire somebody to go there, find this Roxie and Rocky—his mind made a mental pause at the names yet again, despite himself—and somehow convince them to hand over a wedding gift that just happened to be priceless to a complete stranger.

He couldn't even count all the ways that scenario could go wrong.

Or he could take the chance of waiting for the honeymooners to return in a few days. That option ran the risk of the necklace getting lost or stolen through their travels. Or, heaven forbid, tossed like a carnival toy into the rushing waterfall. Though unlikely, anything was possible with giddy newlyweds. He remembered reading in some travel magazine that people threw all sorts of items into the falls on the superstition that it brought about good luck. A shudder ran down his spine at the image of Esther's priceless rubies and stones being pummeled by thousands of tons of water until they disintegrated into fine dust.

He released a resigned sigh before answering Vivi's question. "There doesn't seem to be much of a choice from where I'm standing."

Vivi slowly shook her head. "You can't mean what I think you're saying."

He shrugged. "You heard your friend as well as I did. If we want to get that necklace back to its rightful owner, we're going to have to go to Niagara Falls."

The look of consternation on her face matched his own. But they really did have no choice. By this time tomorrow night, they would have to be in Niagara Falls.

Vivi led Zeke out of the café at a loss for words. It had become almost comically complicated trying to get Esther's necklace back.

"We should probably talk about our exact game plan,"

Zeke said behind her as they stepped onto the sidewalk. "And I could use a drink. How about you?"

"I'm guessing you don't mean the caffeinated kind."

"You'd be guessing right."

Despite the late hour and the toll of the day's events, Vivi knew she wouldn't be able to get any sleep if she tried to go back home now, anyway. Plus, Zeke was right. They had some things to go over if they were to be traveling across the country sometime tomorrow. "I know just the place. Follow me."

A solo saxophonist played a sultry tune on the corner just past the café as Zeke paused to drop several bills into the man's open instrument case. Some teens were doing acrobatic stunts in the grassy area across the street to a rapt audience. Vivi led Zeke down past the park toward Canal Street. Finally, they turned down Bourbon, where the noise level ratcheted up several notches all at once. It was a pretty good crowd for this time on a weeknight.

"You seem to have a lot of competition out this way," Zeke commented, pointing to a neon sign above a shop door that said Tarot and Palm Readings. "How does one end up in that line of work, anyway?" he asked. Maybe she was being oversensitive, but she could swear she detected a note of derision in his voice at the question.

She cleared her throat, trying not to sound defensive as she answered. "One of my foster mothers was into it. She taught me about the cards."

Zeke's response could be described as a grunt.

Despite herself, Vivi paused in her tracks to try and explain what people like him were so unlikely to see. Zeke stopped and looked at her in question.

"It's about more than the cards, you know," she told him, not that he was likely to understand.

"I don't get it." Bingo, she was right.

"It's about the person you're reading for. Their fears, their anxieties. Things they want to get off their chest. Just to have someone safe to talk to."

His eyes flickered over her face. "Then I can see why you'd be good at that."

Vivi felt a warmth flush through her chest straight down to her toes. "That sounded suspiciously like it might be a compliment."

"You should take it as one."

His words sent a ridiculous giddiness through her.

Not trusting herself to respond without saying something embarrassingly cringey, she continued toward their destination. Several moments passed in awkward silence until Zeke finally cleared his throat and broke it with a question.

"We seem to have taken the long way to Bourbon. Any particular reason?"

"I just thought we could use the air," she answered with a shrug, though it was a bit of a fib. Just one more thing Zeke was unlikely to truly understand and would be too risky for her to tell him. She didn't want to explain why she'd gone out of her way to avoid walking past a certain pawnshop. The sight of the place still sent her pulse shooting sky-high and anxiety surging through her core. Zeke didn't need to know that it was where she'd found herself arrested and in handcuffs, the only thing she'd been guilty of being that she'd trusted the wrong man.

"New Orleans could definitely give New York City a run for its money as the city that never sleeps," Zeke commented as they made their way farther down Bourbon Street.

"I wouldn't know," Vivi answered. "I've never been there."

He was about to say that they would have to rectify that, that perhaps he could bring her to Manhattan one day and have her visit his penthouse apartment. But he stopped the words from leaving his mouth.

There was no sound reason for Vivienne Ducarne to visit him once this business with the necklace was over and done with. The notion sent a wave of strange emotion rushing through him, but he didn't want to explore why.

"That's too bad," he said simply instead.

They passed several smoky bars and taverns that looked like they served perfectly good spirits, but Vivi kept walking. Finally, they came upon a rather empty club that could aptly be described as a hole in the wall. Vivi walked through the open door and motioned for him to follow. The inside was dark and misty with walls painted blue and mirrored panels along the ceiling.

This was the place she had in mind?

He had to ask. "Not to question your judgment as a local, but why here?"

"Why not?"

"Well, we passed several other places that were much busier."

She led him to a table booth as she answered. "Like you said. I'm a local. Those other places are teeming with tourists who don't know where the best drinks, food and entertainment really are. Or where you don't have to wait several minutes just to put a drink order in."

That made sense. Zeke sat across from her on the vinyl-padded bench and a server immediately appeared as if to verify Vivi's statement about not having to wait.

"Hey, Vivi," the woman said as she smiled at them both in turn. "Your usual, I'm guessing. And what can I get for this fine specimen of a man you've brought in with you tonight?" She gave Zeke a not-too-subtle wink.

"I'll just have whatever she's having."

Vivi gave him a wide smile when he turned his attention back to her. "What?" he asked as the server went to get their drinks.

"I'm impressed. How spontaneous of you, to not even ask what my usual is before ordering it for yourself."

That was just it, wasn't it? He was acting very uncharacteristically today. Ever since he'd first laid eyes on Vivi, to be precise. Spontaneity wasn't a quality he was normally associated with. But so far he'd taken an unplanned cruise on a steamship, had followed Vivi to a dive bar in a hidden corner of Bourbon Street and was headed for an unexpected trip the next day.

"I'm not going to regret it, am I?" Zeke wasn't even sure if he was referring to the drink order or something else entirely.

He had part of the answer when the server reappeared with two goblets full of a red liquid accompanied by mini bottles of hot sauce.

"Two Cajun Cannons," the woman announced, placing everything on the table in front of them.

Vivi poured the hot sauce into the drink and took a small sip, and he followed suit. It was good. Surprisingly so. The spiciness hit just the right spot after all the sugar from the beignet earlier.

"So we're really doing this, huh?" Vivi asked after another sip of her drink. "Traveling to Niagara Falls."

He nodded. "I'll have a car pick you up tomorrow and take you to the jet at the airport."

She blinked at him. "The jet?"

"We'll be flying private. I'll have to have my pilot see about getting emergency clearance for a flight plan."

"Your pilot." She clasped her hands together over the table. "Am I to understand that we'll be heading to New York in your very own private jet?"

He could only nod again. Every once in a while, in moments such as this one, it occurred to Zeke just how much he took for granted in the life he'd managed to build for himself.

"How does one come about owning one's very own jet?" Vivi asked.

"I appraise some very valuable estates for some very knowledgeable people. Along the way I picked up a little bit about how to invest in valuables and other portfolios. It's all paid off rather well."

She blinked at him again, then took several gulps of her cocktail. "I see."

But she didn't. Vivi had no idea just how little he'd come from. Suddenly, he found himself wanting to explain it to her. But where would he start, exactly? "Things aren't always as they seem, Vivi."

To his surprise, she responded with a peal of giggles, then finally added, "Trust me, I'm not one who needs to hear that."

He had no doubt Vivi had a story that would likely match his own. Zeke hoped he might hear it someday. Maybe she didn't know exactly where to start, either.

A band began setting up on the small wooden stage in the corner. Soon, the sounds of bluesy jazz began to fill the air.

Vivi started to sway to the music in her seat. It was hard not to stare. She sat up straight. "You know what? I think we need to dance."

"Dance? Now?"

She was already standing as she answered. "Yep. You're being spontaneous, right?"

Without waiting for a response, she strode to the dance floor. What choice did he have but to follow her?

The cocktail must have been stronger than he thought.

Because after the second or third number, Vivi was some-how in his arms as they moved to the music.

Zeke forgot about the circumstances that had led them to this moment. None of it mattered. Vivi felt right in his embrace, fit perfectly up against his length. They'd only just met, but everything about holding her felt familiar. Like she'd been in his arms his whole life, like she belonged there.

"You know, you're not such a bad dancer," she told him. "For an attorney," she added with a mischievous smile.

She was teasing him. For any outside observer, they might look like a couple out on a date. With a night full of possibilities ahead of them.

He really couldn't allow himself to think along those lines. "Thank you for the compliment. I guess us attorneys just need the right partner."

Vivi's gasp at his answer was almost imperceptible. But there was no mistaking the way her hands tightened where they were resting on his upper arms. Reflexively, he pulled her tighter against his chest. He could feel her warmth against his skin, smell the fruity scent of her sham-poo. Her lips parted on a soft sigh and he had to wonder what those lips would taste like against his.

Heaven help him, he wanted to kiss her. But something told him there'd be no going back if he gave in to that temp-tation. So he would settle for simply holding her.

Zeke lost track of time as they moved together. His sole focus was on the woman he held in his arms.

He hardly noticed when the last song faded to a finish, because he didn't want this night to end. But Vivi stopped moving moments after the music ended. She slowly stepped out of his embrace. He felt her loss like a cold gust of wind.

"We should probably call it a night," she said, not quite

meeting his eyes. "I'm guessing we have a long day ahead of us tomorrow."

She was right, of course. But Zeke found it hard to refrain from reaching for her again, and had to clench his fists to keep from doing so.

None of this made any kind of sense. Who would have thought when he'd met Vivienne Ducarne in the magic shop that he'd be slow dancing to jazz music with her in his arms less than twenty-four hours later?

Or how hard it would be for him to let her go?

This was so much more than she'd bargained for. What had possessed her to ask Zeke to dance with her last night?

And how in the world had she ended up here? Vivi could count on one hand all the times she'd flown on an airplane and still have a couple of digits left over. Now here she was, sitting on a private jet as it taxied down the runway at Louis Armstrong International Airport en route to Buffalo, New York, of all places. It was a city she'd only heard about on the news, watching reports of record snowfalls.

She'd tossed and turned all night with indecision, had reached for her phone countless times to call and tell Zeke that she couldn't go to Niagara Falls with him, after all. Slow dancing with him in a darkened club after having a strong cocktail had been a foolish and impulsive move. How much worse might it get if she was traveling with him across the country? But her conscience had won out in the end. The sad truth was, she felt more than a little guilty for Esther having lost such a valuable possession.

Also, there was the other much more pressing issue—if the necklace wasn't returned and the authorities became involved, that could cause a dangerous turn as far as she was concerned. Everything she'd worked so hard for, the peaceful and fulfilling life she'd managed to build for herself, could all be in jeopardy. Of course, she couldn't share any of that with Zeke. He would never understand and he'd probably jump to all the wrong conclusions without so much as listening to her end of the story. He might have been a charming and attentive partner last night on the dance floor, but Vivi knew how he would view her if he found out about her past. Like so many others in her life, Zeke would assume the worst.

Just like when he'd stormed into Lucien's Magic Shop and Gift Store.

In any case, it was much too late to be second-guessing things now, she figured as the airplane's tires ate up the runway and the aircraft accelerated before it began to lift off.

"I've taken the liberty of having some breakfast prepared and brought on board for us," Zeke said, interrupting her thoughts. "As soon as we reach a cruising altitude, the flight attendant will bring a few trays out. Along with hot coffee."

Vivi definitely could use the coffee given her restless night. All night long she'd wondered if agreeing to go with him on this trip was a wise decision. The man was so charming it was downright disconcerting. She thought about their time together the night before at the blues club. For such a straitlaced and conservative type, Zeke wasn't too bad a dancer. Color her surprised, but he'd thrown her off with his footwork. Being around him threw her off in ways she couldn't explain in general.

And if she needed any reminders that they came from two completely different worlds, the fact that she was traveling as his companion on his very own private jet certainly fit the bill.

"You look unsettled," Zeke said, studying her. "Are you a nervous flyer?"

"I'm not any kind of flyer," she admitted. "I've never

actually left Louisiana. I have a passport but it's just for ID. And I certainly haven't flown private before."

Zeke ignored that last comment. "Maybe something to calm your nerves instead of coffee, then. A mimosa perhaps?"

Vivi shook her head. "No, thank you." How odd it was to be sitting here as Zeke offered her drinks and snacks. Usually, she was the one pouring coffee or mixing mimosas if she happened to be working a morning shift at the Crawdad Café. To have someone on standby somewhere in the cabin, waiting to serve her breakfast, seemed surreal.

It was certainly a far cry from the old days. She would have never guessed when she was a teen being bounced from one foster home to the next with nothing but the clothes on her back that she'd be in such a luxurious aircraft with a handsome businessman asking her what she desired.

A bubble of ironic laughter gurgled up her throat before she could suppress it. Not that she was forgetting how temporary all this was.

Suddenly, she felt completely out of place—underdressed and ill-prepared. She hadn't given much thought to clothing, just packed an overnight bag with toiletries and some extra unmentionables. A tank top with a cartoon crawfish under a light sweater seemed like a reasonable enough getup to travel in. Worn but comfortable Chucks rounded out her outfit.

Yep, downright peasant-like in comparison to her travel companion. Zeke was clad in pressed gray dress pants and a silk navy shirt that brought out the deep hue of his eyes. The laced leather shoes he wore were polished to a gleam and probably cost more than her entire wardrobe.

Despite what he'd said yesterday about giving her the benefit of the doubt, she knew someone like him would be way too quick to jump to believe the worst when it came to people like her.

"Will you be missed?" he asked, confusing her with the question before he clarified. "By your employers, I mean. I know this was a rather unexpected trip."

She shrugged. "Lucien just announced online that the tarot readings would have to be rescheduled. The new girl said she would take over my shift at the café and I'm not due to sing on the boat cruise until next week."

Zeke loosened his seat-belt buckle and leaned back in his seat. "I see. Is any of that going to set you back? We should be able to work something out. For all practical purposes, you're here traveling with me to assist with a job. As such, I'd be happy to compensate you for your time."

He may as well have struck her.

Vivi tried her best not to visibly bristle with offense. He was essentially looking at her as an employee of his. How right she'd been about the way he must see her. A working-class girl who could hardly afford to miss a shift here and there. Never mind that his assumption stung because it happened to be so close to the truth.

To think, she'd entertained the notion that they might be developing some kind of friendship last night. How silly of her. Zeke was a wealthy estate attorney who owned a private jet. He may not have said it out loud, but she knew he looked down upon her tarot-reading work. She knew he didn't see it as a legitimate way to earn money. Just because he'd told her she must be good at it, didn't mean he respected it.

Well, she was proud of the way she could support herself. Proud that she'd been so often tempted to take the easy way out and had steadfastly refused, even if it didn't look that way on paper if anyone dug deep enough.

She really didn't want Zeke Manning to ever want to look deep enough.

"That won't be necessary," she said, unable to keep the iciness out of her voice. She didn't follow up with a thank-you because she hardly felt any kind of appreciation for his offer.

Luckily, he didn't push it any further.

"What about you? Aren't you missing some important boardroom meetings?" she asked, to change the subject.

He laughed at her mocking tone. "I had my administrative assistant change my schedule so that I could do this."

"Why?"

"Why what?"

"Why is it so important to you?" She hadn't known she was going to press the matter, but something had been nagging at her about his determination to get Esther back the item that she owned. "I mean, I know it's technically your job." She bit her bottom lip, contemplating exactly how she wanted to ask the question. She decided it was best to just blurt out what was making her curious. "But you seem personally invested."

Zeke was silent for so long that the air between them grew thick and awkward. Eventually, rather than answer, he glanced at his watch. "I think we've ascended enough to have the food brought out." He pushed a button on his armrest and the flight attendant appeared within moments carrying a tray of steaming eggs, toast, various pastries and a silver carafe of aromatic coffee.

Vivi decided not to push, either. It appeared she wasn't the only one good at changing the subject of an uncomfortable conversation.

He'd been right about how intuitive Vivi was. Zeke couldn't recall anyone in his life who'd been able to read him at all.

Yet here was this virtual stranger who seemed to be able to do just that. Maybe there was something to the idea that people could read cards, after all. Maybe someone like Vivi really had the kind of talent where she could look at illustrated pictures on a few cards and interpret what those pictures might mean for the person sitting across from her. Who was he to say?

"How long have you known Esther?" he asked her as she took a small bite of her toast. He wanted to get a better feel for this woman, wanted to know more about her. Asking about her relationship with their mutual friend seemed a good enough segue.

She swallowed the bite she'd taken before answering. "She came into the shop one day about six months ago. Just to browse and shop for souvenirs for her staff, she said. When she noticed my table, she asked for a reading. She started coming in once a week after that."

Zeke poured himself more coffee. They were both already on their second cup.

Vivi continued without further prompting. "One day she came in and said it would probably be her last time. That it was just too hard for her to make it into the French Quarter—she wasn't as mobile as she used to be, even with a driver. She seemed really sad about it."

He could extrapolate the rest. "So you offered to go to her."

Vivi set down her toast on the porcelain plate. "It wasn't a burden for me to take the trolley to her place. She didn't seem interested in the cards so much as she was the conversation. I got the impression she gets lonely."

"That was kind of you," Zeke told her, and he meant it. Not many twentysomethings would give up a part of their day once a week to spend it with an old woman looking for a companion.

A less-than-generous voice nagged in his mind that plenty of opportunists or fortune hunters would do just that. But he squelched that voice before it could grow louder. He'd decided yesterday that he'd give her the benefit of the doubt and he had no reason to go back on that decision. Not just yet, anyway.

She shrugged. "Like I said, it wasn't any kind of burden. Even if I wasn't getting paid for the 'reading,' quote unquote, that I was there for."

That took him by surprise. "What do you mean you weren't getting paid for the reading?"

"Esther said the staff, on the direction of her nephew, didn't allow her to write checks. She'd made too many mistakes. And she didn't want them handling her personal affairs, which she considered me a part of. I think she was embarrassed that she was paying someone to essentially just talk to her. Plus, it wasn't like I could swipe her card if we weren't at the shop. She also didn't keep much cash on the premises for obvious reasons."

"I see."

"That was why she liked to give me odd items from time to time. Because I wasn't officially getting paid."

Zeke rubbed his forehead. What an innocuous explanation. Both Esther's and Vivi's hearts had been in the right place. "It's why she mistakenly gave you a priceless necklace."

Vivi nodded, picked up an orange and started to peel. "That's right."

A wave of fresh guilt washed over Zeke as he listened to Vivi. Here was the explanation all along about how Vivi had come in possession of the necklace. All he'd had to do was ask. He should have done just that, asked Esther to explain to him exactly how this whole fiasco had come about. Instead, he'd stormed to Vivi's place of employment to confront her. No wonder she still held a grudge about it.

He had to make it up to her somehow. As soon as he could, he'd find a way.

CHAPTER SIX

VIVI COULDN'T QUITE describe the way Zeke was looking at her. But something about his gaze made her stomach tie in strange little knots. Suddenly, the air in the plane's main cabin felt warm and stuffy. She unbuttoned her cardigan and peeled it off. With all the nervous squirming in her chair earlier, the tank top she wore had ridden up above her belly button. Before she could pull its hem back down, Zeke's gaze fell to the blemish above her left hipbone that was the size of a quarter. Curiosity immediately filled the depths of his eyes.

Vivi sighed. The dermatologist had done the best she could. She'd had a rather amateur tattooist's work to deal with, however. "Go ahead and ask," she prompted Zeke, who was trying and failing in several attempts to not look at the spot.

"Only if you care to tell me," he said.

"I had a tattoo removed," she explained. "Sometimes the procedure leaves a permanent scar."

He merely lifted one eyebrow in response.

"I'm guessing you don't have any tattoos," Vivi continued. "Let alone felt regretful enough to need to remove one."

He nodded once. "You would be guessing correctly."

"Yeah, well. It was the only one I've ever gotten." She

tried not to grimace as the memory came flooding back. Todd urging her incessantly as he sat in the chair waiting for his scorpion to be colored in. Telling her how much it meant to him. Eventually, she'd succumbed to his less-than-gentle insistence. Hard to believe she'd ever been that impressionable, that downright stupid.

"Did you regret it right away?"

"Pretty much." Though it had taken her months to save up enough to pay for the doctor's visit. She was still paying off the remainder of what she owed.

She regretted the tattoo so much that she occasionally wore makeup to hide the blemish and wished she'd done so this morning. This wasn't a path of conversation she wanted to head down with the man sitting across from her.

"Let me guess," Zeke began. "A cute bumblebee. But one day not long after you got it, you were stung by one. And in your ire, you had it removed."

Vivi had to laugh at his guess. "One flaw in that theory. Bumblebees don't sting."

"Of course. A butterfly, then. But one day you tripped and fell as you were chasing one to admire it."

She chuckled again. "It wasn't an animal or insect," she clarified, not quite sure why she felt the need to. It was fun talking to Zeke. Despite their first meeting, he had a fun, easygoing style that somehow put her at ease. Even under these strange circumstances. "It wasn't a picture at all, in fact," she added.

He steepled his fingers in front of his chin. "I see. A word, then. A word you wanted removed from your person. So it had to be a name."

Vivi swallowed. He was too sharp by half. "Let's just say things didn't exactly work out with the bearer of said name."

That had to be the understatement of the year. The man

had nearly destroyed her life. He'd certainly destroyed her reputation and left her with a criminal record.

For one insane moment, she wanted to tell Zeke all of it. She wanted to just confess and get it all off her chest in the hopes that he would be compassionate enough to understand. But she couldn't take that risk. He was being charming and pleasant right now, but she couldn't forget the angry man who had barged into the magic shop and confronted her with his accusations. Something told her the edginess he succeeded in holding at bay was all too close to the surface. A sleeping predator she didn't want to risk poking.

After all, Zeke was an attorney first and foremost. She had enough experience with them to know how things might play out if he found out the truth. No doubt, his first instinct would be to think the worst of her and notify the proper authorities about what he suspected. He'd probably consider it his professional duty.

In fact, she'd shared too much already. Zeke Manning didn't need to know one more thing about her past or her disastrous relationship.

Unclasping her seat belt, she stood up to momentarily step away from the conversation and from Zeke's all-too-observant eye. "I think I'd like to stretch my legs a bit—"

Before she got out the last word, the plane hit a turbulent bump hard enough to have her nearly toppling over. She windmilled her arms in a failed attempt to try and regain her balance. There was nothing for it, she was about to go down and probably take the breakfast tray with her.

But suddenly a set of strong, steadying arms had gripped her around the waist and she found herself colliding against Zeke's chest. How in the world had he moved so fast?

"I got you," he said softly, his breath warm against her cheek.

Vivi didn't need to look up to know how close his face

was to hers. If she moved her head so much as half an inch, their lips would be a hair's width apart.

A mischievous, naughty voice inside her head told her to do just that. To succumb to the desire to see what a man like Zeke might taste like, how his mouth would feel on hers.

His frame felt strong and solid against her body, and she could feel his pulse pounding under his skin. Or maybe that was just her heart beating in her chest. It seemed to be throbbing double time.

"Uh, thanks," she muttered. "That could have been messy. I was heading right for the tray of food."

"And painful," he added.

His grip loosened ever so slightly and she felt a strange sense of loss and regret. Pushing past it, she slowly unfolded herself from his side and took a moment to compose herself. It wasn't easy.

"I think I'll do that stretching once we land," she said with a weak attempt at a smile as she sat back down. Her legs were wobbly, all right, but not because of any air pockets in the sky.

"Good idea," Zeke said, taking his own seat.

Vivi made a pronounced show of studying the view of the clouds outside the small oval window. What had just happened between them? Whatever it was, it couldn't happen again.

She just had to keep her head together and her wits about her until they got back to New Orleans. She's made too many mistakes in the past when it came to falling for the wrong man. She couldn't do that again. It had taken her too long to put her life back together to risk it all now.

But there was no denying the fact that she'd wanted to kiss him back there. And, heaven help her, she still did.

Vivi's resolve to maintain a physical distance from Zeke grew only harder when they landed and entered the private town car that would take them to Niagara Falls. Her heart had only just now reached a normal, resting state. By contrast, Zeke seemed completely unaffected by what had transpired between them. Or almost transpired. Not that she should be surprised. This was the man who had offered to compensate her for her time this morning. He viewed her as nothing more than some kind of employee. While she was still out of sorts about the way it had felt to be in his arms, he'd probably forgotten about the incident completely.

She studied him now as they drove away from the airport and the driver merged onto the expressway. Zeke had his tablet open and was typing furiously on the keyboard.

"I apologize," he said without looking up from the screen. "I don't mean to be rude, but I have to fire off some emails before we get to our destination. I'm due in France in a few days to oversee an estate sale, a family winery that's being bought out by a US conglomerate. Some of the paperwork is having lost-in-translation issues."

"You don't have to entertain me," Vivi told him. What a life he must lead. In just a week's span he would be traveling from New Orleans to Europe with a cursory stop in between where she was accompanying him. And here she was almost giddy to be able to fly to one of the great natural wonders of the world.

"Almost done. Sorry," Zeke said in a conciliatory tone.

"There's no need to apologize for trying to get your work done."

"Hmm," he replied absentmindedly, still not looking up.

Yep, he was barely aware of her presence. Whereas sitting in such close quarters with him was wreaking havoc on her senses. They were in much closer proximity now than they had been on the plane and that had been close enough.

"I'll try Roxie one more time." Vivi pulled out her phone just to give herself something to do. Though she knew the task was futile. Roxie had yet to answer several texts and voice mails Vivi had left since last night. For all she knew, the other woman had locked up her phone in the hotel room's safe to focus solely on her honeymoon.

To be that enamored with a man. Would she ever know how that might feel?

Like a fool, when she'd first met Todd, Vivi had entertained the possibility that she might finally have someone in her corner, someone she might pursue a future with. Instead, he'd very nearly destroyed her future altogether.

Now her gaze shifted to the man sitting across from her. She got the feeling countless women had been enamored with Zeke Manning over the years. A bunch of them probably still were.

She sucked in a breath. It could be argued that Vivi was headed in that same direction and might even be counted among that group.

She shook off the thought. She was just being silly. It was no wonder she felt drawn to someone like him. Compared to her last boyfriend, or anyone else she'd dated, for that matter, he was a whole separate breed.

Smart, successful, well educated. He had material wealth that he'd obviously worked hard for and led the kind of life most men would admire.

Focus.

She made herself look away from Zeke's profile and concentrated on hitting the redial button on Roxie's contact entry. The same three chords sounded immediately through the speaker, followed by the same annoying automated message.

And now the voice-mail box was full.

Great. They would have to follow their original plan. Head to the chapel Roxie's mom had provided and check the handful of hotels nearby where the newlyweds might be staying.

"No luck, huh?"

Vivi looked up to find Zeke had put away his tablet and was focused solely on her now. Only a foot apart on the seat, his closeness was really starting to feel disconcerting. She liked it better when he was distracted with work.

"I'm afraid not," she answered, then focused her attention out the window. Outside the glass there was just so much green. All that grass and lush trees for miles. She'd grown up near the French Quarter. Sure, there were parks and fields in New Orleans, but she'd never seen such a long stretch of shrubbery as far as the eye could see.

She wasn't in Louisiana anymore.

"Penny for them," Zeke prompted. "Your thoughts, that is."

"I was just admiring the view," she answered vaguely. "The scenery out here is lovely." The comment was a bit of a fib. It was much too quiet out this way. Where was everybody? The small houses that dotted the side of the road had no one outside in the yards. Porches were well-kept but empty.

She thought about how busy the streets would be back home this time in the afternoon. All the crowds mixed up of tourists and locals alike. Music would play from every angle.

"If you think it's pretty out here, wait until you see the falls," Zeke said.

"What's it like? Majestic, I bet." Probably breathtaking, she added mentally. "I've gone hiking in Carrs Creek, which has a few, but I'm guessing those would look like a trickle in comparison."

"I've only been here a handful of times myself. But you're right. It's hard to describe. There's just so much water."

The way he said the last word had her giggling once again. "Yes, that's typically what waterfalls are composed of. Hence the name."

He chuckled along with her. "You'll see what I mean when we get there."

She hesitated to voice her next thought. Then decided she'd just bite the bullet. When would she ever get a chance again to come back out this way?

Probably never, was the most likely answer. Clearing her throat, she began her question. "I know we're not exactly here on a pleasure trip. But maybe we could spend some time sightseeing? The pictures I saw of the falls online were breathtaking. I'd love to see it up close if possible."

Zeke's grin spread wide and she had to suck in a breath at the responding reaction in her middle. "Say no more," he answered, giving her a playful wink.

Zeke didn't want to examine too closely why he'd agreed so quickly to Vivi's suggestion just now. After all, what was he supposed to do? Look into those rich, deep hazel eyes and turn her down? The woman simply wanted to spend some time admiring one of the most memorable wonders on earth. He'd be a monster to say no.

Right. Like that was the only reason he'd agreed.

Recalling the way she'd felt in his arms had his skin tingling. This was bad. Things had gone much too far. He was attracted to her. Like he'd never been toward another woman. He had to admit that.

The smart thing to do would have been to ask the driver to take her where she wanted to go while he got some work done in the hotel room until they located the wayward couple who had Esther's necklace. Heaven knew he had enough to do. He was due in France in a few days to finalize the estate transfer for a winery. As much as he loved visiting the French countryside, this was one trip he wasn't looking forward to. First, this little wild-goose chase to upstate New York had thrown quite a wrench in his schedule. Second, the winery owners insisted on trying to set him up with their middle-aged single daughter. Zeke was running out of ways to politely decline their innuendos and the woman's unwelcome advances.

Well, there was no point in dwelling on any of it now. He'd already made his promise to Vivi. As for the pushy French winery owners, he would deal with that when the time came.

He packed up his tablet and shrugged on his jacket as the car pulled into the circular driveway of the hotel they'd be staying at. Zeke was hoping they wouldn't be here more than a day, but he'd booked a couple of rooms just in case. Worst-case scenario was he and Vivi might have to leave empty-handed. He honestly didn't know where they might go from there. The authorities would probably have to get involved at that point.

If that happened, Zeke would wash his hands of the whole matter. Of course, he'd check in on Esther from time to time. But there was only so much he could do. He'd leave New Orleans not knowing when he might return.

His gaze shifted to the woman accompanying him. One way or another, this little adventure they were currently on would be over. The thought brought a pang of regret along with it. He'd never met anyone like Vivienne Ducarne. Probably never would again. There was no doubt she'd been burned in the past. The erased tattoo was proof of that. And she clearly hadn't led the easiest life. But she didn't seem bitter or hardened in any way. No, she was definitely soft. All over. He knew firsthand.

Zeke squeezed his eyes shut. He couldn't go there again. Had to make sure to keep his hands off her.

Geography aside, Vivi wasn't the type of woman he could pursue any kind of relationship with. She was too free-spirited, too unpredictable. She had no clear goals that he could see, despite having immense potential as a gifted jazz singer. Zeke needed more structure in his existence—the woman he needed in his life would be as committed to a life of stability as he was or it would never work. And, as tempting as it was, Zeke had never been one for flings or one-night stands. It just wasn't in his nature. No, he and Vivi were only here for one thing—to retrieve the necklace and return it to its rightful owner.

Everything else was just a distraction he didn't need.

Hopefully, she didn't take any more stumbles and literally fall into his arms again. Not that he'd complained. She'd smelled of fruity shampoo and fresh clean soap. In fact, the scent of her had tickled in his nostrils in the tight confines of the car. An alluring and flowery scent that was distinctively her own.

Enough, already.

As soon as the car came to a stop, Zeke wasted no time in opening his door and hopping out. The driver was already at the other side, assisting Vivi out of the vehicle.

"I thought we could freshen up a bit before we head out and start asking about Roxie and her groom."

"All right."

She paused suddenly before they reached the revolving doors that led to the hotel lobby.

"That sound? Is that…?"

He had to smile at the look of wonder on her face. "Yes. It's the falls. It can be heard from more than a mile away."

"That's incredible. I can't wait to see it."

Zeke realized with a start just how much he wanted that, too. More accurately, he wanted to see *her* as she saw the falls, silly as it sounded. Looking around them, it was hard not to notice the many couples strolling in and out of the hotel. Many held hands or walked snuggled tight up against each other.

This city really did attract newlyweds like bees to a hive. It was hard not to feel somewhat envious. Though he knew that made no sense at all. He wasn't looking for any kind of relationship, knew he wasn't equipped for any kind of long-term union, let alone marriage. Not with the kind of baggage he carried. These useless wayward thoughts really needed to stop.

"I already said we would, didn't I?" he answered rather curtly, madder at himself than Vivi's excitement. She seemed taken aback but didn't respond. Just as well.

"Come on. We should go check in."

Silently, she followed him into the lobby, where they were greeted at the main desk by a dapper-looking attendant with a pencil-thin mustache and a friendly smile below it.

Zeke gave him the reservation number.

"One key or two, sir?" the other man asked.

The question made no sense. "I don't understand," Zeke admitted. "We were supposed to have two separate rooms."

Had his administrative assistant misunderstood the request? The woman was a relatively new hire—he should have followed up.

"Apologies, sir," the attendant began. "They are indeed two separate rooms. But they are adjoined by a common suite with one entry door."

Without asking again, he handed Zeke and Vivi each a separate plastic key card.

Vivi stiffened ever so slightly next to him but took the card without comment. Zeke wasn't going to bother arguing the situation with the staff. It wasn't worth it. All that mattered was that they had two separate rooms. It wasn't as if they would be sharing one. They didn't even need to see each other when they were indoors.

And if the temptation to step into the common area in the hope that she might also be there became too much, he would just have to ignore it.

How hard could it be?

CHAPTER SEVEN

VIVI NEARLY FELL running out of the shower when she heard the ding of her cell phone. The alert sound was the one she'd assigned to text messages. Roxie! Finally!

But when she finally reached it, she saw it was just a short message from Bessa asking how their flight had gone. Wait until she told her friend how different a private jet was than flying commercial. Before she had a chance to respond, her phone rang with an incoming call. Zeke, this time.

"Hello, Zeke."

"Hey, there. What do you think about heading out? Have you had enough time to freshen up?"

Vivi looked about the luxurious room she'd walked into about forty-five minutes ago. She'd spent about a third of that time just lying on the large, sumptuous bed, staring at the patterned ceiling.

Zeke hadn't given her any kind of time window and now she was standing here dripping wet with her hair a mess of tangles.

She'd lingered in the shower, too. But it was so hard to leave the large marble stall with the scented bodywash and waterproof radio that had been streaming music from her favorite app. Oh, and also the showerhead with six different settings that ranged from "massage" to "gentle mist."

A girl could get used to this.

"Vivi? You still there?"

She shook her head. "Um. I could use a few more minutes. I was in the shower."

"Take your time. I'll be waiting for you," he said before disconnecting.

A shiver ran along her spine as she tossed her phone on the bed. It had nothing to do with being soaking wet in an air-conditioned hotel room. No, it was more the tone of Zeke's voice and the exact words he'd used.

I'll be waiting for you.

Vivi knew she was being silly. There was absolutely no reason to read in anything to Zeke simply telling her that he'd be patient while she got ready. But her mind couldn't help but replay an imaginary scenario where she was one of the women they'd passed by on their way through the hotel. A new bride. One whose groom was waiting for her as she got dressed. Against her will, her mind replayed the previous night in the club, when he'd held her in his arms as they swayed to the music.

She blew out a breath and plopped down on the bed, then rolled over onto her stomach. The duvet smelled freshly laundered, with the scent of lavender. The sooner she got those pictures out of her head, the better. Logic dictated that she wasn't about to be a bride anytime soon. And certainly not one wed to the likes of someone like Ezekiel Manning.

Zeke shoved his phone back into his pocket and tried to push away the images that were running through his head. Images of Vivi in a steamy hot shower, soap suds slowly moving over her curves. Water cascading over her skin.

Stop. It. Now.

What was wrong with him? He was acting like a hormonal high-school student with his first crush. He needed some air.

He threw open his door and strode through the common sitting area of their suite, making his way to the balcony. A sunny bright sky greeted him when he stepped outside. A fine sheen of mist hung in the air from the waterfall in the distance. He breathed in deep, trying to make sense of the myriad of emotions pummeling his center.

He didn't have time for the complication of being so attracted to Vivienne Ducarne. His life was finally one of order and normality. He was his own boss, made a very decent living and had a contact list full of willing women he could call when he wanted companionship.

Vivi would never be one of those women. First of all, he doubted she would be up for any kind of fling. He might not have known her for long, but he'd grown to know her enough to surmise that much. Not that he'd ever consider asking her.

No, once they left Niagara Falls, he would have to be on his way back home and leave Vivi completely and unequivocally behind him.

Just like so much of his past. And also like his past, it was for the best. He repeated those last five words like a mantra as he watched the pedestrian traffic in the square below. Yet more couples. A few families mixed in for good measure. Did no one single ever come to this town by themselves?

Several moments passed before he heard light footsteps behind him.

"Something down there making you out of sorts?" she asked from over his shoulder, peering down past the railing.

He hadn't realized he'd sworn out loud. "Just mentally kicking myself for a mistake I made earlier," he answered. That was the complete truth.

"You should go easier on yourself. People make mistakes," she said, her voice tight.

Was it his imagination or was there more to her words than small talk?

"Yes. They do. Some mistakes are bigger than others, however."

"Can't argue with you there." He was about to stand up so they could get going, but she pulled out the other lounge chair and dropped down into it. She'd changed into a light navy blue wraparound dress with tiny red roses dotting the fabric. The color brought out the tanned bronze of her skin and the dark strands of her hair.

On her feet, she still wore the same comfortable-looking sneakers that shouldn't have worked with such a dressy outfit, but somehow on her they worked. Not that he was any kind of fashion expert.

She continued, "For instance, when a sweet, little old lady gifts you a glittery necklace and you don't so much as question it. That was clearly a mistake."

She wasn't wrong. But Zeke's first thought was that he'd have never met her otherwise. Regardless of how this situation played out, whether he ever saw her again after, he was glad to know her. Not something he was about to admit out loud.

"Hopefully we'll be able to rectify that while we're here," he said instead.

She tilted her head toward him, staring out at the horizon. "Silver lining. I get to see a part of the country I never planned on visiting."

"I'm glad for that, Vivi." He turned to fully face her. There was something that had been tugging at him since last night on the steamship. "If you don't mind my asking, why haven't you left Louisiana?"

She shrugged. "It's my home. What else would I do?"

"I've heard you sing, Vivi. I'm no expert but I think you've got a rare skill that should be pursued."

"I do pursue it. I sing on a busy steamboat tour on the lovely Mississippi."

"Don't you think your talent warrants more than that?"

"People from all over the world hear me perform."

"You could have so much more than that. Aren't you even curious about how far you could go?"

Vivi didn't answer, just started picking at a loose thread along the hem of her dress. He knew he might be overstepping but felt compelled to try and explain where he was coming from. "I just don't understand why anyone would bounce from one job to another, simply to try and make ends meet, when they have the means to pursue a real career. And you certainly do, Vivi. You sing like an angel."

She released a deep sigh. "I appreciate the compliment, Zeke. I really do."

Funny, she didn't sound as if she appreciated what he'd said in the least bit.

"I was a toddler when the elderly aunt who'd been looking after me passed," she continued. "I bounced around in foster care after that until I turned eighteen. The life I have now is more than I could have hoped for. I know that's something somebody like you wouldn't understand."

"You might be surprised."

She quirked an eyebrow. "Yeah? How so?"

"Let's just say I couldn't really have imagined the life I have now, either."

"Huh" was all she said in response.

"Don't you ever wonder if your vocal talent might lead you to even more?"

She studied him before responding, then effectively changed the subject. "We should probably get going."

There was more to her story. He just knew it. He also

knew she wasn't going to share any more. Her desire to end the conversation had come through loud and clear.

He would drop the subject, as she wanted, and was rather sorry he'd ever brought it up.

Vivi was afraid to study Zeke's expression too closely as they walked out of the lobby and through the square. She wouldn't be able to stand it if he pitied her. The excitement she'd felt about seeing the falls had waned after their conversation on the balcony. She knew she shouldn't let it get to her, but she couldn't seem to help herself.

He cleared his throat as they meandered through the other tourists. "I'm sorry if I overstepped. I was just very impressed with your voice and your ability when I heard you sing last night."

"Thank you," she said simply.

"I won't bring it up again."

But it was too late, wasn't it? The discussion hung in the air between them now. He thought she was unambitious, with no goals. Well, goals and ambition weren't meant for women like her. She was just aiming for survival.

A career in the spotlight was the last thing she needed or wanted. A life of fame or fortune wasn't in the cards for Vivienne Ducarne. Not with the skeletons she had in her closet. The less attention she called to herself, the better.

There was no way to explain that to Zeke without revealing those skeletons to him.

"So, truce?" he asked.

"I didn't realize we were at battle."

"More of a standoff, then."

Vivi did her best to shake off her irritation. "Whatever you want to call it, consider it over." For now, anyway.

The crowd around them grew larger and larger as they made their way down the sidewalk and crossed the street.

Most everyone was headed in the same direction. The humming sound of the falls increased, so they had to be getting close.

"We must be almost there."

Zeke chuckled at her enthusiasm. "Slow down, I can barely keep up with you."

She hadn't even realized she'd quickened her stride. Finally they turned a corner and there it was. The pictures she'd seen online had not done the view justice. There was no comparing this to anything she'd seen on her hikes back in Louisiana.

It was unlike anything she could have imagined.

A massive sheet of water plunging over the edge like it was alive. A colorful rainbow glimmered at the base, rising high up into the air. A sheen of mist dampened her skin and clothes.

She moved closer to the railing, breathing deeply of the moist, refreshing air. *Majestic* was the only word that came to mind.

"What do you think?" Zeke asked softly in her ear as he reached her side.

She couldn't find the words to answer his question. There was no way to adequately describe what she was looking at. Like a child, she climbed the bottom rail and gripped the top one, leaned over as far as she could, nearly toppling over in the process.

"Whoa. Careful there," Zeke cautioned, grabbing her about the waist to steady her.

The scene quite literally took her breath away.

He was zero for two.

First he'd upset her by asking about her singing. Then he'd broken his vow to avoid touching her. That second one he could be forgiven for. He had been trying to save her from falling over a metal fence, after all. Never mind that his hands had lingered on her waist a second or two longer than needed.

Now they were making their way along the paved pathway trailing the viewing area of the American Falls. They'd been there close to an hour and Vivi didn't seem to be tiring of the excursion in any way.

"This is just awe-inspiring," she proclaimed, stopping to face the falls and admire it yet again.

He would have thought she'd run out of adjectives by now.

As awe-inspiring as the scenery was, Zeke was ready to call an end to the outing. Duty called and all. Plus, he was starting to get hungry. His time in New Orleans, with all its wonderful cuisine, had trained his stomach to expect rather frequent meals.

"How about we grab a bite?" he asked.

Vivi's face fell. "Already?"

As if on cue, his stomach grumbled loud enough to be heard over the rushing water. She chuckled in response. "I guess that's my answer."

"We're here for a while yet. We can always come back."

Her expression looked doubtful. How many people had broken their promises to Vivi over the span of her lifetime? "I'm a man of my word. We'll come back if you'd like."

"Okay. But one more picture." She pulled out her phone and aimed the screen.

Zeke stepped over to her, held his hand out for her phone. "Here. Let me. You should be in it."

She placed it in his hand just as an older couple approached them with wide, friendly smiles. "Let us take the photo," the woman offered. "We'll get both of you. You should have a couple's photo in front of that beautiful view."

Vivi immediately began to correct her. "Oh, there's no need. We're not actual—" But the lady wasn't listening.

"Nonsense." She took the phone out of Zeke's hand. "I'm Marge. Go stand together in front of the water."

Marge sure was a bossy sort.

Zeke gave Vivi a pointed look, one that hopefully conveyed the message that it was probably easier just to comply and move on with their day. Vivi must have gotten the hint. She nodded with a smile and followed Zeke to the railing.

Zeke did his best to pose as an adoring boyfriend/husband without actually making physical contact. It wasn't easy. Luckily, neither Marge nor her husband seemed to notice.

Several snaps later, they thanked the older couple and started making their way back to town.

"What are you in the mood for?" Zeke asked her, trying to recall which eating establishments they'd passed along the way.

"What's this area known for?"

"Burgers and hot dogs—believe it or not. And root-beer floats."

"You know what they say, when in Rome…"

Within minutes they were ordering at the window of a sidewalk diner with outdoor seating. Zeke ordered burgers and franks for both of them and a large basket of fries to share. They each carried a large plastic red tray laden with food and plenty of napkins.

"This should get me to my quota of grease for the month," Vivi remarked as they sat and began to eat. She moaned with pleasure after the first bite. Did the same after eating her first fry.

How did the woman make eating fast food look so darn sexy? Zeke made himself look away and focused instead on his hot dog.

"We should head to the chapel after this," Vivi said between bites.

He nodded in response. "It's as good a place as any to start. See if we can chart Roxie and Rocky's path."

"And if we can't find them?" she asked, dabbing a fry in a mound of runny ketchup. Worry laced her voice.

"Let's hope we get lucky."

She harrumphed out a humorless laugh. Zeke got the impression she wasn't used to seeing much luck come her way. Maybe one day he'd get her full story. But he wasn't about to ask now, not after the fiasco with asking about her potential singing career.

Zeke polished off his frank and moved on to the burger. But Vivi seemed to have lost her appetite.

"Do you want something else? I know this isn't exactly refined fare."

Another ironic laugh. "Refined is overrated. It's not that."

"Then what? Aren't you hungry?"

"I would just feel bad if we can't get Esther back what's rightfully hers."

He patted her hand. "Don't worry. One way or another that necklace will find its way where it belongs."

She mumbled something under her breath he couldn't quite make out. Zeke stood. This wouldn't do. She'd barely eaten anything, and they had a long afternoon ahead of them still. "I'll be right back," he told her and went back to the ordering window.

He returned with a large root-beer float in a tall plastic stein and two long straws. "Dessert," he announced.

"I'm rather full…" Vivi protested, but her words held no real conviction.

"Come on," he prodded. "Who can resist the combination of creamy ice cream and bubbly, sugary soda?"

She clasped a hand to her chest with a dramatic shake of her head. "Not I."

He set the concoction in front of her and pulled a chair close. Even with the scent of grease and sugar lingering in the air, he could still smell the fruity fragrance of her hair. He had to clench his fists tightly to resist leaning in and inhaling deeply the alluring scent that had now become so familiar. Being close to her always seemed to wreak havoc on his senses.

For the life of him, he didn't know what to do about it.

CHAPTER EIGHT

AN HOUR AFTER their salt-and-sugar-laden lunch, they headed back toward the square. The chapel was in the center of town. Vivi hoped for the best. But now that she thought about it, what were the odds they would actually locate Roxie and her new husband? Niagara Falls was bigger than she would have thought. And it was crawling with tourists, domestic and from other countries. Just on their walk right now, she could hear a myriad of different languages and accents.

Finding anyone in such a setting seemed to be the proverbial needle-in-a-haystack scenario.

Somehow, Zeke seemed to have read her thoughts. "Have faith, Vivi. Don't assume failure yet."

"How do you know that's what I was doing?"

He motioned to her, waving his hand up and down. "You've got your hands clasped in front of your middle and you've gone stiff as a board. It's not hard to tell you're stressed."

"I'm starting to wonder how feasible it is to think we might find them among this crowd of people."

"One task at a time. Assume success until proven otherwise."

Quite the lesson in how to approach life. "Is that how you've achieved all your success? With that motto?"

He shrugged. "That and sheer determination. I had a lot to prove."

To whom? Vivi wondered. Maybe the world in general.

Within minutes, they'd reached the small brick building that housed the Niagara Bridal Chapel. A colorful sign hung by the door that read: No appointment necessary. First come, first served.

"Not much different than how we ordered lunch earlier."

"Not everyone's into ceremony," Zeke said.

"Or they just can't wait to get married."

A matronly middle-aged woman with her gray hair piled high in a bun atop her head greeted them as soon as they opened the door.

"Come in! Come in! So nice to have you."

Zeke guided Vivi forward and introduced them both.

"I'm Penny," the woman replied. "Apologies, we're running a little behind, but the minister will be here in just a moment."

She glanced down at Vivi's empty hands with something of a frown. "Let me get you a bouquet." She pivoted on her heel before Vivi could process exactly what was happening.

"I'm afraid we only have plastic flowers," Penny added over her shoulder.

Horror washed over her as realization dawned. Before she could stop the other woman, a gentleman in a dark suit and neck collar appeared through the door.

"Welcome. Let's get started, shall we?"

"No!" Vivi and Zeke both yelled in unison. The minister startled and Penny stopped in her tracks, a bouquet of fake flowers in her hands.

"That's not why we're here," Zeke quickly explained.

"Hmm," Penny said. "Why else would you be in a chapel at two o'clock in the afternoon? In Niagara Falls?"

Zeke stepped forward. "Sorry for the confusion. We're

actually looking for some friends of ours. We were told this is where they eloped."

Penny's lips thinned with disapproval. "We don't use that term here, sir. Every marriage is sacred, and we pride ourselves on providing a quality ceremony for all our couples."

"Of course. I apologize," Zeke offered with a slight conciliatory bow.

"We happen to be in town and we wanted to congratulate them," Vivi added. It was true enough.

Between the two of them, they managed to give a quick summary that left out anything about a priceless necklace, so that it didn't sound as crazy as the truth actually was.

The minister rubbed his jaw when they were done. "I don't know. We get a lot of couples through here."

"My friend has fiery red hair," Vivi said. "And her new husband wears his hair in a ponytail. Sometimes a man bun."

"That could describe a third of the couples we've had in here in the last week," Penny said with a click of her tongue.

"They would have been in here yesterday. Maybe the day before."

The minister squinted his eyes in concentration.

"Maybe the names will help," Zeke said. "Roxie and Rocky."

That seemed to do the trick. Both the minister and Penny nodded in recognition. "Of course!" the man said. "I remember them. Thought they were joking about the names until I saw their paperwork."

"They were a hoot!" Penny added. "Lovely couple."

"Those two couldn't keep their hands off each other," the minister told them. "Even more so than the usual couples we get in here," he added with a wink.

That certainly explained why Roxie couldn't be bothered to pick up her phone or check her messages.

"Do you happen to remember where they said they were staying?" Zeke asked. "So we can send them a bottle of champagne with our congratulations."

"I think they said the Borderside Inn," Penny answered.

The minister shook his head in disagreement. "No, I don't think so. I think they said Niagara Nightly."

"That's okay." Zeke told him. "We'll try both." He extended his hand to shake the minister's. "You've both been very helpful."

Vivi nodded her thanks as well, then followed Zeke out the door with a nearly overwhelming sense of relief. Maybe they'd be able to find the necklace after all. It was just like Zeke had advised earlier: assume success until proven otherwise.

A bubble of laughter escaped her lips as they stepped back out into the sunshine.

"What's so funny?" Zeke asked.

Vivi sat down on the front steps—she just needed a second to gather her thoughts. The whole day had been one continuous whirlwind. "First of all, I can't believe that actually worked. Second, we were almost married just now."

Zeke sat down next to her on the concrete step, bumped her shoulder with his own playfully. "Maybe I should call you almost-wife from now on."

A wayward thought popped into her head at his joking suggestion. Her stomach quivered with an achy longing at the term. *Almost-wife.* Saints above, but it had a nice ring to it.

They decided to try the Borderside Inn first. It was closest of the two places Penny and the minister had mentioned and conveniently on the way back to their own hotel. A buffet was set up out in the lobby when they arrived about ten minutes later. The place was quaint and charming. Zeke figured it did well enough, given its location. It certainly seemed to be full now. Several children scurried about, so the place clearly attracted families as well as honeymooners. Not that that was any kind of useful fact he might need. Zeke didn't really have any family and he certainly had no plans to become a honeymooner anytime soon.

His gaze drifted to the woman next to him and scenes he had no business imagining flooded his mind before he pushed them away. A solitary attendant worked the front desk, so it took them a while to get past the line of guests checking in and out. Finally it was their turn.

Zeke summoned his most charming smile as the woman greeted him. The silver nameplate she wore said *Mindy* in curvy black lettering.

"Good afternoon. I was hoping you might help us with a gift. I wanted to send a bottle of your finest champagne to two of your guests. They just got married. But I don't happen to know their room number."

Mindy returned his smile with a warm one of her own. "Oh, how lovely of you. That's not a problem." She clicked away at her keyboard. "Just give me the last name."

Vivi stepped in. "Clairmont. Roxie Clairmont."

Mindy clicked away some more, but then her warm smile turned downward. Zeke felt a tightening in his gut. The woman's expression did not look promising. "Hmm," she began. "I'm not seeing anyone checked in here under that name."

"What's Rocky's last name?" he asked Vivi. "Maybe they used his."

If they were even at the right hotel. Vivi gave him a blank look. Zeke resisted the urge to swear out loud. To have come this far only to be sidelined because they didn't have even the most basic of facts…

"I'm really sorry," Mindy said with a woeful look at

each of them in turn. "I can't find the room without a last name. Wish I could help."

Zeke released the curse he'd been holding in as soon as they stepped away from the desk.

"I have an idea," Vivi said when they reached the lounge area by the glass double doors of the entrance. "I'll text Bessa so that she can text Roxie's mom and ask what Rocky's last name is."

He must have gone to sleep the other night and woken up in a sitcom. So many degrees of separation.

"There's just one problem," Vivi added.

Of course there was. "Bessa's at work at the Crawdad. Where she doesn't have—"

"Access to her phone," Zeke said, completing the sentence for her.

Honestly, were people from Louisiana just not as attached to their phones as the rest of the country? Roxie wasn't even answering hers.

"Go ahead and give it a try," he told her. Not like they had any other options.

She sent the text then slipped the phone back into her cross-body purse. "Guess now we just wait and see."

"May as well take a walk outside," Zeke suggested. "This hotel happens to be behind one of those rose gardens this part of the country is known for."

Vivi gave a noncommittal shrug. "Sure. Why not. May as well look at some beauty while we wait."

Zeke didn't say out loud what he was thinking. That he'd been looking at something beautiful since this morning. Their quick jaunt from the chapel to the hotel had brought a hint of red to her cheeks, bringing out the golden hazel of her eyes. The humidity of this climate had added gentle curls to her dark hair. Her skin seemed to glow with the sheen of mist from the falls in the air. And the way she smelled. He couldn't seem to get enough of that fruity scent. It reminded him of lazy afternoons in the tropics.

What in the world was wrong with him? He was usually not the type to daydream about a woman's looks or the tone of her skin. It must be the effect of being around all these newlyweds and besotted-looking couples.

They followed the signs down a wooden pathway by the side of the inn that directed them to the rose garden. When they reached the entry gate, Zeke realized what an inadequate name that was for the place. There were certainly roses, but a variety of bushes bearing other flowers dotted the landscape.

"Wow." The simple comment came from Vivi. She looked almost as impressed as she'd been at the Horseshoe Falls earlier.

The colors alone were enough to take away anyone's breath. But what was really noteworthy was the pleasing scent of several floral varieties that filled the air.

"It's like we've stepped into some kind of Eden," Vivi commented.

A bucket of roses for sale sat by a nearby bench. Zeke threw several bills in the payment bin and handed one to Vivi. "A piece of Eden for you, then."

Vivi took the long-stemmed red rose and inhaled deeply. Something squeezed in his middle. The look of pure pleasure on her face had his senses tingling. He could put that look on her face. He could bring her pleasure and take what she had to give in return. A slight breeze rippled the air and blew several strands of curls onto her cheek. Zeke couldn't seem to help himself. He reached over and gently tucked a strand back behind her ear.

What was that vow about not touching her again?

He really needed to pull his hand away from where it still lingered at the base of her delicate ear. But she looked up at him, and heaven help him, he saw the same desire shining in her eyes. She tilted her head up toward him, bringing their lips a needle's breadth apart. Thoughts of any kind of self-imposed vow flew out of his head. Before he could allow himself to think, he lowered his mouth onto hers and finally indulged in what he'd been fantasizing about for so long.

She tasted as good as he'd been imagining. And, oh, had he imagined it. Probably since that first time he'd laid eyes on her. She tasted of berries and honey, like a delectable exotic candied berry. A slow moan escaped her mouth under his lips and he thought it might be his undoing. The kiss was suddenly deeper, more wanton. He couldn't even tell which one of them had caused it.

They were interrupted when a shadow fell over them where they sat on the bench. Someone cleared their throat softly above their heads. With nearly painful reluctance, Zeke made himself pull away from her. Mindy, from the main desk. "I've been looking everywhere for you two. I asked my colleague about your friends. He knew exactly who you were referring to."

It took several moments to regain any sense of thought, or to even process what the woman was saying. Then he remembered why he and Vivi were even there in the first place.

Vivi managed to find her voice first. "He did?"

Mindy nodded with enthusiasm. "He knew right away when I mentioned their first names. He checked them in and recalls which room they're in. Would you like to send them that champagne now?"

Vivi was finding it hard to focus as they followed the hotel's front-desk attendant back to the main lobby. She knew this was cause for relief. They'd managed to find the proverbial needle in the haystack! But all she could think about right now was the way it had felt to be in Zeke's arms. How he had tasted against her lips. The pleasure he'd made her feel deep in her core. She couldn't recall ever reacting to a man's kiss with such abandon. She still felt the tingle along all her nerve endings. Her heart still pounded in her chest.

She squeezed her eyes shut. Right now they had a more pressing matter. They were about to finally get that cursed necklace back.

Vivi waited as the arrangements for the champagne were made and Zeke handed Mindy his credit card. "Could you send my friend a message along with the gift?"

"Of course!" Mindy immediately agreed.

"Could you please tell her to check her voice mail and that we're down here to see them? We'll be in the lobby when they're ready."

The other woman blinked in confusion but then simply gave a small shrug. "I'll make sure they get your message," she assured them.

"Looks like we're in yet another holding pattern," Zeke remarked after they'd moved back to the lounge area of the lobby. Had he been as affected by their kiss as she was? That certainly didn't seem to be the case. He looked calm and collected. As if nothing had happened.

While her stomach was still overrun with butterflies.

She was still clutching the rose he'd given her in her fingers. How did a man give a woman a rose, kiss her silly the next instant and then only moments later act as if nothing had happened?

The better question was, why was she exerting any of her energy right now on anything but getting Esther's necklace back?

She paced from one corner of the lobby to the other, her thoughts a jumbled mess darting between that mind-blow-ing kiss and the astounding fact that they'd finally found Roxie and her groom.

Vivi didn't know how much time had passed before she heard the ding of the elevator arriving followed by a very familiar Southern twang.

"Oh, my God, Vivi. Are you playing some kind of prank on me?"

Roxie, clad in a long silk robe with a feather collar, jogged across the lobby to where she and Zeke waited. She gave Vivi a shoulder squeeze in greeting then gave Zeke a swift nod of acknowledgement.

"No prank, Roxie. I'm so sorry for the misunderstanding. But we need that necklace back."

"Of course. Heavens. This is so hard to believe. My heart jumped to my throat when I finally listened to your messages." She slammed a hand to her chest. "When I think about how careless I've been with it."

She motioned for them to follow her. "Come on up. Rocky's getting dressed."

Yep, they'd certainly interrupted a couple on their honeymoon.

"This is Zeke," Vivi said when they were all in the elevator.

"Hey there, sugar. Thanks for the champagne."

"It's the least we could do. So sorry for interrupting your honeymoon."

Roxie waved off his apology.

"He's the estate attorney who discovered what Esther had done," Vivi explained.

Roxie shook her head slowly from side to side. "That poor woman. She just wasn't thinking straight, huh?"

"No. She wasn't."

"Well, all that matters is we get her rightful property back to her."

The inflection of Zeke's tone held just enough of a hint of accusation that it gave Vivi pause. Surely, he wasn't blaming Roxie for any of this. The poor woman had had no idea. She'd simply accepted a wedding gift from a friend.

In case Zeke hadn't noticed, Vivi and her circle of friends weren't exactly the type of crew who would recognize a priceless antique when they saw one.

"You can have it back," Roxie told them. "It's giving me hives to think I had something that valuable in my possession all this time."

When they got to the hotel room, Rocky was waiting for them with the door open. The men quickly shook hands.

"So this isn't some kind of prank, then?" Rocky asked, his accent thick Louisiana Creole.

"I'm afraid not."

Roxie went to the bureau and pulled out a drawer. Finally, she lifted out the object that had caused so much angst and rushed it over to Zeke. She handed it to him with a visible shudder.

"Thank you."

"No problem."

The exchange was so normal that Vivi couldn't help but think how anticlimactic all of it was. But like Zeke said, all that mattered was getting the darned thing back where it belonged.

"Here." Rocky handed them a velvet bag with a thick drawstring. "Don't forget its container."

Vivi took Roxie in her arms and enveloped her in a tight hug. The relief surging through was indescribable. To finally have this nightmare over with was a divine gift from heaven.

"Enjoy the rest of your honeymoon," she told the other woman. "Bessa and I owe you a real wedding gift as soon as you get back."

"I'm-a hold you to that, sugar."

Out in the hallway, Zeke placed the necklace carefully into the velvet pouch, then slipped it gently into his pocket.

Vivi released a pent-up sigh. "I can't believe something that fits in your pocket has caused us so much hassle."

"Hassle over, for the most part. Let's go. We should get dressed."

Vivi blinked up at him in confusion. Did he want to head back to Louisiana already? Of course, it made sense. Zeke Manning was a busy man. Now that he'd gotten what he came for, he had no more time to dally around staring at waterfalls with a café waitress who read tarot cards and did some singing on the side to make a living. As for that kiss, she'd read much more into it than she should have. A wave of disappointment waved over her heart and she silently chastised herself for it. How pathetic. Cute towns for honeymooners and aromatic rose gardens weren't her life. It was high time she got back to all that was.

"I won't be long," she said as they made their way to the elevator. "I don't have much to pack up. We can leave as soon as you'd like."

"Leave? Why would we do that?" He patted the pocket that held Esther's necklace. "Roxie and Rocky aren't the only ones who have something to celebrate tonight."

CHAPTER NINE

"YOU PROBABLY DIDN'T pack anything too dressy, but there's a boutique a few doors down from the hotel," Zeke explained as they stepped into the lobby of their own hotel about fifteen minutes later. "While you shop, I'm going to get this to a safe-deposit box at the local bank until we can pick it up tomorrow."

Vivi could ascertain two things from what he'd just told her. One, they would be spending the night in Niagara Falls. Two, he planned to take her somewhere fancy, a place that required a dress from a boutique. The latter posed a bit of a problem, as she probably couldn't afford anything there.

Maybe if she maxed out her credit card. Who was she kidding? Even if she did take the hit, and run her card so high that she'd be paying it off for the next forty-eight to sixty months, her limit probably wouldn't even cover it.

Well, she'd figure out something. She was good at that. Figuring out ways to adapt. She certainly wasn't about to admit to Zeke that her pocketbook precluded her from visiting any type of boutique. There had to be a discount store in the more touristy section of town. "How dressy are we talking?" she asked.

He must have read something in her voice, because he quickly added, "You can charge your purchases to my account. It's the least I can do for your aid in helping me get Esther's property back."

So they were back on this again. He was offering to compensate her once more. He really did view her as some kind of employee who'd simply helped him with a project. A man like Zeke would never view her as an equal. To him, she would always be from the wrong side of the tracks. He'd mentioned that it might surprise her how much he understood about the hardships she'd endured in her life. That may be so. But they weren't the same. Unlike her, Zeke had always had at least one person who'd wanted him. And he'd made something of himself. Whereas Vivi had to struggle every day just to get by. No wonder he saw her as nothing more than a temporary employee.

Which begged a major question—did he often go around kissing his employees?

Forget about the kiss. Zeke clearly had.

"That won't be necessary, Zeke. I wanted that necklace found as much as you did." If anything, she had a lot more riding on this quest they'd been on. Her reputation had hung on that necklace being returned to Esther. Maybe her very freedom.

To be returning to Louisiana with it safely in Zeke's possession really was the best-case scenario. She shuddered to think what might have happened if the authorities were involved. The last thing she needed was to have the law poking around in her life. Those days were long gone and she'd do all she could to ensure that they stayed safely behind.

"Vivi, I ins—" Zeke began before she cut him off with a palm up. He really didn't understand that she wasn't some charity case. Not for him, not for anyone. It was uncomfortable enough that he'd be paying for a restaurant that was sure to be pricey.

"It's not up for discussion," she said flatly, leaving him

no room for further argument. "Just tell me what time to be ready."

He sighed with resignation but luckily didn't push any further. By now, they'd reached the door of their suite. "Let's meet back here in the common room in about three hours. Will that give you enough time?"

Vivi honestly didn't know. She was pretty certain this restaurant would be out of her league. The same way Zeke was out of her league. But she would make do with what she had to work with.

That was another thing she was good at.

Twenty minutes later Vivi put her resourcefulness to full use. The boutique Zeke mentioned was just as pricey as she'd imagined. But they had a rack of quality silk scarves that she could actually afford. Just barely.

She picked out one in a beautiful ocean-blue that she knew would bring out the specks of aqua in her eyes.

"Lovely choice," the young blonde at the register told her when she brought it up to be paid for and packaged.

"Thank you. It's about the only thing I can afford in here," she admitted. The clerk didn't seem like one of the pretentious ones so often employed in a place like this. Rather, she had a warm and pleasant smile that made Vivi feel at ease.

"The prices are outrageous," the other woman said with a mischievous smile, cupping her hand around her mouth as if divulging a state secret.

"Too high for me, I'm afraid. I was told to buy a fancy outfit for dinner tonight, but it won't be one of those." She gestured to the rack of beautiful gowns hanging along the wall. This was the kind of place that didn't even have visible price tags. She'd had to ask what the scarf sold for.

"Say no more." Vivi watched as the woman pulled out a

slip of paper and started scribbling. She handed it to Vivi with a glance around the store to make sure no one was watching. The action struck Vivi as highly comical, seeing as they appeared to be the only two people in the store.

"Go there," she instructed, pointing to the sheet of paper. "They have the cutest outfits and they're always running discount sales. Not the best quality, but no one can tell."

That could be an apt description for a lot of things about her life, Vivi mused.

Zeke tucked the ticket for the safe-deposit box in the hotel room's safe and dialed the code to lock it. What a relief to know exactly where Esther's necklace was and that it was safe and secure.

He'd been less than certain more than once throughout the day that their efforts would be fruitful. Particularly when Vivi had been unable to provide Rocky's last name.

Luckily, it had somehow all worked out. Now he could relax and enjoy the evening. With Vivi. It was foolish of him to be so ardently looking forward to an evening out with her. But he figured they could both use it.

Without any kissing.

How in the world had he let that happen? He'd completely lost himself. She'd just looked so alluring in the garden, surrounded by flowers. And the way she sniffed the rose he'd given her, like a goddess bequeathed with a flower from heaven.

There he was waxing poetic again. He had to stop.

And it absolutely could not happen again. That much was certain.

As soon as he stepped into the common room to find Vivi waiting there, he realized just how much an effort it was going to take to stick to his resolutions.

She was absolutely stunning. Movie-star stunning. She

wore a silky jumpsuit of some sort. Black material that somehow glittered navy blue when the light hit it a certain way. A sea-blue scarf hung low from her neck, and was tied in a complicated knot above her breastbone. Delicate tendrils of hair curled around her face. She wore that same red shade on her lips that had so vexed him that day in the French Quarter.

She did a mini twirl then spread her arms out. "What do you think? Will this work for where we're going?"

Think? Who could think? Not any warm-blooded male with eyes who caught sight of her. Clearing his throat, Zeke somehow managed to find voice enough to answer. "Yeah. That will work just fine."

The smile she gave at his response had his body tightening in all sorts of spots that had no business reacting in any way.

"Phew! I was worried a jumpsuit might not fit the bill."

"That one sure does," he mumbled.

Get a grip, already, buddy.

A beautiful woman shouldn't hamper his ability to speak coherently, for heaven's sake.

"Good. Because I'm starving."

Right. They should probably get a move on. While he was standing here on the verge of drooling at a woman he'd met only the day before, yet had already kissed, they were risking missing their reservation time. And the reservation had taken no small amount of string-pulling given that it had been made at the last minute.

"You mentioned you had your passport."

She nodded. "It's my primary form of ID. I don't drive. Why?"

"I figured we'd make this an international trip and head over to the Canadian side."

A dazzling smile appeared on her face and Zeke felt

pleasure clear to his toes. The decision had been rather impulsive, but the look on Vivi's face told him he'd made the right call.

He held his elbow out to her. Vivi didn't hesitate before putting her hand on his arm and following him out the door.

The same driver that had picked them up at the airport was waiting for them outside and drove them through the border crossing into Ontario, Canada. They were at the restaurant moments later. The night had grown dark and the city was lit up at every turn. Just as many people roamed the streets as there had been this afternoon.

Vivi looked around her as they exited the car. A tall tower loomed several feet in front of them. The only structure in a square otherwise occupied by various vendors and street performers. "This is it? Where we're eating?" Her tone was one of curiosity and uncertainty. She had to be wondering if he'd had her get dressed up and cross the border to dine on another hot dog from a street cart.

"Sort of," he answered.

"What does that mean?" she asked, her eyes full of merriment. She was enjoying this. Knowing that made his heart do a little jump in his chest.

Zeke pointed up to the circular podlike structure at the top of the tower. "We'll be eating up there."

Her reaction was exactly as he'd hoped. She gasped out loud and clasped her free hand on her chest. "Oh, Zeke! I can't even imagine the view!"

"You won't have to imagine it. Let's go see it firsthand."

"I can hardly wait." She tugged on his arm, practically dragging him to the entrance.

"What a relief," he said on a chuckle. "I don't know what I would have done if you said you were afraid of heights." The statement was something of a fib. The thought had actually never crossed his mind. He'd known Vivi would be thrilled, that she wouldn't be bothered by the height one bit.

In fact, it was downright uncanny just how much he felt like he did know this woman.

Whatever winning a star meant in restaurant speak, this establishment deserved it. The place was opulent. Shiny silverware gleamed on crisp white tablecloths. The servers were all clad in tuxedos with starched, white-collared shirts and polished leather shoes.

But what Vivi really fixated on was the view. The entire city sat majestically before them, including the falls! She felt like a regal queen sitting atop her royal tower. And it was revolving! The scenery changed by the second. Food wasn't even necessary. She'd be perfectly content to just sit here and admire the scenery for hours.

She was so transfixed by the scene, she almost missed her chair when the server pulled it out for her to sit. Her bottom landed perilously close to the edge and she had to adjust herself to avoid toppling over.

You could take a girl to a fancy restaurant…

A waiter immediately appeared to fill their glasses with sparkling water. A different one showed up to hand them each thick leather-bound menus. Yet another came by after that and introduced himself as the sommelier. There appeared to be an entire team just to serve the two of them.

Zeke ordered a bottle of something Italian she couldn't pronounce while she looked over the menu. Just like the boutique, there didn't seem to be any prices listed anywhere.

If you have to ask the price, then you can't afford it.

She startled at Zeke's laughter, not realizing until that moment that she'd actually said the words out loud.

"Quite the quote," he commented.

"It's something one of my foster moms would say often. She used to watch those reality fashion makeover shows where the recipient always looked shocked when the over-all cost of their transformation was revealed at the end."

Zeke's smile slowly waned. "One of your foster moms? How many houses were you sent to, exactly?"

She began a mental count before giving up. "About a dozen or so, I guess. I was a toddler when I entered the system, so I had time to bounce around before I aged out."

"That couldn't have been easy."

She shrugged. "Some houses were easier to leave than others. The toughest part was losing touch with some of the other kids. It was like repeatedly having to make friends only to never see them again once I left."

One girl in particular she still thought about often would always claim a spot in her heart. Lola. She'd been much younger. Vivi had felt more responsible for the child than their assigned mom. That's when Vivi's brushes with the law had first begun. But she didn't regret trying to help another child who'd needed it, and would probably do the same if she had to live it over again. The last time was a different story. She'd only been playing the fool for a man when that arrest had happened.

"It must have been a relief when you were able to leave," Zeke said, pulling her out of the unpleasant memories.

"It was and it wasn't. Then I had to figure out where to live and how to afford it. All on my own."

She knew she should try and change the subject. She was treading on very thin ice. One slipup and she'd be reveal-ing more about herself than she wanted to. Zeke wasn't the type who would understand some of the things she'd done or why she'd had to do them. He would probably look at her the way some of those judges had over the years. Like she was lower than the tiled floor of the courthouse.

"Looks like you did just fine from where I'm standing."

It was silly, really. But the pleasure she felt at his compliment warmed her all over, from the top of her head right down to her toes.

"Thank you for that."

They grew silent as yet another tuxedoed server, female this time, appeared at their table with a bottle of wine. Uncorking it with expert skill and efficiency, she held it to Zeke, who sniffed then nodded approvingly. Vivi watched the ruby-red liquid pour into her glass, then Zeke's. The woman rested the bottle on a side table before walking away.

Several more moments went by in silence. Finally, Zeke spoke. "For what it's worth, I didn't exactly have what one would describe as a normal childhood, either."

Oh? That was surprising news. She would have pegged him as the type who'd lived in a perfectly tidy home surrounded by a picket fence and at least one, probably two, beloved household pets. Who'd had a set of adoring, attentive parents that exerted just the right amount of discipline without curbing their child's spirit. But that assessment wasn't a fair assumption now that she thought about it. She knew firsthand how deceiving looks could be.

He didn't elaborate further and Vivi was itching to ask but didn't want to push. Heaven knew she had things about her own past she wanted to keep close to her chest.

So she willed Zeke to continue, silently prodding him with a fixed gaze he didn't even seem to notice. She wanted to know everything about this enigmatic, charming man who swore too much and went out of his way to help little old ladies who'd carelessly given away their valuable antiques.

Probably best just to address the proverbial elephant in

the room. She would take a guess and leave the ball in his court. "Parents' messy divorce?" she ventured.

He huffed out a humorless laugh. "Believe it or not, that would have been a blessing in comparison."

CHAPTER TEN

He hadn't meant to sound so cryptic. But what he'd said was the absolute truth. He and his sister would have preferred a messy, loud, battle-driven divorce to what their parents had put them through. His mother, to be more precise. His father had just been too weak to do anything to fix what was happening right in front of his nose. The man had been too cowardly to fight for his family, to protect his kids. A bitter surge of bile rose in his throat, almost ruining his appetite. He washed it away with the sparkling water, downing half the glass before setting it back down.

Vivi was looking at him expectantly. He had to give her something, he supposed. Fair was fair—she'd confided in him about her struggles as a foster child.

He waited while their salads arrived and more wine was poured in both their glasses. After taking a fortifying sip, he cleared his throat before beginning. Trying to put into words what he'd so carefully tucked away in a locked corner of his mind would take some effort. "In her attempt to live a more exciting and fulfilling life, my mother put her trust in the wrong person. People, to be more precise. It ended up costing us everything. We went from living a comfortable and affluent lifestyle to one of desperation and destitution." And filled with fear, he added silently. So much of his childhood had centered around the fear of one man and what he could get others to do for him.

Without a word, Vivi put down her salad fork and reached for his hand across the table. Her touch felt soft and comforting. Like the feeling of coming home after a long and arduous journey. He turned over his palm, taking her entire hand in his so they were clasped. To any outside observer, they probably appeared to be a besotted, loving couple out enjoying a special evening. For one insane moment, Zeke let himself pretend that was the reality. Several moments passed with them just holding each other's hands over the table. Almost as if they were a real couple.

Gently, he pulled his hand away and picked up his own fork. Vivi inhaled deeply before returning to her salad. "It's quite something, isn't it?" she asked.

"What is?"

"The complete and utter havoc others can wreak on our lives when we're not paying attention."

She was right but her words didn't really apply to him. He'd been paying attention, all right, as his world had slowly come crumbling down all those years ago. He'd just been too young and powerless to do anything about it.

Their head waiter appeared at their table to take their order. He opted for the night's special, a braised rack of lamb with fingerling potatoes. Vivi chose the sea bass, which was the chef's signature dish, they were told. Zeke took the liberty of ordering another bottle of wine. He wouldn't be driving anywhere, and the direction of their discussion seemed to warrant more liquid courage.

"Would your earlier statement have anything to do with your former tattoo?"

She chewed slowly, methodically, as if weighing her words. The guy must have done quite a number on her, since she couldn't even bring herself to talk about him.

An irrational and unexplainable anger swelled in his chest at the faceless, nameless man who'd clearly hurt Vivi so deeply that she still carried the wounds. What kind of fool would have let a woman like her go? She'd cared for tattoo guy enough to have his name engraved on her body in permanent ink. His ire began to turn to outrage the more he thought about it. Outrage that had nothing to do with jealousy. He just didn't like to see those who didn't deserve it get hurt. Maybe if he repeated that enough to himself, he'd eventually be convinced.

Finally, she spoke after a rather generous gulp of her wine. "It's a classic story, I suppose. Foolish, gullible girl trusts the wrong man. The repercussions of which follow her for years after. And probably will for the rest of her life."

So they'd both been burned by those who should have done better by them. Kindred spirits with respective painful memories they'd both rather forget.

A disquieting, uncomfortable feeling settled in his gut. This conversation had gotten too heavy, too personal. They were supposed to be two new friends enjoying the successful resolution of a rather stressful matter that they no longer needed to worry about. The mood at the table right now was anything but celebratory. He was racking his brain for a way to fix that when the universe did it for him.

As if on cue, the wall of glass in front of them revolved so they had a perfect view of the falls. Just then illuminative lights went on. The entirety of the falls turned into a massive kaleidoscope. It was a spectacular display of lights and color and rushing water. Like something out of a brilliant painting. Only the art here happened to be vibrantly changing and moving.

Vivi's gasp was audible. "Oh, my," she said on a breathless sigh. "Would you look at that."

But he wasn't watching the display of lights that had

taken her breath away. He couldn't take his eyes off *her*. Her breathing was heavy and quick, at a near pant. The excitement was practically buzzing from her as she stared at the stunning light-and-laser display in wonder and amazement. She was mesmerized.

And so was Zeke. But that had nothing to do with the view from their table.

He was falling for her. Sometime over the last couple of days, his feelings toward Vivi had gone from mere attraction to affection. An affection he had to fight. For a woman like Vivi could ruin him if he let her. Like Vivi said, he could really get burned if he wasn't paying enough attention.

Vivi reluctantly pushed away her plate after taking one last scrumptious bite. The meal was a culinary masterpiece, every morsel delivering a burst of flavor on her tongue. Very likely the tastiest meal she'd ever had—and she lived in New Orleans, one of the food capitals of the world. But she couldn't eat any more. Her tummy was resoundingly, soundly stuffed. It had taken years, but she'd finally taught herself to stop eating when she was full. Before that, it had felt like such a waste to let any food go uneaten considering how many nights she'd gone to bed hungry.

"Dessert?" Zeke asked, pulling her out of the memories. There'd certainly been a lot of those unearthed this evening. She wasn't quite sure how she felt about that. Somehow she'd managed to keep most of her past buried while still confiding in Zeke to some degree.

"I can't eat another bite," she replied, tapping her middle.

"I say we walk a bit and enjoy the night air. You game?"

She definitely was. A walk in the fresh air might help clear her head. "Definitely."

No bill had arrived for their meal, but Zeke stood and

walked over to assist her out of her chair. All their waiters nodded politely as they left the table, and no one gave chase when they made it to the elevator. Vivi concluded that payment had probably been arranged beforehand.

The rich certainly lived differently than the rest of the world.

When they left the tower, the square outside was just as busy as when they'd arrived earlier this evening. If anything, it appeared even more crowded. A band had set up in the center, playing instrumental versions of current top-forty popular hits. Several people were dancing in front. Vivi had to hop out of the way of one couple doing some kind of complicated tango.

She suddenly felt a strong hand on her shoulder. Zeke gently turned her to face him. "Care for a dance?" He held his hand out, palm up. Vivi took it and stepped closer. With a chuckle, he took her in his arms and together they began to move to the beat. He'd undone the top button of his dress shirt, revealing a tanned triangle of skin. She itched to touch him there, imagined trailing her fingers from the base of his neck down lower, to where a small sprinkle of chest hair peeked out from under his shirt. The aftershave she'd grown so fond of tickled her nose and she inhaled deeply, trying to get her fill.

She looked up to catch him staring at her. Something shifted in the air between them. Though the music remained up-tempo and bouncy, Zeke pulled her closer and slowed his steps, his arms tight around her waist. She could feel his hot breath on her cheek, his pulse pound under her palm. Was he going to kiss her again? Dear heavens, she wanted him to. She really, really wanted it.

The tangoing couple barreled into them in that instant. Vivi felt herself falling into Zeke's body, sandwiched between the couple and his chest. Somehow he kept his balance despite the three people crashing into him.

The other gentleman straightened and gave them an apologetic smile. *"Excusez nous."*

Zeke answered the man in French, then proceeded to have a brief conversation with the couple in the other language. He was clearly fluent. Was there any talent the man didn't have?

"You're bilingual," she said as the other couple moved on.

He still held her in his arms. "Trilingual, actually," he answered without any hint of grandeur. "I do a lot of business in Europe. Particularly France." He tilted his head toward the other couple, who were still tangoing despite the change to a slower song. Something told her they'd indulged in some liquid courage as well at some point. "Though their dialect was a little different than what I'm used to as they're French Canadian."

"What other language are you fluent in?"

"Just Italian and French," he answered. Vivi had to chuckle at the *just*.

"It was easier to learn the languages seeing as I'm in those countries so often. In fact, I'm due in Provence in a couple of days."

The comment brought Vivi hurling back to reality. This was all fun and games, dining with Zeke Manning. Dancing with him outside while an amateur band played cheerful music. But she couldn't forget how unreal all this was. How temporary. Fantasyland would come crashing to an end in about forty-eight short hours. Zeke would leave for France and leave her life. Probably never to think of her again.

She suddenly didn't feel like dancing anymore.

"I think I'm ready to move on," she told him, stepping out of his embrace. He let her go, but stopped her with a hand on her arm after a few steps.

"Let's go a bit further before returning to the car."

She followed him away from the partying dancers and out of the square. It only took a few steps for her to determine they were headed back in the direction of the falls. The prospect of visiting it again lifted her spirits somewhat. But not by much. She'd never be able to forget Zeke Manning. Would wonder every day where he was and what he was doing.

How had this happened? She'd fallen for him. And she hadn't even seen it coming. She'd been caught completely unaware.

"Thank you," she said a few minutes later as the sound of the falls grew louder the closer they came.

"You already thanked me for dinner."

"Now I'm thanking you for bringing me back to see the water."

He gave a small shrug. "I promised you we'd go back. What kind of man doesn't keep a promise to his almost-wife?"

Zeke regretted the words as soon as they left his mouth. He really had no business calling Vivi any kind of wife. Not even jokingly. They were simply two people enjoying some time together before they had to go their separate ways. And he and Vivi absolutely had to go their separate ways, being from different worlds that could never collide in any kind of positive way. They both had way too much baggage. And the bags he had were much too heavy to burden anyone else with.

Vivi deserved better.

Now his words hung heavy between them, too late to take them back.

"You shouldn't say such things to me," Vivi told him, confirming his regret. "Calling me a wife implies permanence." She motioned around her. "None of this is permanent. By this time tomorrow I'll be back in New Orleans and you'll be getting ready to fly to another continent."

Heaven help him, that last sentence came out on a sob. He'd never meant for her to become so emotionally invested, wasn't even sure how or when it had happened. He would have to do better. He wanted to get closer to her, to hold her and comfort her. But touching her was the last thing either of them needed.

"You're right. I was careless. It won't happen again."

"No?"

He shook his head. "No."

She visibly swallowed. "And what about earlier today? With what happened in the rose garden."

Right. Their kiss. He should have known that would come up. Yet another transgression to apologize for.

"That won't happen again, either. Consider it another promise."

The color of the lights illuminating the falls changed right then. They went from neon rainbow colors to a combination of soft reds and ambers. The hues brought out the warm hue of Vivi's eyes, and there was no missing the moisture in them.

Her tongue darted out to lick her lips. People strolled by them—all around them the world continued on. But they may as well have been the only people on earth. Nothing mattered now but the woman in front of him and what she was telling him.

"What if I don't want you to make that promise?"

Zeke's breath caught in his throat. Had he heard her correctly? "Vivi, what exactly are you saying? I need to be certain here."

She stepped closer to him, then tilted her head up to his. "I'm asking you to kiss me again, Zeke."

Zeke felt his mouth go dry, his heart beat like a bass drum in his chest. He wouldn't make her ask twice.

His mouth was on hers in the next instant. Vivi wrapped her arms around his neck and held tight. He couldn't get enough of her. And when she ran her tongue along his lower lip, he thought he might collapse from the sheer pleasure.

A low groan vibrated against his mouth. He wasn't even sure which one of them it had come from. Finally, Vivi was the first one to pull away. He felt her loss as if a bucket of cold water had been thrown at him.

She stood before him, breathless and panting, and it took all he had not to drag her back into his arms and repeat what had just happened.

Heaven help him, but he wanted more. Much more.

It was impossible to sleep. Zeke gripped the cold metal bar of the hotel suite balcony railing and watched the lights of the city below gradually go out one by one. He'd lost track of how long he'd been standing there when only a handful of shops' lights remained lit. The town was slowly going to sleep.

Unlike him. Insomnia had cursed him for close to two hours until he'd finally admitted defeat and come out here for some fresh air. He couldn't get that kiss out of his mind. Either kiss.

The way Vivi had tasted, how she'd felt in his arms. The vulnerability on her face as she'd so boldly asked for what she wanted. It all ran in a continuous loop in his mind. The fact that their time together was coming to an end was affecting him more than it should have.

He had no idea what he was going to do about it.

She didn't realize, of course, but he'd never so much as spoken about his past with anyone who wasn't his sister.

And his only sibling preferred to avoid the topic of their shared trauma even more than he did.

Somehow, Vivi had pushed through defenses he hadn't even acknowledged he'd built around himself. He couldn't even pinpoint when it had happened. She visited old ladies and didn't charge them for readings. She elicited fierce loyalty from those who seemed to know her the best. She listened without judgment or expectation.

Zeke hadn't realized just how much he'd wanted that from someone until it was right there in front of him in the form of one Vivienne Ducarne.

Zeke rubbed a hand down his face and grabbed the icy bottle of water he'd brought out with him, emptying it in a few quick gulps. The rich dinner and all the wine had left him parched.

He turned to go back inside for another bottle from the mini fridge when the balcony door suddenly swung open and Vivi stepped outside. She startled when she saw him. In a spaghetti-strap tank and boy shorts that showed off her shapely legs, she looked better than any woman should at this time of night.

"Sorry, I didn't realize you were out here. I'll go back in. You probably want to be alone."

Before she could turn away, he reached for her, gently taking her by the shoulder. "Vivi, stay. I'm just getting some air."

She hesitated for the briefest of seconds before slowly shutting the door and reaching for one of the lounge chairs.

"You couldn't sleep, either, huh?" he asked as she sat down with a thump.

"Been tossing and turning since I crawled into bed an hour ago."

He could certainly relate. They were both probably preoccupied by the same thoughts. "Ditto."

Maybe neither of them wanted the night to end, considering they'd both be returning to their ordinary lives tomorrow. Or later today to be more accurate. It was already almost two thirty in the morning.

Damn it. He had a nice life to go back to. He'd worked hard to get to where he was after burying his tumultuous past. He had no business begrudging it in any way. Even if his time in France in a few days would involve thwarting the unwanted advances of a lonely former winery owner.

But there was no denying that the thought of going back to normal held zero appeal at the moment.

And that feeling had everything to do with the woman sitting in front of him.

She'd said while they'd been walking after dinner that whatever was happening between them wasn't permanent. Was that so wrong? What exactly was so wrong with temporary, anyway?

"Come to France with me, Vivi."

She jerked her head up in shock. Well, he was pretty surprised himself. He had no idea he'd intended to utter those words until they'd left his mouth.

Vivi stood staring at him, slack-jawed. He scrambled for a way to continue. "You'd be doing me a favor."

"A favor? How?"

"My clients in France are a rather traditional family. They think I'd make a perfect match for their single daughter. They've tried several times in the past to set me up with her."

She blinked in confusion. Of course she was confused. He was making a mighty mess of this. How many times could he behave so uncharacteristically unprepared around this woman.

"I see," she simply said.

"It gets distracting and uncomfortable. I'm only there on

business and don't need the added complication of fending off such requests," Zeke explained, hoping he was making some kind of sense.

"What has that got to do with me going to France with you?" Vivi asked.

He shrugged. "Simple. It might help if they think I'm already involved with someone. I figure we can pretend to be a couple."

CHAPTER ELEVEN

Two days later

"TALK ME OUT of this before I do something I'm going to regret, Bessa."

Vivi paused in the act of packing when her roommate walked into her bedroom.

"I'll do no such thing. I think you should go for it. I just came in here to offer you these." She held out a plate of steaming hot hush puppies. "I just made them fresh."

Bessa was known in the neighborhood for her hush-puppy recipe, one she kept secret even from the woman she'd shared an apartment with for the last three years. Vivi reached for one and tossed it from one hand to the other as the ball of fried dough burned her palms.

"Careful, they're hot."

"Fried dough isn't the only way a girl could get burned, you know."

As far as metaphors went, it was kind of lame. But it pretty much captured the way Vivi felt about her decision to say yes the other night on the hotel balcony. Like she'd been impulsive and might be risking irreparable harm to herself.

Mainly to her heart.

Zeke had completely shocked her when he'd asked her to accompany him on his trip to France. She knew she should have given it more thought. But the idea of being able to spend more time with him, in a setting as romantic as the French countryside, had been too tempting to ignore. She simply hadn't the will to turn him down, though that would have been the wisest move. Hindsight, as they said.

"Huh," Bessa responded, taking a bit of one of her creations and plopping down on Vivi's bed while she chewed. "Some fires are worth getting close to."

Vivi wasn't so sure about that theory. Look how badly her relationship with Todd had scarred her. Not that it made any kind of sense to compare the two men. Zeke was everything Todd could ever hope to be. Smart, eloquent. Someone who knew how to treat a woman.

Oh, and Zeke didn't have a rap sheet the length of a swamp gator.

"Said the unsuspecting moth right before his wings were singed," Vivi answered, folding another pair of jeans and tossing them in her bag. She was apparently full of bad metaphors today.

"How did this come about, anyway?" Bessa asked. "He just out and asked you to fly to France with him."

That was exactly what had happened. "Yes," she answered Bessa simply.

"You two must have really hit it off."

That was one way to describe it. "He said the client he deals with in France always tries to hit on him. To the point where it's gotten awkward for a professional such as himself," Vivi explained. "So bringing me along when he goes to their estate might cool her jets a bit."

Bessa barked out a sharp laugh. "He wants you to pretend to be his girlfriend? I'm thinking there won't be much pretense needed."

"It's not like that," Vivi lied, recalling the way he'd kissed her by the falls. How his mouth on hers had melted her insides. Even thinking about it now had her knees nearly buckling.

"So what happened when you told him about...you know?"

Realization dawned on Bessa's features at Vivi's continued silence to her question.

"Oh," Bessa finally said, not needing an actual answer anymore.

"I probably should have. And maybe I will on this trip. But there never seemed to be the right time in Niagara Falls. Especially not during the time a valuable necklace had gone missing."

"I see your point."

Vivi sighed and checked her purse yet again to ensure her passport was there. Not being a driver, she relied on it as her primary form of identification. Which had certainly come in handy when a man she'd met just last week had taken her into another country then asked her to fly to Europe with him.

Another wave of doubt flushed through her center. "Maybe I should call off the whole thing. Tell him I can't go after all."

Bessa popped a whole hush puppy in her mouth. "Isn't it kind of late?" she asked between bites. "You said he's due to pick you up at three. It's one thirty now."

Bessa had a point. It would be unfair to cancel on Zeke at the last minute. Why was she overthinking it, anyway? He wanted her to help him out with an overflirtatious client. It just so happened that she'd be helping him in one of the most romantic and awe-inspiring spots on earth.

Bessa seemed to read her thoughts. "Why don't you just go and enjoy yourself. Leave all the worrying for when you get back. This is a dream vacation to Europe and you're thinking about passing it up."

She was right. There'd be plenty of time to regret her decision later. When the trip was long over and Zeke was back in New York, and she didn't know if or when she'd ever see him again, no doubt the mighty beast of regret would rear its head. Vivi happened to do regret really well. But at least this time, she'd have a visit to France to remember.

"You might be right."

"I always am. As for the rest, wouldn't you rest easier if you just confided in him? Just told him what happened in the past and explained it wasn't really your fault."

Vivi stepped over to the bed and gave her friend a tight hug. Bessa was usually spot-on. But not this time. Not about this. Zeke would never understand that her ex-boyfriend had duped her into waiting in a getaway car while he committed armed robbery inside a pawnshop. That fateful day was the reason she still couldn't bring herself to sit behind the wheel of a car.

And he certainly wouldn't understand that she'd done a short stint in juvie simply because she'd wanted to make sure a younger child had clothes on her back and enough food to eat.

He probably wouldn't even listen to her version of events. The same way the cops, lawyers and judges hadn't listened.

Bessa's description had been an apt one. Vivi really felt as if she might be in some kind of daydream the next day as she sat in a rental sports car—a cabriolet—with Zeke in the driver's seat. He maneuvered the car expertly along cliffside curves and the French countryside while Vivi admired the view. Now that she was here, she couldn't believe she'd almost turned down the opportunity. She may live to regret her decision, but for now she was going to enjoy every moment she could.

Like her roommate had also said, "Deal with the worrying when you get back." Wise woman, that Bessa was. Most of the time.

They were headed to meet the winery owners to finalize the sale to Zeke's American corporate client.

"We shouldn't be there long," he told her now over the wind. "Once I get the paperwork signed and sealed, we can take some time to sightsee."

"That sounds wonderful," she shouted so that he could hear her, then laughed at how comically loud she'd just sounded.

Zeke responded with a grin in her direction before turning his attention back to the road. "What's so funny?"

"Nothing, really. I'm just having a really good time so far." Which made almost no sense, as they'd only been in the country a short while after having landed at Marseille Provence Airport earlier today.

"Not too jet-lagged?"

"Not at all." That was the truth. Rather, she felt energized and ready for the adventures that lay ahead while they were here. She'd never been to an authentic winery or a lavender field before. Let alone done those things in the south of France.

Several minutes later they turned onto a dusty dirt road surrounded by the greenest grass she'd ever seen. The smell of the sea permeated the air. When the house appeared in front of them a few moments later, Vivi had to suck in a breath. It looked like something out of one of those foreign dubbed movies Bessa made her go to occasionally. A sprawling mansion with a tall, round center building flanked by a wing on each side. Behind the structure she could see the rows and rows of lush grapevines on a rising hill.

"Welcome to the Château de Seville," Zeke said as he put

the car in Park and killed the ignition. "I know I thanked you earlier, but I'm doing so again."

"You've flown me to France and our first stop is a gorgeous château. I'm the one who should be thanking you, Zeke."

"You're doing me a favor, remember? This visit will go much quicker and much smoother if I don't have to keep finding creative ways to turn down Michelline's offer of a romantic dinner over and over."

Vivi had to feel for the other woman she hadn't met yet. She understood firsthand how easy it was to fall for Zeke Manning. A small, foolish part of her wished there didn't need to be any pretense. And that she really was here as Zeke's partner. But she was nothing more than a decoy. A fake.

This Michelline couldn't know, but the two of them had a lot in common—pining for the same man who didn't feel the same about them as they felt about him.

Sisters in spirit, Vivi thought as she followed Zeke up the pathway to the large wooden door of the main building. It flung open as soon as Zeke knocked. An older, rotund woman stood on the other side. She greeted them with a warm smile, though the smile directed in Vivi's direction faltered ever so slightly.

"Madame Seville, *bonjour,*" Zeke began, then continued with a slew of more French words Vivi didn't have a hope of understanding. He motioned to her with his hand and said her name.

The other woman took Vivi's hand and shook it just as her husband appeared at the door. She said something to her directly in French. "She wants to apologize for speaking a language you can't understand," Zeke explained, translating.

Within minutes the four of them were seated around a

rustic wooden table enjoying wine and a platter of various cheeses and dried fruits.

Zeke stuck to mostly water, since he was driving.

Vivi could only nod and smile politely, having no clue what was transpiring around her. Occasionally, Zeke threw her an indulgent smile.

The Seville home was cozy and comfortably decorated, despite being an official château. Pens were pulled and mounds of papers were signed.

Michelline had still not made an appearance.

A twinge of guilt settled in Vivi's middle. She knew Zeke had his reasons for this charade. And this family really had put him in an awkward spot if they consistently tried to set him up with their daughter. Still, she couldn't help but feel sympathy toward the other woman. She was in a rather similar situation, wasn't she?

Finally, Zeke began to pack up all the paperwork and slid it back into his leather carrying case. He stood and shook the hands of their hosts. The scene served to alleviate Vivi's guilt somewhat—clearly there were no hard feelings and from what little she could tell of the conversation, the Sevilles had made quite a bit of a profit on the sale of their estate. Monsieur Seville even gifted Zeke a bottle of their special reserve from the previous harvest as a token of thanks.

They were headed to the door to leave when a tall, elegantly dressed woman turned the corner from the hallway. Vivi could only stare in stunned silence. She had to be the mysterious Michelline.

Whatever Vivi had been expecting, it didn't compare to the woman who stood before them with a friendly yet tight smile. She looked like something out of a fashion spread in a magazine. Rich honey-blond hair fell in waves over her elegant bare shoulders. She was dressed in a strapless dress that hugged her delicate curves just so. Her nails had been perfectly manicured, including the ones on her toes.

This was the woman that Zeke was trying to avoid?

"Zeke," she began, and her thick French accent made his simple name sound regal and exotic. "So lovely to see you. And you have brought a guest." She clasped Vivi's hand in hers then air-kissed both her cheeks.

"Th-thank you," Vivi stammered. The woman was clearly fluent in English but Vivi had no idea what else to say.

"Michelline, we missed you during the signing," Zeke said, smiling in return.

"It is done, then?" Michelline asked.

"*Oui.* Your parents can live comfortably the rest of their lives without worrying about the demands of running and upkeep of a successful winery."

"We have you to thank for that, don't we?" Michelline said with clear gratitude, then she turned back to Vivi. "You know, despite the fact that he works for the other party, Zeke convinced our buyers to up their offer and sweeten the deal on behalf of Mama and Papa."

"Wow" was all Vivi could manage to say. She wasn't surprised by what Michelline had just said. She hadn't known him long, but she knew Zeke would fight for the underdog no matter what side he was technically on.

It was one of the many things that had her falling for him.

And she was falling for him—there was no denying it any longer. Somehow along the way, in the span of a few short days, Vivi had gone from attraction to admiration to something much more.

Rather inconvenient.

She studied Zeke's profile now as they drove away from the Seville home. His hair was a windblown mess, but somehow on him it looked rugged and masculine. He'd taken off his jacket and rolled up his shirtsleeves about the elbow.

Her heart did a little flutter in her chest and she made herself look away before he could see the longing in her eyes.

"Ready to tour those lavender fields now?" he asked her, pulling her out of her thoughts.

"I'm looking forward to it."

"It's about a half-hour ride from here," he informed her.

Before even half that amount of time passed, it was clear that fate had other plans. A massive storm cloud appeared in the sky, churning and angry. Vivi ducked her head to get a better look. Not good. It seemed to go on for miles and miles in the sky.

"What in the hell?" Zeke groaned. "There was no thunderstorm or any kind of weather event in the forecast. It's supposed to be a sunny and clear day."

The fact that he'd made sure to check the weather forecast before setting up a plan to take her to a lavender field seemed so true to his character. Zeke Manning didn't seem to like leaving anything to chance. But meticulous planning only went so far at times. Times like right now, for instance.

Vivi pointed up. "I don't think Mr. Cloud up there cares what the meteorologists predicted."

Zeke frowned and hit the button to pull up the cover on the convertible. It closed just in the nick of time. A sheet of heavy rain dropped like a waterfall from the sky. It reminded her of the Horseshoe Falls back in Niagara Falls. Only now it felt like they might be standing right under it.

Zeke slowed the car to a crawl. "I can't see a thing. And it doesn't look like it's going to let up anytime soon."

Before he even got the last word out, a flash of lightning lit up the air around them, as if someone had flipped on a massive light switch then shut it right back off. The following thunder noticeably shook the small car. Zeke pulled out his phone. His lips tightened as he clicked on an icon on the screen and studied what loaded up.

"This doesn't look good," he announced.

She could have surmised that from the messy conditions outside, as well as the concerned look on his face.

Another bolt of lightning struck through the air, this one perilously close to where they were, followed by thunder so loud it made Vivi jump in her seat. The sky grew so dark it may as well have been nightfall. How had all this come about so quickly and without any kind of warning?

Vivi was no stranger to rough weather. She lived in New Orleans, for Pete's sake, where the seasonal hurricanes had devastated the city in previous years. But right now they were in the middle of nowhere, completely isolated.

"We need to find shelter," he told her, putting the car back in gear and moving slowly. The wipers may as well not have been running. They weren't helping in any way to be able to see out the windshield.

"Is there anything out here even?" Visibility was zero at the moment, but they'd been driving for miles before the cloud appeared and there had been nothing but fields and greenery.

"According to my map icon, there's a structure up ahead."

Vivi didn't like the word he'd just used. What did he mean by *structure*? Why didn't he say *cottage*? Or *pub*? She took out her own phone to see for herself what was nearby. The no-signal warning greeted her when she clicked the button. Icy dread ran up her spine. If they needed help, there'd be no way to call for it.

"We just lost cell reception," she informed Zeke.

"Not surprising. If we could just get to this building and get a roof over our heads."

"What kind of structure are we talking about?"

The road they were on was steadily flooding now and Vivi could feel the vehicle actually hydroplane underneath them.

Zeke released a deep breath, his fingers in a death grip on the steering wheel. "It appears to be an abandoned château."

CHAPTER TWELVE

ZEKE WANTED TO kick himself for putting Vivi in such a harrowing situation. That she was in any kind of peril because of his decisions made him feel like an absolute heel. In his defense, the storm seemed to have come out of nowhere. Even the weather reports hadn't seen it coming.

At least he'd found them some shelter. Even if it was in the form of a damp, dusty and moldy abandoned brick mansion that probably hadn't seen any human activity in years, aside from the occasional squatter.

He handed Vivi his jacket from the back seat of the car. "Here. Cover your head. We're both going to get soaked, anyway, but it's something, at least."

She didn't protest, but took it from him with a quick thanks. Luckily he'd thrown their carry-on bags in the back seat as opposed to the trunk. He grabbed them both in one hand and braced himself. The château was only a few feet away, but in this mess it was going to be a harrowing jaunt.

"Ready?" he asked Vivi.

Her lips were tight, her eyes apprehensive, as she nodded. "As ready as I'm gonna get."

"On the count of three."

He hadn't even gotten to one before she threw open her door and leaped outside.

Zeke watched in admiration as she ran to the gaping

hole in the front of the building that had once been a front door. Way to rip off the bandage without any preamble or hesitation. Why had he expected anything less from her?

She disappeared into the building and he rushed to her side. They were both soaked to the skin in just the few seconds it had taken to make it from the car.

He'd been right about the state of the building. Cobwebs hung from the high ceiling. Moldy grime clung to the walls. Several wooden beams were strewn about. But it appeared sound and steady. And it was a roof over their heads in a storm.

He turned to see Vivi shivering with cold. Her hair was wet and plastered to her head. Her clothing a soaked, disheveled mess.

She looked absolutely adorable.

How did a woman manage to look so sexy shivering and soaking wet?

"Hope we're not here long," she commented, studying the dank and dark space. "Not that I'm not grateful to be out of that tin can of a car." She paused, then added, "No offense."

"None taken. It's a rental."

A harsh gust of wind brought some of the rain through the open doorway and they moved farther inside. Zeke dropped the bags he was carrying on the floor and unzipped the one that belonged to him. Reaching inside, he pulled out one of his long-sleeved T-shirts and a gym towel he always carried in the side compartment with his toiletries. He handed the latter to Vivi.

"It's small, but it's absorbent."

"Thanks."

She did her best to dry off and the shivering seemed to abate if only a little. He handed her the shirt. "Here. Something dry."

He turned around so she could change, but not before he could stop the images from flooding his mind. Images of him helping her to take off her wet top, running his hand down her rib cage and over her lips. Pulling her tight against him.

Steady, there. The lady was just trying to get warm and dry.

A few moments later, he heard her clear her throat. "All set. Thanks. That's much better."

The shirt was about three sizes too big for her, and hung like a curtain off her shoulders with the sleeves draped down past her hands. Again, somehow she made it look fetching. In fact, he itched to take her in his arms and devour those damp lips until she was shivering again, but this time for all the right reasons.

He clenched his fists at his side instead. He yanked out another dry shirt, then peeled off the wet one and tossed it aside. As soaked as it was, the Italian silk was most likely ruined, anyway. He pulled the dry one over his chest and torso. Vivi made a deliberate show of looking down at her toes until he was done.

"Well, we could be here for a while," he said, studying the layout of the place to see what they had to work with. "May as well make ourselves comfortable."

Vivi looked around. "How, exactly, do you propose we do that?"

He reached inside his bag again, and found the wine Monsieur Seville had given him just a short time ago. "This should help."

"Merci, Monsieur Seville," she said with a smile.

Zeke unzipped the side pocket and pulled out the granola bar he kept there for nights when he didn't have time to grab a real dinner. "And there's this."

"Resourceful. I'm impressed."

"Tonight, we feast."

"Only one problem." She pointed to the bottle he held. "How do we get that open?"

Like a cartoon, Zeke literally scratched his head in concentration, earning a hearty chuckle from Vivi.

"I saw someone online use a key once to twist off a cork," she offered.

"Worth a try, I guess." Zeke yanked the car-key fob out his pocket and clicked it open to remove the metal key inside.

Twenty minutes and several attempts later, he finally managed to pull out the cork, though some of it had broken apart and fallen into the bottle. Vivi cheered and clapped at his success and he gave her a small bow. "Now we can finally feast."

"Let's see if we can find a dry corner somewhere." When they did, Vivi set down her travel blanket on the ground and they both did their best to fit on it together. Her shoulder and hip rubbed tight against his side as they took turns biting the granola bar and taking sips straight from the bottle.

Warmth spread along his skin everywhere her body touched his. She smelled of fruity shampoo and damp skin. His fingers itched to run his touch over her shoulders and down her arms, and he longed to taste the wine on her lips. Somehow, he made himself resist the urge to pull her closer against him. This wasn't the time or place. They were caught in a raging rainstorm, for heaven's sake.

A storm that showed no signs of letting up. In fact, it seemed to have only grown stronger and more formidable outside. But Zeke found he didn't really mind. He was in no hurry to leave.

If someone had told her a month ago that she'd be huddled up in the corner of an abandoned castle in the French countryside eating a granola bar and drinking wine straight out of the bottle with a man she'd recently met, Vivi would have laughed until her stomach hurt.

Her life had been a series of unexpected twists since Zeke had arrived in it. Had it really been only a number of days since Zeke had stormed into the magic shop demanding to know where Esther's necklace was? It seemed like it had happened months ago.

Even their visit to the winery felt like it had occurred sometime in the distant past rather than just a short while ago. Every minute with Zeke Manning seemed to pack a myriad of experiences.

She recalled what Michelline had said about Zeke making sure her parents got the best deal they could from his client.

"That was very noble of you," she said to him now. In her desire to get warm using his heat, she'd given up fighting the urge to snuggle into his warm chest, her back against his front with his arms around her. Who was she kidding? It felt nice to be snuggled up against him, to feel his rock-hard chest against her back. If she was being fanciful, she might have said they fit together well.

"Noble?" he asked.

"How you made sure to take care of the Sevilles rather than try to shortchange them in any way on behalf of your client."

"My client is a conglomerate of successful wineries throughout the world. The Sevilles ran a family winery and worked hard their whole lives to make it succeed. It was easy to make sure they were given their due."

He was trying to minimize it, but not many attorneys would have even taken such factors into consideration, let alone work to ensure fair play. No lawyer she'd ever had the misfortune to deal with would ever have gone to any such trouble. Even the ones whose job was to defend her couldn't wait to rush to a plea then wash their hands of her. Zeke was a rarity indeed from what she'd encountered throughout her life.

"What you did for them was commendable, Zeke. So was making sure Esther got her necklace back."

He nuzzled the top of her head with his chin. "Any other attorney would have probably done the same in both cases."

That wasn't true and he had to know it. "Why?" she asked simply, counting on him understanding exactly what she was asking.

He was silent for so long that she thought he might not answer. "I don't like seeing people taken advantage of," he finally responded.

Vivi didn't want to push. But she was so curious about what made him tick. How had Zeke Manning become the man that he was today? Maybe it was the wine. It seemed to be going to her head with nothing but half a granola bar to soak up what she drank, but she found herself asking the questions that were running through her mind. "You said your family went from comfort to destitution. What happened to cause that, Zeke. May I ask?"

His arms tightened around her waist. "It didn't happen all at once. My mother was the type who was always bored. Always needed to feel excited about something."

That sounded like a pretty exhausting way to grow up. Vivi didn't voice the thought out loud, just remained silent to allow Zeke the chance to share what he wanted to share. Or to end the discussion if he wanted to.

He went on, "She held these grand parties at our house. Hosted artists and singers and writers. She considered herself a grand patron of true talent. Certain she was about to discover the next best thing."

Vivi felt him take a deep breath behind her before continuing. "All the while, my dad just did what he had to do to make sure we could afford it all. He worked for a major law firm and invested well, but eventually it wasn't enough. Not after my mom met an up-and-coming painter. Rex Waltham. He had my mother convinced he was the next Andy Warhol. She bought everything he painted or drew."

Vivi could just guess where this was going. And it broke her heart. "Eventually, Rex moved in. I actually had to give up my room so he could stay there with us. At the awkward age of thirteen I had to share a room with my younger sister. And my father didn't do anything about it. Just continued to bring in the money to keep my mother happy. He wasn't a strong man. Too weak to fight and too complacent. It was easier to just try and indulge her. And my old man always took the easy way out."

"But it wasn't enough," he added after a pause. "It was never enough."

The pieces that made up the puzzle that was Zeke Manning started to slowly fall in place. His protectiveness and fierce desire to ensure fairness. His lack of trust and propensity to think the worst of others. The way he had about *her*.

"That man used her and spit her out," he said after another long pause. "He finally left after finding the next, much richer mark. But by then it was too late. My father was a shell of his former self. Sick and weak. He wasn't with us long after that."

Tears stung her eyes at the pain in his voice. He'd been so young. To have his whole life turned upside down by those who should have loved him enough to protect him. "You must have been so strong. To just even survive that."

He grunted out an unamused laugh. "I had to do more than survive. After my dad was gone, I had to pick up all the pieces. Make sure my mother got help for her issues and that my younger sister was taken care of."

"What did you do?"

"As soon as I was old enough, I worked for anyone who would hire me. My sister and I ended up moving in with my grandmother. All four of us crammed into a tiny condo in Brunswick. At that point our house had been taken. An unoriginal McMansion, but it had been home. Then one day it was just gone. Any savings or investment was already long spent. Rex somehow convinced my mother to keep investing in him until there was nothing left."

She felt his muscles stiffen behind her. His heart was beating like a drum against her back.

"I somehow managed to put myself through college and then law school. Last I heard, my mother had traveled out to the West Coast, living in some kind of co-op or commune. None of us have heard from her in years."

Vivi let everything he'd just told her sink in. She'd thought he was accomplished before. She'd had no idea. Just thinking about all he'd had to overcome just to survive. But he'd gone on to do so much more than that.

One thing was for certain—Zeke had been taught from an early age that trust was never to be given lightly. How could she ever expect him to trust someone like her if he ever found out the truth?

Amazingly, they'd both fallen sleep. It was the cramping pain below the back of his skull that woke him up. Zeke stirred and tried to roll out the kink in his neck muscles. Sleeping against a hard stone wall while sitting upright was not ideal for a man his size or age.

The wine bottle sat empty by his right thigh. The granola-bar wrapper was crumpled up on Vivi's lap.

A small ray of sunshine shone through one of the square

window holes on the second floor, casting light on the ground next to his feet. And it was quiet. No thunder, no steady beat of rainfall. The storm seemed to have passed.

What time was it?

Zeke tried to lift his arm to peek at his watch, but he couldn't quite move with Vivi sprawled on top of him. They'd been sitting next to each other against the wall, but at some point she'd ended up square in his lap. Not that he was complaining. Despite the muscle cramps and his uncomfortable position, one thing did feel right. The feel of Vivi's warm body nestled against his as he listened to the rhythmic sound of her breathing while she slept. He couldn't recall the last time he'd felt such a deep sense of peace.

Was that because of all he'd told her about himself?

There was no denying a feeling of calm and catharsis had seemed to settle over him. For the first time in a long while, he didn't feel tense or wound up, like he constantly had to be on the alert for the next catastrophe.

He had no idea how long it might last but knew he had Vivi to thank. Somehow he'd opened up to her about the most painful details of his life and the world hadn't come crashing down to an end. There'd been no judgment in her reaction. No words of sympathy or—heaven forbid—pity. She'd just listened.

He hadn't realized how badly he'd needed someone to do that.

His phone vibrated in his pocket and he felt the ding of several messages and emails downloading at once. Apparently they'd just regained cell service.

He had to check to see what those messages were. After the meeting with the Sevilles he was technically off the clock, had penciled time off to spend the day with Vivi. But his work never actually stopped. He couldn't just lounge here enjoying the feel of Vivi sitting on his lap for hours. As tempting as that was. Plus, a killer migraine was in the process of forming in the center of his head because of his awkward position against the wall.

He gently rubbed a hand down her cheek to rouse her awake. "Vivi, the storm has stopped. We can leave."

She stirred ever so slightly before settling back. Zeke took a moment to indulge himself in studying her. Long thick lashes as dark as midnight. Tanned skin kissed by the Southern sun. Ruby-red lips that she chewed absent-mindedly from time to time when she was deep in thought.

He knew exactly what those lips tasted like.

Another text vibrated on his phone. He really had to look at those messages. There might be something important that needed his attention.

He tried again to awaken her, rubbing his palm down her upper arms until she finally stirred. It took several moments but eventually her eyes slowly drifted open. Her lips thinned as she looked around in question.

She certainly looked adorable when she first woke up, all confused and flustered from sleep.

"It's done, sweetheart. The storm has moved on. We can finally get out of here."

She gave her head a brief shake and rubbed the drowsiness out of her eyes. "How long have we been in here?"

"I'm not quite sure. But I'd say it was long enough. We can head back to my place and relax by a fire after a nice hot shower."

That sounded like he intended for them to shower together, then cuddle up in front of his fireplace. He hadn't meant for it to sound so intimate. Not that the idea didn't sound downright heavenly.

Vivi looked up at him then, the longing in her eyes so

deep and clear that he felt the breath rush out of his lungs. Her desire was clear on her face and matched his own.

When she tilted up her chin to angle her face closer to his, he took it as the clear invitation it was. In the next instant, he was kissing her, his hands roaming over her luscious curves as he relished the feel of her hot breath in his mouth.

She turned to fully face him, straddling him in the process, and he thought he might die from the pleasure. She had the heart of an angel and more spirit than anyone he knew. He'd never met anyone like her, and she called to him on every level.

Sweet heavens, he wanted her. Like he'd never wanted any other woman in the past.

But they were in an abandoned castle propped up against a damp, cold wall. None of that would do.

There was no longer any denying where things were headed between them. But this wasn't the time. He wanted their time together to be right. Not rushed and frenzied under a leaking stone roof.

Somehow, he found the discipline to pull away and gently nudge her back. She blinked up at him in confusion and hurt. He couldn't have that at all. Cupping her chin, he brushed another soft kiss against her lips.

"You can't think I don't want you."

She blinked twice more.

"But not like this." He gestured around them. "Not here."

He knew he was making the right call. But, man, pushing her away like that had felt ever so wrong.

CHAPTER THIRTEEN

VIVI COULD STILL feel the warm flush on her cheeks as they loaded up the car with their carry-ons and drove away from the château.

Hard to tell if the heat on her face was due to the effects of Zeke's earth-shattering kisses or because of her horrified embarrassment. She'd practically mauled him back there, after throwing herself at him. How utterly mortifying that he'd been the one who'd had to pull away.

Not her classiest moment. But she didn't have too many of those.

"I can't believe we just spent part of the afternoon stranded in an old abandoned mansion," she said, just for some semblance of a conversation. Being in a tight car in such close proximity to Zeke after what had just happened was unnerving her and making her tense.

"There's quite a few of them dotted around the country-side and all throughout France."

"Oh?"

He nodded. "During the revolution, when the elite were forced to flee, they had to leave everything behind. Including their luxurious palace-style homes."

Of course, she remembered studying that period of history in school. "It must have been beautiful once."

"Maybe some wealthy retiree will buy it and fix it up."

"I hope so," Vivi answered. "The place did save us from a rather frightening storm. It deserves to be restored to its original grandeur."

An hour later, mostly spent in awkward silence, they pulled up to a quaint little cottage with a gravel road and small patch of grassy yard in the front. The house was surrounded by tall trees and thick, leafy bushes. It sat in front of a rolling hill dotted with yellow flowers. *Charming* was the first word that came to mind. "Do you rent this place or something when you're in town?" she asked as he slowed the car and came to a stop.

"I used to," he answered. "Then I just bought it outright to make things easier. About a couple of years ago."

Every time she seemed to turn around, Zeke did or said something to impress her even more than she already was by him.

"I have a service that comes in to maintain and stock it for me regularly. There should be plenty to eat and drink."

Again, that sounded like him. No unplanned shopping trips, for Zeke's life was planned and orderly. Seemed to be working out well for him. He owned a cottage in the French countryside. Bessa and Vivi scrambled every month to make their rent and pay the utility bills.

He pulled out his phone and punched some keys on the screen. The garage door started to rise up, opening to reveal a tidy one-car bay area with wooden steps against the side wall leading to the main house.

Zeke came around to help her out of the car. "I, for one, can't wait to get out of these damp, filthy clothes," he told her.

Right. He'd mentioned showering. Was it her imagination or had he inferred that they'd be taking said shower together?

Her insides quivered at the thought. But she wasn't going

to go making any assumptions. And she certainly wasn't going to make the first move after she'd practically attacked him back there upon awakening.

You can't think I don't want you.

As soon as they went up the steps and Zeke shut the door behind them, all her questions were answered and her doubts vanished. He pulled her toward him and crushed his mouth to hers in a hard, satisfyingly punishing kiss.

She could feel the strength of his desire, and it sent a feminine thrill down her spine. This enigmatic, compelling, attractive man wanted her. He couldn't take his hands off her. No one had ever made her feel this wanton, this desirable. She could let it go to her head if she wasn't careful.

Right now, however, it was time to throw all caution to the wind.

Her arms wound around his neck and she pushed closer to his length. She would never be able to get enough of him.

"Now," he whispered against her mouth, then took her hand and led her farther inside. "About that shower."

"We never did make it to the lavender fields," Vivi said an hour later, her voice wistful and sad. They were under the warm down comforter of his king-size bed. It was a far cry from the hard, cold floor and the stone wall they'd been forced to endure during the storm earlier. The shower had helped warm them up at first, though bathing hadn't exactly been the primary activity.

"Tomorrow is another day. Those flowers aren't going anywhere."

She ran a finger down his chest, sending desire surging through him once more. "So we'll go sometime tomorrow?"

"We can head there right after breakfast."

"Promise?"

It was hard to think with that wayward finger of hers

running along his skin and tempting him all over again. "Absolutely. Though it pains me."

She lifted her head to look at him in question. "What? Why?"

He kissed the tip of her nose before answering. "Because, I'd much rather stay here. In bed. Just like this."

She grinned at him, like the cat who'd just gotten away with slurping up spilled milk. "We'll be sure to make it a very quick trip."

"It will have to be," he answered, gently nudging her on her back and settling over her.

He couldn't seem to get enough of this woman.

Remember, temporary, an unwelcome voice reminded him from the deep recesses of his mind. He pushed it away, focusing on Vivi's soft, luscious welcoming lips instead.

Temporary didn't have to mean short-term.

The aroma grew stronger and stronger the farther they drove. A rich flowery scent that reminded Vivi of expensive perfume. They had to be getting close.

Zeke confirmed it when he spoke. "Just about five more minutes."

A moment later he turned into a dirt road at the base of a tall hill. When they cleared the top, a sprawling complex of buildings came into view.

"Welcome to Roge Abbey."

When Vivi stepped out of the car after Zeke parked on a grassy knoll, she felt as if she'd crawled into a bottle of lotion.

"The tour will start in a few minutes," Zeke informed her. "But we can take a peek at the flowers first."

He led her down the side of the building and Vivi's breath caught in her throat after they rounded the wall. Rows and rows of rich, deep purple flowers that appeared to go for miles. "It's breathtaking," she said, overcome by the wonder she was looking at.

Again, the pictures she'd called up on her phone and on Zeke's laptop earlier hadn't quite caught the beauty of the scene before her. And, of course, the scent in the air wasn't something one could appreciate by reading about it.

"It's late June," Zeke said. "So we timed it right. Flowers are blooming and ripe with aroma."

Vivi inhaled deeply, savoring the exotic scent. "Careful," Zeke warned. "It can get overwhelming after a while."

Like the feelings she'd developed for him. The silly thought popped into her head and gave her pause. They'd shared an incredible night together. He'd held her like fine valuable china, been affectionate and gentle. Though there had also been those moments when he'd been less than gentle, but in the best of ways.

Overwhelming.

He continued explaining. "This is real lavender," he told her. "Only grown in very specific regions. Most of the world grows a different variety of flower. It's not the same thing."

"Like champagne versus sparkling wine."

He tapped her nose playfully. "Exactly like that."

Vivi bent down and rubbed her finger down the tiny, soft delicate petals. He was right—the flowers even felt different than the lavender she'd handled in the past. Smoother, like soft delicate velvet.

Zeke gently took her by the elbow to help her up when she began to straighten. "We should get to the main building," he said with a glance at his watch. "The tour's about to start."

She followed him back down the side path to the front of the abbey. Before they rounded the wall's corner, Zeke's phone rang.

"I don't mind if you get that," she told him, already rather guilt-ridden that he'd taken so much time out of his schedule just to play tour guide for her. She was only here because he'd needed her to help him out of an awkward business situation with the Sevilles. Their growing intimacy was another matter entirely.

His eyebrows drew together when he looked at the screen. "I think I will," he told her. "Go ahead on the tour without me if they start. I'll find you as soon as I'm done with the call."

Vivi couldn't resist planting a small peck of a kiss on his chin before she turned away and he clicked on the call. The day was already one for the scrapbooks. She'd woken up to find Zeke had surprised her by running out to fetch them a delicious breakfast of chocolate croissants and fresh baguettes smothered in brie. Along with rich, satisfying French-roast coffee. A girl could get used to such gestures.

Now they were here in this majestic abbey surrounded by so much beauty, it took her breath away.

She couldn't recall the last time she'd felt so content. So…dare she say it? So happy.

The day had just begun and she was going to enjoy every minute of it. In the company of the man she'd fallen in love with.

The thought had her stopping short. There was no denying it. Somehow, when she hadn't been paying attention, she'd fallen head over heels for Zeke Manning. A man utterly wrong for her—the polar opposite of her free-spirit personality and hopelessly out of her reach. But, nevertheless, she was completely in love with him.

Not that she would ever be able to tell him that.

Zeke gripped the phone so tight in his hand it was a wonder the screen didn't crack. Bill Wolfson was calling him.

Why now, after all this time?

Zeke had figured that he hadn't found anything when he hadn't heard from the other man. Then he'd sort of forgotten that he'd even asked him to look into one Vivienne Ducarne of New Orleans, Louisiana.

But now Bill was calling. There was no other work he'd been doing for the firm. This call had to be about Vivi.

Zeke swore out loud, knowing he was going to regret answering. But he knew deep in his core that he had to. Sooner or later he would have to face what he was about to hear.

"Hey, Bill," he answered.

"First of all, I have to apologize."

"For?"

"I would have called you much sooner. But I had a bit of a family emergency."

"Is everything all right?"

"It is now. My kid had to have an emergency appendectomy. Then he had a bad reaction to the anesthesia. But he's fine now."

"I'm glad to hear it," Zeke said to be polite. But inside he was screaming for the man to get on with it already and explain the reason for his call.

"Anyway, I would have contacted you before with this information if it wasn't for all that."

"What information?" Zeke asked, though he could feel in his core that he didn't really want to know.

"You asked me to look into that young lady. I've sent a file to your inbox but figured I'd call as well."

Something shifted in Zeke's gut. A cold dread ran down his spine. He had an urge to pretend to lose the connection and drop the call. Then ignore the ring when Bill called back. But that would just be putting off the inevitable. Bill had found something in Vivi's past. Something she had kept from him. "What did you find out?"

The sound of Bill clearing his throat sounded through the tiny speaker. This was clearly going to take a while. Zeke leaned back against the door of the rental car and braced himself.

"She's got a pretty serious criminal history."

The breath rushed out of Zeke's lungs as the word pounded through his ear. *Criminal.* His investigator was informing him that the woman he'd been falling for was a criminal.

Bill continued, "Starting when she was a juvenile. But those files are sealed."

"And as an adult?"

"Let's just say I'm surprised she hasn't done any time."

"What exactly has she done? How serious?" Zeke asked, trying hard to ignore the loud pounding of his heart. His vision had gone dark, his palms had grown clammy with sweat.

"She was an accomplice in an armed robbery. That's pretty serious."

A young gentleman wearing a smock and beret-style hat greeted her when she walked through the abbey door, introducing himself as Rainier. She was one of half a dozen others taking the tour. After a quick introductory spiel about what to expect, Rainier began leading them down a long corridor to another door that led outside.

Vivi hesitated, wondering if Zeke might perhaps finish up the call and join her, but ultimately she decided to follow the others. Getting lost in a sprawling abbey would not be a good turn of events. And Zeke had told her to go on without him if need be.

The minutes ticked by as Vivi tried her best to listen and

pay attention to everything Rainier was telling them. He talked about the monks and how they meticulously tended to the flowers, and how much prep the soil needed before each season. Even the properties of the plant that gave lavender its unique spicy scent.

But Vivi could hardly absorb much of it. Where was Zeke?

The phone call must have been important. Or some kind of emergency. Maybe she should head back and look for him to make sure everything was all right.

But she couldn't just walk away from the group. On top of being rude, she wasn't even sure which way to go. They'd meandered around the building, as well as a greenhouse, and through several rows of fields.

Still no Zeke.

Just when she thought she couldn't take it much longer, Rainier finally led them to a small gift shop and bid them *au revoir*. Vivi exhaled a sigh of relief. Was Zeke all right? What had happened to keep him from the tour?

The tour had ended by the entrance of the abbey. She ran outside to finally get some answers. There had to be a good reason why Zeke had just stood her up.

He was standing with his arms crossed, leaned up against the passenger side of the rental, when she stepped out the door.

"Hey, is anything the matt—" She didn't get the last word out. The look of utter contempt on Zeke's face stopped her in her tracks.

He had no idea who she was. She'd been lying to him all this time. About her past, her very identity. He didn't even know anymore what was false and what was real. Questions hammered in his brain. How much had she kept from him? What crimes had she committed where she hadn't been caught?

What had really happened with Esther's missing necklace?

She stared at him now in desperate confusion. Even now, though he wanted to kick himself, he couldn't help but think how beautiful she looked. How innocent and naive.

Looks could be so deceiving.

"Zeke?" she asked, her eyes clouded with questions. She looked genuinely concerned. But he couldn't be certain that it wasn't all part of the same act.

"Not here," he growled and flung open the driver's-side door. Leaning across the seat, he opened the passenger door for her and waited for her to get in.

"Please tell me what's going on," she pleaded, buckling her seat belt.

"We can talk when we get back home."

This was going to be a most uncomfortable forty-five-minute drive back to his cottage. Just as well. He would need at least that amount of time to calm down and gather his thoughts enough to form a coherent sentence or two.

They hadn't even been on the road for ten minutes when she whirled on him in her seat. "Please pull over. This is ridiculous."

He grunted at that. *Ridiculous* was one way to describe how he'd been acting. Letting down his guard, taking everything he'd been told at face value. Putting his trust in someone he didn't even really know.

What a fool she must have taken him for.

"Zeke. I am asking you to pull this car over right now so that we can talk about whatever has you so heated."

No hint of pleading or confusion in her voice now. She sounded determined and firm. Wow, she really was good.

Perhaps she was right. Maybe it was better to get this confrontation out of the way. He drove until they were next to an empty field and slowed to a stop. Without a word, he shut off the car then got out and sat on the hood.

Vivi appeared in front of him within seconds.

"What's going on?" she demanded. "Why are you acting like this?"

"I have a question for you before I answer any of yours," he told her bluntly, earning a stunned gasp.

She crossed her arms in front of her chest, met him eye-to-eye. "What question would that be?"

"Tell me the truth about what happened back in New Orleans."

"I don't understand."

"I think you do. I think you've been acting a part this whole time. I think you took something that didn't belong to you and then had your friends help you cover it up."

Her mouth fell open and her skin turned the color of fresh snow.

"It's time you stopped lying to me, Vivi."

Vivi wanted to clamp her hands over her ears to keep from hearing anymore. Every word Zeke uttered landed like a physical blow. How could he be telling her these things? Asking her such accusatory questions?

She managed to find her voice, though her tongue felt heavy in her mouth. "Where is all this coming from?"

"I have an investigator who works for me occasionally. Does jobs for the law firm as needed. He found out some very interesting things when looking into your past."

She couldn't have heard him correctly. He'd been having her investigated all this time?

"You were paying someone to dig up dirt on me?"

"He didn't have to dig too deep."

Vivi couldn't believe what she was hearing. On wobbly legs, she paced in a circle as she tried to absorb exactly what was happening here. "When, exactly, did you hire him? Was it the day you kissed me for the first time? Did you call him between courses when we were having dinner in a tower overlooking Niagara Falls?"

"Don't be silly," he said, brushing off the questions. "I hired him that first day. When I first learned Esther had given you that darned necklace."

"But you never called him off. All the time we were together, you had someone out there looking into my past. You never put a stop to it even after…?" She couldn't even complete the sentence. It hurt too much to think about how intimate they'd been, given what he was doing to her right now.

"I'd say it's a good thing I didn't. You certainly weren't telling me about your past as an accomplice to armed robbery. Not even after I shared so much with you." The last few words hung in the air between them, full of accusation. He shook his head slowly, looked her up and down as if she was a worthless piece of litter he might have to step over in the street. Vivi felt the hot sting of tears behind her eyes.

"You don't understand. I had nothing to do with that. I was clueless about what he intended."

"He? Who? Ah, yes. The tattoo guy."

So he was going to be downright cruel about this. He wasn't even listening to what she had to say. "Yes. Him. He asked me to take him to the pawnshop because we were low on cash and he had some things that might sell. He asked me to wait in the car. Next thing I knew, Todd was running out of the building just as a squad car pulled up from behind with its lights flashing."

Zeke actually smirked at her. "So let me get this straight. You didn't know your boyfriend was inside robbing a business while you waited. And you also didn't know that you were in possession of a priceless antique after an old lady had given it to you."

"Yes! You know that was a simple misunderstanding."

He shrugged. "I know that's what you told me."

She literally stomped her foot in frustration on the soft, damp grass. "I told you that because it was the truth!"

"What about before?"

"Before what?"

"When you were younger. I've been told there's a sealed file."

"Wow. Your man did a very thorough job, didn't he?"

"It's why I pay him so well."

He'd paid the man to set up her betrayal. Her heart felt like it might shatter in pieces at the thought. "I had a young foster sister at one of the houses. The girl was being neglected. Barely given enough food, wore the same ragged sweater for days on end."

"What's that got to do with why you ended up with a juvenile file?"

"I took some things from a superstore so that she could eat and have clean clothes without holes in them."

Zeke tilted his head. She could tell by the curtain behind his eyes that her words held no weight whatsoever where he was concerned.

"How noble of you," he said, his voice dripping with sarcasm. "Did it occur to you to maybe notify someone? To get help of some sort?"

"You of all people should know better than to ask that. I was a teen, barely more than a child. Do you think anyone in a position to do anything was going to listen to someone like me?"

"So your first impulse was to break the law."

"I was a kid in a tough spot. I thought I had no choice."

"Why, Vivi? Why wouldn't you have told me any of this?" He rammed his fingers through his hair. "You had so many chances to come clean. Why keep it all from me if you're really as innocent as you say?"

Just the fact that he was asking such questions told her there was no answer she could give that would satisfy him. He'd already come to his conclusions. Nothing she told him now would make a lick of difference, not after what had just transpired between them by the side of this road.

Why should she even bother to try and defend herself? Zeke didn't care about what she had to say. His reaction right now was exactly the reason he hadn't confided in him about any of this. Her whole life, no one had ever had enough faith in her to believe anything she had to say. Zeke was no different.

But this time it *felt* different. Her heart felt shattered in her chest. She'd fallen for this man, had trusted her heart to him. And he was so ready to think the worst of her. Wasn't even giving her a chance to explain. Todd had betrayed her and taken advantage of her trust. What Zeke was doing was even worse. Because she loved him in a way she'd never felt for anyone.

Her legs had only grown wobblier, and it was hard to remain upright. But they were in the middle of nowhere in a field, and sitting on the hood of the car wasn't an option when he was already perched there. She refused to collapse to the ground. She wouldn't give Zeke the satisfaction.

"I'd like to go back now. I think this conversation is over."

He nodded briskly, jumped off the hood. "I agree. There's nothing more to say."

"I don't mean back to your cottage. I'd like to go back home to Louisiana."

She couldn't stand to be here in France with Zeke Manning for one more day, let alone under the same roof. She never should have agreed to come in the first place.

CHAPTER FOURTEEN

"EVEN FOR SOMEONE at a blues festival, you're looking particularly gloomy."

Against her better judgment, Vivi had allowed Bessa to convince her to come out to one of New Orleans's most popular summer events. An event she usually enjoyed every year. But not so much today. She was in no mood to be in a crowd of this many people, would much rather wallow by herself in front of the fan in their apartment. Lafayette Square was bursting with tourists and locals alike out to enjoy the day and hear the bands who'd come here to perform from all over the country.

"Sorry, Bessa. I have a lot on my mind."

Bessa sat back down on the bench next to her after dancing to the last song. Now they were waiting for the next set to begin, by a quartet called the Bayou Baritones.

"Girl. Just stop." Bessa gave her a nudge on her knee. "We both know you only have one thing on your mind. And it's not a thing at all. It's a who."

"That obvious, huh?"

"Wanna talk about it?"

"Aren't you tired of hearing me yet?"

Her friend gave her an indulgent smile. "Never. You know that."

She may not have been lucky in love, but Vivi had the

greatest friends a girl could hope for. Bessa being top of the list.

"Maybe you should just call him," Bessa suggested, not for the first time. "Just get everything off your chest."

"I don't think it would do either of us any good. No, the best thing to do would be to move on. Forget I ever met the man."

"How do you plan to do that?"

Vivi sucked her bottom lip. "Just keep reminding myself of why it went so bad between us, I guess. Repeat in a continuous loop how different we are. How someone like me would never fit in the world a man like him inhabits. He would have never accepted me for who I am."

"What's that mean? Sounded like he accepted you just fine until that blasted investigator ruined everything."

Vivi shook her head with regret. "Not really. Zeke hired the man in the first place. And he never really did find me acceptable. One of the first times after we met, he said he couldn't understand why I wouldn't try and make more out of my singing."

Bessa clasped a hand to her chest in mock horror. "No! Not that! He paid you a compliment by saying you were good enough to try and go pro. Why, the man's a veritable demon!"

Vivi ignored the heavy sarcasm. "You know I'm not interested in pursuing any kind of professional singing career."

"Sure. For all the wrong reasons."

"What's that supposed to mean?"

Bessa turned in the bench to face her fully. "You don't want to call any attention to yourself. You want to lay low and stay out of any kind of spotlight. Because then people might figure out who you are and discover what happened in your past."

Vivi wasn't quite sure what her friend's point was. So what if all she'd just said was true? It made perfect sense. "Do you blame me? Look what happened with Zeke. As soon as he found out, he sent me back to the States in his jet while he stayed behind in France." That wasn't quite the truth. Vivi had demanded she fly back commercial, but Zeke wouldn't hear of it. He'd arranged for his jet and pilot to fly her back home while he'd returned to Manhattan on a commercial flight.

Bessa knew all that and sure enough, she called her on it. "The man arranged for a private flight for you because you demanded to leave."

"Fine," she begrudgingly admitted. Why did Bessa have such a strong recall of details? "None of that exonerates him."

"He was angry you didn't tell him the truth yourself. Whether or not he's justified in that is another story."

"And that's why you think I should call him?"

Bessa nodded. "Yep. You know what else I think?"

"What?"

"That you should rent out that sound studio uptown for an afternoon like you always talk about doing. And you should cut a track."

"And then what?"

Bessa threw her hands up in the air in frustration. "I don't know. Send it out to producers. Upload it to a streaming platform. How do aspiring recording artists get heard by the masses these days?"

Vivi squeezed her eyes shut. "I don't want to be heard by the masses. I don't want people to know who I am."

"That's not accurate, though. You don't want people to know what you did. What you did is not who you are. And you should tell this Zeke Manning that."

CHAPTER FIFTEEN

ESTHER SOUNDED GOOD on the phone. Zeke wasn't sure what to expect when he'd called her to follow up on the estate assessment, but to his relief, her voice came through clearly. She sounded alert and aware, so different than that fateful day he'd told her about the necklace two weeks ago back in New Orleans. He knew from speaking with various family members that she'd been receiving treatment from a team of neurologists and her prognosis was good in general.

Plus, apparently a grandniece who'd just gotten out of a messy divorce would be moving in with her for the foreseeable future. Hopefully, all of that meant no more priceless pieces of jewelry or antiques would be carelessly given away.

"I have to go, dear," she said now over the speaker of his office phone. "I have someone coming to the house in a few minutes. I'm going to have my cards done."

Zeke stiffened in his chair. She had to mean Vivi. Vivi was the one who made house calls to Esther to read her cards. Yet another reminder to jab at his wounds. Not that he needed any. Not that much time went by that he didn't think about her.

The last words they'd said to each other had been vicious and hurtful with no taking them back. He'd replayed the scene over and over in his head.

Esther continued, confirming what he'd suspected about

Vivi's visiting her. "You met Vivi, didn't you, dear? Such a sweet girl. I had to find a way to pay her though she insisted no payment was necessary. I had to practically force that necklace on her that day. If only I'd known what I was actually giving the poor child."

With that, she clicked off the phone call.

Esther's words resonated throughout the walls of his mind—*had to practically force that necklace on her.*

Vivi had insisted on her innocence.

He'd never actually called up that cursed file to read it. There didn't seem to be any point. He'd heard all he needed to hear from Bill Wolfson.

What did it really matter what the file actually said? The end result would have been the same, wouldn't it? Vivi had a criminal record that she'd kept from him.

But now, curiosity was getting the better of him.

How had she been involved in an armed robbery, for heaven's sake? Without giving himself any time to think, he called up the email and downloaded the file Bill had sent him all those days ago. It only took reading one page to decide it was time for him to do some investigating of his own.

Less than twenty minutes later, Zeke knew two things for certain. One, he needed to call a recruiting firm to see about finding another PI for his business. And, two, he should have given Vivi the benefit of the doubt when she'd tried to explain everything that day by the side of the road.

Bill had only told him part of the story when he'd called Zeke in Provence.

It was all there in black and white. It had only taken a few clicks of a standard search engine to find news reports about the family Vivi had stayed with in foster care during the time in question. Years later, they'd been charged with neglecting the children in their care. So Vivi was telling the truth when she'd said she'd felt driven to steal.

Her actions hadn't been right. But her motives were pure and she was just a child.

As for the armed robbery, tattoo guy's real name was Todd Felton. In return for a lighter sentence, he'd turned in all the other criminals in his circle. But he'd steadfastly stuck to the same story about Vivi. That story being that she had no idea what he was up to in the pawnshop that day. The man would have had no motivation to say she wasn't involved if it wasn't the truth.

The guy was bad news, but at least in that sense, he'd done the right thing. And he'd stuck by it.

If only Zeke hadn't taken that phone call from the PI at the abbey. If he'd taken the time to look at the file the man had sent instead of answering the phone, he may have had time to process and think things through. He'd been so shocked and hurt that he hadn't been thinking straight.

He had to accept that Vivi hadn't actually meant to take Esther's jewelry. The truth of that was staring at him in digital format on his laptop screen and had been echoed in Esther's words just now in their phone call. He should have never accused her of outright theft and would regret it the rest of his life. It had been a heat-of-the-moment reaction based on the anger and shock he'd been feeling that day. Everything she'd been trying to tell him was verified by the file.

She should have been straight with him, but he should have given her a chance by the road in Provence to finally make that right. He could have handled it all so much better.

Zeke swore out loud and slammed his laptop shut so hard that the penholder on his desk fell over to the floor.

He'd been a fool. And he had to make it right somehow.

"Did the cards cooperate today, Vivi?" Lucien walked over to her table in the corner of the magic shop as Vivi gathered up her tarot set.

"They always do."

"You packing up for the day?" her boss asked.

"Yeah. I think I'd just like to get home." She'd had several walk-ins and the last client with an appointment had just canceled on her at the last minute. "Unless you need help closing later?"

Lucien shook his head. "Nah. Go get some rest. You've been looking kinda tired lately. If you don't mind my sayin'."

Lucien had never been one to pry, but Vivi knew he was always ready with a shoulder to cry on, if and when she needed it.

Vivi was done crying, though. She'd always carry a torch the size of a wildfire for Zeke Manning, but she knew she had to move on. What's done was done.

They'd both done their part in wrecking what had sprung between them.

She should have been straight with him from the beginning, but he should have had more faith in her. Not to mention, the things he'd said and the words he'd used still stung like salt in a fresh wound every time she thought about the events in Provence.

Even if more than two weeks had gone by already. Every time she closed her eyes, she relived the scene by the field after the abbey tour. It was like picking at a scab, but she couldn't seem to help herself. Maybe she would stop doing that someday. No doubt about it, it was going to take a while to feel any kind of normal again.

Bending below the table to retrieve her pocketbook, she heard the chime of the front door, signaling the arrival of a customer. Vivi crossed her fingers and uttered a silent prayer that whoever had just arrived was a shopper in search of a souvenir and not here for a tarot reading. She really just wanted to get home and crash on the couch with a pint of praline caramel. But footsteps approached closer and closer until they stopped about eight inches away from where she was still crouched down.

Looked like she couldn't cut loose just yet. Pasting a reluctant smile on her face, she straightened to greet the newcomer.

Then did a double take at the sight that greeted her.

"Zeke?"

It couldn't be. Surely, she had to be seeing things. Her mind was conjuring what she wanted so badly. She rubbed her eyes just to be sure, but he was still standing there when she looked back up.

"Hey, Vivi."

Yep, it even sounded like him.

"What are you doing here?"

He pulled up the chair across from her table. "I was hoping to get a reading. If you have time, that is."

"You want a tarot reading? From me?"

"That's right." He pointed to the cards in her hand. "Is there a card in there that symbolizes a stupid, thoughtless man who should know better than to let the woman he loves get away?"

Vivi's heart felt ready to pound out of her chest. "The woman he what now?"

"Huh. I guess there's no such card, then."

She could only shake her head. "There's the Fool."

"That's close enough, I guess."

Lucien stood staring at them from the crystal-gemstone aisle, a knowing smile plastered on his face. Vivi had to wonder about the last-minute cancellation of her final client for the evening.

Zeke had taken the time and effort to arrange all this. Despite herself, she felt moved and touched.

Not so fast, a small voice cried the warning in her head.

She couldn't let her heart be so open and vulnerable when it came to this man. She still hadn't recovered from the last time Zeke Manning had been careless with it.

"Here…" He reached into his jacket breast pocket, and to her utter surprise pulled out an engraved wooden box, like those custom-made to hold personalized tarot cards. It resembled a small treasure chest, complete with a copper key. "Use these."

She reached for the box with a shaky hand. "What are these?"

"I commissioned an artist to custom-make them for you. She dropped all her other projects to make these a priority."

Vivi gently opened the box and glanced at the signature on the cover card. A surprised gasp escaped her lips.

"Ranita Jackson drew these? She's the most sought-after visual artist in Louisiana. Maybe all of the South."

He nodded. "She said she'd make each card a work of art."

Vivi gently removed the deck, studied the delicate patterns and intricate details. Zeke was right—every card was an individual masterpiece.

"So what do you say? Are they telling you to forgive me?"

Vivi took a deep breath. As much as she wanted to jump into his arms, her heart felt heavy and weary. "I don't have to pull a spread to know what they should say."

He merely quirked an eyebrow.

She swallowed past the dryness in her mouth. "They'll say I should be careful, guarded." Heaven help her, she had to bite back a sob before she could continue. "They'll also say I can't handle being hurt that way again."

Zeke exhaled a deep sigh. "I can't deny any of that, sweetheart. I know how wrong I was to react the way I did."

"You didn't even give me a chance to defend myself. I'm

not my past. I did what I thought was right and made some bad decisions in my lifetime. But I've learned from them and become a better person in the process."

He rubbed a hand down his face. "Vivi, I was an idiot back in France. I should have never forgotten even for a minute what a strong, willful and determined woman you are. I'll never forget again."

Well, he was certainly saying all the right things. Vivi took a moment to study him carefully. Dark circles colored the skin below his eyes and his hair was a mess of waves, as if he'd been running his hand through it repeatedly. He looked like he hadn't shaved in at least two or three days.

Maybe he'd been missing her as much as she'd been pining for him.

"What made you rethink this? Why did you come here, Zeke?" She had to know the answer, had to hear him say it.

He rammed a hand through his hair, only adding to the disheveled mess it already was.

"I was afraid, Vivi."

"Afraid?"

"Yes. Afraid of what I was feeling, afraid it wasn't real. That *you* weren't real. And then when I found out you'd been keeping things from me…"

She lifted a hand to stop him. He was right. But he'd never given her a chance to fix it or redeem herself. "I should have told you," she admitted, then had to suck in a breath before she could continue. "But I was afraid, too."

He gave her a wistful smile. "What a pair we make, huh?"

Vivi could only nod, at a loss for words.

"I promise to do better in the future," he told her. "If you'll just give me a chance."

Vivi couldn't take any more. She wasn't made of stone, after all. She'd really missed him. It had been so long. And now, here he was in the flesh. With a cry of resignation, she ran around the table and let him take her into his arms.

What she hadn't told Zeke was the true meaning of the Fool card. It meant new beginnings.

EPILOGUE

One year later

WHAT WERE THE odds of another freak thunderstorm striking in the exact same spot where they'd been caught last time?

Vivi ducked her head to look out the windshield of the convertible sports car as they made their way to the Sevilles' former estate. Zeke said he wanted to head out there to see how the transition was proceeding after his clients had taken over several months ago. He'd asked Vivi to accompany him so they could enjoy a complimentary wine tasting during their visit. He didn't have to ask twice.

Vivi could use the distraction. They were in town for her audition the next day for one of Europe's most popular vocal-audition shows. She still couldn't believe she'd actually made it this far in the process.

"I know it didn't help much last time, but did you happen to check the forecast?" she asked. "The sky looks like it might be getting kind of dark."

Zeke looked away from the road just long enough to give her a wolfish grin. "If a storm hits again, we know exactly where to take shelter."

"I'd prefer to stay warm and dry, unlike last time."

Though she had to admit, waking up in Zeke's arms for the first time that day had not been without its merits.

"Afraid you'll be stranded and miss your audition?" He was joking, but just the mere thought of that happening had a brick settling in her stomach.

"Don't even jest about such a thing."

"You know, maybe we should stop at the abandoned château, anyway. Relive the past a bit," he added with a wink in her direction.

Vivi thought he'd made the comment as a flippant suggestion. But as they approached the structure, Zeke slowed the car and turned in the direction of the building.

"You're serious? I thought we were headed to the winery."

He came to a stop and killed the ignition. "We are. This will only take a minute."

Her confusion grew as they stepped out of the car and several other vehicles appeared from down the road, eventually stopping near where they stood.

Utility trucks with construction equipment and an excavator. Several men climbed out of the vehicles and began unloading supplies.

What in the world was going on?

"Zeke?"

"The cottage is a bit small for both of us. And chances are good we'll be in France quite often. Especially when you win tomorrow night."

"*If* I win tomorrow." And it was a big if.

"When," Zeke insisted. "In any case, I thought we could use a bigger place."

Her mind didn't seem to be able to absorb exactly what was going on. And then it finally clicked. She felt her jaw drop.

"You—you bought an abandoned château? *The* château?" She stammered out the questions, too stunned to have her mouth work properly.

He nodded. "The renovations will take a while, but I think the wait will be worth it."

For one of the very few times in her life, Vivi found herself at a loss for words.

Before she'd recovered from the confusion of what was happening around them, he shocked her even further. Taking her hand, he pulled a small velvet box out of his pocket.

"We almost got married by mistake about a year ago. Will you marry me for real this time, Vivienne Ducarne?"

Vivi's heart felt as if it might explode in her chest. She loved this man with every fiber of her being. Her mind played back to the scene in the chapel that afternoon in Niagara Falls, when the minister was ready to perform a marriage ceremony before realizing why they were really there. Zeke had called her his almost-wife.

She'd known, even then, that she'd somehow fallen in love with him. And she'd loved him ever since and always would.

"Yes," she answered with a breathless gasp, throwing herself into his arms. "Yes. I will be your forever wife!"

* * * * *

GREEK HEIR TO CLAIM HER HEART

JENNIFER FAYE

MILLS & BOON

CHAPTER ONE

CHANGES WERE AFOOT.

Changes that didn't bode well for the immediate future.

Hermione Kappas wanted to be optimistic, but at the moment she was too tired. She was the general manager of the exclusive Ludus Resort. As she'd settled into her position this past year, she thought at last her life would be peaceful and predictable—two things she hadn't had growing up. And they had been for a while, but as quick as the flip of a coin everything had once more changed.

On this particular Monday evening, darkness had come early. She yawned as she gathered her things. She hated working this late. Thankfully it was a rare occurrence.

On her way to her car, she paused in the resort's spacious lobby. "How are things going, Titus?"

The nighttime desk clerk looked up. His gaze rose over the rim of his reading glasses. His older face, trimmed with a gray mustache, lit up with a friendly smile. "It's another quiet evening, just the way I like them." He removed his glasses. Concern reflected in his eyes. "You've been working late a lot recently."

She nodded. "I have been. I hope this evening is the end of it."

She'd been coordinating all of the requested information for the independent auditors. Now that the resort's owner had unexpected died, the resort's future was uncertain. And an audit was being conducted.

She hadn't been privy to the details of the will—only the part about her having the authority to keep the resort in operation until the estate was finalized, whatever that meant. She just did as instructed by the resort's legal team.

Titus nodded in understanding. "I'll miss chatting with you each evening, but I'm sure you're anxious to have life return to normal. Be careful out there. It's an ugly night."

"I will. Good night."

She paused at the front door and stared out at the pouring rain. With it being winter, she longed for just a little snow. In the northern part of Greece where she'd grown up, there was snow in February but down here in the south, the snow was replaced by periodic rain.

So be it. It wasn't like she'd melt. She pushed open the door. Once she stepped outside, the wind immediately caught her unzipped jacket. She grabbed the flaps and held them closed. When she reached the edge of the portico, she ran across the garden area to the nearby parking lot.

The rain fell in large drops, flattening her bangs and soaking her clothes. She hurled herself into the car. Wet and disheveled, Hermione sat in the driver's seat. As she wiped the wetness from her face, the raindrops pounded on the roof.

Hermione loosened her hair from the French twist at the back of her head and finger-combed her long hair. She leaned her head back against the seat and closed her eyes, letting the constant rap-a-tap-tap of the rain lull her into a state of relaxation. After being hunched over her desk since early that morning, her body ached.

With a sigh, she started the car and set off for the ferry that would transport her to the mainland. She couldn't wait to get home. There were some leftovers in the fridge so she wouldn't even have to prepare dinner. She could even eat in bed. The tempting thought had her pressing harder on the accelerator.

Just then there was a brilliant flash of lightning. It lit up the entire sky as though it were daytime again. A crack of thunder rumbled through the car. Then as though the heavens had opened up, the rain came down even harder and faster. The car slowed to a crawl. She increased the speed of the wipers as she squinted, trying to see the roadway.

A chill of apprehension raced down her spine, leaving a trail of goosebumps in its wake. In the glow of the dashboard lights, her knuckles shone as she clutched the steering with both hands. As the wipers failed to keep up with the deluge of rain, she leaned forward, trying to see better.

A blur of white light blinded her. This time it wasn't lightning. It was a constant light and getting brighter. Headlights? Was there a vehicle headed toward her?

Her foot tramped the brake.

The weather was foul.

Just like his mood.

Atlas Othonos braked as a branch crashed onto the roadway in front of him. Luckily the road from the ferry to the Ludus Resort was deserted. He carefully wheeled around the debris and continued on his way. The strong winds pushed against the small car as though trying to shove him off the road.

Why hadn't he checked the weather forecast before deciding it was a good idea to pick up his brand-new car today of all days? He groaned in frustration. Weren't Greek islands supposed to be sunny and warm year-round?

The truth of the matter was that he didn't want to be on this small island—even though by some ironic twist of fate, it was all his. He owned an island—an exclusive island—the playground for the rich and famous. And he didn't want it. He didn't want any part of it. The sooner he could rid himself of it, the better.

His estranged mother, Thea as he called her, had died nearly two months ago. Not having seen her since he was young, he refused to acknowledge any feeling about her passing. Was that wrong? Perhaps.

Since it took Thea's attorneys a while to track him down in the States, the funeral was over before he knew what had happened. It was for the best. But the fact that she'd left everything in her will to him was not for the best. Not at all.

He'd dragged his heels as long as he could. The attorneys warned him the longer he took to sell the resort, the greater the chance of the business running into trouble. The only catch to selling the place was that he needed to oversee the estate.

The more he thought about it, the faster he drove. He'd worked so hard to avoid any of this, and in the end, he was to spend the next two weeks on the island going through his mother's personal finances and belongings. The thought twisted his gut up into a tight knot.

Atlas squinted, trying to make out the road. With the rain coming down in sheets, it was hard for him to see.

A flash of lightning or was that of headlights? Definitely headlights. They were headed straight toward him. They weren't slowing down. And they weren't moving over.

His body tensed.

He swerved.

His foot stomped the brakes. The tires slid forward over the wet pavement. He cut the steering wheel hard to the right. The car wouldn't respond. There was too much water on the road. His heart lodged in his throat. The car kept careening forward.

His body stiffened for the impact.

His car slid off the roadway and went down a small embankment. It finally slowed to a stop. With the windshield wipers rapidly swishing back and forth, he stared out into the darkness. He didn't spot the other car. Where were they?

He put the car in reverse. He pressed on the accelerator. The engine revved but the car didn't budge. Not about to give up, he tried to drive forward. But once again, the car refused to move.

A groan emanated from the back of his throat. He was stuck. He wasn't going to get his new car out of this mess without some help.

Tap-tap.

He glanced to the side to find the outline of a person holding a flashlight as they rapped on his driver's-side window. So he hadn't imagined the other car—a car that had been headed straight for him.

He rolled down the window.

"Are you all right?" a female voice called out over the noise of the wind and rain.

He squinted at her flashlight. She lowered the beam. "I'm okay. But my car needs help. Can you call for a tow?"

She straightened and checked her phone. "There's no cell service."

They were on their own on this dark stormy night. As though to confirm his thoughts, the whole sky lit up. A crack of thunder shook the ground.

Atlas's gaze moved to the crop of tall trees surrounding them. This was not a good place to be during an electrical storm. They needed out of there as quickly as possible.

There was another brilliant bolt of lightning followed by a crack of thunder. This storm was sitting right over them.

As though reading his thoughts, she said, "Come on. My car is over there."

He hesitated. "I can't just leave my car."

"Sure, you can. It's not going anywhere—at least not tonight. Are you a guest at the Ludus Resort?"

"Yes."

"Good. Let's go." She turned, and in her rush up the embankment she slipped in the mud. She landed on all fours.

"Are you all right?"

Before he could exit the car, she got to her feet and acknowledged that she was fine. By now she was soaked and muddy from her effort to help him.

With great reluctance, he grabbed his travel bags from the passenger seat and got out of the car. It was raining so hard that he was instantly soaked. As he carefully climbed the embankment, he could feel the rainwater seeping into his shoes. His back teeth ground together. Could this evening get any worse?

Once inside the car, he said, "You should learn to drive more carefully."

She hooked her seat belt. "What are you talking about?"

"You were driving in the middle of the road."

"I was not." Her restrained voice failed to mask her indignation. "Perhaps you were driving too fast for the road conditions—"

"I was not." Was he? He had been distracted. And perhaps he was taking his bad mood out on her.

He sat quietly while she slowly and carefully turned her car around. When she finally had the car straightened on the road, she barely pressed the accelerator. They were never going to reach the resort tonight if she didn't pick up the speed.

With a huff, he sat there stiffly. He stared straight ahead at the rain pounding the windshield. When they finally reached the resort, he'd insist they get someone out there to tow his car. He just hoped it wasn't damaged.

While she gripped the steering wheel with both hands,

they rode on in silence. At last, the glow of lights hovered in the distance. Seconds later they came upon lampposts lining the road that led to the resort.

They parked beneath a fully lit portico. He glanced over at the woman as she undid her seat belt. Her long hair hung well past her shoulders. Even though it was wet, it had loose waves.

And when she glanced at him, he was immediately drawn in by her eyes, but she turned away before he was able to fully appreciate her beauty. She didn't say a word as she got out of the car.

He rushed to do the same. The large glass doors swept open, bidding them entrance to a marble floor that gleamed. In the center of the spacious lobby was a water fountain with lights that played off the droplets of water. It was surrounded by groups of light aqua upholstered chairs.

He glanced down at his wet clothes and shoes that were making a mess of the floor. He couldn't wait to go to his suite and get cleaned up. Except there was no one at the reception desk. He found a bell at the end of the counter. He banged his palm down on it, over and over again. He hoped the rest of the resort's service was better.

The woman covered his hand with her own. The touch jolted him from his thoughts. It felt as if an electric current had arced between them before racing up his arm and making his whole body tingle. His gaze met hers. It was then that he noticed the color of her eyes, brown with gold flecks. And right now, agitation radiated from them.

"Stop." She kept her voice low but firm.

He glanced down to where her hand rested on his. Her touch was warm and soft. As though realizing they were still touching, she swiftly moved her hand.

A door off to the side of the counter area opened. An older man rushed out. He struggled to place his black-rimmed glasses on his face. When his gaze collided with Atlas's glare, his eyes widened. And then the man took in Atlas's appearance. By the horrified expression of the desk clerk, he must look quite the mess. But it was his car he was worried about right now.

Before the clerk could utter a word, Atlas said, "There's been an accident."

The clerk's gaze moved from Atlas to the woman and then back again. "Is anyone hurt?"

"My new car. It's stuck out there in the mud. Someone has to remove it from the side of the road. And then I need to check in."

"Yes, sir. I can call for a tow and get you registered." The man hesitated as though not sure what to do first.

"Call them," Atlas said in his get-it-done-now voice.

That seemed to stir the man into action. A phone call later, the clerk wordlessly hung up. "No one answered."

"Surely there has to be someone working at this hour." He started to wonder how there could be a five-star resort in a place that was so far removed from a major city that they didn't have twenty-four-hour road service.

"I'm afraid not, sir. But I assure you it'll be a priority in the morning."

The morning? That wasn't good enough. The clerk had no idea how valuable his car was, but he would know soon.

Atlas opened his mouth to explain when the woman intervened. "That will be good, Titus. Perhaps we should get the gentleman checked in."

"Oh." Titus appeared startled out of a stupor of uncertainty. "Yes, I can do that." The man visibly swallowed. "Do you have a reservation?"

"I do."

The clerk typed something into the computer. "Last name?"

"Othonos."

"First name?"

"Atlas."

He waited, wondering if the man recognized the name. Moments passed. "There you are." The man's fingers moved rapidly over the keyboard. "You have one of our finest suites—the jungle suite."

"Sounds intriguing." Atlas glanced over to find the woman had moved toward the doors. Was she leaving? Atlas called out to her. "Surely you aren't thinking of going back out there."

"I need to go home."

"The ferry just left. It's the last trip tonight," Titus said.

The woman approached them. Her shoulders drooped. "What am I supposed to do now?"

"You could get a room for the night," Atlas suggested.

"That's not possible. The resort is fully booked." Titus sent the woman a hesitant look. "I'm sorry—"

"It's okay. I understand." A flicker of emotion reflected in her eyes, but she blinked it away before he was able to discern it.

Atlas told himself he should be happy that he'd inherited a profitable business, but he didn't think anything about his inheritance was going to make him happy—not until he signed the sales agreement. And that wasn't happening fast enough.

But in the meantime, he felt bad because if this woman hadn't stopped to help him—if she hadn't given him a ride to the resort—she would be on her way home. And now there wasn't even an available room for her to spend the night.

He turned his head, taking in the spacious lobby. There wasn't even a comfortable couch to stretch out on.

The last thing he needed was to feel bad because this

woman had to sleep in her car. She'd done him a good deed, and so he'd do her one in return. "You can stay with me."

"I don't even know you."

He stepped up to her and extended his hand. "Hi. My name's Atlas Othonos. I'm the CEO of Atlas Securities. I can give you references. There's my assistant and—" He stopped himself from mentioning that his mother had owned this resort. It was a subject he wasn't prepared to delve into that night.

She eyed him up as though trying to make her mind up about him. "Thanks. But no thanks." She turned to the desk clerk. "Could you have a cot and linens sent to my office?"

Titus nodded. "Of course." And then the clerk turned to him. "If I could have your keys, sir, I'll see that your car is taken care of."

Atlas hesitated before handing over the car keys. "Thank you." He turned back to the woman. "You aren't planning to spend the night like that, are you?"

Her muddy clothes clung to her, and there were goose-bumps lining her arms. Her face and lips were pale. A sense of responsibility passed over him.

She glanced down at her disheveled clothes. "I'll be fine."

As the air conditioner kicked in, she started to shiver and his concern grew. "No, you won't. Not like that. You need a hot shower and some dry clothes. If you won't stay in my suite, at least stay long enough to get a shower and warm up." A flicker of interest shone in her eyes. "Let's go."

Even though she was shivering, she shook her head.

"If this is about us being strangers, I'll wait here in the lobby while you use my shower."

Her eyes widened with surprise. "You'd really do that?"

"I would."

"But you're wet too."

"Not as wet or cold as you."

"There are actually two bedrooms in your suite, so you wouldn't have to wait your turn."

His thoughts suddenly took a steamy turn. "I hadn't planned to share my shower, but if you're offering—"

"I'm not!" Her cheeks took on a rosy hue. "That isn't what I meant."

The rumble of laughter started low in his chest and burst forth. His amusement resulted in her fine brows knitting together in a frown.

He subdued his amusement. "I'm sorry. It's been a really long day. If there are two bedrooms, it's all the more reason for you to warm up. I promise to be a perfect gentleman."

"I don't know."

"I'll just have a seat over here until you come back." He started toward one of the chairs in the lobby.

"Wait." When he turned back to her, she said, "You need a shower and dry clothes too. Let's go."

He thought of asking if she was sure but then thought better of it. He quietly let her lead the way. A hot shower would feel really good. The truth was he was exhausted and had absolutely no interest in sitting around the lobby. He'd been up extra early that morning to head to the airport. Maybe some sleep would make him less irritable.

"Here we are." The woman stopped next to an oversize wood door.

He opened it and gestured for her to go first. His gaze followed her into the room. She was unique, and he liked all things unique from cars to women.

CHAPTER TWO

TONIGHT HAD CERTAINLY taken an unusual turn.

Hermione stood in the suite not quite sure what to say to her undeniably handsome host. Maybe it was her being cold that had her tongue-tied. She rubbed her upper arms, hoping to chase away the chill that had taken hold of her.

Her gaze caressed his chiseled jawline before moving to linger on his kissable lips. Her attention swept up past his straight but prominent nose and came to rest on his light blue eyes framed with dark lashes and brows. He was drop-dead gorgeous. If he were a Greek god, she could imagine him being Zeus with his many lovers.

Why was a sexy man like him checking into the resort alone? It didn't happen often at the Ludus. Most often the resort hosted couples and families. It wasn't known as a singles spot.

Atlas ran his hand over his clean-shaven jaw. "Do I have something on my face?"

Heat flared in her cheeks. "Um, no. Sorry. You just remind me of someone."

"You already know who I am but I don't believe you introduced yourself." And then he sent her a dazzling smile that made her insides melt into a pool of desire.

"Hi. I… I'm Hermione Kappas." Good grief. Now he

had her stuttering. And she realized she was once again staring at him. She quickly averted her gaze.

"It's nice to meet you." He held his hand out to her. She hesitated. What was it about him that had her feeling off-kilter?

She refused to let him know that his presence got to her. She placed her hand within his. His long, lean fingers engulfed her hand. His touch was warm, and it sent an electrical current up her arm that made her heart pitter-patter. As he gave her hand a gentle shake, she came to a conclusion—this man was dangerous to her common sense. She should get away from him as fast as her mud-covered heels would carry her. And yet her feet refused to cooperate.

He released her hand. "Thank you for the help tonight."

"Glad I was there to help."

Just then her stomach decided to rumble its complaint about its lack of nourishment. Lunch had been many hours ago. And she thought she'd be home by now.

"I...ah...should go get that shower." Her gaze moved between the two bedroom doors. "Do you have a preference of which room you want?"

He shook his head. "Help yourself." As she started to walk away, he said, "Wait. You need some dry clothes."

He was right but she'd make do. She'd already imposed on him enough. But when she turned to tell him so, he was pulling clothes out of a bag.

"These will be big on you but at least they're dry." He tossed some drawstring shorts and a T-shirt at her.

She hesitated. The thought of warm, dry clothes was too much to resist. "Thank you."

She knew she should feel grateful for him going out of his way for her and leave it at that, but she had to question why he was trying so hard to be nice to her. Maybe it was just that she'd been on her own since she was seventeen when her mother had died. She'd learned the hard way that the only person you could count on was yourself.

The last man she'd trusted was her ex-boyfriend, Otis. Things had been good in the beginning. Then he'd moved in and she'd started to think they had a future together. What was the saying? Love makes you blind. That must have been what happened to her because in the end, she'd seen his true colors and she didn't like what she saw. That's when she'd kicked him out.

But she wasn't about to get involved with Mr. Tall and Sexy. However, it didn't mean she wasn't curious about the man. She wanted to know everything about him from where he came from to what he was doing on the island. And she was curious about one other thing… Her gaze strayed to his hands. No rings. Interesting.

He looked as though he wanted to say something more when his phone buzzed. "Sorry. I need to get this."

"No problem. I'm just going to go get that shower."

With his phone pressed to his ear, he moved toward his room. She turned and headed in the other direction.

She stepped inside her bedroom and closed the door behind her. Even though she'd previously been in this suite, it felt so different to be here as a semi-guest. She looked around, seeing her surroundings differently. She admired the beauty of the room and anticipated the luxurious comfort awaiting her. As a resort employee, staying in a guest suite was frowned upon.

But what did she have to worry about? It was only a shower and she was the boss…for now. Until the will was resolved, she could do as she pleased and there was no one to reprimand her. A smile pulled at her lips.

As she moved to the bathroom, she noticed that it was practically the size of her entire flat. No expense had been spared when this resort was built. And updates were completed on a regular basis.

She stepped farther into the room and admired the enormous white soaking tub. It beckoned to her. She really shouldn't give in. But she was already here, so why not indulge?

As she filled the deep white tub with warm sudsy water, she unwrapped a purple bath bomb and smiled as she dropped it in the tub.

She quickly undressed. An inspection of her stained and torn clothes had her placing them in the garbage. Then she stepped into the warm and inviting tub. As she soaked, her thoughts drifted to Atlas. She was quite certain he wasn't soaking in a tub, though that didn't stop her mind from conjuring up the very steamy image. Her heart beat faster. Oh, what an image!

His broad shoulders had hinted at a muscular physique. Not even his tailored suit could hide the fact that he worked out, probably daily. And boy did it pay off. Not that she was interested. Not even a little. Okay, maybe just a little.

But she had her career to think about now. And with the future of the Ludus up in the air, she had to be prepared to fight for the livelihoods of her employees. She just hoped it didn't come to that drastic measure.

CHAPTER THREE

SHE WAS UNFORGETTABLY BEAUTIFUL.

And an indulgence he couldn't afford right now.

Atlas wasn't at the Ludus Resort for a holiday. He was here to conduct business—at least that's the way he'd come to regard his mother's estate. Because to consider what it truly meant would mean scratching back scabs on old wounds. It would mean dragging to the surface emotions he'd worked for years to bury.

Now with room service ordered, he'd showered and changed into a fresh button-up and jeans. He rolled up his sleeves as he stepped out of his bedroom into the living room. He glanced around the suite, taking in the details from the palms and trees that soared up to the second-story ceiling with fake cockatoos and parakeets in the trees to the forest green wallpaper. He couldn't help but wonder how the other rooms were decorated. Or what Thea's private apartment was like—not that he wanted to spend time there. He wanted nothing to do with her things.

He turned his thought to his security business. For him, working was like breathing. His business was the reason he got out of bed in the morning.

Whereas people were unreliable, his business never let him down. It was there for him each day, and it rewarded him for all of his efforts. As it was, if he didn't work another day in his life, he would never want for a thing in his life.

But at this late hour, business was concluded in Europe. He grabbed his phone to check his messages and answered a couple of emails that he'd received while he'd been in transit to the island.

He decided to send a text message to his old friend, Krystof.

Have arrived. This resort has a lot of promise. Will send pictures soon.

He slipped the phone back in his pocket. No sooner had he done that than it vibrated. He withdrew it to find a response.

Looking forward to them. Can't wait to see in person.

Come now. We can see it together.

Can't. Playing cards in Monaco.

Krystof was always moving from one challenge or game of chance to the next. He was a nomad much like himself. But he was the one person Atlas knew and trusted that had the funds to buy this place.

Come as soon as possible.

I'll check my calendar. Maybe next week.

See you then.

Atlas returned the phone to his pocket. By next week, he planned to be finished with this part of his life. The sooner, the better.

He sat down on the hunter green leather couch, finding it surprisingly comfortable. In his vast experience of traveling from one place to another, he'd found most hotel furniture looked nice but ended up being terribly uncomfortable. Not so with the Ludus Resort.

Was it Thea who'd put all of the thought into this resort with its themed suites and furniture that not only looked good but felt good too? Not that he cared what Thea did. Just as she'd never cared what he did.

Knock-knock.

He welcomed the interruption. Thinking about Thea only angered him. Why she'd left this island to him seemed like some sort of cruel joke.

When he opened the door, he found a server wearing a black-and-white uniform pushing a white linen-covered cart with two covered dishes, and yellow and purple flowers in the center. Once the food was placed on the dining table next to the window overlooking the stormy evening, the cart was removed.

Atlas turned to find Hermione had emerged from her room. Her long hair was wet and hanging down her back. His clothes engulfed her petite frame. Even so, she looked adorable.

"Would you care to join me at the table?" He gestured to an empty chair.

She hesitated. "I don't want to intrude any further."

"You won't be. And I ordered enough for two. What do you say? Will you join me?"

She hesitated as though considering her options. "I did miss dinner."

"All the more reason for you to join me." He pulled out a chair for her before taking a seat himself.

She lifted the lid from her plate. "Breakfast food?"

He nodded. "I travel a lot, and I've found this food appetizing at any hour. I wasn't sure what you'd like, so it's a little bit of everything. But if you want something else, I'll call down to the kitchen. They are open twenty-four hours a day, but you already know that."

"This is fine. Thank you."

They ate quietly as though each were lost in their own thoughts—thoughts of the accident, thoughts of how their lives had collided and thoughts of what tomorrow would bring each of them. He turned his gaze to the window and stared out at the turbulent night as lightning etched against the dark sky.

If not for the storm, he would have missed meeting Hermione. She was different from the other women who'd passed through his life. Hermione wasn't chatty. She hadn't told him her whole life's story in the first five minutes of their meeting.

Instead, he found her to be a mystery of silent looks. Her eyes let him know there was a lot going on in her mind, but whatever her thoughts were, she was keeping them to herself. The quieter she became, the more he wanted to know what was going on behind her captivating brown eyes.

"Was your meal good?" he asked.

She nodded. "It was."

And then she looked at him like she was trying to read his thoughts. She wasn't the first one to look at him that way. But he liked to think of himself as unreadable.

"Will anyone be joining you?" she asked.

He couldn't help but wonder where this conversation was headed. He thought of his invitation for Krystof to join him here on the island, but he knew that wasn't what she meant. But she didn't appear to be trying to hit on him. So what was her angle?

Curiosity got the best of him. "No."

"No wife? Or girlfriend?"

She surprised him with her very pointed questions. "Just me."

It wasn't that he didn't have relationships—if that's what you wanted to call them—it's that he wasn't any good at them. At least that's what he'd been told as the women exited his life.

Maybe he didn't try hard enough to make any of the relationships work. Or maybe they saw what his mother had seen in him—he wasn't worthy of love. Either way, he focused all of his energy on his business. It hadn't let him down.

Hermione nodded as though he was giving all of the right answers. "This just doesn't seem like the sort of destination for a single man."

He sat up straighter. "Why not?"

She shrugged. "The resort doesn't exactly have much of a nightlife or an abundance of single women."

His gaze moved to her hands. No rings. He ignored the excitement that raced through his blood. He hadn't intended to have a holiday fling, but now he was reconsidering his options.

"What about you?" If she could ask personal questions, so could he. "Are you single?"

She hesitated. "I am."

He smiled. "See. I didn't even have to look around and yet I found the most beautiful single woman on the island."

That's all it took to bring a rosy hue to her cheeks. And it made her even more attractive. Oh, yes, a holiday fling was becoming more appealing by the moment.

"You probably say that to all of the women." She reached for her water glass and took a sip.

"Trust me. I don't throw around compliments lightly." It was true. He used them sparingly and only when he truly meant them.

As his phone vibrated in his pocket, it reminded him that he had his hands full while he was on the island. He had to stay on top of his security business while cleaning out Thea's apartment and retrieving all of the documents in her personal safe. In addition, he had to make sure the property was ready to hit the market. And he planned to have it all done in less than two weeks.

In order to meet his aggressive timetable, he had to stay focused on his mission. But maybe Hermione could help him in a different way. "How much do you know about the island? I mean you must know most everything, right?"

She shrugged. "What are you curious about?"

"This is my first visit here." *And my last.* "As you probably know, this resort doesn't have a website. And there really aren't many pictures of it online."

"That's because the island has a privacy policy. It gives the rich and famous a chance to unwind and enjoy themselves without the risk of ending up in a tabloid."

"But doesn't it make it hard to lure in new visitors?"

"Not really." She frowned at him. "You make it sound like you're a journalist." And then her eyes narrowed in on him. "Listen, if you're here to write some exposé—"

"I'm not a journalist." When she continued to stare at him with suspicion reflected in her eyes, he said, "I swear. I'm not."

"You sure sound like one."

How was he supposed to convince her that he wasn't a journalist? "Do you really think a journalist could afford to stay here?"

She paused as though giving the idea consideration. "Your publisher could pick up the tab."

He inwardly groaned. She wasn't going to give him any slack. And then he had an idea. "Wait here." He moved to his room and quickly returned. He sat down and handed her a card. "This is my business card."

She read it. "You install security systems like they sell on television?"

He couldn't help but laugh at her underwhelmed expression. It'd been a long time since someone didn't recognize him or his company. "Not exactly. Atlas Securities develops and installs very sophisticated systems."

She yawned. "I'm sorry."

He found himself smiling at her bored expression. She was definitely unique. The more he got to know her, the more he liked her. "It's okay. My business doesn't excite everyone."

"No, it's not that. It's just been a really long day. I had to finish a special project and it wiped me out."

"What sort of project?"

She shook her head. "You don't want to hear about that tonight or I'll put us both to sleep." She yawned again. "We should call it a night."

"Agreed." He set aside his napkin and got to his feet. "Are you sure I can't convince you to stay in the guest room?"

She shook her head and then walked away. At the door, she turned back. "Thank you for the shower and food." And then color bloomed in her cheeks. "And the clothes."

When she started out the door, he asked, "Will I see you again?"

"It's a big resort. Probably not." And then she was gone.

He was sorry to see their evening end so soon. They were beginning to be friends and he liked that idea. Having a friend on the island might make his job here less painful. Maybe tomorrow he'd seek her out—to help him find his way around the island. Yes, that sounded like a fine idea.

CHAPTER FOUR

HAD LAST NIGHT been some sort of dream?

When Hermione opened her eyes the next morning, she glanced around, finding herself in her office, wearing clothes that most definitely weren't her own. Last night had been no dream.

She wasn't ready to move. Not yet. She closed her eyes, and her mind filled with the image of the handsome man she'd met last night. At first he'd been rather testy, but then he'd offered her a hot bath, food and the clothes off his back. Okay, maybe they weren't off his back, but it had been a kind gesture. She lifted the T-shirt to her nose and inhaled the faint spicy scent that clung to the soft material. Mmm... She inhaled again, deeper this time.

The alarm on her phone went off. She reached for it on the floor and checked the time. As her gaze focused on the numbers, she groaned. She needed to get moving.

The first thing she did was call one of the resort's boutiques and request they send over an outfit. Next she located some sample toiletries in her bottom desk drawer. She took them to the ladies' room where she styled her hair into her usual French twist. She liked its sleek professional look and the way it kept her long hair out of her way as she leaned over her desk to review reports.

After rushing through her morning routine, she returned

to the office and called the car garage about Atlas's…er…
Mr. Othonos's vehicle. They promised to immediately see
to towing and detailing it.

Knock-knock.

She swung open the office door to find a young woman
with a rack of clothes. Hermione didn't recognize her. Her
gaze moved to the name tag: Iona. She must be one of the
new hires. Now wasn't exactly the right moment for an in-
troduction.

She quickly sorted through the selections. The clothes
that had been chosen for her were of bright, cheerful colors,
everything Hermione wasn't feeling right now. She picked
the least vibrant shade, a peachy-pink-colored outfit. She
thanked the young woman and sent the rest of the clothes
back to the boutique.

Her gaze moved to the price tag on the outfit. She stifled
a moan. The clothes cost as much as her monthly rent, but
what choice did she have? Her navy-blue business suit had
been stained, and there had been a tear across the knee
from when she'd fallen. She'd left it in the trash back at
Atlas's suite.

When she was ready to face the world—ready to face
Atlas—she headed for the door. She moved quickly through
the quiet hallways. The closer she got to Atlas's suite, the
faster her pulse raced. Last night, she told herself she wasn't
going to see him again, but…well…she did have his clothes.
And she really should thank him again for all he'd done
for her last night.

When she stopped in front of his door, her palms grew
clammy. Before she lost her nerve, she knocked.

When Atlas opened the door, his gaze met hers. She
felt as though she could drown in his mesmerizing blue
eyes. Her heart thump-thumped in her chest. And when

he smiled, she noticed how his eyes twinkled. She subdued a dreamy sigh.

She forced herself to look away. If she didn't get the words out quickly, she feared she'd forget her reason for being at his door.

"Here are your clothes." She handed them to him. "Thank you for last night—"

Someone cleared their throat.

Oh, no! He isn't alone.

She glanced past him and into the room. Hermione's heart sunk down to the white canvas shoes she'd been supplied by the boutique. There before her stood Adara Galanis, the resort's concierge and her friend. When their gazes met, Adara's eyes momentarily widened in surprise.

Atlas stepped back and bid her entrance to the suite. Hermione didn't know what to say as she stepped forward. Heat engulfed her cheeks as he closed the door behind her. How was she supposed to explain any of this?

Atlas cleared his throat. "This is Hermione. She came to my rescue last night and ended up stranded on the island."

Adara's startled gaze moved between her and Atlas. "I heard about the accident and as the concierge, I wanted to personally offer my services. If there's anything I can do—"

"Yes, you can make sure my car is detailed and inspected," Atlas said.

"I've already taken care of your car," Hermione said. "It was the first thing I did this morning."

Adara sent her a concerned look. "Hermione, are you okay?"

"Perfectly fine. Not a scratch on me." She tried to sound calm and in control, but being this close to Atlas made her insides shiver with nervous energy. "His car was the only one involved in the accident."

His gaze moved between the two women. "You two know each other?"

"Of course," Adara said. "Hermione is the resort manager. She didn't tell you?"

His gaze narrowed on Hermione. "No. She failed to mention it last night."

At first she'd kept her position from him because he'd been agitated about his car. And later it was just easier to keep things casual. The muscles around Hermione's chest tightened like a vise.

"I can explain," she said.

Atlas shook his head. "I don't have time for explanations. I'm expecting a very important business call." He turned to walk away. "Just go."

"Wait. Give me a moment to explain." Hermione moved to block his exit.

His gaze caught hers. The anger reflected in his eyes stopped her in her tracks. He walked around her and strode into his room. The door closed behind him with a resounding thud.

The breath trapped in her lungs. She had totally messed this up.

First, there had been the downpour followed by his accident. And now she'd made a huge miscalculation by not admitting last night that she ran the entire resort. A little voice in her head said to just walk away. It didn't matter if he liked her or not. They would never see each other again. But there was this other part of her that had started to like him.

Resort manager.

He was still surprised to learn Hermione was in charge of the resort. He couldn't help but notice how she'd purposely left out that detail last night. He couldn't help but wonder why.

Had she recognized him? Had his mother shown her a press release of him? Surely not. Thea's life hadn't had room for him.

The questions mounted one right after the other. He raked his fingers through his hair as he tried to discern what sort of angle Hermione was working. Usually he was able to see a con from afar but with her, he hadn't sensed a thing.

Whatever. He had work to do—contracts to review, emails to answer and that phone call that still hadn't come. All in all, he didn't have time to play games. In his spacious bedroom, he sat down at the large desk facing the wall of windows overlooking the beach, but he didn't take the time to appreciate the beauty of the scenery. Instead, he opened his laptop and set to work.

As his fingers moved over the keyboard, his thoughts repeatedly drifted back to Hermione. He replayed their meeting in his mind. Perhaps he hadn't made the best first impression. He wasn't usually this agitated.

Perhaps Hermione hadn't announced her position because he hadn't made her feel comfortable enough to reveal her true identity. And there was the fact that he hadn't admitted who he was either.

Knock-knock.

When he didn't immediately respond, Hermione called out, "Mr. Othonos, can we speak?"

He pressed Send on an email to his assistant in the London office. "I'll be out."

Her heels clicked over the marble floor as she retreated. He didn't rush out to speak to her. He wasn't used to being summoned. He was the one who did the summoning. And so he answered one more email.

Then he quietly joined her in the living room. He glanced

around, finding that they were now alone. As though she sensed his presence, she turned. Their gazes met and held for a second too long. In that moment, he forgot about his irritation with her.

Her dark hair was pulled back in a much too severe style. He imagined unpinning her hair and letting it flow down over her shoulders. Definitely better. His fingers tingled with the temptation to comb through her long silky locks.

And then there was her beautiful face with dimples in her cheeks. High cheekbones led to a pert little nose, but it was her brown eyes that drew him in. His pulse spiked. And when a smile pulled ever so slightly at her lips, he realized that he'd let himself get distracted for much too long.

He glanced just past her left shoulder and out the window at the gray sky. He cleared his throat. And then proving to himself that he had control over his reaction to her nearness, his gaze met hers again. "Why weren't you honest about who you were last night?"

Emotions flickered in her eyes, but in a blink, they were hidden behind a wall of diplomacy. "I'm sorry if you feel I was in some way dishonest with you."

Her restrained manner and resistance to admit her error only succeeded in further agitating him. "I didn't ask for an apology. I want an explanation."

"You were dealing with enough last night with your car going off the road—by the way it will be delivered a little later this morning."

"I hope they're careful." He frowned at her. "You know none of this would be necessary if you had stayed on your side of the road last night?"

She opened her mouth to argue with him but wordlessly closed it. In the light of day, she couldn't deny that she forced him off the road.

He expected to feel some sort of satisfaction at her acknowledgment of fault, but he didn't. Okay, it wasn't exactly an acknowledgment. It was more like a lack of denial. Either way, he'd been in the right and her in the wrong.

She blinked and then two lines formed between her fine brows. "I can assure you the garage does exceptional work."

"You don't understand. That car is unique. There's not another one out there like it." When she still looked confused, he said, "It's a kit car with every upgrade you can imagine. I just picked it up. I'm planning to have it shipped back to London."

She looked at him like he'd just spoken a foreign language. She obviously wasn't a sports car aficionado. "I thought you would be happy to have it back as quickly as possible."

He raked his fingers through his hair. She was right. He wasn't usually this on edge. It was being here in this place—Thea's place. He didn't want to be here.

"Of course," he said. "Thank you for seeing to it. This place just unnerves me."

The words had crossed his lips before he'd realized that he'd said too much. His pulse raced. It was though the earth had shifted beneath his feet. A moment ago he'd been Atlas Othonos, founder and CEO of Atlas Securities, and soon he would be known on the island as Thea's son. It was a title he hadn't worn since he was a little boy. It was a title he never thought he'd have again.

Hermione's gaze searched his. "I don't understand."

"Thea is, er, was my mother."

Her eyes widened. "We heard the island had been inherited, but we weren't even sure Thea's son was still alive."

"Why wouldn't I be alive?" His voice came out harsher than he'd intended.

Had his mother told everyone he was dead? The thought sickened him. It was one thing not to want to be a part of his life but quite another to want him dead. Could his mother have been that cruel?

"I'm sorry," Hermione said. "It's just none of us have ever seen you around the resort."

How did he explain this? And then he decided he didn't have to explain any of it. It was none of her business.

"My mother and I weren't close." That was as much as he was willing to admit. It wasn't anything Hermione couldn't surmise on her own. "But I would appreciate if you kept this information to yourself."

"You don't want anyone to know that you now own the resort?" Hermione asked.

"No, I don't. At least not yet."

"But you'll want to get to know the staff right away—"

"No, I won't."

Her diplomatic expression slid from her face. In its place was a look of surprise. "Why not?" Her eyes widened as though she realized she'd just vocalized her thoughts. "I mean is there a better time for you to tour the resort?"

"I don't need to see it. I'm selling it." He pressed his lips together.

He hadn't intended to tell anyone about his plans yet, but there was something about Hermione that had him acting out of character. Now he braced himself for a barrage of reasons that selling the resort was a bad idea.

"What? But why?" Her gaze searched his.

"I can't keep it." Still she sent him an expectant stare so he added, "My life isn't here. It's in London." It wasn't the whole truth but it was enough of it.

Concern reflected in her eyes. "But what about the resort? Will it be kept the same?"

Once again he raked his fingers through his hair. She wanted answers from him that he didn't have. "I don't know. That will be up to the new owners."

"But you haven't even seen the resort yet. You might change your mind about selling it."

He shook his head. "The sale is going to happen. The only question is when. Now if you don't mind, I have work to do."

He walked her to the door. He could tell the wheels of her mind were turning. This conversation might be over for the moment, but he had no doubt she would broach the subject in the near future. And his answer would be the same—the resort was for sale.

CHAPTER FIVE

THIS MORNING WAS not going well.

That was one of the biggest understatements of her life.

Hermione wondered what else could go wrong. Her steps were quick as she hurried down the spacious hallway. She forced a smile to her face as she greeted everyone she passed. It wasn't her staff's fault that she'd had the most unfortunate run-in with the resort's heir. Or the fact that he was the most stubborn, annoying man to ever walk the earth. Okay, maybe that was a bit over the top, but he really got under her skin.

How could Atlas not even slow down and consider keeping the island? Who wouldn't want their very own island? Wasn't that what dreams were made of?

But, no. He didn't even want to hear about how profitable the resort was, or how it basically ran itself, so his immediate intervention wasn't needed…or wanted.

Now what was she supposed to do? Start looking for a new position elsewhere? The thought left a sour feeling in the pit of her stomach.

The Ludus Resort was more than her place of employment. It was her makeshift home. Without having any relatives of her own, she'd adopted the resort employees or rather they'd adopted her. She wasn't quite sure of which way it'd happened. But the point was she would be lost without this great big, loving group of people.

She glanced at her smartwatch. She had almost two thousand steps already. It was the pacing she'd done in Atlas's suite. And now it was five minutes before the start of the workday. She'd meant to get to her office much sooner, but the run-in with Atlas had taken longer than she'd anticipated. Not that her pleading had done a thing to sway his decision about the fate of the resort.

Her assistant, Rhea, glanced up from her desk as Hermione walked through the doorway. "Good morning."

So far there was nothing good about it. Still, it wasn't Rhea's fault. Hermione forced another smile to her lips. "Morning."

Rhea's gaze followed her as she crossed the outer office to her doorway, but her assistant didn't say another word.

With the door closed, Hermione's thoughts returned to Atlas. She'd always wondered what had happened between Thea and her son. Her friend was always light on the details of their estrangement, but Hermione was starting to figure things out. And she didn't like what she saw.

In fact, she was really worried. She sank down on her desk chair. Whereas the Ludus was steeped in traditions from the employees' monthly luncheon to the annual regatta, Atlas didn't seem to care for tradition.

She blew out a frustrated sigh. More changes were coming to the Ludus. And she would predict that they weren't going to be good for her or the staff. Even worse, she didn't know how to stop Atlas. How did you stop an heir from doing what they wanted with their inheritance?

"Hermione?" Rhea's voice interrupted her troubling thoughts.

She glanced up. "What did you say?"

Rhea hesitantly stepped in her office. "I asked if everything is all right."

"Uh, yeah. Perfect." Everything was so not perfect. It was anything but perfect.

"That outfit is pretty. Is it new?"

Hermione glanced down and wanted to say that it was just something she'd pulled out of the back of her closet, but she couldn't bring herself to lie. It just wasn't who she was. Instead, she nodded.

Rhea smiled. "I was tempted to buy it."

She was so busted. "I… I just decided to splurge."

Rhea's eyes sparkled with amusement. "What's his name?"

"What?" Heat immediately rushed to her cheeks. "It's not like that. There is no he. Surely you don't think I had a one-nighter with a guest." She pressed her lips together to keep from rattling on and digging a hole deeper for herself.

"It's okay. Relax. I heard about the accident."

"You did?"

She smiled and nodded. "Titus let me know you had a rough night."

The heat in her cheeks increased until the roots of her hair felt as though they might instantaneously ignite. "It's not like you're thinking."

"I'm thinking that you got stranded on the island and there weren't any available rooms so you slept in your office."

"Oh." Hermione was caught off guard. It took her frenzied mind a moment to catch up with reality. "It is exactly what you were thinking."

Rhea stepped out to her desk and soon returned with a pair of scissors in hand. She approached Hermione. "Stand up and turn around."

"What?" She really needed some caffeine because she was having problems following Rhea's words. "Why?"

She continued to smile at her. "Trust me."

And so Hermione did as she was told. There was a distinct snip and then Rhea adjusted the neckline on Hermione's top.

"Okay. You can turn around."

When she did Rhea was standing there holding a tag. Oops. She'd been in such a rush that morning that she'd forgotten to remove it. She inwardly groaned. She wondered how many people had seen the tags hanging off her clothes.

Atlas! He would have seen her blunder. The heat rushed back to her cheeks. The best thing she could do was just keep her distance from him. It was obvious she didn't think clearly around him and in turn she rubbed him the wrong way.

"Thank you."

"Anytime. You would have done the same for me."

Hermione nodded. Friends watched out for each other. "Now I'm going to go hide in my office all morning. If anyone wants me, I'm not here."

Rhea arched a brow. "Seriously?"

Hermione sighed. "No. But it is tempting."

Rhea closed the door on her way out, giving Hermione a chance to gather herself. Perhaps she took more comfort in her morning routine than she'd realized because she felt utterly rattled and out of sorts.

She moved to her coffee maker and brewed a cup. She was never more grateful than now that it only took a couple of minutes to create a steaming cup of coffee. She added some sweetener and creamer and gave it a stir before carrying it to her desk.

It was there that she settled into her work, and soon she was caught up in reviewing department budgets and approving large disbursements. For a moment, she forgot about everything, including the man with the sky-blue eyes.

She didn't know how much time had passed when there was a knock at the door. She glanced up to find Adara standing there. "Do you have moment?"

Hermione waved her in. "What's up?"

"I just wanted to tell you how sorry I am about this morning. I didn't mean to make things awkward for you."

If she was upset with anyone, it was herself. "Don't worry about it. And just for the record, I didn't spend the night with him." She explained how she'd used the shower and then slept in the office. "Thank goodness I didn't. He's Thea's son."

Adara's eyes widened as her mouth gaped. "He is?"

She nodded. "It came out after you left. He was upset that I hadn't told him I was the manager."

Adara settled on the arm of the chair across from Hermione's desk. "Why didn't you?"

"Because he was really upset last night, and I didn't want to make things worse."

"And how are things with you two now?"

Hermione leaned back in her chair. "Not good. He's selling the resort."

Her eyes widened. "He is?"

She nodded. "I offered to give him a tour but he declined. He said he had work to do."

"So he's in his suite working instead of enjoying all of the resort's amenities?"

"I guess so. I haven't checked on him."

"Don't you think you should? I mean if he sells this place, everything is going to change. You need to show him that he's making a big mistake."

Hermione shook her head. "You didn't hear him. He's

very determined. And he's angry with me because he thinks I ran his precious car off the road last night."

"Oh, no. That's not good. Did you apologize?"

"No." Her response came out harsher than she'd intended. "I didn't do anything wrong. The road was flooded. He must have overcorrected and gone off the road. Anyway, I had the garage tow his car today. They're cleaning it up and having it delivered this morning."

Adara nodded. "So then he had nothing to be upset about. You should try again and show him that the Ludus is special."

Hermione resisted the urge to roll her eyes. "I don't think anything will convince him of that. Certainly not me saying it. It's like he arrived on the island all set to hate the place and anyone associated with it."

"Then give him things to like about the Ludus—like the employees." Adara smiled brightly. "We're a great group, if I do say so myself. Once he meets us, he'll have to like us."

At last Hermione smiled. "You think that highly of this group?"

"I do. I really do." Adara pondered the idea for a moment. "You know the best way to immerse him in the atmosphere is to bring him to lunch today."

"Today?" She shook her head. "I don't think he'd be interested in a covered dish lunch. He doesn't strike me as the social type."

"We'll see about that." Adara stood. "You get him to the lunchroom and I'll spread the word that we need to melt his frosty exterior. After all, he's Thea's son. Surely he has a heart in there somewhere." She made a quick exit.

"I wouldn't count it," Hermione muttered under her breath.

The last thing she wanted was to deal with that man again. He was like a grumpy old man. Only he wasn't old;

in fact, he didn't appear to be much older than her. And maybe he did have a reason to be grumpy. After all, if she'd just picked up a new car, she'd probably be upset if it went off the road and got stuck in mud.

And then there was the death of his mother. Close or not, that had to hit him hard. At the very least, it had to make him feel his mortality. It was one of the many things she'd felt when she lost her own mother.

She sighed. Had she really just talked herself into giving him another chance? It would appear so. She just wondered how she felt about home cooking because that's what they served for their monthly employee luncheon.

His phone rang nonstop all morning.

Atlas frowned as he stared blindly at his laptop. The voice of his vice president sounded over Atlas's speakerphone. He knew he shouldn't have come to the island. He'd only been gone one night and there were already problems. He should be back in London so he could go to the office and straighten out this mess in person.

But on a good note, by midmorning a resort employee had returned his keys. His car was now safely tucked away in the resort's private garage. Atlas had immediately given it a thorough personal inspection as well as a short test drive. Thankfully no damage had been done.

"What do you want to do?" The VP's voice drew Atlas from his meandering thoughts.

He gave his company's problem some serious thought. "I want the head of our installation department to fly to the embassy, and I want him to do what needs to be done to fix this problem. And I want him on a plane today."

"Yes, sir. I'll see to it."

"Make sure you do. Because as of now, this is your highest priority. No. This is your only priority. The embassy is counting on us to get this right or we can forget about any future national security contracts."

"I'm on it."

"On second thought, I want you on the plane too. I need someone on the ground who can smooth things out." He'd do it himself, but that would mean dragging out the mess with Thea's estate even longer.

There was a distinct pause on the other end of the line. "Yes, sir."

"Keep me updated."

Ding-dong.

"What was that, sir?"

"That is an interruption I don't need right now. See that this problem is corrected." And then Atlas ended the call.

Ding-dong.

Someone was certainly impatient. He couldn't imagine who it might be. He swung the door open and was surprised to find Hermione had returned so quickly. For a second, his voice failed him. Had they set up a meeting and he'd forgotten about it? No. Not possible.

"Can I help you?" he asked.

She sent him another tentative smile that didn't go all the way to her eyes. Then as a happy couple strolled by, Hermione waited until they'd moved further down the hallway before speaking. "Can we talk?"

He opened the door farther and stepped aside. "Come in." After she'd stepped inside, he said, "I don't have much time. You'll have to make it quick."

"Have you been in this suite all morning?"

"Yes. I have work to do."

"So why come to the island?" She looked at him expectantly.

His body stiffened. So much for them starting over. "You know why I'm here, to deal with my mother's things."

"You could have just had someone box up her things and ship them to you."

She was right. Why hadn't he done that? Why hadn't the thought even crossed his mind? When he'd received news of her death via his office, his first thought was to come here. But by the time he'd heard the news, the funeral was over. He was left figuring out why he suddenly felt so much more alone on this great big planet.

His brain said he shouldn't feel anything about Thea's passing. After all, it wasn't like they were a part of each other's lives. And that had all been her decision. She's the one who walked away and left him behind.

And yet there was this hollow spot in his chest that felt as though something was now missing. He refused to explore that feeling further. He was here to do a job, nothing more.

He cleared his throat. "Is there a reason you're here, Ms. Kappas?"

"It's Hermione. And yes, there is a reason. Have you eaten lunch yet?"

Was it that late, already? He consulted his Rolex. Yes, it was that late. "No, I haven't."

"Then come with me." She started for the door without even waiting for his response.

He started after her, prepared to set her straight. "Listen, I don't have time to go to lunch with you." He was out the door, trying to catch up with her. "I have work to do."

She paused in the hallway to glance back at him. "And you have to eat in order to do your work." She gestured behind him. "Don't forget to close the door."

He glanced over his shoulder to find she had him so distracted that he had walked out the door without a thought to closing it. He retraced his steps and did just that. Then he took long, rapid steps to catch up to her.

"I don't think you understand," he said. "I run a huge

international security company. I have things that need my attention." Just then his stomach growled as though in protest to him trying to skip out on another meal.

She glanced over at him and arched a brow. "You need to take care of you. And besides, I think you'll enjoy this lunch."

He sighed. "Couldn't we just order room service?"

She shook her head. "This is better than room service. Trust me."

That was the problem. He didn't trust her. He didn't even know her. Still, he walked with her. Maybe he'd order some food to take back to his room.

They appeared to be heading away from the lobby and common areas, which he found odd. Why wouldn't the restaurants be in highly trafficked areas? Perhaps it was something the new owner should correct.

Hermione swiped her employee card to open a set of heavy steel doors. He caught the placard on the door that said: No Entrance. Employees Only.

"Where are we going?" He glanced around the brightly lit hallway, taking in the buzz of voices mingled with the hum of machines.

"You'll soon see. We're almost there."

Maybe he had been a little too focused on his work, but that was how he'd built his company to be one of the biggest and best in the world. The only problem with being the biggest and best was that there was nowhere to go from there. It was though his drive was starting to wane and he found himself looking for a new challenge. He just didn't know what that would be. Nor did he have time to figure it out—not with the embassy problem to sort out.

Just as he was about to tell Hermione that he didn't have time for this expedition, she stopped in front of a door. She turned to him with a smile. "We're here."

Here? He glanced around. This wasn't a restaurant.

Hermione opened the door and stepped inside. He followed her because he'd come this far, he might as well see what this was all about.

The first thing he noticed were the delicious aromas. They smacked him in the face and sent him spiraling back in time to when he was a little boy. He recalled how much his mother used to love to cook. Their kitchen used to be filled with the most delicious aromas of fresh herbs, clove and allspice. He hadn't thought of that in a long time.

Another memory came flooding back of his mother saving him leftovers from his favorite meals. She would say growing boys needed extra helpings. His father didn't agree. And so she would hide the food and let Atlas eat it when his father was at work. He'd felt so special, so loved—

He gave himself a mental shake, pushing away the unwanted memory. Because the only thing that mattered was that Thea had left him.

His gaze scanned the room as he tried to figure out why they were here. The room was filled with tables and people—lots of people. Most were dressed in work uniforms from maid outfits to cooking staff and some in janitorial coveralls.

Atlas stopped and turned to Hermione, feeling as though he'd somehow been set up. "What are we doing here?"

"I thought you'd want to meet the employees. They are excited to meet you." And without giving him a chance to say that it was the last thing he wanted to do, she turned to the people. A hush had come over the crowd as they stared at him as though trying to decide what to make of him. "Hi, everyone. I'd like you to meet Thea's son, Atlas. He is the new owner of the resort and I hope you'll give him a big, warm welcome."

Suddenly people surged forward with their hands outstretched. Some wore smiles while others sent him hesitant looks. They all wanted one thing from him—the knowledge that their lives weren't about to change. This was exactly what he'd been hoping to avoid. They wanted a promise he couldn't give them. And so he artfully darted around the subject of the future of the resort. Instead, he found himself focusing on the here and now—which meant promising them that he would tour the resort.

It felt as though he'd just fallen into a trap—a trap set by the beautiful manager. He'd most definitely underestimated her. He glanced around for Hermione, but she'd disappeared into the sea of Ludus employees.

It would appear this was some sort of special employee luncheon. He missed the part about why they were holding such a luncheon, but he was handed a plate. Food was heaped on it, so much so that it took both of his hands to hold it.

Now he felt obligated to view the resort because one thing he wasn't was a liar. And he had Hermione to thank for this latest development. So if he could miss work to tour the grounds, so could she. Although the thought of spending more time with the crafty manager didn't sound so bad; in fact she intrigued him.

It was working.

Or perhaps it was a bit of wishful thinking.

Hermione couldn't decide if Atlas was putting on a good show for the employees or if he was starting to let down his guard with them. She hadn't spoken to him throughout lunch. It wasn't that she was avoiding him, it was that he was constantly surrounded by employees greeting him.

But now that lunch was over, the crowd was thinning. Atlas approached her. It was impossible to tell what effect the luncheon had on him. His poker face gave nothing away.

He leaned in close to her ear. "That little trick wasn't very nice of you."

"Would you have agreed to come if I'd have told you we were eating with the employees?"

"No. Because it won't change my mind about the sale."

She resisted the urge to sigh. She'd never met such a stubborn man. Maybe Adara could reason with him because she was done with him. "Well, I need to get back to my office—"

"Not so fast. Thanks to your plotting, I've now promised the employees that I'd tour the resort and I've chosen you to be my guide."

"Me." This had to be a joke. He didn't even like her.

The corners of his mouth lifted in a devious smile. "Where shall we start?"

Her phone buzzed, distracting her. She withdrew her phone from her pocket and checked the screen. "Something has come up. I must go."

"Not so fast. If I'm going to miss work for this tour, so are you."

She shook her head. "You don't understand. The royal jewels have arrived. I must go sign for them."

"What are royal jewels doing at the resort?"

"I don't have time to explain now. Do you remember how to get back to your suite?"

"I can manage. But I'm coming with you."

So all it took were some famous jewels to spark his interest in the resort. If she'd have known, she'd have mentioned their pending arrival for the upcoming Valentine's Day Ball much sooner. The holiday was not quite two weeks away. She couldn't help but wonder if Atlas would be attending.

Perhaps there was more to this resort than he'd originally thought.

There was definitely more to its general manager than he'd first suspected.

She wasn't above pulling out all of the stops if she felt something was important, not only to herself but to those around her. He respected her determination, but it wasn't enough to change his mind. Nothing would convince him to keep this island.

Still, he was curious to learn why royal jewels had been delivered to the resort. It could possibly be a selling point. He was quite certain most resorts didn't play host to royal gems. Perhaps he'd been too quick to dismiss the idea of touring the resort.

His security expertise might come in handy. He liked the thought of doing some manual labor instead of answering the unending list of emails awaiting his attention. And it would give him a chance to know the general manager a little better—from a business standpoint of course.

"Do you really expect me to believe these jewels are royal?" It had to be some sort of PR campaign to draw in more guests.

As they made their way along the hallway, she glanced at him. "You really don't know much about your mother, do you?"

He'd made a point not to know anything about her. If Thea could so easily forget him, he could forget her. "What is that supposed to mean?"

Hermione shook her head. "The jewels are real, and they are from the royal family of Rydiania."

He vaguely recalled hearing of the country, but he couldn't place where he'd heard the name. "Why would they send the resort jewels?"

"The prince visits every year."

So they'd worked out some sort of arrangement with this prince. Interesting. "I want to know why this prince would agree to such an arrangement."

Hermione stopped walking and turned to him. She waited for a family to pass, and then she lowered her voice. "Which part would that be—the part where the prince is your step cousin? Or the part where your mother married a former king?"

He didn't recall his mouth opening but it must have happened, because a little bit later when his mind came out if its stupor, he pressed his lips together. This couldn't be right. Thea had married royalty? No. Really? None of this was making sense to him.

Hermione continued walking. "Your stepfather, Georgios, had already abdicated the throne by the time he'd met your mother. In fact, they met right here on this island. She was a maid and he was a lonely, sad man, who missed his family as they'd disowned him. In that way, Georgios and your mother felt as though they had something in common—"

"I didn't disown my mother. If that's what she told you, it was a lie." His words were quick and sharp.

"No. I'm sorry. That isn't what I meant. I shouldn't be telling you any of this. It isn't my story to tell."

He sighed in frustration. "It's me who should be sorry. I didn't mean to snap. This is just a lot to take in."

Sympathy reflected in her eyes. "I can't even imagine what you're going through. When my mother died, our circumstances were different. We were very close. I'd been able to say goodbye."

"I'm sorry for your loss."

She resumed walking. "Thank you. It was quite a while ago. Although there are times when something happens and she's the first one I want to tell. And then the loss comes washing back over me. We were as close as a teenager can be to their mother."

"I didn't know my mother when I was a teenager. She took off when I was five. And my father and I were anything but close." It wasn't until he'd spoken the words that he realized he'd never admitted any of this before. But there was just something about Hermione that made it easy for him to open up. Perhaps too easy.

It was best to focus on business. He didn't want to dredge up any more memories of himself at five years old, crying into his pillow for his mother—a mother that would never come back for him—at least not for many years.

He cleared his throat, hoping when he spoke his voice didn't betray the raw emotions raging within him. "Having the jewels here, it's quite a liability for the resort to take on, perhaps too much. What if something were to happen to these royal jewels? It'd put the resort in quite a difficult position."

She stopped walking and turned to him. "It's what your mother wanted."

He opened his mouth and then closed it. He had a sinking feeling this wasn't the first or the last time Thea's memory or wishes would be an issue. "But she's not here now and I am."

Hermione's eyes narrowed. "What are you saying?"

He wasn't going to delve back into the subject of his relationship with Thea. The fact was this island and the resort were now his responsibility. And until it was sold, he had to do what he thought was best for the business.

He met her gaze straight on. "I'm saying that I'm not

comfortable with this arrangement with a prince I've never heard of."

"And yet you're the one that didn't want to get too involved with the resort or its employees, remember?" Her eyes glinted with agitation. "This resort is my responsibility—at least until the resort is sold."

He didn't want to make an enemy of her. He'd already heard the employees sing her praises. They would go to battle for her. And all of that would hamper any hope of a sale.

He needed to divert this conversation. "We should get moving. They'll be waiting for you."

She gave him an intense stare. "I know you have your reasons not to like this place, but I love it and its people. You would too if you let down your guard. Regardless, I will fight to maintain our ways."

"Change is inevitable, whether it's coming from me or someone else. Now let's not be late."

She was nothing if not observant. He'd prefer if she didn't read so much in him. It made him feel exposed and vulnerable. It was a position he wasn't used to being in. And one he hoped not to be in again.

CHAPTER SIX

SHE DIDN'T THINK she could do it.

There weren't many things that defeated her, but Atlas's stubborn disposition about retaining ownership of the resort might be one of those things.

Hermione grew quiet as they approached the large glass doors of the Ludus Gallery. She was still processing the fact that the rift between Atlas and his mother went so much deeper than she'd ever imagined. While her heart went out to him, she still had an obligation to her employees. No matter what, she couldn't give up on changing his mind about keeping the resort.

Perhaps he needed to remember the good parts of his relationship with Thea. Were there good parts? She thought of Thea—kind, generous and caring Thea—yes, there had to be good parts. Maybe he'd forgotten them. Maybe he didn't want to remember them. But Hermione knew that until her dying day, Thea had loved her son.

Something awful had gone wrong. Hermione couldn't fathom what it might have been. Atlas might try and tell himself that it didn't matter after all of this time, but it did matter to him. If it didn't matter, he wouldn't be here.

She wanted to help him find some peace. She told herself that she would be doing it in memory of her dear friend, who had given her a hand up when she'd needed it most. It was her chance to pay back Thea's kindness.

She stopped next to the thick frosted glass doors before she reached for the oversize brass handle. Atlas grasped it. He opened the door for her. She thanked him as she stepped inside the gallery.

"This part is currently open to the resort guests," she explained. "But if you'll follow me to the back area, it's where we're preparing for the Valentine's Day reveal."

There were a few people here and there, admiring the latest watercolor acquisitions. Hermione glanced over at the six-piece collection of seascapes. Though they were all of the same scene, each displayed a different time of day, from a morning scene to an evening sunset. Each was so detailed that she could stand there for an hour or two and still not catch all of the minute details.

"Do you do these special exhibitions on a regular basis?" Atlas's voice drew her from her thoughts.

"While the resort owns the pieces on display out here, the ones in back are the ones on loan from other museums or countries." She stopped and turned to him, hiding her excitement that he was finally showing some interest in the resort. "We try to always have something special either on display in the back room or in the planning stage."

She used a key to open the door to the sealed-off section. She held the door for Atlas. He was intently inspecting the door, which she found surprising when there was so much else to see back here.

"Is everything all right?" she asked.

"I was just surprised that there isn't higher security for this section."

"We haven't had any problems with it so far."

"That's what everyone says before they're robbed."

She frowned at him. In a low voice she asked, "Are you saying we're going to be robbed?"

"No. I was just thinking that your security needs to be upgraded."

She glanced around, hoping they weren't overheard. "Perhaps you should think about those matters a little quieter."

"We can discuss my ideas for the new system later."

She didn't speak for a moment, not trusting what would come out of her mouth. "I don't think that's necessary. This system was just installed last year."

"And as you pointed out, this is now my resort."

She wondered when he would play that card. "The jewels are this way. I can't wait to see the Ruby Heart. I've seen pictures, but that is never the same as seeing it in person."

She didn't think of herself as the jewelry type. There was only one piece of jewelry that she cared about—her mother's locket. But it was lost to her forever. Still, there was just something exciting about viewing jewels that have been worn by queens and princesses.

An armed guard stood in front of the room where the Ruby Heart was to be displayed. He nodded at them.

"Is it in the display case yet?" she asked.

"They're waiting for you before they unpack it."

"Understood." She started past him.

The guard stepped in front of Atlas, impeding his entrance. "You can't go in there. Only approved employees."

"I'm with Hermione."

"There are no exceptions."

"Are you serious?" Atlas's voice grew deep with agitation.

"Absolutely."

"It's okay," Hermione said. "He owns the resort."

"It doesn't matter if he's the president. If he hasn't had a full background check and been added to my list, he can't go inside."

Her gaze moved to Atlas. "I'm sorry. We can get this straightened out later. The security firm doesn't work for the resort."

"It's okay. Do what you need to do. I'll be fine here."

She wasn't so sure he would be fine. He looked more like a caged animal as he started to pace. But people were waiting for her, so she moved into the secure room. While the rest of the gallery had white walls to make it feel airy and spacious, this section was done with black walls and ceiling.

Spotlights were used to highlight the specific items on display. Nothing was to distract from the features of the show. And it worked. It drew people's gazes where they needed to go. But the spotlights hadn't been set up yet as the star of the show had just now arrived.

A couple of royal guards stood with the locked box. She knew the procedure. She had to produce two forms of identification and have her fingerprints scanned. Then she signed the digital receipt. Once all of that was complete, one of the guards entered the security code that released the digital lock.

The Ruby Heart was revealed in all of its sparkling grandeur, and Hermione was left speechless. She didn't know a gem could look that impressive. She felt bad that Atlas wasn't able to see it. But if he stayed until Valentine's Day, he could see it once it was secure in its display case.

"Did I miss anything?" Atlas's voice came from behind her.

Hermione spun around. "What are you doing back here? How did you get past the guard?"

He held up his phone. "Remember, I own a security company. I have connections around the world. I called up the owner of this security firm, and I was immediately added to the list."

"You were?" She blinked. "But it normally takes weeks for the background checks."

"I have top security clearance in a number of places, including Greece. I have to for my work." He moved closer and stared at the gem. "So this is the beauty that's causing all of the problems?"

"Isn't it beautiful?" She was still in awe over it.

"It's not bad."

"Not bad? Are you serious? It's one of the biggest rubies in the world."

"I'm just giving you a hard time. I think it is quite impressive."

"And look, there's a brass plaque with it." She moved closer to read it aloud. "'The legend of the Ruby Heart. If destined lovers gaze upon the Ruby Heart at the same time, their lives will be forever entwined.'"

Heat warmed her cheeks. She suddenly regretted reading the legend. Not that they were lovers—far from it.

"Whatever works," he said.

"What does that mean?"

"It's clearly a gimmick. A lure to draw in an audience." His gaze moved to her. "Surely you don't believe it, do you?"

Did she believe the legend? Of course not. Did she want to believe it? Maybe. Was it so wrong to believe in eternal love?

"No." She wasn't about to tell him how she truly felt. After signing for the other royal jewels, she turned to Atlas. "We should get moving and let these men take care of things."

"Now that I know there are priceless gems on the

grounds, I'm definitely having my people upgrade the security. You can never be too safe."

"That won't be necessary."

"Sure, it is."

She pressed her hands to her hips. "Are you saying the current security isn't good enough?"

"I'm saying it could be better."

What she heard was that the security system that she'd painstakingly researched and ultimately chosen wasn't any good. Was he right? Had she made a costly mistake?

She stopped herself. He was doing the same thing to her that Otis used to do—make her doubt herself. The current security was more than sufficient.

She opened her mouth to tell him that, but then she realized this might be a way for Atlas to invest himself in the resort. And though it took swallowing a bit of her pride, she chose to put the future of the Ludus first. "It sounds like you have a plan. Let me know what you'll need from me."

"I will." He grabbed his phone and started texting someone.

She could only imagine he was contacting his office. For a man anxious to keep his distance from this resort, he was getting more involved by the minute. But she resisted pointing this out to him. She didn't want to scare him off. In fact, she was looking forward to him staying around much longer.

This place could definitely use his expertise.

The next day, Atlas had gone over the resort's blueprints and made arrangements to fly in his best crew. A resort this size was going to take a lot of work, but it was doable. And then when the place was sold, it would be a selling point. In his book that was a win-win.

But he'd gotten so caught up in the security aspect of

the resort that he still hadn't toured the place. And the tour would let him scope out the best type of security for the different areas.

At least that's what he told himself when he went to track down Hermione and collect on the tour she still owed him.

He had just opened his suite door when he spotted her walking down the hallway. "Do you have a moment?"

"Sure." She followed him into the suite. "What do you need?"

"I believe you owe me a tour of the resort. After all, we wouldn't want me to lie to the employees, right?"

She opened her mouth as though to disagree with him, but then she wordlessly pressed her lips together. He noticed her pink shimmery lip gloss and her lush lips. They were so tempting. So very tempting. He wondered what it'd be like to kiss her. Would one kiss be enough? And then realizing where his thoughts had strayed, he raised his gaze.

He couldn't help but wonder if she knew what he was thinking. He hoped not because it wasn't like him to let pleasure get in the way of business. And right now, this was his most important business. Because the sooner he wrapped things up here, the sooner he could leave the past in the past.

"I don't have a lot of time. Where do you want to start?" she asked.

"Wherever you choose will be fine."

She reached for her phone. "Let me update my assistant."

He knew showing him around was the last thing she wanted to do. But then again, she'd been the one to get them into this situation. He checked his phone while he waited for her. Just then a message popped up from Krystof.

We need to talk.

Agreed. If you don't want the island I need to find another buyer ASAP.

Commence your search for another buyer.

That wasn't the news he wanted to hear. A sale to Krystof would be fast and painless. But trying to line up another buyer wouldn't be so simple.

You still planning to visit?

I'm not sure.

A frown pulled at Atlas's mouth as he slipped the phone back in his pocket. He moved to the floor-to-ceiling windows. Now that the rain had moved on, he noticed the lush green foliage. So this was after all a beautiful sunny Mediterranean island. Buyers would fight to own it. Wouldn't they? There might even be a bidding war. Or was he being overly optimistic?

"Sorry about that." Hermione slipped her phone back in her purse. "Shall we go?"

They entered the spacious hallway with plush red carpeting that silenced people's footsteps. Hermione led the way. She hadn't stated their destination and he hadn't thought to ask. All the while, he was taking in his surroundings from the expensive and notable artwork on the walls to the crystal chandeliers.

"Are all of the rooms normally booked?" He hated the fact that he knew so very little about this property. He had a lot to learn and quickly.

"Yes. The reservations fill in well in advance."

"Really?" His voice came out quite loudly in the quiet hallway.

"This is an exclusive resort that offers privacy and pampering. Our clients return regularly."

"It can't be that great."

Hermione arched a fine brow. "You'll soon see."

A couple of employees passed by them. They smiled and silently nodded in greeting. This appeared to be the time of the day when the resort was abuzz with employee activity as suites were cleaned.

An older woman pushed her cleaning supply cart toward them with a big, friendly smile on her face. When she reached them, she paused. "Hermione, I'm so sorry I missed the luncheon. We're shorthanded this week so I picked up a few extra rooms. You know, if everyone pitches in it makes it easier for everyone."

"Thank you, Irene," Hermione said. "Your efforts are greatly appreciated."

Irene turned her attention to Atlas. The smile slipped from her face as she stared at him. He wanted to ask what she was doing, but he already knew—she was looking to see if he had any resemblance to his mother. He didn't.

"You must be Thea's son." As his back teeth ground together, she continued, "We're happy to have you here. My condolences on the unexpected passing of your mother. She was the kindest woman. You were lucky to have her for a mother. I always thought she died from a broken heart. I just wanted to say how sorry I am for your loss. I'll let you two get on with things. I have another room to clean."

The woman's well-meaning words tore at his scarred heart. The Thea these people knew was not the same person he had known. He knew he should thank the lady, but the words bunched up in the back of his throat.

As they continued walking, Hermione asked, "Are you okay?"

He nodded. No, he wasn't, but he refused to let on to Hermione.

He swallowed the lump in his throat. "The people are friendly here."

"Yes, they are. It's a really great place to visit and work."

"If the resort is so great, why haven't I heard of it?"

"We have no need for the media…" Her voice trailed off as though she were lost in thought. "We have a mailing list that goes out regularly to our select clientele. And from there our guests use word of mouth to spread the news to other visitors."

It was inconceivable to him that in this day and age a resort could be amazing enough to generate sufficient business by guests returning regularly and recommending it to their family and friends. After all, it was just a giant hotel. Right?

Okay, so maybe the suites were on the lavish side, but there was no way they could do that for the rest of the resort. After all, there had to be limitations. No place was that incredible. He didn't believe it.

He glanced at Hermione as they walked through the resort. "How long have you worked here?"

"Since I was eighteen. In some ways, I feel as though I grew up here."

He noticed that she didn't feel the need to elaborate. He wondered in what ways, but he didn't ask. If she were to confide in him, she would expect him to do the same in return. And he'd already said more than he'd intended.

Atlas rubbed the back of his neck as memories of his youth came rushing back to him. They hadn't had much money growing up. Whatever they had his father spent on expanding his auto business.

Atlas hadn't always enjoyed his current state of creature comforts, including a small fleet of unique sports cars. He knew what it was like to do without. His father had withheld money as a way of controlling him. It was only when Atlas had finished university and went into business for himself that he became wealthy. But it never stopped him from getting his hands dirty if the need arose.

If he were to keep the island, he would change things. He would make the island less exclusive and open to everyone. It wouldn't be as lavish as it was now, but it would still be a fun destination. But it wasn't like he was entertaining thoughts of keeping the island. No way. He wanted the sale to go through as quickly as possible.

"Are you staying for the Valentine's party next weekend?"

"I don't think so." The idea most definitely didn't appeal to him. He didn't do hearts, flowers and romance. "Even if I am still here, I won't be attending."

"You won't want to miss it. The party will be spectacular."

"I'll be too busy." He averted his gaze.

He hadn't planned to share any of this with Hermione, but he was quickly finding it was very easy to talk to her. He'd have to be cautious around her or he'd be opening up about all of his secrets. And he didn't want to do that.

CHAPTER SEVEN

SHE WAS DOING FINE...

If fine included the imminent possibility of losing her job.

But it was the resort employees that Hermione worried about the most. Some of them had worked at the Ludus longer than she'd been alive—talk about devotion to their occupation.

She knew what it was to get bounced around in life and having to reinvent herself time after time. Even though she'd grown quite comfortable working here, she could re-invent herself again as a hotel manager or something else, but she didn't want to do it.

She chanced a glance at the heir to the Ludus Resort. As her gaze touched upon his handsome face, her heart raced. He was busy taking in his surroundings, giving her a chance to study him. He wasn't smiling. There was a firm set to his jaw. What was he thinking? Was he calculating the resort's monetary value?

It was as though the happiness had been sucked out of Atlas. She felt bad for him, which most people would find odd since he was the one who was about to upend her life. What had happened to him?

Buzz-buzz.

She lifted her phone to find an urgent message from

Nestor, the resort's event coordinator. It was regarding the special effects for the Valentine's party. "I'm afraid the tour will have to wait. There are some urgent disbursements that require my signature."

"Perhaps I could come with you." His gaze met hers, sending her heart rate into triple digits.

She wanted to tell him no. She needed some space so her pulse could slow to a steady pace. But when she opened her mouth, she said, "It won't take long."

"Even better."

She messaged Nestor that she'd meet him at her office. And so they set off for the administrative suite. Hers was the largest office, as well as having the prime spot in the corner. When she passed by her PA's desk with Atlas hot on her heels, Rhea arched her dark brows as unspoken questions reflected in her eyes.

Hermione paused and made introductions.

Rhea was her usual sweet and charming self. And to Hermione's surprise Atlas soaked up Rhea's pleasantries and returned them. It was though he'd transformed into another person on the way here. Because if that wasn't the case, it meant he didn't enjoy her company. The last thought nagged at her.

After a minute or two, Hermione moved into her office. She wasn't sure if Atlas was going to follow her or stay in the outer office chatting with Rhea. But then he joined her and closed the door behind him. He made himself comfortable on a chair facing her desk while she took a seat behind the desk. As she logged onto the computer system, she found herself glancing over the top of her monitor and noticing that he'd retrieved his phone and appeared to be scrolling through messages.

She got to work, but she kept finding her attention drawn

to Atlas. When he'd glance up and catch her staring, heat would flood her cheeks.

Knock-knock.

"Come in." Hermione pressed Send on an email.

Nestor stepped into the office. His tan face lit up with a warm smile. She noticed how he was starting to take on some gray at his temples even though he was in his early forties with a young family.

She introduced Atlas and the men shook hands.

"How's the party coming?" she asked.

Nestor's face lit up. "It's on track to be our biggest and best. I think the guests will be impressed."

That was the kind of news she liked to hear. "What would we do without you?"

He continued to smile. "Hopefully you'll never have to find out."

Hermione resisted giving Atlas a sideways glance. "Do you have the disbursements and backup?"

He nodded and handed them over.

These were sizable payments. She tied in each number, initialed where required and then signed the bottom of the requisition.

After Nestor left, she continued to work. A half hour later Hermione was finally done. She pushed her chair back and stood. "I'm all set to go."

Atlas glanced up from staring at his phone with a confused look on his face as though he'd been totally lost in his thoughts and had no idea what she was talking about. "Sorry. What?"

"I didn't mean to interrupt you." She wondered what had him so preoccupied.

"No problem." He got to his feet and opened the door to the outer office.

"Do you still want to tour the resort?"

His dark brows furrowed together. "Why wouldn't I?"

"It just seems like you have something else on your mind."

"My mind is on seeing the resort. I have a promise to keep."

She had a feeling there was something he wasn't telling her. Well, she knew there was a lot he wasn't telling her, seeing how they were virtually strangers. A niggle of worry ate at her.

Thea had once encouraged Hermione to follow her dreams wherever they would lead her. In fact, she'd pushed for Hermione to finish her higher education and even paid for it. She owed Thea a huge debt of gratitude.

Thea had been so nice. She would speak with all of the staff just like they were family. She'd inquire about the staff's children, grandchildren and pets. Thea was very down-to-earth, so much like her husband.

But Atlas was nothing like his mother. Where Thea was open and welcoming, Atlas was closed off and distant. Where Thea had a fair complexion and was short in stature, Atlas was dark and tall. The only glimmer of Thea that she could spot in Atlas were his eyes. He had his mother's sky-blue eyes.

"Where are we going?" His voice drew her back to the present.

"I thought we would start with a visit to the spa."

"The spa? Do I look like the spa type?"

"Honestly, I don't know what type you are as I just met you last night, but you wanted to see the resort and the spa is a huge part of the resort. It's near the lobby."

"That seems like an odd place for a spa."

"Why? It's not like people wonder around in their robes. Trust me, the spa is a world unto its own." She walked a little farther in silence and then came to a stop in front of two large wooden doors with oversize brass handles. "Here we are."

He remained quiet as they stepped inside. The young woman behind the desk practically drooled at the sight of Atlas. The woman's obvious infatuation with him aggravated Hermione. She told herself it was the woman's obvious lack of professionalism that bothered her and nothing else. She would have a discreet word with the woman's supervisor later.

After Hermione had stated the purpose of their visit, the young woman said, "I'll send someone out to give you a tour."

Once the woman walked away, Atlas turned to Hermione. "I thought that's what you were going to do."

She shook her head. "I can't."

"Why not?" His tone carried a note of displeasure.

"Because I... I'm not that familiar with the spa." The surprise that flashed in his eyes made her feel embarrassed.

Did he think she wasn't good at her job because she didn't know the intimate routine of the spa? Because she was very good at her job. She had department heads and supervisors that saw to the little details. And when there was a problem they couldn't resolve, she stepped in.

Suddenly she felt as though she didn't measure up in Atlas's eyes, and that bothered her. She'd worked very hard in her life to get this far. She was proud of how she'd gone from having nothing after her mother died to being able to put a roof over her head and now she was in charge of one of the world's most glamorous resorts. But she supposed none of that would impress Atlas. Wait. Did she want to impress him?

Part of her screamed out that yes, she did. But she quickly silenced that little voice. She didn't need his approval or any other thing, except her job.

"But you work here," he said.

"As the general manager." Why was he making a big deal of this? She lowered her voice. "Staff doesn't make use of the spa. It's reserved for guests only."

He frowned at her response. "That's a silly rule."

At that moment, a young woman in bright aqua scrubs approached them. "Mr. Othonos?"

"Yes." Atlas turned to the woman.

"We're ready for you."

"Good. Right now, we—" he gestured to himself and Hermione "—are going to have massages."

"I can wait here," Hermione said softly.

"Nonsense. You are my guest. I insist."

"You mean you won't get a massage unless I do?" She'd never faced such a predicament.

A smile spread across his handsome face. "That's exactly what I mean."

Adara's words echoed in her mind about making him comfortable here. But a spa treatment? Really? And during work hours? This was totally unheard-of.

"If it makes you feel better, as owner of the resort, I'm giving you the afternoon off and free access to the spa." His gaze dared her to challenge him.

It didn't make her feel better. She hated how he picked when he wanted to play the owner card. If he wanted to be involved in the resort's policies and management, he needed to fully commit himself. Otherwise, he needed to leave things to her.

Both Atlas and the attendant looked at her expectantly. She knew to back out now would cause even more tension with Atlas. Maybe it was best to indulge him this once.

"Fine. But I don't have long."

He sent her a satisfied grin. He seemed to like challenges

and especially winning them. She tucked that bit of information away. She might need it in the future.

And so they took a tour of the sprawling two-story spa followed by chocolate massages. Hermione opted for a hand massage with a mani-pedi with *Kiss Me Pink* polish. Atlas agreed to a full-body massage. She could only hope it left him in a much better disposition.

Things needed to change.

Atlas didn't like the resort's atmosphere of haves and the have-nots. It reminded him too much of his childhood. His father had it all, and he had to beg for what little he got.

His father was big about the haves and have-nots. His father, being a small business owner, believed he was part of the "haves." He'd preached to Atlas that if he wanted to be someone in this world, he had to be rich like him—rich being a relative term. Back then his father made Atlas beg for new clothes or shoes when the old ones no longer fit.

These days Atlas tried not to waste his time thinking about his father—a father who said Atlas would never amount to anything just like his worthless mother. Atlas wondered what his father would think if he knew how much Atlas was worth now. He could buy his father's auto dealership many times over. And the fact that his mother had gone on to own and run this impressive resort would really get to his father.

But money hadn't changed Atlas. He hadn't become rich because of his father; he'd become successful in spite of his father. All he'd ever wanted to do was help people. And that's how he'd gotten started in the security business. He wanted to give people a sense of security—something he never had growing up. A state-of-the-art security system wasn't quite the same as the safety of a loving family, but it was as close as he could get.

And then he reminded himself that it wasn't his job to approve or disapprove of things at the resort. That particular responsibility would belong to the new owner. He just didn't know who that would be at this point.

He hadn't given up hope on changing Krystof's mind. But this was too important not to seek out other potential buyers.

As they passed by a poster advertising the grand Valentine's Day Ball, Atlas started to get an idea. He pulled out his phone and texted his real estate agent.

I want to invite potential buyers to a party at the Ludus Resort.

People like parties. When?

Valentine's Day. But there's a problem.

What sort of problem?

The resort is booked solid. Guests would have to stay on the mainland.

Not good. Let me think about it. Talk soon.

He slipped his phone back into his pocket. He was pretty proud of himself for coming up with a potential way for buyers to see the resort at its finest and with the royal jewels on display.

But his next thought was that if they worked out the logistics, he'd be obligated to attend the Valentine's ball. It was the sort of scene he worked hard to avoid. But if he focused on business, perhaps it wouldn't be so bad.

His gaze moved to Hermione. She would be at the ball. Suddenly he imagined her in a glittering dress with her long hair down around her slender shoulders. He imagined taking her in his arms and holding her close. The image was so tempting. Maybe a main course of business with a side of pleasure wouldn't be so bad after all. He didn't allow himself to think of what dessert might be.

"What did you think?" Hermione's voice drew him from his thoughts.

Having lost track of their conversation, he asked, "Think about what?"

Hermione's brows scrunched together. "The spa."

"Oh. It was nice."

"If you would like, I can arrange for you to spend more time there."

He shook his head. "I'm afraid the rest of the tour will have to wait for another time. It's getting late, and I have some urgent calls to return."

"I understand. I, too, have work awaiting me. I'll see you tomorrow."

"Yes."

And then she was gone. Suddenly he felt very alone. It was as though she were all bright and sunny and now with her gone, a long, dark shadow had fallen over him.

Which was utterly ridiculous because he was used to being on his own. It'd been that way since he was a child. He didn't need someone in his life—someone to share his time. His business was all he needed.

He used to be able to sell that line to himself, but lately it wasn't ringing as true. For a second, he thought of going after Hermione and asking her to have an early dinner with him.

Buzz-buzz.

He glanced at his phone. It was a call from the embassy where he'd sent his men to resolve a problem with their system. With a sigh, he took the call and started walking in the opposite direction from Hermione.

CHAPTER EIGHT

HE WAS GETTING DISTRACTED.

And that wasn't good.

Thursday morning, Atlas had set up his temporary office in his suite. The problem at the embassy was more elusive than originally imagined. He'd done his best to help troubleshoot from afar. It was very frustrating not to be there.

That's why his very next phone call had been to his real estate agent. The sooner the resort was sold, the sooner he could get back to his life.

"So far there hasn't been a lot of interest in the island, but it's still early in the search," the agent said. "The lack of publicity has buyers hesitant."

"But the place is booked solid."

"That's definitely a selling point, but when it comes down to your island resort, well, it's remote and doesn't have a reputation with world travelers. The big hotel chains are going to go with a known location over something that isn't easy to reach. And I have to be honest with you. A lot of the properties are changing hands right now, so your resort is going to have competition."

He raked his fingers through his hair. "So what you're saying is that you can't sell the resort?"

"No. What I'm saying is that we need to build a portfolio, starting with the resort's history. I did an internet search but couldn't find much. Do you know the history?"

"Uh, some of it." He thought about his mother's marriage to a former king. But he wasn't ready to share that information. "I'll find out more."

"Good. And I'll arrange for one of our best photographers to come out and take photos. The images will be used for prospective buyers as well as growing a social media presence. Does this place even have a website?"

He hesitated. She wasn't going to like his answer. "No."

She clucked her tongue. "That's not good. I'll hire a designer and be in touch."

"When will the photographer arrive?" He didn't want to drag out his stay.

"I'd have to check on his schedule, but I'd say in a week or two—"

"Two weeks?" He once again raked his fingers through his hair as he stood and started to pace.

"I could try and find someone with an earlier opening on their calendar, but I couldn't vouch for their talent."

They couldn't be that bad, right? "Good. Do that."

He promised to forward her the required information. After he disconnected the call, he couldn't concentrate on business matters. He was frustrated that getting rid of his mother's island and resort was proving to be so difficult.

He needed to see Hermione. Maybe the resort had a professional photographer who could speed things up. At least that was the excuse he told himself when he went in search of her.

When he arrived at her office, her PA informed him that Hermione was dealing with a problem in the resort's gallery. He didn't have to request directions; he recalled how to get there.

He made his way across the resort. When he found

Hermione, she was in the back of the gallery signing paperwork.

"Another delivery?" he asked.

Her gaze lifted to meet his. "As a matter of fact, yes." She gestured to the large canvas behind her. "It's called *Clash of Hearts*."

He gazed at the artwork with its hot pink and silver hearts entangled together. The conjoined hearts were repeated in varying sizes all over the canvas. "It's different."

She smiled. "You're not a modern-art fan?"

He shrugged. "Art is okay."

"So it's the hearts you have a problem with?"

This was not a subject he wanted to delve into. He cleared his throat. "I need your assistance."

"I'm sorry. I really don't have time. We're a bit short-handed right now."

"Is that why you're here signing for a painting?"

"Yes. The woman who oversees the gallery went out on maternity leave." Hermione pulled out her phone. "I'll message Adara. She can help you with whatever you need."

"No. It has to be you."

She drew in a deep breath as though subduing her frustration. "Why me?"

"Because you knew my mother."

Her brows drew together. "Yes, I did. We were good friends." She hesitated. "What do you need help with?"

"A couple of things. First, does the resort have a professional photographer on retainer?"

She shook her head. "We've never needed or wanted one."

Of course they didn't. That would have made things easier for him.

The silence dragged on before he spoke again. This was

something he'd given a lot of thought. "I want to know if you'd assist me on going through Thea's things."

"Oh." She was quiet as she absorbed this information.

"I need the help and with you being her friend, I thought you might know what she'd want done with her things." Not giving her a chance to back out, he said, "What can I do to convince you to help me? Name your price." That was how badly he didn't want to face his mother's things alone.

This was his fourth day on the island, and he hadn't even stepped foot in Thea's apartment much less started sorting her items. He knew if he didn't get help that he'd keep making excuses to avoid it.

He could see the wheels in Hermione's mind turning. She was going to turn him down, and he couldn't really blame her. This wasn't her mess to clean up. And she'd already taken time out of her busy schedule to make sure he enjoyed his stay.

"If I help—" her voice drew his full attention "—will you make sure the resort's staff is retained by the new owner for at least six months?"

And there she went again, impressing him with her generosity. Most people would have asked for something for themselves, but Hermione thought of others instead of herself.

"Done." He was unable to deny such a selfless request, even though it would hamper any sale negotiations.

"And the employees won't lose the seniority and benefits they've so rightly earned." Her voice was firm.

"Done and done. Anything else?"

She shook her head. "If you help them out, I will help you, but it will have to be in the evenings. I still have a day job."

He held his hand out to her. "It's a deal."

She looked at his hand before her gaze rose to meet

his. And then she placed her hand in his and gave it a firm
shake. For an instant, he considered tightening his grip
and drawing her to him. He had this growing urge to kiss
her—to feel her lush lips pressed to his. He wondered how
she'd react.

As he continued to stare into her eyes, he felt his heart
pound. What was it about this woman that had such an effect over him?

And then he realized he was making too much of things.
After all, he was already out of sorts with being here on
his mother's island with the dread of having to go through
her personal items hanging over him. As well as learning
how happy she'd been here—without him.

It was a lot to deal with at once. It was no wonder his
mind was so quick to find a diversion. And that's what
this infatuation with Hermione was—a break from reality. He withdrew his hand, already missing the softness
of her touch.

His mouth grew dry. He swallowed hard. "Why don't
we continue the tour of the resort?"

She frowned at him. "Right now?"

"Is there a problem?"

She hesitated as though she were thinking up an excuse
to get out of it. "No. Of course not. Let's go."

And off they went on a walking tour of the resort, from
the play area for the children and those who were young at
heart with their ballroom and art room to the casino, which
looked as though it belonged in Monte Carlo with its gold,
flashy slot machines and table games to the gold-trimmed
ornate ceiling and enormous crystal chandeliers. The staff
was all dressed up in pressed white dress shirts, wine-col-
ored vests, gold neckties and black pants.

Atlas started to get an idea. "Would there happen to be
a high rollers room?"

Hermione arched a brow. "You like to play cards?"

"No. I'm not asking for myself."

She led him outside the casino. They walked a little way and then turned a corner. There stood one of the largest bouncers he'd ever seen. The man was taller than Atlas as well as wider.

Hermione stopped at the end of the hallway. "The private room is there. I believe there's a poker game in progress. You'll need to wait until it ends to go in."

"That won't be necessary." This might be just what he needed to lure Krystof to the island. "What's the buy-in?"

"It's high."

"How high?"

"A hundred."

"Thousand?" When she nodded, he said, "Interesting."

"Would you like a seat at the table?"

"No. I don't gamble on games of chance, but I do know someone who would be very interested."

They continued walking until they came to the indoor pool area that had not one or two but four long slides with skylights overhead. The area was filled with smiling people and rambunctious children. He had to admit that the resort did a fine job of offering entertainment for most everyone.

Next to the pool area was a food court with cuisine from around the world. They decided to have a late lunch there. Hermione opted for fish tacos while he chose a gyro with lettuce and tomato topped with *tzatziki* sauce and a side of *sfougata* cheese balls.

"What do you think of the resort?" Hermione asked after finishing her two tacos.

"I think it's like a small city with a lot to offer the guests."

"And you haven't even seen the outside."

"I still can't believe Thea owned all of this." There was

a part of him that wanted to know more about her. "Was she happy here?"

"Very much so. She loved her husband dearly, and this island was her whole world."

He shouldn't have asked. He didn't want to hear about Thea's perfect life—a life that didn't include him. What was it about him that made her reject him? Was he that unlovable?

"I don't understand why Thea left this place to me." He was still asking himself why she'd done it.

"I'm not. She never stopped loving you."

He wanted to believe Hermione, but his mother's actions or rather her lack of action where he was concerned told him all he needed to know about his mother's feelings toward him. There was something inherently wrong with him that his own mother rejected him.

"My mother and I had a lot of unresolved issues."

"Is that why it took you so long to come to the island?"

"I was away in the States when I was notified of Thea's passing." As he said the words there was a twinge of pain, but he refused to acknowledge it. "I should have dropped what I was doing to deal with the solicitors but..."

"But what?"

He was about to brush off her inquiry when his gaze met hers and he saw the genuine concern reflected in her eyes. "But my mother and I hadn't been close since I was a little kid. I... I didn't, well, I didn't realize what all was involved with her will."

"You didn't know that she owned an island much less a hugely profitable resort?"

"I had absolutely no idea about any of this. When I knew her, my mother didn't have much—certainly not when she walked away from my father." Atlas rested his elbows on the table and gazed at Hermione. "But you knew someone different."

She smiled, but it didn't quite reach her eyes. She missed his mother; that much was obvious. "We all knew and liked her. Thea was very involved in the resort."

His back teeth ground together. Thea had been very involved with what mattered to her—the resort—not him. He'd already been dismissed by not just his mother but his father as well. His father was all about his auto business and stroking his own ego. If you didn't look up to his father and regard him highly, he didn't have time for you—even if you were his own flesh and blood.

Atlas preferred to be on his own because then no one could hurt him. It also gave him the ability to come and go as he pleased, never staying in one place for too long. Never getting too attached to anything or anyone.

"Atlas, what is it?" The concerned tone of Hermione's voice drew him from his thoughts.

He shook his head. "Nothing."

"You know you can talk to me. I'm an okay listener."

He couldn't help but smile. "Just okay?"

She smiled and shrugged. "A great listener sounds like bragging, and if I said I was a terrible listener you wouldn't say a word. So I went with the middle of the road description."

He laughed at her explanation. Hermione was exactly what he needed right now. She was like a ray of sunshine on a cloudy day. And what they were about to do was going to be so hard. Thankfully Hermione would be there to hopefully take the edge off the painful task.

Hermione nodded. "What would you like to see next? I can take you to our indoor golf driving range or our tennis courts."

He shook his head. "As tempting as that sounds, I have something else in mind."

"What would that be?"

"I... I'd like to see my mother's apartment."

"Certainly. Let's go."

Hermione quietly led the way from the food court. All the while he took in the decor of the building. A lot of it was old, but it was all elegant and well cared for. It was like being in an older home that had been loved and preserved through the years.

Atlas couldn't help but think that there was still room for updates. He was certain the buyer would want to do a total remodel to bring the place up-to-date with the rest of their global properties. Of course that would mean the resort would lose some of its unique charm, but there were always trade-offs to keep things modern. It's what he told clients when his team had to make adjustments to properties for their security equipment.

Speaking of security equipment, not only the gallery but the entire resort could use a complete overhaul. He was a bit surprised they hadn't hired his company in the first place. They were the best in the business. Or did his mother purposely not hire him? It was another prick to his heart.

After stopping by her office to pick up the key card to Thea's apartment, Hermione led them to the back of the resort. She stopped next to two steel doors with a sign that read: Authorized Personnel Only. She inserted a master key card in a reader. The lock on the double doors clicked as they released.

"I thought we were going to my mother's apartment," he said in confusion.

She held the door open for him. "This is the way to the private entrance."

Interesting. They entered a service hallway. So this

was the inner workings of the resort. Signs in the hallways clearly marked each entrance to the massive kitchens, to the laundry and to the janitorial services.

"Do you want to go to the apartment alone?" she asked.

Atlas didn't speak, not that he was being rude but rather his vocal cords were frozen. Instead, he shook his head. The last thing he wanted right now was to be alone.

His body filled with dread. The closer they got, the faster his heart pounded. If he was smart, he'd turn around and request that everything in the apartment be disposed of. But he knew it wouldn't be that easy. There would be legal papers and whatnot in the apartment that he, as the heir to his mother's estate, would need to sort out.

At the end of the lengthy hallway was a private elevator. This time he slid the key card that Hermione had given him into the reader. The silver doors silently slid open.

"Are you sure you want to do this?" she asked.

"I have to." His voice was monotone as he refused to let Hermione see just how much this bothered him. He had gotten through worse—like when Thea left him alone with his neglectful father.

On wooden legs, Atlas stepped into the small elevator car. There were no buttons to press as it had only one stop, Thea's apartment. The seconds it took to ride to the third floor were silent as he prepared himself to deal with his mother's things.

The door slid open, and he stared out at the large foyer. It was all done up in white with a large painting of the colorful sunset reflected over the sea to add a splash of color to the room. She certainly did love art.

The glass door leading to the apartment was propped open as though it were always open to visitors. He wondered what his mother would say if she knew he was about to enter her private space.

"Atlas?" When he glanced at Hermione, she asked, "Are you going to step out of the elevator?"

He swallowed hard and then took a step forward. "I never thought I'd be doing this."

All he could surmise about Thea's motives was that since she didn't have any other children, he had become her heir by default. Still, another prick to his scarred heart.

"I'm sorry it's come as such a shock. I have some idea what you're going through."

"Because you lost your mother too?"

She nodded. "When I was seventeen. She had a brain aneurysm. One moment she was fine, the next her head hurt so bad she went to the hospital. I didn't know what was going on at first. Who thinks they'll die from a headache?"

He reached out and took her hand in his. His thumbs gently stroked the back of her hand. He didn't say anything. He didn't know what to say. He felt helpless.

"They…they, um, rushed her to surgery. I never prayed so hard in my life. But…but it had ruptured by the time they got in there. She hung on for a little bit but…"

Her words failed her. She held up a finger as she gathered herself. "When it came time to discuss when to turn off life support, I'd never felt so alone in my life."

Atlas drew her to him. Her cheek came to rest on his chest as his hand slowly and gently rubbed her back. Her arms wrapped around him as though he were an anchor to the present, who kept her from getting swept away in the painful memories of the past. He'd never been someone's anchor before. He liked the feeling of being needed—being able to comfort her in some small way.

She drew in an unsteady breath and then pulled away. "After she died, I lost everything."

For a moment, this wasn't about him. Hermione's loss

was so much greater than his. "I'm sorry. That must have been awful."

"It was. My mother was my best friend. I miss her all of the time. I'm sorry you didn't have that closeness with your mother."

He shook his head. "She walked away from me when I was very young."

"I bet she wishes she hadn't done it."

He shrugged. "She came back once years later, but the damage was done by then. I wanted nothing to do with her."

"She never gave up on you."

His gaze swung to her. "Why would you say that?"

"Because she left all of this to you."

He shrugged it off. "That's only because she didn't have any other children."

"Maybe. But I don't think that's the reason. I think she wanted you to have this place because it brought her such happiness." When he shook his head, refusing to accept what Hermione was saying, she continued. "If she didn't want you to have it, she could have donated it to a worthy cause."

That was true. Maybe Hermione had something there, but in order to accept Hermione's theory, it would mean he'd have to accept the fact that his mother still cared about him. And he wasn't ready to do that. He wasn't ready to forgive and forget.

"Let's see what we have to deal with." He stepped past her and entered the apartment.

The living room was huge. Size-wise it put his penthouse in London to shame. He stepped forward, finding a wall of windows that gave an unobstructed view of the beach. The view was priceless.

"It's beautiful, isn't it?" Hermione stepped up next to him.

"You've seen this view before?"

"I have. Your mother liked to host parties for the staff. She called us her family. After your stepfather died, she felt very alone up here. She spent more and more time working with the staff."

"She didn't have to be alone," he muttered under his breath. He refused to feel sorry for her. She'd made her choices—she'd walked away with barely a glance back.

"I think I see some rays of sunshine poking through the clouds," Hermione said. "We can go out on the deck."

She led him to the door that opened onto a partially covered deck. They quietly stared out at the sea for a couple of minutes. The sea breeze had warmed up a bit. It was like being on top of the world up here. But he wasn't here to vacation or enjoy the view. He was here to pack up his mother's belongings and dispose of them—just like she'd disposed of him.

"I better get to work." He held the door for Hermione.

Once back inside the living room with its white-and-aquamarine decor, he looked around, taking in all of the artwork from statues to wall hangings. He had no doubt the art in the apartment alone would be worth a fortune. This was going to be more involved than he'd originally thought. Did he auction it all off? Or donate it to the Ludus Gallery?

There were so many decisions to make. What would Thea want? Why hadn't she left detailed instructions? Why did he even care about what she'd want?

His head started to throb. He needed to think about something else—anything else. He turned to Hermione. "How did you come to work here?"

"Your stepfather was the one who hired me after my mother died. I was so happy to no longer be living on the streets that I was willing to do what was asked of me, and that was good enough for him. I started at the front desk and under your mother's guidance I worked my way up to the administrative offices. Then they offered to pay me to go back to school."

"It's impressive. Not everyone could have come through what you did and remained standing. The more I learn about you, the more you amaze me."

He stared into her eyes, seeing the pain those memories brought to her. And then he felt guilty for feeling sorry for himself. From the way he saw it, Hermione had it so much worse than him because she'd not only lost a mother who had loved her, but she'd been homeless. He couldn't imagine how horrific that must have been for her.

"I'm so sorry," he said.

"For what?"

"For acting like I had it rough because my mother rejected me."

Hermione's gaze narrowed in on him. "Don't do that."

"Do what?"

"Feel sorry for me. I'm fine." Her voice took on a hard edge. "I'm taking care of myself. And I haven't done too bad. I don't need you or anyone else feeling sorry for me. Got it?"

He didn't blame her for being defensive. It's probably what got her through those long, cold nights on the street. Sympathy welled up in him.

He held up his hands in surrender. "Got it."

"Now, what is your plan for this place?"

He told her how he wanted everything in the apartment inventoried. And then he would take the list and split it into trash, donations, and at Hermione's insistence there would be a keep category. He didn't want to fight with her so he went along with it, but he already knew there wouldn't be anything he was keeping.

And then they agreed to meet back at the apartment as five o'clock. He realized the sooner he finished his time on the island, the sooner he'd have to say goodbye to Hermione. The thought sat heavy in his chest.

CHAPTER NINE

IT HAD BEEN a rough evening.

At least it had been for Atlas.

In that moment, Hermione did what she'd just yelled at him for—she'd felt sorry for him. But it was different. Really it was.

Going through a parent's belongings no matter how good or bad the relation, it was never easy. It was like an emotional jack-in-the-box. And you just never knew when you opened something what emotions were going to be attached to that particular item.

He'd started working in one of the guest rooms while she set to work in the living room. She'd had the forethought to have Rhea track down some colored stickers to mark items after they were inventoried on their computers. They worked nonstop for a few hours.

When they decided to call it quits for the night, she decided to take him to a late dinner at the Under the Sea restaurant. But when she found it was booked solid, she did something she rarely did—she exerted her executive privilege. Minutes later there was a text message that the best table in the restaurant had just opened up.

"Can't we just order room service?" Atlas asked when she'd prodded him to dress for dinner.

"No. We can't. You came here to see the resort. Consider this part of your tour. Now hurry. We can't be late."

"Why?"

She sighed. "Because I had to pull some strings to get this reservation. With the resort fully booked, reservations are at a premium."

"Which restaurant are we eating at?"

"You'll see." And then she smiled. "Trust me, you'll like it."

Twenty minutes later, she exited her office dressed in a little black dress. After being caught without a change of clothes the night of the storm, she'd decided to keep some outfits in her office. The dress wasn't too fancy. And it wasn't boring either. It was cut to fit her curves as though it were specially made for her.

And then there were the black heels. They were...well, they were stunning. It's the reason she'd splurged on them. And they fit her perfectly. She rarely had an occasion to wear them. But dinner at Under the Sea seemed like the perfect occasion.

Rhea had already gone home for the evening when Atlas had arrived to escort Hermione to dinner. He had relented and changed clothes. He now wore a dark suit with a light purple dress shirt and a vibrant purple tie. It was different and yet it looked quite attractive on him. When her gaze rose and met his, her heart fluttered. It was getting hard to remember that this was a business dinner and not a date.

"You look beautiful." It was though his deep voice caressed her.

Heat swirled in her chest. It rushed up her neck and set her cheeks ablaze. "Thank you. You clean up really well too."

He held his arm out to her. She couldn't remember the

last time a man had done that for her. Otis never had. He thought chivalry was a waste of time.

She should resist Atlas's offer and keep a boundary between them because he was far too sexy and he made her pulse race. But she threw caution to the wind as she slipped her hand in the crook of his arm. She noticed the firm muscle beneath her fingertips. Her heart thump-thumped as they set off for the evening.

As they stood in the elevator, he said, "I didn't realize there was a lower level. What's down here?"

"We're going to Under the Sea."

"We're going to look at fish? But I thought we were eating."

She smiled at his frown. "I promise you will eat soon."

The doors swung open into a darkened room. It was more like a wide hallway that had glass walls and ceiling. The glow of the fish tank cast a blue glow over the room. And on each table was an LED candle. There were only a couple dozen tables lining each side of the room.

"This is amazing," Atlas said, gazing all around, taking in the hundreds of fish in all variety of colors. "Did you see that?"

"See what?"

"I think it was a small shark. But I don't see it now."

They were shown to their table, which sat midway down the dining room. It gave them an amazing view of it all. He lifted his head to watch the fish as they swam overhead.

"No wonder you wanted to bring me here," he said in awe, as though he'd totally forgotten what they'd been doing just an hour or so ago in his mother's apartment. "You must eat here often."

"Actually, I've never eaten here."

He glanced across the table at her. "But why not? Don't you like fish?"

"No, it's not that. I think this is amazing." Then she lowered her voice. "Remember I work here."

"Oh. Sorry. Sometimes I forget that employees aren't able to enjoy the amenities. You know, someone really needs to change that rule."

"You mean someone like the owner." She looked expectantly at him.

"Oh, you want me to change the company policy?"

"Well, you do own the resort."

He shook his head. "I don't think you want me changing things."

She arched a brow. "Why not?"

"Because you seem to like everything exactly the way it is. You take comfort in the routine of it all."

She wasn't so sure she liked him trying to figure her out. And even worse, he was right.

"Maybe I do," she said defensively. "But that's because I know what it's like not to know where I was going to sleep at night or where my next meal was coming from." She hadn't intended to admit all of that, but Atlas had a way of burrowing under her skin and she found herself uttering things she preferred to keep to herself.

"I'm sorry." He had the decency to look sheepish. "I never should have said any of that. I was just trying to point out how different we are."

Perhaps she'd overreacted. "And maybe I'm a bit defensive. My ex had criticism down to a fine art by the end of our relationship. I guess I still haven't developed a thick skin."

"Don't. You're perfect just the way you are."

Her cheeks grew warm. "You don't have to say that."

"I meant it." He smiled at her. "I'm so happy I found you—I mean because you've been so helpful."

But the way he looked into her eyes she couldn't help but

wonder if he meant something else. Because she was starting to develop feelings for him and she knew that wasn't
good. Not good at all.

Once he'd accomplished his business on the island he'd
be gone. And she'd be left with nothing but a broken heart.
She wouldn't put herself through that again. She just had to
keep reminding herself that this candlelit dinner was business. But it sure didn't feel like it.

Dinner was delicious.

The atmosphere was out of this world.

But it was the company that was priceless.

Atlas hadn't thought he would smile again after sorting
through Thea's belongings. At the apartment, he'd been
reminded of how alone he'd been after his mother had left
him.

But now inside this giant aquarium-like room, he was
no longer alone. He had Hermione—as a friend, or course.
Though they'd only known each other a short time, he
didn't know how he'd get through any of this without her.

After their dinner dishes were cleared, he reached across
the table and placed his hand over hers. In the candlelight,
he stared into her eyes. "Thank you."

"For what? Bringing you here? I'm sure you'd have eventually made it here on your own."

"Not the restaurant—though I am glad you refused to
do room service—but rather I meant helping me through
this process." As she smiled at him, he gave her hand a
squeeze. His gaze dipped to her lips, causing his heart to
beat faster. Then realizing what he was doing, he lifted his
gaze to meet hers once more. "It means a lot. And I won't
forget it. If you ever need anything, all you have to do is
phone me."

She withdrew her hand and glanced away.

What had he said wrong? He could speak programming language fluently, but he didn't have a clue how to speak on a personal level to a woman. And he didn't want to mess up this thing they had—this working relationship. Because it wasn't anything more—it couldn't be. He didn't do long-term anything. He liked his freedom—at least that's what he'd been telling himself for years.

"Would you like dessert?" he asked.

She shook her head. "I'm ready to call it a night."

"Not yet." His eyes pleaded with her. "Maybe we could go back to my suite for some coffee. You could tell me more about the resort." When he sensed she was going to reject his invitation, he said, "Please."

She hesitated. "Just a few minutes. I have to get home."

"I understand."

She stood and pushed in her chair. Her gaze never met his. He felt as though he needed to apologize for something, but he just couldn't figure out what it would be.

They quietly made their way back to his suite. Each was lost in their thoughts. Only this time he didn't have a clue what she was thinking.

Inside the suite there was a lamp lit on a side table. It sent a soft glow throughout the living room. They both sat on the couch. Hermione left a great distance between them. For Atlas, it felt as though she were trying to get away from him. And for the life of him, he couldn't figure out what had happened. Whatever he'd said or done, he wanted to take it back. He longed to return things to the way they'd been before the dinner—light and easy.

"I'm sorry if I said or did something wrong at dinner," he said.

"It's okay."

"No, it's not. I don't even know what I did to upset you." He raked his fingers through his hair. "Here's the thing.

I'm not very good with speaking to women, you know, on a personal level."

Her gaze met his. "You seem to do just fine with me."

"Really? Because I'm thinking that if I was better at it, you wouldn't be so anxious to get away from me." He leaned back on the couch. The events of the day weighed heavily on him. "Maybe I shouldn't have drawn you into my nightmare. It wasn't fair of me."

"I don't mind helping you." When he sent her a skeptical look, she said, "I mean it."

"Then what happened between us? Things were going so well, until they weren't." And then he wondered if it was this growing attraction between them that had made things awkward.

"Do you really care what I think?"

"Of course I do."

"Why?"

She wanted him to dissect his feelings and put them into words? His chest tightened. He wasn't good with mushy stuff. But as he gazed into her eyes, he realized that's exactly what she expected. His hands grew clammy.

He cleared his throat. "Because you're my one friend on this island."

She smiled at him. It was the kind of smile that lit up her eyes and made the gold flecks in them twinkle. "Stop overthinking things." Her voice was soft and sultry. "We're good."

He sat upright, rubbing his palms on his pants. He was so anxious to move beyond this awkward moment. "We are?"

She nodded as she continued to smile. "We are."

Maybe there was something to this mushy stuff. When he spoke, his voice came out deeper than he'd intended. "Because when this is all over and I go home, I'm going to miss you."

"You are?"

With his gaze still holding hers, he nodded. "Definitely."

"I'll, ah, miss you too."

His gaze lowered to her lush lips. His heart pounded. As though drawn to her by a force that was beyond his control, he leaned toward her. Surely she had to feel it too. Right? It couldn't just be him.

His eyes closed as his lips pressed to hers. He willed her to kiss him back. Surely he hadn't misread things between them. Had he?

And then her hands reached out, cupping his face. Her touch was feathery soft, as though she was afraid he might disappear in a puff of smoke. Her lips slowly moved over his as she took the lead.

Thoughts of his mother's estate slipped from his mind. Worries over selling the island were swept away. Anxiety about the security of the royal jewels eased. In this moment, his thoughts were only of Hermione and how right this kiss felt.

He wanted this moment to go on and on. Because a kiss was normally just a kiss, a prelude to something more. However, with Hermione, it was all by itself an earthmoving event. His lips gently brushed over hers. He didn't want to scare her off. He wanted to hold her in his arms as long as possible.

As he drew her closer, their kiss intensified. His whole body came alive with the rush of adrenaline. He'd never been so consumed with a kiss.

Hermione was unique in so many wonderful and amazing ways. As her lips moved beneath his, he wondered how he'd been so lucky to meet her.

The reality of their circumstances slipped away. The only thing that mattered right now was him and her. And this kiss that was like a soothing balm on his tattered and torn heart.

He didn't want this moment to end. His hand reached up and gently caressed the smooth skin of her cheek. His fingers slid down to her neck where he felt her rapid pulse. She wanted him as much as she wanted him.

Buzz-buzz.

He didn't want his phone to ruin this moment. He didn't want anything to come between them. It vibrated in his pocket, distracting him from Hermione's tantalizing kiss.

She pulled away. His eyes opened to find her staring at him. He couldn't read her thoughts. Was she happy about the kiss? Or was she angry that he'd overstepped?

She glanced away. "You better answer that. It's probably important. And it's getting late. I'll see you in the morning."

Buzz-buzz.

"But I don't want to answer it. I want us to talk."

She shook her head as she stood. "We've definitely said more than enough for tonight. Good night."

And then she was out the door in a flash. Once more he was left with questions where she was concerned.

Buzz-buzz.

Why wouldn't his phone stop ringing? Surely it must have switched to voice mail by now. He yanked it from his pocket to turn it off, but then he caught sight of the caller ID. It was an important client from London.

Normally, he'd drop everything to answer it. But these weren't normal times. It was his policy to meet problems head-on instead of letting them fester. But this problem wasn't with his client. It was with Hermione.

He'd made a mistake by kissing her. He should have known better, but he'd let himself get caught up in the evening—he'd let himself imagine their dinner had been something more than it was. And now he'd blurred the lines of their relationship.

He needed to focus on business. It didn't confuse him or hurt him. It was a constant that he could always count on. And so when his phone rang again, he answered it.

"Atlas, what's going on?" Krystof practically shouted into the phone.

It was best to find out what he knew before admitting to anything. "What are you talking about?"

"Don't give me that. You left me this urgent message that we had to talk right away. What's wrong?"

"Everything." He raked his fingers through his hair. "And nothing."

It wasn't the reason he'd left the voice mail. But so much had changed since then, and he needed a friend to speak to. Krystof was a very old friend, someone he could confide in.

"What are you talking about?"

Atlas blew out a deep breath. Suddenly, he wasn't so sure he was ready to discuss Hermione with anyone.

"Nothing. It's just been a long day."

"It's a woman."

"What? No." He suddenly felt self-conscious about this avalanche of emotions for Hermione.

"I'm right. I knew it. What's her name?"

"There's no woman," he snapped. "I mean not really. Anyway, that isn't the reason I called. I think the resort has more to offer you than you think."

"I'm listening."

Atlas went on to tell him all about the casino and the high rollers room. "So how soon can you get here? You'll love it."

"Says the man anxiously trying to unload the island. Sorry. I still can't get there any sooner than next week, and this place better be as good as you say it is."

They wrapped up the phone call with Atlas promising Krystof that he would fall in love with the island.

But as Atlas opened his laptop to go back to work, his thoughts turned to Hermione and their kiss. Had it been a mistake? If it was, it was a delicious one.

CHAPTER TEN

WHY HAD SHE done that?

Why had she kissed him back?

Hermione knew the answer, but she didn't want to admit it to herself or anyone else. The truth was she couldn't quit thinking about that kiss and replaying it over and over in her mind. She was drawn to Atlas in a way that she'd never been drawn to a man in her life—not even her ex. And that scared her.

Even to crack open the door to her heart a little and let Atlas in frightened her. Because every time she opened herself up to care about someone, she lost them. They either disappeared from her life or they ended up not being who she thought they were—except for her Ludus friends. They were always there for her.

And worse yet, Atlas was out to ruin the world she'd immersed herself in here at the Ludus. Sure, he might have promised to protect the employees' jobs for six months, but that protection wouldn't include her.

She understood that the new owner would have a different style and require different management. The thought not only saddened her but scared her. Without Adara, Rhea, Titus and the rest of the Ludus team, she would be all alone again.

And so that night at her apartment instead of sleeping,

she worked on her résumé. It needed a lot of updating. And then she went online and set up an account on a professional networking site. She worked late into the night.

Friday morning, she almost slept through her alarm. She rushed through the shower and dressed. She had to get to work early. The employees' future employment hinged on her holding up her end of the bargain. And she refused to give Atlas any reason to void their agreement.

There had to be a way to rewind things. Yes, if they could just pretend the kiss hadn't happened they would be totally fine. They could work together until he left. As anxious as he was to finish cleaning out his mother's apartment, he'd most likely be gone by Valentine's.

Knowing she had to get a move on before a large chunk of the morning slipped by, she jumped in her car and headed for the island. She told herself to focus on her work and not the soul-stirring, heart-fluttering, best ever kiss. Definitely not that.

When she entered the resort, she immediately turned toward her office. But as she deposited her purse on her desk, she realized she wasn't going to get any work done until she told Atlas what was on her mind.

When she went to his suite, Atlas didn't answer the door. She messaged him and he told her to come on in. He was out on the balcony.

Her stomach knotted up with nervous tension. Maybe this wasn't such a good idea. But it was too late to change her mind. She used her master key card and let herself inside.

Atlas glanced up from his laptop when he heard her step onto the sunny balcony. "Good morning."

"Morning." Hermione didn't smile. "We need to talk."

"Have a seat?" Atlas gestured to the chair next to him. She opted to sit across the table from him. Coffee was offered and she declined. Hermione's empty stomach churned. She told herself it was nervousness over what she had to say, and it had absolutely nothing to do with her close proximity to the man whose kisses made her go weak in the knees.

"We need to talk about last night," she said.

"Agreed."

His quick, agreeable response surprised her. "It shouldn't have happened. It…it was a mistake."

His gaze searched hers. "Is that what you really think?"

She glanced down at her hands. "I do."

She couldn't let herself fall for him. He was the enemy of sorts—the man who would steal away the life she'd come to cherish, from the monthly luncheons to the friendly greetings in the hallways. Even some of the guests had become friends.

Her ex may have stolen her money as well as her mother's locket, but Atlas was preparing to steal something so much more valuable—the family she'd worked so hard to create. She couldn't bear the thought of having to start over again.

Buzz-buzz.

Hermione glanced at her phone. There was a message from Adara.

Urgent. Need to talk.

What's wrong?

Adara wasn't one to panic. She was really good at taking things in stride. It's what made her so good at her job of concierge.

Where are you?

I'm meeting with Atlas in his suite.

I'll be right there.

"What's wrong?" Atlas asked.

"It's Adara. She says something urgent came up. She's on her way here." She followed him inside the suite.

Knock-knock.

Atlas opened the door. "Come in."

Adara strode into the suite in her navy-and-white skirt suit and high heels. It wasn't so much her actions or the smile she briefly forced on her face but rather the worry reflected in her eyes that had Hermione on alert.

Adara's worried gaze met hers. "It's Nestor. His wife just called. He's in the hospital."

Hermione knew Adara lived near Nestor's family, and she'd become good friends with his wife. "Oh, no. What happened?"

"A heart attack." Adara's voice was filled with emotion. "They're taking him into surgery. His wife said it was touch and go for a while."

"How awful." Her heart went out to Nestor and his family. He was always so reliable and generous. People naturally smiled when they were around him. He put people at ease, and that really helped him do his job of event coordinator.

Adara nodded. "I just can't believe this happened to him."

"His wife wanted us to know he'll be off work for quite a while."

"Tell them not to worry. His job will be waiting for him when he's ready to return."

Adara nodded. "I will. And I don't want to be crude at this moment, but this complicates matters."

Atlas rubbed his fingers over his freshly shaven jaw. "What's complicated?"

Adara's gaze flickered to him and then back to Hermione. "Nestor is supposed to be planning a Valentine's wedding as well as the Valentine's ball. And his assistant just went out on maternity leave."

Hermione inwardly groaned. What was it with this week? Things just kept getting worse.

Her gaze moved to Atlas to see how he was taking the news. If the frown lines marring his handsome face were any indication, he wasn't taking the information very well. He moved to the glass wall and stared off at the sea.

"I can coordinate the party," Hermione said. "But I can't organize the wedding."

Handling the management of the resort in addition to planning an extravagant party wouldn't leave her any spare time, but this wasn't about her. It was about helping a co-worker at his most vulnerable time.

Atlas turned to them. "Would you even know where to begin?"

She straightened her shoulders. "I can figure it out."

He shook his head. "This is a big event. Have you ever planned a party of that size or grandeur?"

Translated to mean that the party was too important to let an amateur handle. He had no faith in her abilities. No wonder he was anxious to sell the place. He was worried she'd destroy the resort.

"No, I haven't but it doesn't mean I can't do it. Nestor was good at keeping notes." She turned to Adara. "Do you know where his company laptop is?"

"As far as I know, he was never without it. It's probably at his house. I can pick it up for you."

"Thank you. It's the key to everything." Upon seeing the doubt reflected in their eyes, Hermione said, "Everyone stop worrying. I can handle it. Most of the plans should already be in place. The trick is the follow-through. You know, making sure everything arrives on time and is put in its place."

"You really think you're up to this?" Adara asked. "It's a lot with everything else you're doing."

"I do." She ignored the flutter of nerves in her stomach. "But what about the wedding?"

"I'll take care of it," Adara said.

"You can't do that. You also have your hands full," Hermione said.

"Listen to who's talking." Adara crossed her arms and arched her brows in challenge. "If you're going to pick up some slack, so am I."

Hermione knew how stubborn her friend could be. "You're not going to change your mind, are you?"

Adara shook her head. "You know me better than that."

Hermione breathed a little easier. "Okay, now that we have the two big items on his calendar taken care of, I'll have to see what else he has going on."

"And I'll talk to Rhea about setting up a schedule to make sure there's food for Nestor's family," Adara said. "If that's all right with you."

Hermione nodded. "Yes. That's a great idea."

"We could hire a professional party planner," Atlas said. "It'll cost extra at this late date, but it'll be worth it. That's what we'll do. I'll put my assistant on it."

If she had been worried about how she'd stay out of his arms going forward, she didn't have to worry any longer. Anything she'd thought had been started between them had been officially doused with his outright disbelief in her abilities.

Hermione glared at him, but he refused to back down.

"Then I'm no longer needed here." Hermione lifted her chin ever so slightly and strode away.

"Hermione, wait," Atlas called out. "I didn't mean it that way."

He'd meant every word he'd said. Of that she was certain. At every turn, he was questioning her and her choices. The backs of her eyes stung. She blinked repeatedly, refusing to let on that his words had hurt her. She would not give him that power.

Her steps came quickly. The truth was she wanted to be as far from Atlas as she could get. The man utterly frustrated her. One minute he's kissing her like he never wanted to stop—like she was the most beautiful woman in the world.

The next moment he's insulting her abilities. No wonder she hadn't been in a relationship in a long time. Men were utterly exasperating—most especially Atlas.

She walked out the door. She gave it a firm yank but with its gentle close feature, she wasn't given the satisfaction of it slamming closed.

What had he done?

He'd totally messed up everything.

Atlas had watched the storm clouds gather in Hermione's eyes and he hadn't done anything to calm the waters. The reasons—the good reasons—had all been there in his head. But had he used the right words? No.

It seemed that whenever he was in close proximity to Hermione that his mind and mouth had a glitchy disconnect. There were so many things he wanted to say to her, but for one reason or another he'd kept them to himself.

But he couldn't let things stay like this. He couldn't stand the thought of Hermione being upset with him and jumping to the wrong conclusions. He had to fix things or at least try.

After apologizing to Adara, he rushed to the hallway, finding no sign of her. Would she go back to her office? Or would she walk out the front door and keep on going?

Stop. He was getting ahead of himself. After all, she was an employee of the resort. Her address was on record. He could easily track her down if he was so inclined.

Who was he kidding? He was most definitely inclined. He just wasn't sure it was a good idea. After the kiss last night, he knew the volatile attraction ran both ways. He also knew Hermione was in denial of their chemistry. Whether they wanted to admit it or not, it existed.

If he was to go after her now and things got heated—if their attraction spiraled out of control, she'd never forgive him. He wouldn't forgive himself. Things needed to cool off, and then they could talk like rational adults.

After calming down, hopefully she'd see the merits of his plan. She was overextending herself. At the same time, it impressed him the way she was worried about those around her and asked for nothing for herself. There weren't many people that were so selfless.

He returned to his suite where Adara was checking messages on her phone. She glanced up when he entered the room. She slipped her phone in her pocket.

"I didn't handle that very well," he said.

"Did you have a chance to speak to her?"

He shook his head. "I didn't catch up with her."

He sunk down into the chair. "When I came to Ludus I knew it wasn't going to be fun, but I didn't expect things to keep getting worse at every turn."

Adara paused as though not sure she should say what was on her mind. When her phone buzzed, she checked it and then returned it to her pocket.

"It's okay," he said. "Just say it."

"I think you should let Hermione decide how much she

can handle. She'll ask for help before she does anything to damage the resort. She loves this place. It's her home— her family. And we won't let her fail. We'll help her every step of the way."

It sounded nice, but he wasn't sure it was based in reality. "Even though it would be above and beyond everyone's duties?"

"Even then. This group pulls together to help each other."

His business didn't run on such employee devotion. This resort was so different from anything he knew. It was a good thing he was selling it because he knew his management style would clash with the established routine.

"The guests will be unhappy if the party goes awry." When Adara sent him a surprised look, he said, "I've heard them talking in the hallways. This place is abuzz with excitement."

"And you should know that Nestor does have a couple of other staff members. I'm sure they'll pitch in so the party isn't overwhelming for Hermione. And like I said, if more help is required the resort is full of people who would lend a hand."

This whole thing made him uneasy. There was a resort full of famous and influential people who were waiting for a splashy and impressive party. If the party was a failure, it would really hurt the resort's reputation and hamper any potential sale.

He rubbed his jaw. "Even if I could find Hermione, I don't think she'd be willing to hear me out."

Adara sent him a smile. "I think you underestimate yourself. But you have given me an idea."

He braced himself. "Do I even want to know what it is?"

"Don't worry about it. Just go talk to Hermione."

"I don't know where she went."

Adara held up her phone. "But I do. She texted me and mentioned she was stopping by Thea's apartment."

"Really?" Even though Hermione was upset with him, she was still holding up her end of their agreement. He didn't know it was possible, but she impressed him even more.

"Now I have to go." Adara started for the door but then paused to say, "Good luck."

He was going to need it. Hermione had never been this upset with him. And he had no idea how to make it up to her. But that wouldn't stop him from trying.

CHAPTER ELEVEN

SOME PEOPLE WOULD say she was foolish.

Other people would say she was smart.

Hermione really didn't care what people thought of her—well, that wasn't quite true. She cared what Atlas thought. The truth was she cared too much.

She should be in her office right now, but she was too worked up to sit still. She needed some physical activity. She needed to work off some of her frustration.

Hermione carried a stack of books from the bookcase in Thea's living room to the coffee table. There she opened each one, turned it over and shook it to make sure there were no loose papers tucked inside. And then she placed them in a cardboard box to donate as Atlas had instructed.

Though it nearly killed Hermione to admit it, Atlas was right. She couldn't do everything—even if she wanted to. Delegating was the only way she could get through the next week leading up to Valentine's.

She'd had Rhea on speakerphone going over a couple of urgent matters, including the double-booking of the Cypress Room. Once that was sorted, she asked Rhea to temporarily take on some more responsibilities. Her assistant understood that this was a difficult time for the resort and enthusiastically offered to pitch in.

Rhea's kindness and generosity brought tears to Hermione's eyes. Thank goodness they were on the phone. Hermione wasn't usually overly emotional. She blamed the tears on Atlas.

When she disconnected the call, she continued to mull over the scene with Atlas. If she didn't care for Atlas, would his lack of faith in her abilities hurt so much? Unwilling to answer that question, she told herself it was a pride thing. However, deep down she knew it was more than that. She wanted him to be different from her ex, who was always handy with a backhanded compliment. She wanted Atlas to see her as an equal—someone he could share more than a passing moment with—

The breath caught in her lungs. What was she thinking? She was not falling for Atlas. Absolutely not.

"Hermione?" Atlas's voice carried from the elevator into the living room.

She hesitated to answer. If she remained quiet, would he go away? No. Atlas was way too determined when he wanted something. And she would not let him think she was afraid to face him.

"In here." She would just treat him like any other coworker.

The sound of his approaching footsteps echoed in the foyer. And then he was there, filling up the doorway with his broad shoulders. "Can we talk?"

"Now isn't a good time. I'm a little busy." She continued opening books, shaking them and placing them in the box.

It was the same way she'd act with any other coworker. But any other person wouldn't make her heart race just by their presence.

Just ignore it. He'll be gone soon.

"This is important."

She stopped working. Hesitantly her gaze met his. "So is this. I have my end of a bargain to keep. And the sooner I finish, the sooner we'll no longer have to deal with each other."

He sighed. "Hermione, you took what I said out of context—"

"I don't think so." She resumed her task.

Buzz-buzz.

Her gaze moved to her phone, resting on the cherrywood end table. It wasn't her phone. That meant it had to be Atlas's, and she'd never been so grateful for an interruption. His phone went off again. She willed him to answer it.

"I need to get this, but we're not done talking."

She didn't say anything, but she was thinking plenty. None of her testy thoughts would make this situation any easier.

He stepped into the foyer to take the call. He didn't say much. Most of the conversation appeared to be one-sided. Then he stepped back in the study. "I have to go take care of something, but I'll be back."

"Don't rush on my account."

He hesitated as though he were going to say something, but then he'd thought better of it. He walked away, and at last she could take a full breath.

She had to quit letting him get to her. After all, it wasn't like they were a couple or anything. She needed to work faster because once Nestor's laptop was delivered to the resort, she would need to focus most of her energies on the Valentine's ball.

She continued her task with renewed determination. After quickly moving through a dozen or so books, her phone rang. She had no intention of answering it, especially if it was Atlas. But curiosity had her checking the caller ID.

When she saw Adara's name on the screen, she couldn't help but wonder what she would need. Perhaps the laptop had already arrived. She was anxious to see exactly what party details needed to be completed. It would be a lot as no detail was overlooked or extravagance forsaken when it came to a Ludus event. They were the definition of lavish.

She pressed the phone to her ear. "Hello."

"Hermione, I'm so sorry to bother you, but there's a problem at the dock. It's something about a special shipment for the party, and they're insisting on your signature."

Hermione inwardly groaned. This was the last interruption she needed at the moment. Her gaze moved around the study. It wasn't like the work wouldn't be here when she got back.

"Okay. I'm on my way."

Adara gave her the instructions and then hung up. It all seemed easy enough. And with it being an unusually warm, sunny day, it'd be a good day for a walk. It would be a chance for her to clear her mind and figure out how to deal with Atlas in a calm, reasonable manner.

A strange place for a meeting.

Atlas sat aboard the resort's luxury yacht—*The Sea Jewel*. Adara had phoned him and asked him to meet her there. She'd sounded anxious or worried; he wasn't quite sure which but something was definitely not right with her.

He was starting to worry about the resort. Without his mother at the helm, would the service decline? Hermione seemed good at her job, but she was getting spread too thin.

The problem was that she was too fiercely independent for her own good, and that could spell trouble for the resort. And he wouldn't be of much help. He didn't know a thing about running a resort, but he did know how to manage people. Still, his style of management and hers were two very different things.

Should he step in and assume control of the resort? It was the very last thing he wanted to do. He'd only come here to settle his mother's personal affairs and now he felt as though he was being drawn in more deeply with every passing hour.

The captain escorted Atlas to the interior of the boat. It was spacious and appeared to have every amenity a person could want, from long comfy white couches to captain chairs along with a large bar and a giant screen television.

Atlas sat down on the couch but unable to sit still for long, he started pacing. He was forever staring out the long bank of windows, hoping someone would arrive soon.

Tired of waiting, he reached for his phone. There must have been some sort of mix-up. He would call Adara and find out what was going on. His finger hovered over the screen when he detected movement on the dock. *At last.*

He slipped the phone back in his pocket. He headed for the deck to greet Adara and get down to business. But when he stepped outside, he was greeted by Hermione.

When her gaze met his, her eyes widened. "What are you doing here?"

"That's just what I was going to ask you."

"I was told I needed to sign for a shipment, but when I got to the dock, I was guided onboard the yacht." Her brows drew together. "I don't understand. Why are you here?"

"I was told to meet Adara here, but I haven't seen her."

Hermione crossed her arms. "What's going on? I don't have time to play games."

He had a suspicion who might be behind this setup. "Who called you?"

"Adara." Hermione's brows rose as her eyes lit up. "Let me guess. She called you too?"

"Yes. It looks like she set us up."

As though in confirmation, the engine started. The boat started to move away from the dock.

"Hey!" Hermione called out. "Wait."

Atlas shook his head. "They can't hear you."

"What are we going to do?"

"Apparently we're going for a ride." It was certainly one way to obtain Hermione's undivided attention. He just didn't know if this cruise would be long enough for him to convince her to forgive him.

"But...but that's kidnapping." Hermione frowned. "I have work to do. I don't have time to go sailing." She turned to him. "Are you just going to stand there?"

"I was actually thinking of sitting down and enjoying the view." And he did just that.

"You can't be happy about this."

"I will definitely have a word with Adara when we get back." He would thank her for this terrific idea, but next time he wanted to be clued in on her plans ahead of time. Then he was going to give her a well-deserved raise.

Hermione huffed. "You could tell the captain to turn around right now."

Perhaps a change of subject would help. "I didn't know the resort owned a yacht."

"They own many boats but not all are this fancy. This one is brand-new. Your mother ordered it just before she... well, uh, it was just delivered." She looked flustered as she avoided his gaze.

"What you're saying is that we're the first ones to ride in it?"

She shrugged. "I don't know for sure, but I think so. It'll come in handy come June."

"What's in June?"

"The Royal Regatta."

He was intrigued. And the more Hermione talked about the resort the less stiff her posture became. "What does it entail?"

She sat down. "It's a boat race around the island."

He joined her. "And who participates in this race?"

"A lot of people—even the prince of Rydiania. It's his country that cosponsors the race."

"The same country that loaned the resort the Ruby Heart and the other jewels?" When she nodded, he asked, "Why would a foreign country lend the resort what must be priceless gems? I thought Thea's husband had been thrown out of the family and exiled to this island."

"That's not quite how it went down. Even though Georgios had been exiled from his homeland of Rydiania, he was free to travel the world—to make his home wherever he pleased. However, his family preferred that it was a long way from Rydiania."

The more Hermione talked, the more her voice took on its normal bubbly lilt. Her arms now rested at her sides. And the frown lines had smoothed from her face.

"And he picked this island of all places to live?" Atlas didn't want her to stop talking about the island and its history because when she was unveiling the past for him, she wasn't thinking about how angry she was with him.

"Georgios said it was love at first sight. He knew once he stepped on the island that he was home. But he quickly grew lonely, and that's when he got the idea to invest his savings into building the Ludus Resort. He said he never regretted that decision."

"If I had a private island," Atlas said, "I don't know if I'd want to share it."

"But you do have an island. Remember? This is all yours."

"It doesn't feel like it."

"What does it feel like?"

"Some sort of messed-up dream and soon I'll wake up."

"But this is no dream. It's your future—if you want it to be."

He didn't want to think about that now. He'd rather enjoy this truce he'd somehow struck with Hermione. "I'm still confused. If this king was cast out of the family—"

"He wasn't cast out. He abdicated the throne. He said he wasn't meant to be a king. He believed his brother could do a better job."

"Still, he was exiled from the country, so why would they lend their jewels?"

Hermione smiled. "Well, that's another story. The current king and queen of Rydiania have three children. The oldest being Prince Istvan. He had known Georgios when he was very young. You might say those two hit it off. When Georgios was exiled, the prince was deeply upset. The king and queen forbade him from contacting his uncle. But you know how kids can be when they're forbidden to do something."

He thought back over his own troubled youth. "It makes the temptation even greater."

"Exactly. When the prince was old enough to travel without his parents or chaperones, he sought out his uncle. To hear it told, and to have witnessed them together, it's like the two had never been parted all of those years."

"And so all was forgiven with Georgios?" He was hoping there would be a happy ending. He needed to know all families weren't messy and broken like his.

"No. I'm afraid not. Georgios said it was enough to have the prince back in his life, but every now and then when he didn't think anyone was looking, he would get this faraway look in his eyes and then a sadness would come over him."

"So much for a happy ending."

"Oh, I think for the most part Georgios was happy. It was just when he thought of his brother that he realized what he'd lost. And as for the royal jewels, they belong to Prince Istvan. He inherited them from his grandmother. He loved your mother and visited often after his uncle passed on. He knew how much your mother loved Valentine's and thought the jewels might cheer her up."

And yet another person Thea had won over. It would appear he and his father were the only two she didn't care for. The thought weighed heavy on him. Was he too much like his father?

"Now that you know the backstory on the jewels, it's time to turn this boat around. I can't believe Adara would do this." She reached for her phone.

"Don't do that. It's a beautiful day." He stood and moved out to the deck. "Why not enjoy some of it?"

"Atlas, we can't just run off for the day. We have things to do." She followed him.

The sea breeze combed through his hair and rushed past his face, offsetting the warmth of the sun. But Atlas didn't pay much attention. He was drawn to the emerging landscape.

"This is beautiful." He stared back at the rocky shoreline with its lush green foliage. "Is that a waterfall off in the distance?"

"Yes. It's one of them. If you want you could explore the island."

He shook his head. "I have too much work to do."

"You should see it during the summer when the orchids and wildflowers are in bloom. It's a cascade of color."

He opened his mouth to say that he couldn't wait to see it but then wordlessly pressed his lips back together. He wouldn't be here come summertime. By then Ludus Island would be in this rearview mirror...where it belonged.

He swallowed. "So the only thing on the entire island is the resort?"

She nodded. "This all belonged to Georgios. He liked

having the ability to keep the paparazzi at a distance so he and his guests could enjoy the island's beauty."

"Do you offer sightseeing boat rides for the guests?"

"No, we don't. But now that you mention it, perhaps we could work on putting together something. Maybe a lunch and dinner cruise."

"I'm glad we have this moment together."

She arched a brow. "Don't go thinking any of this erases what happened earlier."

"Will you at least let me explain?"

She didn't say anything at first, then she sighed. "Fine. It's not like I have anyplace I can go. And I don't plan to swim back to shore."

"Back at the suite, the things I said didn't come out right."

"It sounded pretty clear to me. You don't trust me to organize the Valentine's ball. All I'm good for is to clean your mother's apartment."

"Whoa. Where did that come from?"

"Isn't that what you're thinking? That I'm not cut out to run this resort?"

He shook his head. "I never thought such a thing. Who put these thoughts in your head?" When she didn't respond, he said softly, "Hermione, talk to me. What's going on?"

"My ex, Otis, was always planting doubts in my mind. Just little things here and there when I went back to school. At first I didn't pay much attention. It wasn't until Adara pointed out how his little comments over time had eaten away at my self-confidence until I doubted myself about almost everything that I realized he was jealous of my career."

Anger balled up in his gut over what that jerk had done to her. Who did such a thing to such a smart, accomplished and caring person like Hermione?

And then he recalled all of his questions and suggestions for the resort. He'd also insisted on upgrading the resort's security over her objection. And finally he'd questioned her ability to take over the Valentine's party on top of all her other responsibilities. Not because he didn't think she could do it but rather because he cared if she took on too much work.

He cared.

The revelation echoed in his mind. It'd been so long since he'd allowed himself to get close enough to a person to truly care about them. In the process, he'd totally messed up everything.

His gaze met hers. "Hermione, I'm not like your ex."

Disbelief reflected in her eyes. "It doesn't matter—"

"It does matter." His voice was soft but firm. "I know I haven't handled any of this correctly." He needed her to truly hear him. That would only happen if he put himself out there and revealed things he'd never shared with anyone. "Coming to this island—Thea's home—is the hardest thing I've ever done." His voice grew gravelly with emotion. He cleared his throat. "And then to find out how much she cared for all of you…it was hard."

Pity reflected in Hermione's eyes. "I'm so sorry. I should have been more sensitive."

"Don't pity me. I'm fine." He didn't feel fine. He felt beaten and scarred. "I've been caring for myself since I was a kid. I'll get through this."

"You don't have to get through this alone. You could let people in."

He shook his head. The thought of setting himself up to be abandoned like his mother had done or rejected like his father had ultimately done made his protective wall come back up.

"I... I can't talk about this." He strode back inside the yacht.

Hermione followed him. "Running from your past isn't working. Once you face it, it won't have any control over you."

"That's not what I'm doing. I only mentioned it because I'm trying to explain the reason I said and did certain things when I arrived. Instead of telling you what I intended to do, I should have asked for your input. Like the security system we're supposed to work on tomorrow. Do you feel it's too much for the resort?"

Her eyes momentarily widened. "We haven't had problems in the past but what you said got me to thinking. If the resort is to grow, it's feasible to update the security. Just don't go too overboard. We're still just a small island resort."

"Thank you for your input. I'll do my best to run my ideas for the resort past you. My input wasn't meant to demean your capabilities. They were about me and my need to prove myself...that Thea was wrong to leave me—to forget me."

"But she didn't. She loved you—"

"No." His voice came out harshly. He made an effort to soften his tone when he spoke again. "Don't say that. People who love you don't abandon you."

He was losing track of this conversation. Why did he keep revealing more and more of himself? This conversation was supposed to be about Hermione, not him.

He sighed. "I'm saying this all wrong."

Her gaze narrowed in on him. "What exactly are you saying?"

"I'm saying I think you're capable of anything you set your mind to, but I didn't want you to take on too much. As it is, I think you should stop working on Thea's apartment so you can focus on the party. Just promise me one thing."

"What's that?"

"If it's too much or you need help that you'll tell me."

"I'll tell you. But don't worry, I've got this. This is going to be the best party ever." And that's when she leaned into him, wrapping her arms around him as she hugged him.

His heart immediately started to hammer against his ribs. His body froze. He was afraid to move or breathe for fear that she'd pull away. Because having her so close was the most amazing feeling that caused a warm spot in his chest.

When at last she pulled away, he said, "Hermione, I—"

She pressed her fingertips to his lips. "Maybe we've done enough talking."

What? There were still things he wanted to say. But when she moved her fingers from his lips, those words escaped him. What exactly did she have in mind? As though in answer, she pressed her mouth to his. He liked the way she thought.

It wasn't a slow and gentle kiss. No, this was a kiss full of need and longing. Her hand slid up over his shoulder and around his neck until her fingertips raked through his hair. It was the most exhilarating feeling. Desire pumped through his veins.

The right and wrong of their intimacy was long forgotten. A driving need to feel her next to him pulsed through his veins. He wanted to explore all of her. He wanted to make her moan with pleasure.

He scooped her up in his arms. He carried her to the spacious chaise longue and gently laid her down. He joined her. His fingertips swept the loose strands of hair behind her ear.

"Does this mean I'm forgiven?" he murmured.

"Obviously I haven't been doing something right if you

have to ask that question. Maybe I should try again." Her eyes twinkled with merriment.

A slow smile pulled at his lips. "Yes, I think we need some definite clarification."

She reached out to him. The backs of her fingers caressed his jawline as desire burned in her eyes. A bolt of need shot through his body.

He'd never had an afternoon tryst. Afternoons had always been for doing business. But with Hermione in his arms business was the last thing on his mind.

CHAPTER TWELVE

HER FEET DIDN'T touch the ground.

At least that's the way it felt.

Hermione's steps were light and quick as she made her way back to the office. She'd never felt this happy—this alive—this, ugh, she ran out of adjectives. Her brain was abuzz with images of being held in Atlas's arms as they'd made love. She had no idea he could be so gentle and loving.

There was so much more to him than she'd ever imagined. She could talk to him—really talk to him. And she felt safe when she confided in him that he wouldn't tell anyone else or use it against her—like Otis had done.

The thought of her ex weighed down her steps. Coming back down to earth, she recalled how excited and certain she'd been of Otis in the beginning. And look how wrong she'd been.

Was she wrong about Atlas too? After all, he still hadn't said he was going to change his mind about selling the resort. But with every passing day, she could see that he was getting more comfortable on Ludus Island. Soon he would realize that it was his destination.

The last thought buoyed her heart once more. It was like his presence on the island was his destiny. He just needed a little more time to figure things out.

Adara headed down the hallway toward her. "I was looking for you."

"Like you didn't know where I was since you're the one who had us whisked away on the yacht." Hermione knew she should be upset with her, but it was so hard when all she wanted to do was smile.

Adara acted as though she hadn't heard her. "I just talked to Nestor's wife and the surgery was a success. Now all he has to do is recover."

"That's the best news I've heard all day. If they need anything, let me know." Hermione was so happy for Nestor and his family. But she wasn't quite done with Adara. "You know I should be really mad at you for pulling that stunt with the boat."

Adara smiled. "But you're not because it worked. You two made up...didn't you?"

"I'm not going to tell you." Hermione resumed walking toward her office. "I can't believe you set us up—set me up. I thought we were friends."

Adara's smile faltered. "We are friends. I... I thought I was helping, but now you've got me worried that it went all wrong."

Hermione chanced a glance at her friend. "You should be worried. That was a very awkward situation."

"Oh." Her shoulders dropped. "So it didn't go well. I'm sorry. I won't do it again. I was just trying to help."

"Actually, it went very well." Hermione smiled.

Adara's eyes widened. "It did?"

"Yes, but you still shouldn't have done it."

"It just felt like you both needed a push, no, make that a shove in the right direction. I've seen the way you two look at each other when you think the other isn't looking. And you've both got it bad."

Her heart did a leap of joy. Atlas was checking her out. "We talked. And we worked some things out."

"Is that what we're calling it these days?" Adara grinned.

Heat flared in Hermione's cheeks. "We aren't discussing that. And I really do have to get back to work. I wasn't expecting to take a boat ride in the middle of the workday."

"So does mean you two are officially a couple now?"

"I… I don't know." They hadn't gotten that far, but she'd like to think they were. There's no way he'd confided in her and then made love to her without feeling anything. But as for labels for their relationship, it was all too new.

"Just be careful around the Ruby Heart. I just saw it— alone, thank goodness—because there's some legend if lovers view it together that their lives will forever be entwined."

Hermione was starting to wonder if there was something to that legend. She wasn't ready to reveal that she'd viewed it with Atlas. "Do you believe it?"

Adara shrugged. "I've heard of stranger things. Why? Are you planning to visit the ruby with Atlas?"

"Stop trying to matchmake."

"But you're totally into him, aren't you?" Adara sent her a hopeful look.

Hermione hesitated. It was as though once she spoke the words it would make not only them but this whole thing with Atlas real. But she knew how silly that was because nothing could have been more real than the love they'd made on the yacht.

With her heart hammering with excitement mixed with a little fear, she said, "Yes." It was barely more than a whisper. She swallowed hard. If she was going to do this, she had to believe in it—in them. "Yes," she said with more force. "How could I not be? Have you looked at him?"

Adara nodded. "He's hot. Does he have a brother?"

"I'm afraid not. He's one of a kind."

Adara sighed. "I guess it's good that I'm happy with my life just the way it is."

Hermione wondered if her friend was as happy with her single status as she'd like others to believe. But considering that Hermione was about to put her tattered heart back out on the line for a man that didn't even live here, much less in the same country, well, she might not be the best person to give relationship advice.

When Monday rolled around, she still couldn't stop smiling.

Hermione felt like she was walking on air ever since Friday when they'd returned from that very special boat ride. She and Atlas had come to a new understanding. They hadn't made love again—not that she hadn't thought of it— but they'd shared meals and updates on their day.

It was as though a wall had come down and they were able to really communicate. She did notice that he didn't mention their relationship or what happened on the boat, but she also knew he was under a lot of stress with having to clean out Thea's apartment.

And though he hadn't spoken of their future or the resort's future, she told herself they still had time. She couldn't rush things—even though that's exactly what she wanted to do.

With each passing day, he was getting more involved in the resort. She shouldn't have doubted that the island would work its charms on him. At this moment, he was off meeting with his security team as they began installing a new state-of-the-art security system. He wasn't one to pass off tasks to others; he was overseeing this installation personally.

But now with the party at the end of the week, she had to focus fully on the preparations. Thankfully Nestor had everything well organized. Her main tasks were to make sure the ballroom had been cleaned from top to bottom and then verify everything had been delivered.

"How's it going?" Atlas stood in the doorway of the event coordinator's office.

She looked up from where she sat behind Nestor's desk. "I just finished a phone call to make sure the ice sculpture would be here on time."

"And what did you learn?"

"It will be here early and stored in our walk-in freezer. Nestor made this job very easy for me."

Atlas lounged against the doorjamb. "Don't go jinxing yourself. You still have a lot to do before everything is set to go."

"I know." She stood up and moved toward him. "But I think a positive attitude is half the battle."

He nodded in agreement. "It's nice to see you in such a good mood." His voice took on a serious tone. "But I have something to ask you."

"Uh-oh." Her mind raced. "If this is about Thea's apartment, don't worry. I'll get back to it after the party. I never meant to pull out of our agreement."

He shook his head. "That isn't it. I have a special guest flying in for the party, and I need to know if there is anywhere for him to stay?"

"No. I'm sorry. The resort is fully booked. The Valentine's ball is always a big draw." She gave the idea some thought. "There's the spare room in your suite."

"I thought of that, but I'm not sure that's the right impression I want to give him of the resort. And I don't know if he'll be traveling alone."

"What about putting them in Thea's apartment?"

Once again Atlas shook his head. Then he sighed. "But I could move there and give him the suite."

She knew he'd had a very complicated relationship with his mother. She also knew he was happier when he spent the least amount of time in Thea's apartment. This couldn't be easy for him. This guest must be very important to him.

And then she thought of an idea. "Or you could stay on the mainland at my flat."

He sent her a barely there smile. "Thank you for the offer. But I need to spend more time sorting Thea's things. If I'm staying there, I won't be able to procrastinate nearly as much."

She nodded. "I understand. I'll have your things moved—"

"Don't worry. I have it under control."

When he didn't move on, she asked, "Did you need something else?"

"I just noticed that with the nicer weather more people are gravitating outdoors." He opened his mouth as though he wanted to say more but then wordlessly closed it.

"When the weather warms up, it's even busier. And the regatta draws a huge crowd."

"Interesting. It'd probably be an even larger crowd if the resort wasn't for select clientele."

"You mean rich people."

"Yes. I'm just not sure why my mother hadn't changed it. I don't recall her being all about status. But then again, I was just a little kid when I knew her. What did I know back then?"

"I'm only guessing, but something tells me your mother kept the resort the same because it's the way her late husband liked it. And it really is nice the way it is. Give it a chance. It'll grow on you."

"I don't know." *Buzz-buzz.* He glanced at his phone. "I've got to get this. We'll talk more later."

And then he was gone. She didn't know what to think

about what he'd suggested. Why would she change things when she loved them as is? Was it possible the island hadn't worked its charms on Atlas like she'd hoped? And if so, where did that leave her?

CHAPTER THIRTEEN

HE DIDN'T KNOW how to act around her.

Atlas could see that their lovemaking had changed things for Hermione. She no longer looked at him like he was the enemy—out to destroy the traditions of the Ludus.

But had things changed for him? He didn't think so. He was still moving ahead with the sale of the resort. But when it came to Hermione, all he wanted to do was to pull her into his arms and hold her close. Still, he resisted the idea because when he left the island, he didn't want to hurt her.

And since she hadn't mentioned their lovemaking, neither had he. He wouldn't know what to say—hey, it was amazing but a mistake. He couldn't say that to her, especially after knowing how her ex had treated her.

Instead, he'd kept a respectable distance from her. It wasn't helping because he noticed that she looked at him differently now, like she was caressing him with her gaze. And the way she spoke was of a softer tone, not to mention her agreeable attitude.

He wasn't much better. When he'd sought her out earlier, he'd almost asked her to go strolling on the beach with him. He couldn't imagine anything better than her hand in his with a gentle sea breeze as the sun warmed their faces.

But then he wondered what sort of idea that would give

her. It was the sort of thing couples did. Was that what he wanted?

No. He was terrible with any sort of relationship; just ask any of the women who'd passed through his life.

The only thing he knew to do was to throw himself into upgrading the resort's security. Once that was completed, he would spend all of his time working on Thea's apartment because he couldn't stay here forever.

It was late by the time he and his team finished working for the day. He fully expected Hermione to have gone home by then, but when he strolled by her office, she was so immersed in her work that she didn't notice him at her doorway until he knocked.

"Hey, it's time to call it a night." He stepped into the office, automatically pulling the door shut behind him.

"I still have so much to do." Her gaze moved over the various stacks of papers and files on her desk.

He glanced around her desk, noticing that it wasn't as neat and tidy as it'd been when he'd first arrived.

"And it will wait until tomorrow." He couldn't believe he had just uttered those words.

He was a certified workaholic. But the more time he spent on this island, the more he was finding an interest in things other than work such as spending as many meals with Hermione as their busy schedules allowed.

She sighed. "Maybe you're right." She began shutting down her computer. "It has been a long day."

"Do you have a moment before you go home?" He'd missed spending time with her and hoped she wouldn't rush off.

"Sure. What do you need?"

"I have something I want to show you." He'd found a photo album full of Ludus employees, and he'd thought Hermione would know what to do with it.

After she gathered her things, she said, "Let's go."

"Right this way." He opened the door for her.

As they walked, she asked, "Did you eat?"

He cleared his throat. "I had something with the guys." And then he worried she'd waited for him. "Did you eat?"

She nodded. "I wasn't sure how late you'd be."

"There was a lot to do, and there were a couple of problems with the installation. In order to have it all up and running by the unveiling of the Ruby Heart on Valentine's, we had to work late." He rubbed the back of his neck.

For a while, they walked in a peaceful quietness. He couldn't help but wonder if this was what it was like for couples after a long day. Did they quietly enjoy each other's presence without having to speak?

He chanced a glance at Hermione as they took the private elevator to Thea's apartment. Her face was drawn with exhaustion and he had an urge to step in and take over the party planning, but he knew that was the last thing Hermione would want. She had promised to say something if it was too much. He had to trust her.

Once in the apartment, he gestured to the couch. "Why don't you come sit down?"

He took a seat next to her. "How's the party prep coming?"

"Good. The ballroom was cleaned until it gleamed. Tables have been set up. Tomorrow we'll start decorating."

"Is there anything I can do?"

She shook her head. "I've got this."

"I do have a question for you. My friend Krystof Mikos arrives tomorrow, and he's very interested in getting a seat at the high-stakes poker game. Is that possible?"

"Sure it is. I'll have Adara make the arrangements." She wrote a note and then paused. "The buy-in won't be a problem for your friend, will it?"

"Not at all." Krystof had more money than a small country, but he didn't act like it.

"Are you sure you wouldn't like to try your hand at cards?"

He shook his head again. "I only take chances on sure things."

"You mean your business?"

"Yes."

"And what about us?" Her gaze searched his. "Are we a sure thing?"

At last she'd broached the ominous subject weighing over them. The word yes teetered on the tip of his tongue, surprising him with his willingness to involve himself in a relationship. He bit back the answer. It was a moment of delusion—a moment when he wanted to believe that happily-ever-after truly existed.

It was Hermione's fault. She made him want to believe in fairy tales and happy endings. The last thing he should do was get anywhere near her.

The memories of their lovemaking were always there, lurking at the edge of his thoughts. And getting close to her would be too tempting. He'd want to pull her close and continue where they'd left off.

But that would be wrong. He couldn't offer her anything but a good time. And Hermione didn't strike him as the type to have a casual relationship. When she cared about people, she put her whole heart on the line.

"Listen, I've been meaning to talk to you but there just wasn't a chance earlier." He struggled to find the right words.

"I wanted to talk to you too. I don't want to rush things."

"Rush things?"

"With us. I've done that before. I led with my heart instead of my head, and it didn't go well."

He didn't like being grouped with her jerk of an ex. "I'm not your ex."

"I know that. It wasn't what I meant." The pained look in her eyes said her ex had hurt her worse than she was letting on. "Otis was handsome and said all of the right words. And he happened into my life just when I needed someone."

"Sounds like you cared a lot about him." An uneasy feeling snaked its way through him.

"I did. At least in the beginning. I thought—well, I hoped he'd fill the hole that my mother's death had left in my heart. The emptiness. The loneliness. It was just so much. When Otis came along, he flirted with me and flattered me. I thought it was meant to be."

The uneasy feeling swelled within him. "You were happy?"

She nodded. "For a time."

"And then what happened?"

"He lost his job. When he had problems finding another one, he grew jealous of my education and my career. Somewhere along the way he stopped looking for work. He sponged off me and then took my money to the bar where he bought rounds of drinks for his friends."

"That must have been rough."

She shrugged. "It wasn't the best, but I thought it was a bad spell and we'd work through it so I put up with it for a time. But even I have my limits. I kicked him out. He stole all of my money and the few pieces of my mother's jewelry before he skipped town."

"That's horrible." Anger replaced the jealousy that had coiled up in his gut. "Who does such a thing?"

She shook her head. "It doesn't matter. It's over. I just wish I could get my mother's heart-shaped locket back. I tried every pawnshop I could find but none had it."

He hoped he never met this Otis guy. It wouldn't be good for either one of them. Though it would make Atlas feel a bit better to knock some sense into the guy.

"What did the locket look like?" he asked.

"I have a picture of it." She pulled out her phone. Her finger rapidly moved over the screen. And then she held up a photo of her wearing the locket.

He took the phone from her and enlarged the photo. It was a heart locket with an intricate engraved design. And in the center was a ruby.

Who would steal the necklace of a dead woman from her daughter? Atlas's gut knotted. Otis was lower than low.

"May I take a copy of this?" he asked.

"Why would you want to do that?"

"I have some friends who are good at tracking down things. I was thinking they could have a look and see if they can find it for you."

"You don't have to go to that trouble."

"But I'd like to. I'm not sure it's possible to find the locket, but I'd at least like to try."

She shrugged. "Go ahead. But I don't think you'll find it. Trust me, I've tried. For all I know, he threw it in the sea."

Atlas reached out to her, taking her hand in his own. "I'm so sorry you had to go through all of that. You deserve so much better. You deserve someone who loves and cherishes you."

Her eyes shimmered with unshed tears. "You really think so?"

"I do."

"No one has ever said that to me."

When a tear splashed onto her cheek, he moved closer and swiped it away with his thumb. "You should have someone who tells you that you're the most beautiful woman in the world." Their gazes met and held. His heart pounded. "You should be told you have the most alluring eyes that look upon the world with kindness and compassion. And most of all you have the biggest heart."

Another tear splashed onto her cheek. This time she swiped it away. "You don't have to say all of that. It isn't why I told you about Otis."

"I know I didn't have to. I wanted to." It was the truth. He meant every word. "The fact that it's taken me this long to say is my fault."

And then he didn't take the time to weigh the right or the wrong of it. He let himself do what felt right. He leaned toward Hermione, intending to place a kiss upon her cheek. But she turned just as he neared her and his kiss fell upon her lips—her soft, luscious lips.

He should pull away, but he didn't want to. He'd been thinking about her sweet kisses all day. They were addictive.

And then her mouth began to move beneath his. A moan swelled deep down in his throat, and he made no attempt to suppress it. In that moment, he didn't care if Hermione knew how much he wanted her.

There was just something about her that had him acting so out of character—acting like someone he didn't quite know. With Hermione, he wasn't shut down and cold. She made him open up and feel things. With her, he wanted to take chances and put himself out there.

He thought of the Ruby Heart's legend. Was it possible there was a bit of truth to it? As quickly as the thought came to him, he dismissed it. This thing between Hermione and him wasn't forever. He didn't do commitments.

The next thing he knew, Hermione was pushing him back on the couch. And then her soft curves pressed against

CHAPTER FOURTEEN

SHE AWOKE WITH a smile.

Her hand reached out, finding an empty spot next to her.

Hermione's eyes sprang open. She rolled over and then her gaze searched the room, finding that Atlas was gone. It took her a moment to realize where she was—a guest room in Thea's apartment. They'd moved to the bed sometime during the night—a night in which they hadn't gotten much sleep. Heat rushed to Hermione's cheeks at the memory.

The sun hadn't even risen yet. She couldn't believe she hadn't heard him get up. She yawned and stretched before settling back against the soft pillow, not quite ready to get out of bed and face the day. Atlas must have a lot to do if he was out of bed so early.

She reached for her phone and sent him a text.

Good morning <3

When an immediate response wasn't forthcoming, she scrambled out of bed and headed for the shower. There was no time to waste with Valentine's Day just a few days away.

She was thankful for having had the forethought to bring extra clothes to her office. The very last thing she wanted to do was walk around in yesterday's clothes. That would be a big announcement to everyone that she hadn't gone home last night. And it wouldn't take her friends long to figure out with whom she'd spent the evening. Heat flared in her cheeks as the memories of spending the night in Atlas's arms replayed in her mind.

She took the back way to her office and sneaked inside to switch clothes. Luckily it was so early that even Rhea hadn't arrived yet. Hermione took the opportunity to delegate some tasks to her staff as well as make a minor adjustment to the Valentine's menu.

By the time Hermione completed her emails, the resort was in full swing.

She grabbed her digital notebook so she could start checking off items. As she rushed back to the ballroom, she nearly ran into Adara. "Sorry. It's a busy morning."

"Good morning. Should I ask how things are going?"

She wasn't sure if Adara meant with the party preparations or between her and Atlas. She opted to go the safe route. "The preparations are on schedule. I just feel like the party needs something else."

"Something as in? The menu? The decorations?"

"That's just it. I don't know. It's just this feeling I have that won't leave me."

Adara sent her a smile. "I'm sure it'll come to you. And how are things with you and Atlas?"

Her body tensed. Their relationship was all so new to the both of them. She wasn't ready to dissect it. She wanted to leave it be for a little longer.

"Things are...are good." She swallowed hard. "Oh, yes, I was supposed to let you know that Atlas's friend, Krystof, has arrived. Atlas is showing him around the resort, but this evening Krystof will require a seat at the high-stakes poker game."

Adara's brows rose. "Does he know that it's a hundred-thousand-dollar buy-in?"

"Atlas said money wasn't an issue."

Adara nodded. "Okay, then. I'll make sure he's on the list."

Hermione gave her Krystof's full name. She didn't know much else about him. The truth of the matter was she'd been too distracted with Atlas as they explored this new facet of their private life to talk about much else. But if Atlas was inviting his friends to the island, that had to mean he was thinking of keeping it.

Adara finished adding the information to her digital notebook. "I'm glad everything is going well with you and Atlas. Let me know if you need anything. I think between the two of us, we might convince him to stay on the island."

Hermione smiled. "I was just thinking the same thing."

"I should be going. I have a meeting with a nervous bride-to-be. If I ever decide to change professions, please remind me that wedding planning is not for me."

Hermione laughed. "It's going that well?"

Adara nodded. "But we'll get through it. And how about you? Are you excited about attending the Valentine's ball?"

Hermione vehemently shook her head. "I'm not going. At least not as a guest."

Adara's eyes reflected her surprise. "But you have to after all the work you put into the preparations. And I know Atlas will be disappointed if you're not there."

Hermione again shook her head. "I can't." She failed to mention that she didn't have a dress for the ball. And she had absolutely no time to shop for one. Plus there was the tiny matter that Atlas hadn't asked her to be his date. "But I'll be working in the background."

Adara studied her for a moment. "Isn't there some way to change your mind?"

"It's for the best. Besides I'd never find anything to wear at this late date." Completely uncomfortable with the conversation, she said, "Can we talk later? I really have to get to the ballroom."

"Don't dismiss the idea of attending the ball. We'll talk more later."

And then Adara was gone. Hermione continued on her way. She knew Adara meant well, but she wasn't going to the ball. She'd have to be content with planning it. Still, why hadn't Atlas mentioned it?

The day had not gone as planned.

This morning's meeting with the photographer for the real estate agent had been agonizingly slow and beyond frustrating. Atlas wasn't good with playing the patient tour guide as the photographer took his time getting the perfect shot.

But the day wasn't a total loss. Krystof had arrived. And Atlas had him on the go most of the day. There was so much to see and do at the resort. It was concluded with a late dinner at Under the Sea. To Atlas, the restaurant felt as though it were part of a great big aquarium. He thought of it as the highlight of the resort.

As soon as the thought crossed his mind, he realized it wasn't true. Hermione was the true highlight of the resort. She kept the place humming along smoothly. And even when they hit some rough water, such as the problem with the Valentine's ball, she did what was needed to keep things going.

She was a true leader—a great leader. And if he were to keep the resort, she'd definitely remain the manager and get a large raise.

"What are you smiling about?" Krystof studied him.

He was smiling? He swallowed and assumed a neutral expression. "What do you think of the restaurant?"

"I don't think it's what had you smiling."

He wasn't going to have this conversation with Krystof. He'd make too much of what was going on with him and Hermione. "I was able to get you a seat at the card table tonight."

"Good. I've been looking forward to seeing what the island has to offer."

"I think you'll be impressed." At least Atlas hoped so. "And then we can revisit the idea of you buying this island paradise."

Krystof rested his elbows on the table and leaned forward. "Paradise? Aren't you layering it on a little thick?"

Atlas shook his head. "I don't think so. You can settle down here and soak up some sun when you're not trying your hand with lady luck."

"I don't know. I'm not one to stay in one place for long."

"Trust me. This place is awesome."

"If it's so great, why aren't you keeping it?"

"I probably would if it wasn't a constant reminder of Thea."

Guilt reflected in Krystof's eyes. "Sorry. For a moment, I forgot."

Krystof knew that Thea had abandoned Atlas as a young boy. It was kind of hard to hide when she was never around for any of the school events, but Atlas never went into details.

"Just give the island a chance. It's all I'm asking. And if you want to pass, I'll understand. I have a real estate agent working on a listing. One way or another, this island will cease to be my problem."

"Unless you find a reason to stay."

"Not going to happen." Hermione's face flashed into his mind. "I can't stay."

When they finished their meal, Atlas showed Krystof to the casino and the high rollers room. And then he passed by Hermione's office as well as the event planner's office. She wasn't in either place. A sensation of disappointment settled over him—was it possible he missed her? He wasn't used to missing people. He used to pride himself on not needing anyone.

But he had things he wanted to tell her. And he wanted to hear about her day. There was also that matter of clarifying things between them. Atlas expelled an exasperated sigh. Instead of clarifying things with her last night, he'd succeeded in making things more complicated.

The one thing he had accomplished was he'd sent the picture of Hermione's mother's locket to have a private investigator put out feelers with a reward for its recovery. And he'd had one of the finest jewelers in Athens start working on a replica. He paid extra to have it completed as soon as possible because he'd wanted to give it to Hermione before he left the island. And his departure hopefully wouldn't be too far off—not if he could get Krystof to buy the island.

He took the private elevator to Thea's, er, his apartment and was surprised to find the lights on. "Hermione? Are you here?"

"Back here." Her voice came from one of the bedrooms.

He strolled back the hallway and came to a stop at the doorway of his room—the room where they'd made love last night. But Hermione wasn't alone. There was another older woman standing there next to a table.

He was confused. "What's going on?"

"I have a surprise for you."

"For me? But it's not my birthday."

"Aren't you even curious what it is?"

He hesitated. "What is it?"

"A chocolate massage."

Though the idea was quite tempting, he shook his head.

"I don't think so." Then his gaze met the older lady's. "Sorry. No offense."

Hermione approached him. "Look at you. You're all tense. This will do you good. Trust me." She clasped her hands together as she pleaded with her big brown eyes. "Please."

He was quickly learning that he had no defense when she looked at him that way. "Okay. But you have to join me."

She shook her head. "I can't."

He reached out for her hand, drawing her close. In a low voice that melted her insides, he asked, "Is there a way I can change your mind?"

She hesitated. "I have plans."

He arched a brow. "Should I be insulted? Or jealous?"

"Neither." She laughed. "It's not that kind of plan. Adara asked me if I'd meet her this evening."

"To do what?"

"I'm not sure."

After she left, he felt as though the air had been sucked out of the room. There was just something about being around Hermione that filled him with a warmth. The thought of returning to his flat in London no longer appealed to him. He just wanted to be near Hermione. But he refused to acknowledge what that meant.

What did Adara want?

Hermione was surprised by her friend's invitation. She'd been unusually mysterious about their plans for the evening. The only thing she'd said in the text was that she really needed some help.

Hermione had no time to spare, but she'd make an exception for her best friend. She just couldn't stay late. With only four days until Valentine's, she had so much to do. Her stomach shivered with nerves. She may run the resort, but it was very different work from planning a lavish party.

What if she hadn't ordered enough champagne? What if they didn't schedule enough servers? This list of worries went on and on.

The party had to be spectacular. She needed Atlas to see the resort at its very best. She knew the place and its people were growing on him. A successful party would be the final touch to convince him to step into his inheritance.

Maybe she'd made a mistake by not taking time from her hectic schedule to hunt for a party dress and asking him to the dance. After all, who said the woman had to wait around for the man to extend the invitation. But it was too late now to worry about it.

She would be content to hear the after-party stories and see the photos. But the best part would be if Atlas was happy with the event.

Hermione paused outside Adara's office and knocked. "Come in."

Hermione opened the door. "Hi. What's going on?"

"I need a little help."

Hermione's gaze took in two glamorous dresses. "These are amazing." She stepped closer to the dresses. "How can I help?"

"I'm having problems deciding on a dress. I was hoping you could help me settle on one for the ball."

Surely she hadn't heard her correctly. "You want me to pick out a dress for you?"

"You sound horrified at the thought."

"No. It's just that I don't know how much help I'll be. I don't wear fancy clothes like these. I'm more of the business casual type."

"They are just material sewn together."

Hermione moved closer to the red and white dresses to

have a better look. "Silky, shimmery, sexy material sewn together in the most amazing vintage styles."

Adara laughed. "I take it you like them?"

"Who wouldn't like them? I don't know how you'll pick just one."

"How about you try them on?"

Hermione pressed her hand to her chest. "Me?" When Adara nodded, she asked, "But shouldn't you see how they fit you?"

"I need to see how they look on a person and not on a hanger. It'll help narrow things down for me. Go ahead. I know you want to."

Hermione sent her a hesitant look. "Are you sure?"

"Positive."

She tried on the white one first. She didn't have enough curves to fill it out properly. And it hung much too long for her. She insisted Adara try it on. It fit her perfectly.

While Adara wore the white one and tried to decide if she liked it, Hermione tried on the red gown. It fit her so much better. Since the office lacked a mirror, they took photos of each other in the dresses. In addition, there were sparkly, stunning heels to wear with the dresses.

"You need to wear the red dress to the ball," Adara said.

"I told you I'm not going."

"I remember your excuse being that you didn't have a dress. And now you do."

"What? No. These are your dresses."

"Not if I give you one. Besides, the red one looks far better on you."

Hermione shook her head. "You're just saying that so I'll go."

"I mean it."

"If I did go and I'm not saying I will, I'd have to pay you for the dress and shoes."

"Fine. Now we have to work on getting you a date." Adara's eyes twinkled as she smiled. "You should ask Atlas to go with you."

Hermione's mouth opened to refuse, but she couldn't think of a reason not to ask him. Wordlessly she closed her mouth.

"See," Adara said. "You like the idea."

Hermione knew Adara was once again matchmaking and she should stop her, but she didn't want to. Instead, she decided it was time to turn things on Adara. "I'll ask Atlas if you ask someone to go with you."

Adara's mouth gaped. It took her a moment to gather herself. "Who would I ask?"

"I'm sure you can find someone." Hermione snapped her fingers as the answer came to her. "Atlas's friend is here. Ask him?"

"He…he probably has a wife or a girlfriend."

"He doesn't. I asked."

Adara looked flustered. "He probably doesn't like dances."

"You won't know until you ask him." When Adara frowned at her, Hermione laughed. "Now you know how it feels. So will you ask him?"

"If that's what it takes to get you to the ball with Atlas, then yes."

With a bottle of wine and a pizza delivered for dinner, it was quite an evening. They talked. They laughed. And they had a great girls' night. She'd miss it dearly if the resort was sold.

Anxious to stop by Atlas's apartment on her way home and tell Atlas about her evening, she told Adara good-night. She might even work up the courage to ask him to the ball. She wondered what his answer would be.

But when she got there, she found his bedroom door

open and him draped across the bed as though he'd been meaning to get back up but never made it. She grabbed a throw blanket and tossed it over him before tiptoeing away. Her question would have to wait until another time.

CHAPTER FIFTEEN

TOMORROW WAS VALENTINE'S DAY.

And it was all coming together.

Friday morning, Hermione stood in the center of the ballroom taking in the amazing scene. When they'd started the prep work at the beginning of the week, the room had literally just been four plain walls with a ceiling and floor. There hadn't been anything else in the room. But the last few days had been a blur as this humongous room was brought to life. It was magnificent.

Love Under the Stars. She loved the theme. She wished she could take credit for it, but it was Nestor's idea.

Buzz-buzz.

She glanced at her phone. It was a message from Adara.

Did you ask Atlas yet?

No. Did you ask Krystof?

No.

Ticktock.

Back at you.

Hermione resisted the urge to roll her eyes. Then she turned her thoughts back to the party preparation. She still felt as though something was missing. She gazed around at the positive words displayed in neon lights on the one wall and then onto the wall of glass that opened onto a patio that led to the beach, and finally to another wall with a giant mural of the night sky with a crescent moon and the various astrological signs. As beautiful as it all was, she was certain they were missing something.

She turned to where the refreshments were to be displayed. The chocolate fountain was already assembled. No. It wasn't that. It was…

Ugh! It was right on the edge of her thoughts but when she closed her eyes to focus, there was Atlas's very handsome face. His image was always there, distracting her from her work. When she opened her eyes, he was standing in front of her looking so handsome in a light blue houndstooth button-up with his shirttail untucked and wearing a pair of dark jeans with his boat shoes. He looked totally dreamy.

She blinked, making sure she hadn't imagined him. But he was still there smiling at her, making her heart go rap-a-tap-tap. "Hi. Did you need something?"

He sent her a sexy smile that made her swoon. "I came to see if you needed a hand. I know this is a lot of work. I've cleared my schedule. All I need you to do is to tell me what needs to be done."

She glanced around, trying to figure out a task for him. But she couldn't think of anything that wasn't already being done.

Then she turned to him. "You could tell me what's missing."

His brows drew together. "Missing?"

She nodded. "I have this feeling I can't shake that something is missing."

He glanced around. "You have all of the food sorted, right?"

She nodded. "And the chocolate fountain is all set to go."

"That sounds good to me."

"Are you serious?" She pressed her hands to her hips. "This is the event of the year. It has to be perfect."

He stepped in front of her. "It will be."

She arched a brow. "How do you know?"

"Because you'll be there, and that's all I need to make my evening perfect."

Her heart rapidly thump-thumped. Heat swirled in her chest and rushed up her neck, warming her cheeks. What was she supposed to say to that? She opened her mouth, but her mind and mouth were at a disconnect. She wordlessly pressed her lips together.

He stepped closer to her. His gaze met hers as he reached for her. "Would you like a demonstration of what makes a perfect evening?"

She stepped out of his reach. "Atlas, stop." But secretly she didn't want him to stop. She wanted to sneak off with him and spend the rest of the day in his arms. "There's work to be done."

One of the workers approached them. "Hermione, where should the champagne fountain go?"

She swallowed hard, trying to hide the fact that Atlas had totally undermined her train of thought. She turned to the young man. "Um, what did you say?" After the man repeated the question, she instructed him to place it on the opposite end of the buffet from the chocolate fountain. Then she turned to Atlas, who wore an amused smile. "You're not funny. I have a job to do. You can't distract me."

"But it's so fun."

This was the moment she should ask Atlas to the ball. Her stomach shivered with nerves. If he escorted her, it would take their relationship public. It would solidify things between them. But if he turned her down...did that mean he wasn't as into her as she was into him?

She swallowed hard. "Atlas—"

"Hermione, we have a question." Two women approached her with inquiries about the buffet table. Once more asking Atlas to the ball would have to wait, but she was running out of time. She'd ask him soon, she promised herself.

A few minutes later she returned to Atlas's side. "Sorry about that."

"No problem. After all, you're the star of this production."

"That's it." She just had a light bulb moment. A big smile pulled at her lips.

"What's it?" Confusion reflected in his eyes.

"Stars. That's what's missing. A few years back there was a big wedding and they'd used crystal stars. There were hundreds of them everywhere. We can suspend them from the ceiling and use white twinkle lights to make them sparkle." She was so pleased with herself.

"Do you think you have time for all of that?"

She nodded. "But I have to hurry. I think the stars were put in the storage room. It's so big though that it's going to take me some time to find them."

"Why not send someone else?" Atlas asked.

She glanced around the enormous ballroom. It was abuzz with activity. There were people rushing here and there. People either had their arms full or they were putting something together.

"Everyone is busy. I'll just go. It'll be faster and easier."

Atlas frowned. "Two people can find them quicker than one. I'm coming with you."

Hermione shrugged. "Suit yourself."

Moments later they were in the maintenance elevator that would take them to the lower level. Hermione had to admit that she'd never liked it down here. The first thing she did was prop the heavy metal door open. No way was she getting trapped down here.

She glanced over her shoulder at Atlas. Okay, so maybe getting stuck wouldn't be the worst. After all, they'd have to find some way to pass the time, right? A smile pulled at her lips.

The overhead lights weren't that effective, certainly not to read the labels on the boxes. They located flashlights in the janitor's closet, and then they split up searching the storage room. She took the left side while he went to the right. Row after row of shelving units were lined with cardboard boxes.

Hermione flashed the light on the boxes that were well labeled. However, there wasn't any rhyme or reason to their placement on the shelf. This was going to take them some time—time she didn't have. They had to hurry.

What was happening to him?

He hardly recognized himself anymore.

Atlas had left his team to finish the security system in the gallery on their own so he could help Hermione. That wasn't like him. His business always came first...at least it used to.

In the evenings, he'd been cleaning out Thea's very large apartment, but it was slow work. So much so that he'd had to extend his stay for another week. His mother, to his utter surprise, was the sentimental type—except perhaps when it came to her only child. However, her apartment was filled with all sorts of photos and mementos.

His first reaction had been to toss it all in the nearest dumpster, but he knew the things would mean something to the Ludus staff, who had been thoughtful enough to give the items to Thea. And so he started returning the gifts one at a time.

In the process, he'd gotten to know more of the staff. They were good people with a willingness to give him the benefit of a doubt, even though he'd never visited the resort while Thea was alive. For the most part, they didn't bother him with probing questions. But there were a few of the older employees who greeted him with a raised brow. Even that hadn't been so bad because he understood their confusion. It appeared Thea didn't say much about him beyond her close circle of friends.

Even though he had other tasks requiring his attention, he couldn't abandon Hermione. He knew she was nervous about the party. He was certain with all of the attention she'd given the event that it would be a huge success. So much so that he'd arranged for the real estate photographer to come back and snap some more photos.

They really didn't have time to waste meandering around this dusty storage room. There were so many boxes that he was fairly certain they weren't going to find the stars. Still he flashed his light on box after box. St. Patrick's Day. New Year's. The names of the boxes were everything but what he needed. They were searching for the Jericho wedding.

Other than holidays, he'd found the Wilson wedding, the Smith wedding and about a dozen other weddings, just not the right one. Where was it? And how long was Hermione going to persist in this search?

He sighed as he kept checking one box label after the next. Bored of this monotonous task, his mind rewound to his conversation with Krystof about the ball. Atlas had a policy about avoiding weddings and dances at all costs, but this was different. He'd seen how excited Hermione was about the ball. How could he not be there to support her?

He wondered what she'd say if he asked her out for Valentine's? The truth of the matter was that he didn't have any idea of her plans. And he wouldn't know until he asked her—

"Atlas! I found them." The excitement rang out in Hermione's voice.

A high-pitched metallic squeak filled the silence. What was she up to now? As he headed to her location, he noticed that she'd found a ladder on wheels. She'd wheeled it over and was already halfway to the top by the time he got there.

As he looked up at her, he noticed she was on the ladder in high heels. "Hermione, you shouldn't be up there. Let me do it."

"Why? You don't think a woman can climb a ladder?" She took the last step to the top little platform.

"No. I think you wore the wrong shoes to be climbing around the storage room."

"It's okay. I'm up here now." She reached for the first box.

"Be careful."

She glanced down at him and smiled. "Are you worried about me?"

Was he? He supposed so. But he wrote it off as general concern, like he'd have for anyone. But with each passing day he was finding that Hermione wasn't just anyone—she was someone special.

"Just pay attention to what you're doing." His voice came out a little gruffer than normal.

"Yes, sir." She smiled down at him again.

He held the ladder, even though the wheel lock was secure. It was the only thing he could do as Hermione pulled box after box and piled them in front of her on the little platform.

"Let me carry them down," he said.

"I've got it." She hooked an arm around the first box and started to back down the ladder.

He stood there with his body tensed and ready to spring into action. But she took one careful step after the next. He was about to take his first easy breath when she was one step from the bottom. Then the tip of her heel caught on a rung. He reached out to her, pulling her and box safely to him.

Her head came to rest on his chest. Nothing had ever felt so right in his life. It was like they were two halves of a whole. She'd shown him that even though his heart was tattered and scarred it was still capable of more emotion than he'd ever dared feel before.

Since their lives collided during the rainstorm, his life had been irrevocably changed. He knew deep down he was never going to be the same man. Hermione had changed him for the better.

Once she regained her balance, she glanced up at him and sent him a sheepish smile. "Oops."

She looked so cute in that moment that he couldn't resist taking the box from her and letting it fall to the floor with a thump. Then he wrapped both arms around her and drew her snugly to his chest.

"What is going to happen to you when I'm not around to catch you?" He stared deep into her eyes, feeling as though he could see his future in them.

The gold flecks in her brown eyes twinkled. "I guess you'll have to stick around just in case I need you."

"And what do you need now?" His voice grew deep and gravelly with desire.

Her arms snaked around his neck as she drew him closer. And then her lips were pressed to his. Oh, yes, that's exactly what he needed too.

Hermione pulled away far too soon. "That should hold you over until later."

"Later? But I want more now."

A soft laugh filled the air. "We have work to do. How about you carry down the rest of the boxes. There are a few more on the shelf. And I'll go find a cart to move these to the ballroom."

She turned and walked away. He was left with the awful thought that one day much too soon, he'd be saying goodbye to her and those delicious kisses. The thought twisted his gut up in a knot.

But what was the alternative? Stay here on Thea's island, living in Thea's resort, in Thea's apartment? No. That was impossible. It wouldn't work. With the constant reminder of the woman who'd rejected him and yet fully embraced the Ludus staff, he would become bitter and it would destroy anything he had with Hermione.

There was another alternative: ask Hermione to leave the island with him. It wasn't ideal because he knew how much she loved it here. But it was an idea that he wasn't so quick to let go of, if it meant a chance to see where things would go with Hermione.

CHAPTER SIXTEEN

IT WAS VALENTINE'S.

The day she'd anxiously awaited.

And yet Hermione was totally bummed. Now that all of the party plans were ready to go, she realized she still hadn't asked Atlas to the dance. She reached for her phone to text him, but she hesitated. This was something she should do in person.

Her memory strayed back to their kiss in the storage room. The memory made her heart thump-thump. That kiss was forever etched upon her mind. It wasn't so much his lips touching hers, it was more the way he looked at her. It was though he too sensed there was something serious growing between them. And it was just the beginning.

Hermione had hit the ground running that morning with no makeup and a messy bun. She headed to the ballroom for the final preparations. Everything must be perfect for tonight.

Speaker system test. *Check.*

Musical acts and comedian. *Check.*

Food and refreshments. *Check.*

Ice sculpture. *Check.*

Twinkle lights and stars. *Check.*

She scanned her checklist one last time. Everything on it had been checked, double-checked and in some cases triple-checked. They were all set for tonight. Her stomach shivered with nerves.

She'd told herself that it'd be okay.

She'd told herself she could deal with it.

But she'd only been lying to herself.

She checked the time. Six o'clock. The party was set to start at seven. Atlas had been sweet to offer her his apartment for her to shower and change into her new red dress instead of having to commute back and forth from her place.

When she stepped into the apartment, Atlas was there. But he wasn't alone. There was another man with him. She recognized him as Atlas's friend Krystof. They both turned to her with a serious expression on their faces.

"Hi. Sorry." Hermione wasn't sure if she should stay or go. "I didn't mean to interrupt."

"Hermione, join us," Atlas said.

The men stood. Introductions were made. She noticed that Atlas didn't introduce her as his girlfriend—in fact, no titles were used. But that was okay. She didn't need a title. They knew what they had growing between them.

"I'm sorry for monopolizing so much of Atlas's time," Krystof said.

Her gaze moved between the two men. She hadn't known they'd spent that much time together, but she was happy that Atlas had a friend here at the resort. It would help him feel more at home.

"Not a problem," Hermione said. "I hope you're enjoying your time on the island."

"So far we've scaled the climbing wall twice, enjoyed the wave pool and visited the spa," Krystof said. "I don't like to sit still. I can only imagine what all we'd have to do if it were summer and the beach was open."

"You'll definitely have to come back in June. We have our annual regatta. Do you have a boat?"

"As a matter of fact, I do."

"Then you should consider entering. The prince of Rydiania enters every year."

"I'm sure you'd enjoy it," Atlas said.

Krystof's eyes widened. "You've attended?"

"Uh, no," Atlas said, "but I've heard a lot about it. Sounds like a good time."

"I'll keep it in mind. But right now, there's a Valentine's ball to attend." Krystof turned to Hermione. "Atlas tells me you've put together a fabulous party—the best in the resort's history."

Heat rushed up her neck and settled in her cheeks. "I don't know if it'll be the best, but I hope everyone will have a wonderful time."

"I'm sure they will." Krystof held out his hand to her. "It was nice to meet you." They shook hands. "But now I have to go because I have a date."

"A date?" Atlas sounded surprised before he smiled and shook his head. "Why am I not surprised?"

So Adara had held up her end of the agreement.

Hermione felt the pressure mounting for her to ask Atlas to the ball. But not in front of Krystof.

Atlas walked Krystof to the elevator. "I'll see you at the party."

"See you there."

Atlas closed the glass door and turned to her. "Looks like you have an admirer."

"Hardly. He was just being nice to me because he's your friend."

"I think you underestimate your beauty. It starts on the inside and glows out, putting people at ease. You're like a ray of sunshine on a cloudy day."

Her gaze strayed to the wall of windows. "But it's dark out now."

He smiled and shook his head. "You know what I mean."

"I do. Thank you for the kind words."

She filled him in on the final details for the party. And he let her know that the new security system was up and running. The conversation was very comfortable, very ordinary as though it were customary for them to fill each other in on their days.

Hermione knew it was now or never if she was going to ask him to the ball. Her heart pounded as her hands grew clammy.

"Will you go to the ball with me?" they asked in unison.

Hermione's mouth gaped as Atlas smiled at her. Had that really happened?

When she gathered herself, she pressed her lips together and swallowed. "Did we just ask each other to the ball?"

"I believe we did."

"Does that mean it's a date?" She needed him to confirm they were having an official date that evening—that they were going to let everyone know they were a couple.

"Yes, it does. Now you better get ready. You don't want to be late for your own party."

Buzz-buzz.

Atlas reached for his phone.

Tonight her very own Prince Charming would be her escort. A smile pulled at her lips. This was going to be the best night ever. And she couldn't help wondering if the Ruby Heart had something to do with it.

Atlas's voice interrupted her musing. "It's Krystof. Something came up and he needs to see me. But I can put him off—"

"No. Go. It must be important. We'll meet up at the ball."

"But this is supposed to be a date."

"It still will be. Now go see what he wants."

"Okay. I'll see you later."

And yet he continued to stand there, looking torn between staying with her and going to his friend. The fact he valued her that much wasn't lost on her. Her heart swelled with…with happiness. She wasn't ready to admit to a deeper feeling—not yet.

CHAPTER SEVENTEEN

HE WANTED TO LINGER.

He longed to be the first to see Hermione all dressed up for the ball.

And yet Atlas had been called away because Krystof said he'd made a decision about buying the island. He'd seen enough and was ready to negotiate. If it were for any other reason, Atlas would have willingly skipped out on the meeting. But he needed to close this chapter of his life—move beyond Thea's long shadow.

First, he needed to change clothes. He'd already show-ered for the second time that day. He changed into his tux. He'd had it sent via special messenger to the resort. He never anticipated needing it when he'd packed for this trip—it seemed so long ago.

The elevator chimed, alerting him to the fact that they had company. He went to meet their guest.

Adara stepped out of the elevator in a white shimmery gown. "Oh. Hi." She smiled at him. "How are things?"

"Good. How's the wedding coming?"

"It was absolutely lovely. Now that it's over, I had a few minutes to slip away and help Hermione get ready for the party."

He was out of excuses to linger around the apartment. And yet he was still hesitant to leave. This wasn't like him.

He used to be the type who didn't let anything stand between him and a meeting.

Business used to be the thing he could count on in his life. It was the one constant. His professional endeavors were what got him out of bed in the morning, what drove him all day long and were the last thing he thought of before he fell asleep at night.

But now, it was Hermione that he rushed out of bed to see in the morning. Her engaging company was what kept him going through this whole trying experience. And it was her image that was the last thing on his mind as he fell asleep at night.

And yet his time at the resort was running out. He just couldn't stay here. And he was torn about asking her to leave with him. He'd witnessed how she fit in here at the resort. Her work fulfilled her, and the people were more than just friends. This was her home and the people were her family. To rip her away from this after all she'd gone through after losing her mother would be so very wrong.

Feeling as though the world were weighing on his shoulders, he left the apartment. As he walked through the resort, memories of his time with Hermione lurked around each corner. When he'd come to the island, he'd never anticipated making memories here. Was he ready to give them up so quickly?

He shoved aside his tormenting thoughts. Right now, he had some negotiating to do with his old friend. Krystof greeted him at the door. Over a couple of bourbons, they haggled back and forth. Coming to a sales agreement was harder than Atlas thought it would be. He said upfront that the Ludus employees would need to retain their jobs for at least six months—including Hermione. Krystof agreed. But Atlas still wasn't ready to shake on it.

Krystof leaned back in his chair and studied him. "You don't want to sell the island, do you?"

"Of course I do," he said with more force than was necessary. "Why else would we be meeting?"

Krystof crossed his arms. "I get the feeling your heart is no longer in it. And if I had to guess, it has something to do with that beautiful manager."

"It does not." *Liar.*

"I don't believe you. You have it bad for her." His friend's eyes lit up as he smiled at him—like he had all of the answers to life. "You're in love."

"I am not." Atlas shot out of his chair and began to pace. His back teeth ground together as his body tensed. He didn't know who he was most upset with at the moment. His friend for having fun pointing out the obvious to him. Or himself for letting things get so out of hand with Hermione.

It would never work between them. He wasn't handsome like Krystof. He didn't have a way with words like his car salesman father, and he didn't have a selfless heart like Hermione.

He was...well, he was unlovable.

It's what he'd been telling himself since he was a kid and his mother left. He'd blamed himself. There was something about him that drove her away, and it kept his father from caring about him. And when Hermione got to know him better, she'd find out she couldn't love him either. He had to put an end to all of this now.

His gaze moved to Krystof. "Do you want to buy the island or not?"

His friend arched a brow. "And you don't care what I do with this place after six months?"

Atlas shook his head because he didn't trust his voice. The truth was that he was more invested in this island than he was willing to admit. But if he were to stay—if he were to keep it—he feared the ghosts of the past would destroy him.

Krystof stood and held out his hand to him. Atlas gripped it.

When they shook, Krystof said, "It's a deal."

Atlas hadn't realized how much time had passed. If they didn't leave now, they'd be late for the ball. And he didn't want to miss this party—the party that Hermione had worked so hard to put together.

With Krystof next to him, Atlas led the way to the ballroom. Though the party had just started, the room was abuzz with people in black tuxes and glittery dresses. Atlas smiled. He was so happy to see that Hermione's party was off to a successful start.

Neon lights in red and white lit up the wall with inspiring words of hope and love. He glanced toward the grand patio. It was lit up with white candles. While inside, red roses adorned all of the tables as well as bowls of heart-shaped candies with printed messages such as *Be Mine* and *Kiss Me*. But it was the crystal stars and twinkle lights suspended from the ceiling that made the whole room appear magical.

But where was Hermione? His gaze searched the room for her. It was so hard to see with so many people in attendance. She had to be here. But where?

He made his excuses to Krystof, who appeared to be looking around for his date. They'd been so caught up in making a deal for the resort that Atlas hadn't even thought to ask him about his mystery date. It must be the reason for his interest in the resort.

Atlas moved about the room, searching for the woman who made this whole evening possible. And still he couldn't find her. He had a feeling with a room of this size, he might be walking around it all night and still miss her.

He moved to the stage where a world-famous K-pop band was playing dance music. He stood off to the side in order to look out over the crowd. Still, no sign of her.

But then his gaze strayed across to Krystof. And not surprisingly, he wasn't alone. The surprise was the identity of the woman he was dancing with—Adara. Both were smiling and appeared to be having a good time.

He'd be having a good time too if he could find Hermione. He was about to backtrack to the apartment to see if she'd changed her mind about attending the party when in through the entrance came Hermione. His gaze latched on to her and stayed with her.

Her long hair hung past her shoulders in loose curls. On top of her head were curls secured with sparkly pins. But it was the smile on her face that drew him to her. He longed for her to smile like that at him.

He hurried off the stage and headed toward her. He just hoped she didn't get away before he made it through the crowd. With a lot of *pardon me* and *excuse me*, he made it to the entrance.

And there was Hermione in an off-the-shoulder red gown. The fitted bodice was studded with crystals that sparkled. The material gathered at her slim waist and then fell loosely down over her hips and stopped at her heels, which also sparkled with crystals. She was…breathtaking.

She stepped up to him. "Atlas, is everything all right?"

He swallowed hard. "Uh, yes…everything is perfect. You…you are perfect."

Color flooded her cheeks. "I don't know about that."

"I do. I've never seen someone so beautiful." As the color in her cheeks intensified, he rushed on to add, "And this party is amazing. Everyone is having a great time."

"Really?" Her eyes lit up with excitement. "You think so?"

"I do." He held his arm out to her. "Will you dance with me?"

A bright smile lifted her lips. "I'd love to."

He had a feeling his feet were going to be sore by the end of the night because he intended on claiming every dance with her. With their time together drawing to a close, he wanted to make more of those happy memories—memories he would carry close to his heart.

As they danced to a slower tune, he drew her in close. He breathed in the delicate floral scent of her perfume. He would never breathe in that scent without thinking of her. How was he ever going to tell her that the sale of the island was in the works?

CHAPTER EIGHTEEN

THE EVENING FLEW BY.

Atlas couldn't remember being so happy. They'd spent the entire evening together. They were making more of those memories that would keep him warm on those long lonely nights ahead of him.

He needed to tell her about the pending sale of the island, but he hadn't found the right moment. And with nine o'clock approaching, the guests had made their way onto the beach to watch the fireworks that would be set off offshore.

And then the countdown began...

"Ten—nine—eight—"

Atlas joined in the countdown. And he couldn't be happier to have Hermione by his side.

"Seven—six—five—"

Though everything had been a disaster when he'd first arrived on the island, they'd taken a surprising turn for the best. And it was all thanks to Hermione. She'd made his visit an enjoyable event.

"Four—three—two—"

Too bad it was coming to an end. Whereas Valentine's was meant to reaffirm one's love and commitment, this thing between Hermione and him, well, it was an ending. And, oh, how he was going to miss her. More than he'd ever imagined possible.

"One!"

A loud boom thundered around them signaling the beginning of the fireworks. A softer *whoosh* could be heard as the fireworks were launched. A cascade of white and red lights glittered in the black velvet sky.

Another *whoosh* was heard, and a sparkling pink heart filled the sky.

Hermione turned to him. "Isn't it spectacular?"

He stared into her eyes and was immediately drawn in by her boundless happiness. It filled his scarred heart and filled in the cracks and crevices—making him feel whole.

Hermione leaned into him. He reached out to her. And the next thing he knew, they were in each other's arms. His lips claimed hers with a need to remember everything about her. He didn't ever want to forget her or this moment.

Even though he wasn't leaving for another week, he already missed Hermione. He pulled her closer, feeling her soft curves pressed to him. A moan swelled in the back of his throat.

There would never ever be anyone like Hermione. She was sweet and funny at the same time that she was fiercely independent and stubborn. It was an intoxicating combination. And he longed to hold her in his arms forever and ever because he was in love with her. The thought startled him.

He pulled back. Hermione didn't seem to notice that the world seemed to have shifted. Maybe it was just him. Because loving Hermione meant loving this island, and he couldn't do that. This was Thea's island, not his. Never his.

He couldn't let himself get drawn into a fantasy where Hermione was concerned. His business was waiting on him to hit the road and land other big deals. That's what he could count on—his business.

He glanced over and noticed that Krystof was still talking to Adara. "Krystof and Adara seem to have hit it off."

Hermione arched a brow. "Is he the one you were thinking of selling the island to?"

"I still am. That's the reason I invited him here."

Frown lines etched her eyes and mouth. "I thought you changed your mind."

"You want me to keep this island?" When she nodded, he said, "You don't know what you're asking of me."

"But isn't that what we've been working toward? You've even gotten to know the staff."

"Hermione, you're asking too much of me. Krystof will do a much better job managing the island than I've done."

"No, he won't. He doesn't have a connection to the island like you do."

She was right. No matter how much he wanted to deny it, he was forever linked to this island via Thea. But not in a good way. Thea chose this life and this island over him. How was he ever supposed to reconcile himself to that fact?

He shook his head. "I'm sorry. I can't do it. This sale is going to happen."

Her eyes grew dark as though a wall had just come down between them. "And that's it? No conversation? No negotiation?"

"This is the way it has to be." It was killing him to say these things. He wanted another option. And even though he knew it was selfish, he said, "Come with me. I can show you the world."

She was quiet for a moment as though giving his suggestion serious consideration. "When we're done seeing the world, I want to come home. I want to come back to Ludus."

He shook his head. "I can't."

Disappointment flashed in her eyes. "Then this is goodbye."

Hermione turned to leave but he reached out to her. His hand caught hers. "Don't go. Not like this."

She turned back to him. Her eyes shimmered with un-shed tears. "Do you want me to wait so you can leave first? Because once you sign the sales agreement you'll be leaving and we'll never see each other again. My life is here. My friends are here." She gazed deep into his eyes. "Have you ever stayed in one place long enough to make close friends—friends who have your back and you have theirs?"

The truth was that he'd been moving around since he finished university. Though he had a flat in London, he was forever on the road making deals. With technology he didn't have to be in one place to do his job.

"I have a home in London." His tone was firm. "Everything I care about is there."

"Except me." The pain reflected in her eyes dug at him. "Goodbye, Atlas."

He stood still as she walked away.

He desperately wanted to go after her—to tell her that he'd changed his mind. But he couldn't do that. This island would slowly but surely eat away his soul. Thea's memory lurked in the paint colors, the wall hangings—she was everywhere—reminding him that the people you loved the most were the ones that hurt you the most.

Right now, he was the one doing the hurting. And he hated himself for it. But it was better now than later. Because the longer this went on, the more Hermione would invest herself in him, in them, and he would eventually let her down. It was in his genes.

He wanted to rewind life to that rainy night when their lives had collided. He wanted things to go back to the way they used to be—easy and fun. And then he wanted to slow time so he could savor their moments together. But none of that was possible. He was left with his few precious memories.

CHAPTER NINETEEN

HE'D MADE THE biggest mistake of his life.

Buzz-buzz.

And he had no interest in hearing from anyone.

Bleary-eyed, Atlas stumbled through Sunday morning. He'd barely slept the night before. He kept replaying the scene at the party over and over in his mind. The kiss had been perfect. Hermione had been perfect. And he—well, was broken.

The more he told himself that he'd done what was best for Hermione, the more his heart told him it wasn't true. The reason he'd been fighting his love for her was much more serious. He'd been protecting himself from being rejected yet again.

He loved the lilt of her voice. He loved the way her eyes lit up when she laughed. He loved how she stood up for herself—believed in herself. And most of all, he loved how she cared for others—putting their needs ahead of her own. And sadly he knew he couldn't give her what would make her happy. He couldn't stop moving around and settle here on this island.

He knew Hermione would find someone else to love her—someone who would make her happy—someone who would share her vision for the future. The thought of her with someone else made his stomach churn.

Buzz-buzz.

What was it with his phone that day? Did everyone think he constantly worked? Even on Sunday. Well, he used to be that way, but since he'd been on the island, Hermione had shown him what it was like to have balance in life. It was something he intended to carry on after he left here.

Ring. Ring. Ring.

His gaze moved to the landline phone, but he made no motion to answer it. Obviously whoever wanted him was getting impatient. He should care, really he should, but he didn't. The business and the rush of closing a new deal no longer had a pull over him without Hermione in his life.

He was supposed to meet Krystof to sign the papers this morning. There was no point in putting off the inevitable. Once they were signed, he wouldn't be plagued by the what-ifs that had bothered him all night.

He showered without bothering to shave. He dressed but in jeans and a dress shirt that he didn't bother to tuck in. He didn't feel the compulsion to worry about his casual appearance. It was what it was.

Ding-dong. Ding-dong.

He thought of ignoring the private elevator too, but the fact that he needed it to go to a meeting made that impossible. With a resigned sigh, he headed for the intercom and pressed the button to allow whoever it was up to the apartment. A moment later the elevator door slid open, and Adara stood there with her fine brows knitted together in a frown.

"I've been trying to reach you," she said.

"We weren't supposed to meet, were we?"

"No." She crossed her arms. "But we need to talk."

"I'm not really in a chatty mood—"

"This is important." Her firm tone brooked no argument. He gestured for her to step into the living room. "Give me a second." He strode over to the bar and retrieved a water. "Can I get you anything?"

She perched on the edge of the couch. "No. Thank you."

He sat down on the chair and turned to her. "What do you need?"

"Krystof's counsel has arrived. There's some question as to the ownership of the resort. They want to know if you have a copy of the will."

"Uh…no. I didn't think I'd need it. My attorney assured me that all of the paperwork had been properly filed."

"I believe you. I just think the gentlemen in the meeting room would feel better if they could see verification."

He didn't want to do it. He didn't want to have to deal with Thea's will…again. "I guess the sale will have to be delayed."

"Maybe not."

He arched a brow. "What do you have in mind?"

"Thea, Hermione and I had become very close over the years. She told us if there were any problems that she'd placed a copy of her will in her safe."

"She told you that?"

"Yes. It was after your stepfather passed on. She wanted to make sure the resort went on as it always had and the employees didn't lose their jobs."

He shook his head in disbelief. "If it means ending this sooner rather than later, I'll go check her safe."

And with that he walked away. In the hallway his strides were long and quick. He'd had it with Thea pulling his strings from beyond the grave. He just wanted his life back the way it was supposed to be—where he was in control. It couldn't happen soon enough. Because being here—being without Hermione—was killing him.

By the time he reached Thea's bedroom and removed the large painting from the wall to reveal the wall safe, he was in a perfectly awful mood. He pulled up the code to the safe from the note he'd made on his phone.

The first time he moved the tumbler too rashly and it didn't work. He took a deep breath and blew it out. And then with a steadier hand, he tried once more. This time the safe opened.

He hadn't explored the safe yet. The truth was that he'd been putting it off. He'd been ignoring Thea's entire bedroom. It was just too personal.

The safe was filled with jewelry boxes. None of that interested him. He scanned the safe, looking for the will. As soon as he got it, he was out of there. He was half inclined to tell Adara to do what she wanted with the rest of Thea's belongings since they'd been friends.

On the top shelf of the safe were some papers. He pulled them out. One by one he glanced at them, looking for the will. And then he happened upon an envelope with his name handwritten on it.

He froze. Why would this be in the safe? And then he realized it must be a copy of the will. Since he was the sole heir, it would make sense to have his name on it. Though the envelope did seem a bit slim for such a document.

He opened the envelope, expecting to find some sort of legal document. Instead, what he found was blue stationery with Thea's handwriting.

My dear Atlas,
If you're reading this it means my worst fear has happened. I have died without us reconciling. And for that I am so deeply sorry.

First, I love you. I've always loved you. You are a piece of me—the best part of me.

But I am human, and I made huge mistakes—mistakes I wish I could undo. I never meant to leave you.

I swear. I left because I didn't have any other choice.
Your father and I couldn't live together any longer.
I'll spare you the details but please believe me when
I say it was bad, very bad.

Atlas stopped reading. He wasn't going to let Thea re-write the past. No way. He was there. He knew what happened.

He tossed the letter aside. He continued his search for the will. That was the reason he was here—the only reason. He wasn't going to give Thea's words any power over him.

He reached back inside the safe and pulled out another stack of stuff. This time there was a book of some sort. Surely the will wouldn't be in there, but curiosity got the best of him and he lifted the other papers off the big bound book. He opened it to find a baby photo of himself.

A voice in his head said to close it and move on, but apparently his body wasn't listening to his mind because the next thing he knew, he was turning the page. Again there were pictures of him as a little boy. Why would she still have these after all of this time?

He turned page after page, finding photos he'd never seen before. His father wasn't big on family photos. But some of these photos were of him and Thea. She was smiling as she cheered him on to blow out candles on his birthday cake. There were others of them at the park.

Page by page, he aged in the photos until they suddenly stopped. And then there were media releases about his company—about him. She'd followed his career from his small start-up company to becoming one of the largest security firms in the world. She had press clippings in here that he'd never seen before.

And then something splashed onto the page. Luckily there was a clear plastic sheath over the clippings so he could wipe away the moisture without it damaging anything. And then there was a drip on his hand. He lifted his fingertips to his cheek and realized the moisture was coming from him.

He swiped at his cheeks as he continued flipping through the pages. Thea had followed his life right up until she'd died. Why would she do that if she didn't care about him?

He set aside the scrapbook and reached for Thea's letter once more. He continued reading as she explained that his father had physically thrown her out. With his father being much older than Thea, he'd had a lot of power over her. He'd threatened that if she ever tried to see Atlas again that both she and Atlas would pay for it. At the time she'd been too poor to fight him in court as he owned a car dealership and had many resources and lots of influential connections in the community.

It wasn't until she met Georgios and fell in love that she was able to fight his father. She went back for Atlas but by then he had been swayed by his father into thinking that she'd willingly abandoned him. He'd wanted nothing to do with her.

She went on to explain that she didn't know what to do. She didn't want to make things worse for him so she left. But she never stopped loving him.

She left him this island because it's where she healed and flourished. She'd hope it would bring him happiness and love. He rubbed his eyes and read the letter again.

All of this time, he'd thought his mother hadn't loved him. And maybe she hadn't handled the situation the way he would have liked, but she did the best she could. No one was perfect, most especially not him.

And that was the reason he'd been holding himself back from picturing a future with Hermione. But the truth was that he couldn't imagine his future without her.

If he left the island now, would he be following in his mother's footsteps? Would he be walking away from the chance to give love and be loved? Shouldn't a lesson be learned from what happened with him and his mother? Sometimes people weren't given second chances—sometimes you had to seize the moment.

Atlas set aside the letter. He had to find Hermione. And he had to find her right now. No, he needed to pause in order to form a plan—proof that he loved her.

CHAPTER TWENTY

A WEEK OFF from work.

Monday morning, Hermione looked around her modest flat and couldn't find a thing she felt like doing. And yet she couldn't go back to the Ludus—not yet. She had a lot of unused time off, and now was the time to use some of it.

In a week, Atlas should have his business wrapped up at the resort. She pushed the painful thought of him to the back of her mind. She supposed she should be happy he hadn't fired her.

How had she ever let herself get caught up in the legend of the Ruby Heart? She blamed it for letting herself fall hard for Atlas and believing that he could change. She had been so foolish.

She needed to stay busy. Her gaze moved around the bedroom. Her bed was already made up without a wrinkle. Everything was in its place. And it all felt so empty.

She told herself it had nothing to do with Atlas—nothing to do with the fact that he'd soon be flying back to London, nothing to do with the fact that she would never again lay eyes on him.

She retraced her steps to the living room. Her heart ached as she pictured his handsome face. She reached for an old faded throw pillow on the couch and hugged it to her chest. Then just as quickly she tossed aside the pillow. She was not going to sit around feeling sorry for herself. She was fine before Atlas and she'd be fine after him.

She moved to the two houseplants she'd bought yesterday at the market. She'd given them names. One was Spike and the other Ivy. Not original names, but she liked them.

She gave them each a drink of water and placed them on the windowsill to soak up some sunshine. She glanced around for something else to do—something that needed her attention. Perhaps she should adopt a dog. Then again, when she went back to work, she wouldn't be home much. Perhaps a cat would be better. She liked the idea. It would be nice to have someone to come home to. Then Atlas's image once more appeared in her mind. She exhaled a deep sigh. How could she have read things so wrong between them?

Knock-knock.

It was probably her neighbor, Mrs. Persopoulos. She was very sweet. And Hermione tried to help her out by carrying her groceries up the stairs or helping to clean her tiny apartment when she was available.

Hermione moved across the flat in just a few steps. She forced a smile to her face as she opened the door, only to find it wasn't Mrs. Persopoulos. There was a delivery person holding a bouquet of red roses.

"Ms. Kappas?"

"Yes."

"These are for you." He held the arrangement out to her. She automatically accepted them. "Thank you."

Her heart raced. No one had ever sent her flowers—certainly not her ex. Could these be from Atlas? No. Of course not. Why would he send her flowers?

She rushed to her small table and placed the vase of

flowers atop it. There was a note attached. She pulled the card from the envelope.

I'm sorry!
Atlas

They were from him. Her breath caught in her throat. What did that mean? He was sorry for what? Hurting her? Walking away?

The questions continued to roll around in her mind. Hope began to swell in her chest. She knew that was dangerous. She didn't want to get her heart broken. But wasn't it already broken?

Because she loved Atlas, even if he didn't love her in return.

She leaned over and inhaled the flowers' delicate scent. She had to know what this was all about; she reached for her phone. Her hand had a slight tremor as she dialed Atlas's phone.

It rang once. Twice. Three times.

Knock-knock.

She rushed to the door and swung it open. There stood another delivery person. "Ms. Kappas?"

"Yes." This was beginning to take on a sense of déjà vu.

He held out a small brown-paper-wrapped package. She thanked him and closed the door. She moved to the couch and sat down. What was it this time? She assumed it was also from Atlas. Why was he showering her with gifts?

She tore off the paper to find a box of specialty chocolates and an envelope. She opened it, finding a gift certificate for a chocolate massage at the resort's spa. And a note in Atlas's handwriting.

I know how much you love chocolate. I hope you will enjoy these and maybe you will find it in your heart to forgive me. Please. Perhaps a chocolate massage will help. I know I enjoyed the one you planned for me. You are so thoughtful—so kind. And I miss you!

Hermione read the message again. And again. What was he trying to tell her? Had he changed his mind about keeping the island—about their relationship?

Knock-knock.

CHAPTER TWENTY-ONE

HE WAS TAKING a chance.

This was a risk he'd never taken in his life.

In the past, when a woman was tired of his workaholic and nomadic ways, she walked away. He never followed—never asked for a second chance. And yet with Hermione, he was willing to risk it all—his pride and most of all... his heart—if it meant a chance for him to win her back.

He'd done a lot of soul-searching over the past two days since she'd left, and he knew his life just wasn't the same without her in it. But would he be able to convince her to give him a second chance?

His heart thump-thumped as he knocked on her door. He braced himself for the possibility of having the door slammed in his face. He wouldn't blame her. He'd made an utter mess of things.

Each second dragged on. And then he heard footsteps and the door swung open. Hermione looked adorable in her blue jeans and pink cotton top. Her long hair was swept back in a ponytail. And there wasn't a trace of makeup on her face—not that she needed any. She had a natural beauty about her. But he did notice the shadows beneath her eyes.

"Atlas, what are you doing here?"

"I'm hoping you'll come somewhere with me."

"I... I don't know." She worried her bottom lip. "Where?"

He noticed she didn't invite him inside. "Back to the beginning."

"What beginning?"

"Ours." His gaze searched hers. "Please."

There was a moment of silence as though she were deciding what she should do. All the while, he willed her to agree. He wanted so badly to make things right between them.

"Okay." Her voice was so soft that for a moment he thought he'd imagined it. "Let me grab my stuff."

A moment later she had on a light jacket, white tennis shoes and a gray purse slung over her shoulder. He led her downstairs and outside to his one-of-a-kind black sports car. As he zipped along the streets, she peppered him with questions but he held her off.

He wanted to do this right.

And so he distracted her with talk of the warm weather and trivial matters. The fact they were communicating on any level he took as a positive sign. Soon they arrived at the dock. A short ferry ride and they were on Ludus Island. He navigated the car along the winding road until they came to the spot of the accident. He pulled to the side of the road and turned off the engine.

"What are we doing here?" Hermione asked.

He got out but when he rounded the front of the car to open the door for her, she was already exiting the vehicle. "I thought we should go back to the beginning of you and me."

"You meant it literally." She gazed around.

"Signs of the accident have all been washed away with the flooding rains, but one thing wasn't, the initial feelings I had for you. They've only grown since I've gotten to know you."

She eyed him suspiciously. "The only thing you felt for me that night was anger."

He shook his head. "I'm sorry I was so grouchy in the beginning, but you didn't let it run you off. You stood your ground and made me see sense during one of the darkest times of my life. You're the strongest woman I know. And I'm so much better off by knowing you."

Her eyes shimmered with unshed tears. She blinked repeatedly. "You really think I'm strong?"

Once more he nodded. "So much stronger than me because you were willing to admit that what we had wasn't just a holiday fling—it was so much more. But I was afraid to put my heart on the line—afraid I wasn't worthy of your love."

She reached out to him, cupping his cheek with her hand. "How could you think that? You are amazing and sweet. Any woman would be lucky to have you in their life."

He leaned down and pressed his lips to hers. The kiss was short. He didn't want to get distracted. He needed to get this all out there. He needed to fix what he had broken.

Summoning all of his strength and determination, he pulled away from her sweet kiss. Her eyes fluttered open and stared at him with confusion reflected in her eyes.

Her heart raced.

Hermione could hardly believe she was here with Atlas and that he was kissing her. Hope and excitement swelled within her, but she refused to let it take over. She had to know that Atlas was fully invested in their relationship. She had to hear him say the words.

She loved him, but she wasn't going to make this easy for him. She wasn't going to assume what he meant by this grand gesture. If he was going to be in this for the long haul with her, he had to be willing to put himself out there—the whole way.

"Why did you bring me here?" she asked.

"I told you, so we could start over. Come back to the resort."

"You mean to continue running the place until the new management can take over?"

He shook his head. "There isn't going to be any new management."

She was confused. "There isn't?"

"Krystof and my mother helped me see that this place, this island—and you are my future. That is if you still want me."

Oh, boy, did she ever. It would be like a dream come true. Wait. Had she heard correctly? "Your mother?"

He nodded and explained about the letter and the scrapbook. "I just wish she'd have reached out again and that I would have been mature enough to hear her out." His gaze searched hers. "I don't want to repeat my mother's mistake and walk away from someone I love. Will you give me another chance?"

A tear splashed on her cheek. "You love me?"

He held up a finger for her to wait a moment. Then he reached in his suit jacket and pulled out a black velvet box. Her heart leaped into her throat.

"Go ahead," he said. "It's for you."

Another gift? The gifts were really sweet. He was trying really hard to get this right. She accepted the box and opened it. Inside was a locket. The breath hitched in her lungs. She knew this locket. She looked closer. It looked so much like her mother's missing locket.

"It's not the original," Atlas said. "I had a duplicate made until we can recover the original."

No one had ever done something so thoughtful for her. She lifted her gaze to his. "Thank you for being so sweet."

"Open it."

She swiped at her cheeks and then she did as he asked.

Inside were two little heart-shaped pieces of paper with the words *I love you* written on them.

Her gaze lifted to his. "You do?"

He nodded. "With all of my heart."

And then she had the most incredible realization. "It's true."

"What's true?"

"The legend of the Ruby Heart."

"Is it?" His gaze challenged her. "Will you come back to the resort with me?"

She smiled and nodded. "I love you too." But then she realized that she now had other responsibilities. "But can Spike and Ivy come with me?"

"Spike and Ivy?" He shrugged. "Bring whoever you want. My home is your home."

"Good. Because I've kept those houseplants alive for two days now and I'd hate for anything to happen to them."

He laughed and shook his head. "Maybe we should think about getting you a dog."

"Or a cat."

"Or one of each." He pulled her close. "I've always been a bit of a nomad, but I can't wait to set down roots with you. And Spike and Ivy."

"Before we do that, how about we do some more of this?" She lifted up on her tiptoes and pressed her lips to his.

EPILOGUE

Four months later... Ludus Island

EVERYTHING WAS LOOKING UP.

The resort was bustling with sunseekers.

And Hermione had never been happier in her life.

Right now, she was gearing up for the resort's biggest event of the year—the Royal Regatta. It was due to kick off tomorrow, and Hermione was a nervous wreck. Everything had to go perfectly with Prince Istvan of Rydiania in attendance.

Additional staff had been hired to make this year's regatta bigger and better than ever. Nestor was back at work, seeing to all of the event's details. While Atlas was splitting his time between his security business and running the resort. He was very busy, but Hermione had never seen him happier. And that filled her heart with joy.

Hermione stood outside on the veranda taking in the view of smiling guests enjoying the beach. June was her favorite time of the year. There was an energy that flowed through the resort—

"Excuse me, Miss Kappas. Where do you want me to set up?"

Hermione turned to their latest hire. She searched her memory for the young woman's name. It took Hermione a second to recall it. "Good morning, Indigo. We're so happy to have you as part of the Ludus family. I've had a large umbrella set up for you on the beach. Just let us know what else you need—"

"Good morning, Hermione." The deep male voice had a distinct foreign accent.

Hermione would know that sexy voice anywhere. She immediately turned and then curtsied. "Your Royal Highness."

He smiled. "Hermione, I told you curtsying isn't necessary."

"But it feels wrong not to. After all, you're a prince."

"Don't remind me. I have those guys to constantly remind me." He gestured over his shoulder to the small army of dark suited men with sunglasses and earpieces. His gaze moved to Indigo. His smile broadened. "And who might you be?"

Hermione noticed how the young woman's eyes widened. When Indigo appeared to be shocked into silence, Hermione intervened. "This is Indigo. She's a talented artist."

"Is that so?" The prince's gaze studied the woman. "A beautiful artist."

If Hermione didn't know better, she'd think the prince was drawn to Indigo. But he was normally smooth and flirtatious with all of the pretty ladies. This meeting was no different. Or was it? "Perhaps she could do a sketch for you."

"I'd like that." He was still staring at Indigo, who was now blushing. "But it'll have to wait. I have some business to attend to." He turned his attention to Hermione. "I wanted to say hello and find out how things are going now that Thea's son owns the island."

"Things are going well." She smiled as she thought of Atlas. "Very well. I'll have to introduce you to him."

"I'd like that. Now I must be going." He gave Hermione's hand a butterfly kiss. And then he did the same for Indigo. "I look forward to our next meeting."

After he was gone, Indigo still hadn't spoken a word. Hermione couldn't blame her. The prince was quite charming. And then there was that sexy accent.

"You can go set up," Hermione said, jarring the woman out of her stupor.

"I… I can't believe I didn't say a word to him."

Hermione smiled. "It's fine. I'm sure he's used to it."

Once Indigo moved on, Hermione checked her email on her digital tablet. She should be in her office working, but the sunshine and sea breeze had called to her. She'd have to go inside soon, but she just needed a minute or two more of fresh air.

"Here you are." Atlas stepped up next to her. "Are you busy?"

"I'm never too busy for you." She lifted up on her tiptoes, pressing her lips to his. When she pulled away, she asked, "What do you need?"

"More of those kisses." He smiled at her.

"I'm afraid you'll have to wait until later."

He sighed. "In that case, I need you to come see something."

"Please tell me nothing's wrong. The prince just arrived. Oh, and he wants to meet you."

He arched a brow. "Should I be jealous that you're buddies with a prince?"

"No. I already have my prince." She gave him another quick kiss. "Now what's going on? Is it the security system?" She followed him inside to the elevator. "We assured the prince that everything was now state of the art."

"It's not the security system." He pressed the down button.

"We're going to the Under the Sea restaurant?"

Atlas turned to her. He cupped her face in his hands. "Stop worrying. I promise you everything is going to be perfect."

"But you said I had to see something."

"I didn't say it was something bad. Did I?"

"But—"

He leaned over and pressed his lips to hers. Immediately her stress started to dissipate. She leaned into him and returned the kiss. She would never ever get tired of kissing him.

The elevator dinged as the door slid open. With great reluctance, she pulled away from Atlas. But he in turn took her hand in his.

"Come on." He led her past the waiting area.

The restaurant was only open for dinner service so with this being noon, it should be empty. But when they stepped into the dining room, there was a table in the middle of the room. There was a few candles and a huge bouquet of red roses.

Hermione turned to Atlas. "I don't understand."

He smiled. "I have a surprise for you." He drew her closer to the table that was set for lunch—a champagne lunch. He picked up a black velvet box. He held it out to her. "This is for you."

She smiled. "You have to quit spoiling me."

"But I enjoy it. I love making you smile."

She opened the box. Inside was a locket, exactly like the one she was wearing. "You got me another locket?"

"No. I got you the real locket—your mother's locket."

"You found it!" Tears rushed to her eyes as her finger traced over it. "I never thought I'd see it again." Her watery gaze moved to his. "Thank you."

"Open it."

This definitely felt like déjà vu. But she did what he said. Inside, resting on top of the photos of her parents, were two little pieces of paper.

On the left it said: *Will you...*

The right read: *...marry me?*

She read it twice, just to make sure she'd read it correctly. When she looked at Atlas, she found him on bended knee. He held out a smaller black velvet box with a big beautiful emerald cut diamond ring.

"Hermione, I fell for you from the first time I saw you. I didn't need a ruby to tell me how special you are. I just had no idea how much you would change my life for the better, and now I can't imagine my life without you in it. Will you marry me?"

By now the tears of joy had rolled onto her cheeks. Her heart went pitter-patter with love. "Yes. Yes, I'll marry you."

He straightened, slipped the ring on her finger and then pulled her into his arms, claiming her lips with his own. She had found the love of her life. How had she gotten so lucky?

* * * * *

COMING SOON!

We really hope you enjoyed reading this book.
If you're looking for more romance, be sure to
head to the shops when new books are
available on

Thursday 3rd February

To see which titles are coming soon, please visit

millsandboon.co.uk/nextmonth

MILLS & BOON

MILLS & BOON

Coming next month

BABY SURPRISE FOR THE MILLIONAIRE
Ruby Basu

All the different instruction leaflets scattered on her counter said the same thing—the best time to take a test was first thing in the morning. Saira knew this already. She didn't need to read the instructions to know what to do. But reading them was a good distraction from thinking about why she needed the tests...

She ran her fingers through her hair. She could be worrying about nothing. Probably was. This was a situation she was all too familiar with, and each time she was left disappointed.

Saira picked up one of the boxes. How many times had she bought one of these, full of excitement, full of joy, and then seen Dilip's crestfallen face each time she told him the negative news?

Apart from that one time. Which she didn't let herself think about. Couldn't let herself think about.

She took a couple of deep, centring breaths and focused on the boxes in front of her. After all those times when she'd yearned for a positive result, she couldn't be pregnant from a fling. Could she?

She hadn't even considered it a possibility until that morning. When Dilip died, Saira had put away her ovulation kits and thermometers and trackers, never expecting to need them again.

It was only when she saw her stock of unused sanitary

supplies and put them together with her dizzy episodes and mild morning nausea that she even entertained the thought.

The hope?

The previous times she'd taken these tests she'd been part of a loving, committed couple, for whom a child would have been a much-wanted addition to their family.

This time it couldn't be more different.

She'd returned to England to start again. Get a job. Find her own place. Be independent. Her future plans hadn't included having a child.

But those plans were based on her false assumption she would need to be in a relationship before a child could be part of the picture. Life didn't care about her assumptions. If she were pregnant she could easily adjust those plans, and would happily do so.

Pregnant.

Could it be possible?

She half-laughed, half-cried at the prospect. The fear, the worry, the doubts had already started to creep in.

She needed to be practical. She deliberately turned her thoughts to Nathan. To how he would react. She had no idea how to handle this situation. Was there some etiquette for telling someone you'd had a fling with that you might be pregnant with their baby?

Continue reading
BABY SURPRISE FOR THE MILLIONAIRE
Ruby Basu

Available next month
www.millsandboon.co.uk

MILLS & BOON

THE HEART OF ROMANCE

A ROMANCE FOR EVERY READER

MODERN

Prepare to be swept off your feet by sophisticated, sexy and seductive heroes, in some of the world's most glamourous and romantic locations, where power and passion collide.

HISTORICAL

Escape with historical heroes from time gone by. Whether your passion is for wicked Regency Rakes, muscled Vikings or rugged Highlanders, awaits the romance of the past.

MEDICAL

Set your pulse racing with dedicated, delectable doctors in the high-pressure world of medicine, where emotions run high and passion, comfort a love are the best medicine.

True Love

Celebrate true love with tender stories of heartfelt romance, from the rush of falling in love to the joy a new baby can bring, and a focus on the emotional heart of a relationship.

Desire

Indulge in secrets and scandal, intense drama and plenty of sizzling hot action with powerful and passionate heroes who have it all: wealth, status good looks…everything but the right woman.

HEROES

Experience all the excitement of a gripping thriller, with an intense romance at its heart. Resourceful, true-to-life women and strong, fearless m face danger and desire - a killer combination!

To see which titles are coming soon, please visit

millsandboon.co.uk/nextmonth

MILLS & BOON
MEDICAL
Pulse-Racing Passion

Set your pulse racing with dedicated, delectable doctors in the high-pressure world of medicine, where emotions run high and passion, comfort and love are the best medicine.